Safina

DAUGHTER OF ISLAM, BOOK I

A Novel by

S. Smart

Cover Illustration by D. Scott

DEDICATION

The members of my writers' critique group inspired me, and made it possible for me to complete this project. I am very grateful to them for their support and honest commentary.

TABLE OF CONTENTS

PREFACE

"The American soldiers hunker down in their fox holes, inside armor plated Humvees, and in their tents – and wait. Grimacing, they bear the burdens of wars they only slightly understand. Too bad no one is brave enough to tell them these are absolutely just and necessary wars; wars that are driving away the vultures until the revolution; holding the line until reinforcements take their place, finally allowed to win! Those who survive will be proud, and those who do not make it will see their sacrifice through the eyes of Nomad, and they too will be glad they stood unflinching for us, and for their children."

President Safina Morelli Abussani
United Federation of Arab States

CHAPTER I

Being a Wife

Safina awakened curled on her side, pressed against the cool stone floor, exposed, and stripped of clothing. She unfolded her arms from around her thin body and moaned. Her frail girlish shoulders were darkened with purple splotches where his hands had held her down.

She pushed herself up to a standing position, and gathered the ugly black dress from the end of the bed. Clutching it tightly against her chest with both hands, she looked across the room, and saw her own image in the large mirror, and did not recognize herself. The reflection was of an old woman, bent in pain. A reddish brown line of dried blood ran from her cheek all the way down her body to the thigh. The eyes in the mirror stared at her from an empty sunken black void.

"*Allah hu Akbar*," The muezzin from the sky-piercing minaret of the nearby mosque sounded the midday summons. Safina knew that Abdul Khaliq Abu-El-Haj would return home soon after prayers, and the torture would resume.

She walked to the basin of water at the entrance hall, and took one of the towels kept there for guests. Dipping it in the water, she wrung it out and wiped the blood from her face. She stood there for several minutes, seeking a thread of sanity to seam herself back together into the person that she had once been. Safina slipped the black *abāya* over her head, letting it fall in a straight line to the floor. She tied the neck closure and waist ties to make sure they could not fall open. She found her pantaloons on the floor where Khaliq had stripped them from her so easily yesterday as the sun went down in the sky.

Vivid pictures played over in her mind. She remembered the awful nauseating odor of Khaliq. Her eyes squeezed shut. Between her legs she was torn and bleeding. This was not new to Safina. Night after night he would thrust his "man thing" into her again and again, into all the orifices of her child body. He would crush her with his hairy belly, leaving her wet and stinking. As she lay naked on her stomach, Safina would think of dying. She would drag herself from beneath his suffocating weight, and inch her way on hands and knees into the farthest corner of the room.

The attacks continued each day and each night, as she prayed to Allah for her own death. Safina understood now. *This was the meaning of being a wife.* Safina opened her eyes; she forced the scenes from her mind. She was 11 years old.

⌘

"Safina! Safina!" Khaliq's powerful voice pounded in her ears like Persian cannon fire.

Safina ran from the entrance vestibule into the villa's central hallway, on painfully injured small narrow child's feet, as she looked for a place to disappear. She squinted, adjusting to the darkness. Her flat chest heaved in and out. Her skin was clammy and she shivered. To the right of the foyer she could make out the long hallway and the row of closed doors to the sleeping rooms. Safina moved hesitantly; she

2

stumbled on the rough hewn stone floor but managed to stay upright. The massive iron entrance gates to the courtyard swung closed with reciprocating metal-on-metal clunks. When Khaliq entered the villa, Safina could hear his heavy footsteps as his wooden soles thudded along the corridor toward her. She crept into one of the rooms, and slipped into an over-sized wardrobe closet, pulling the heavy cedar door closed behind her. Safina hardly dared to breathe in her hiding place among the man's long stripped *galabia* dresses. The closet reeked of Turkish cigarettes and the stench of sweat, which permeated all of his clothing. Rows of house shoes with the backs crushed down onto the soles, where the man walked on them, were lined up along the bottom of the wardrobe like prison guards on both sides of her.

"Come to me. Where are you hiding, my little chicken? You must come to me!" She heard him crashing about the rooms, pushing heavy wooden furniture that scraped and screeched against the tile floors in the sitting room. Overturned clay pots smashed into the walls and shattered like exploding firecrackers. Safina held her hands over her ears and gritted her teeth so tightly that her cracked tooth from a previous beating, broke off and fell onto the floor of the wardrobe closet. She was gripped in a vice of fear.

"May your father have boils on his privates, and may your sisters be barren," Khaliq bellowed.

Safina pressed herself against the back panel of the wardrobe, and willed herself to fuse with the wood. The door jerked open, and the man's fat hairy hand waved wildly among the hanging dresses. Long tobacco-stained yellow fingernails barely missed her face. She froze, a cornered animal, panting silently. She heard him moving away, his footsteps lurching and shuffling down the corridor. Urine ran down her legs onto the wooden floor of the closet. She could not move a single muscle for fear that Khaliq would hear her and return to attack his captive prey.

꧁✥꧂

Safina had tried to run away from Khaliq after the first two weeks of the marriage. He caught her a kilometer from the villa and dragged her back home, beating and cursing her all the way.

When he got her back inside of the villa he tied her feet to the table leg and dropped a heavy grinding stone on her toes. Most of them were broken and crushed. She removed her anklet to wash the blood away. The swelling of her wounds prevented her from returning it to her ankle and toe. The pain was excruciating. She wrapped the jewelry in a cloth and hid it.

When her bones healed, more than a month later, her feet were crooked and grotesque looking. Safina could no longer run. She walked by keeping most of her weight on her heels. Instead of deterring her from escape this only frightened her more and heightened her flight instincts. A woman who lived nearby told her that Khaliq's two previous wives had died: one from a severe beating, and the second girl died during childbirth along with her unborn baby. The second wife was 12 years old. Safina knew he would kill her if she did not escape soon.

Inside the wardrobe among the smelly dresses her thoughts focused on survival. Since her marriage she had endured months of severe physical abuse. Her body was weak, but despite the torture her primal instinct to flee became stronger and more compelling.

After a while the thrashing noises stopped. Cautiously, she pushed aside the *galabias*, and slowly opened the door of the closet and stepped out. Pain racked her bruised body as she gasped, taking in the cool air. All of her senses were heightened; the fine hairs on her arms and neck stood up. Her aching bare feet pressed the floor as she made her way out of the sleeping room, and along the corridor. From the hallway she saw Khaliq sprawled on the flowered brocade couch among the blue satin cushions. A bottle of Arrack, the sweet licorice alcohol of Lebanon, was cradled against his bloated stomach.

Although publicly he adhered to the laws of Islam that forbade the drinking of alcohol, he guzzled Arrack nightly. Khaliq's breathing rattled jaggedly, gurgling through his saliva. A greasy *kafia* turban unraveled, and came slithering down to the floor from his sweaty head, as if it were a serpent seeking a cooler place. Its black woven design of the *Haj* (signifying his pilgrimage to Mecca) was ominous.

On an ornate three-legged brass table the *nargilla* (water pipe) charcoals still glowed in the dim light and sporadic bubbles rose one by one inside the glass sphere, popping at the surface of the water. Safina hoped that Khaliq had inhaled deeply and his opium-induced stupor would last until the morning. No matter how long he remained passed out, this was her best opportunity to flee.

Under the stairs, at the entrance hall to the villa, Safina retrieved a small worn leather bag containing her belongings. She reached into the bottom of the bag and felt around with quivering fingers until she found it – her mother's photograph, dim and yellowed. A tear splashed onto her hand, and she pushed the photo far down into the deep pocket of her black dress. She checked to make sure her anklet and toe ring were still in her bag. On top of these she added a dozen "woman rags". She put her sandals on her feet, and wrapped the pliable leather thongs around her slender ankles. They gave strength to her shaky legs, as she tucked the worn leather ends under the last coil. Safina covered her hair and face with a scarf and veil, and hastily threw a large black shawl around her shoulders.

In the kitchen she carefully removed the lid of an earthenware pot. Deep in its dank interior, she grasped a piece of salty goat cheese, and from a small clay jar she scooped up a handful of fat purple olives. She wrapped these, with a pita, in a clean rag and stuffed them into the bag. After pulling the long drawstrings tight, she tied them around her tiny waist where the shawl covered the bag. These provisions would sustain her for a while.

Safina moistened a clean rag with water from a basin that she had prepared earlier. She lifted her robe, pulled down her pants, and washed herself as best she could. She then pushed some clean dry rags between her legs to staunch the bleeding, pulled her black pantaloons back up and repositioned her robe. She threw the washing rag into the cesspool hole near the back of the villa, and returned to wash her hands with a mixture of coarse salt, lemon juice and olive oil. Wiping them on a rag, she looked around the sparsely stocked pantry. There was nothing else she wanted to take with her.

Safina passed through the rear door of the villa, out of the inner courtyard, and walked down the dirt alley along its central open sewer trough that fed into the main line in the street. She was afraid to leave, but even more terrified to stay with Khaliq. It was nearly dark now. Khaliq might be roused again to pray, but he would probably fall back to sleep immediately after performing the evening ritual.

Safina knew that she must get as far away as possible from Khaliq or she would be dragged back to him with more brutal beating and raping than before. She had no real plan, and she could barely concentrate on making her legs carry her forward. He would come looking for her when his Arrack induced stupor wore off.

She removed her golden nose ring, working it into the hem of her shawl. A thief might notice it under her veil, and she knew it was one of the few items of value that she possessed.

As Safina made her way along the edges of the streets and alleys blending into the ancient shadowy passages, she remembered when Allah forsook her - that wretched day when the hand of Khaliq reached out and caught her many months ago...........

CHAPTER 2

Sandstorm

(Six months earlier)

Months before Safina was traded by her father to Khaliq, one of his wives took her aside. She brushed her fingers affectionately against Safina's cheek, and spoke in a hushed tone, "This was your mother's, Safina." She fastened a silver band to Safina's ankle with a ring attached by a delicate silver chain, and slipped the ring around Safina's middle toe.

She led Safina into the kitchen, and together with another wife, they pierced her nose with a sharp hollow needle dipped in fermented pomegranate juice. Tiny drops of blood dripped onto Safina's shoulder. The pain was sharp when one of the wives pushed a gold ring through the pierced skin. But Safina was glad and she did not cry out. It was a sign of status in her tribe to be worthy of wearing a golden nose ring. She was proud to have these things that had belonged to her mother.

"You are old enough now, 11 years have passed since your birth. Know who you are Safina. Your mother was a woman of great beauty, loved by the wives and children of your father, El Sighi. We were filled with tears when she was taken from us."

"Where did you get that nose ring and ankle bracelet?" El Sighi demanded a few days later when he happened to notice her bringing in water.

"Fatima gave it to me. She told me that they belonged to my mother. Your wives kept them for me. It is all I have to remember her, please allow me to keep them," she begged, with her head down in a subservient posture.

El Sighi looked uncomfortable. He rubbed his stubby beard with his fat fingers.

"Father, I wear them to honor you and to show your generosity to the lowly daughter of a concubine. Surely those who see these adornments will know you as a man of fairness and a protector of your family in all things," Safina spoke in a gentle and hesitant voice. She meant to pacify her father and to negotiate this small compromise from him. It was the first time in her life that she actually valued something material, and she wished with all of her heart that she might keep them.

"Very well. She wore them when I took her in as a widow. Just don't flaunt them among the women – or they will all be asking for such things. Go finish your chores." He flicked his hand up in dismissal, and she hurried away before he might change his mind.

Once a year the village members gathered their small herds together, and packed up whatever handcrafts they made during the year. They journeyed south to Baghdad where Safina's father sold and traded goats, sheep, camels, horses, and occasionally even a prized Saluki dog, if the price were right. He often engaged in the Islamic practice of *muta'a,* "the taking of temporary wives" to relieve a man's physical stress. His permanent wives traded their colorful baskets and embroidery for spices and perfumed body oils at the open market bazaar. The women and girls marveled at the beautiful hand-woven horse and camel blankets made from sheep's wool, and dyed the bright colors that were so admired by the tribe's people.

El Sighi's sons boasted of the horse races they would win, and wagered among themselves as to who would have enough money to have their mares serviced by the fastest stallions in all of Arabia.

Safina, drawn to her eldest brother, Youssef, would sneak out of the tent and linger near the makeshift corral to be near him. She loved the way he talked to the animals, so gentle and kind. Sometimes he would give Safina a sugar cube meant for the horses. Once he gave her a small carving of her favorite mare, Quallil. He winked at his sister and patted her on the head.

He was the horse whisperer of the clan. He would talk with the Arabian mares in his father's small herd as he groomed and fed them, "The superiority of Kulbarq, Parador and Manifik is unparalleled – and then there is the glorious Djendel, sired by Maganate and foaled by the French Mandor, a delightful saucy mare of great distinction. Djendel was the foundation of the Al Shahania stables of Qatar. This most beloved stallion is the origin of the greatest Arabian bloodlines in the entire world. These stallions are owned by the Saudi Prince Khaled bin Sultan bin Abdul Aziz Al Saud. One day, one of you will be bred to the Djendel line and you will bear the world's fastest Arabian race horse. The name of Youssef bin El Sighi will fall from the royal lips of Prince Khaled and from all who strive for perfection."

His brothers laughed at him and called him a stupid dreamer who would rather talk to the mares than arrange for *muta'a* for the night. Safina heard him tell his brothers that he refused to rape a girl or woman and pretend it was his Islamic right to do so, "The thought of forcing myself on another being, or an animal," he glared at his brother Ahmed, "is disgusting and wrong."

Once while brushing Quallil he spoke to Safina, "I dream of the day I will leave the tribe and travel to Al Khalediah Stables with my best mare, Jamiilah. The Prince will marvel at her speed and balance, and will call for his servants to bring out his best stallion to service her."

Safina loved her brother Youssef because he had a sincere heart and because she believed in his dreams. She prayed they would come true.

On their annual trek to Baghdad, El Sighi led his people to an oasis where they were camped for the next few days to rest before continuing on their long journey. Excitement among the villagers was running high, and there was much chatter among the wives, "Put out his favorite cushions Safina, and make sure the deserts, *Baklawah min Semsem Wah Fistuk* (baklava pastry with sesame seeds, pistachios and raisins), are extra sweet."

The youngest wife of El Sighi, Farka, told Safina, "I will not be beaten tonight. I will work especially hard to setup the tent exactly the way he likes it."

The first time Safina saw Abdul Khaliq Abu El Haj, she was on her way to the water hole. A storm was advancing from the east. Wind driven, invading shards of pulverized desert stone and coarse sand stabbed and tormented the soft skin of Safina's neck. They filled the hollow places of her ears as her head scarf flapped in the ever increasing velocity and power of the impending might of the sandstorm. As she struggled to find her way to the well, she spat the orange clay-sand from her lips, clutching the veil covering her nose and eyes.

Peering out through the loosely woven black fibers she saw a rider approaching the water hole on horseback. He rode stiffly, his body shifting from side to side, out of sync with the long smooth strides of the large animal. Because she had observed her brothers who were expert horsemen, she could see that the rider was clumsy and uncomfortable on the black horse.

A long caravan of heavily laden camels and pack horses followed him. The men leading the animals were holding scarves over the eyes and nostrils of the horses and pulling them forward. The camels were roped together one behind the other, and appeared oblivious to the blowing particles. Men and beasts advanced with heads down as the camels' wide flat feet plodded their way through the drifting sands in a long resolute queue.

Safina was sorry for the horses who were struggling with the sand-filled wind, but she had no concern about the camels. She knew the sand could not penetrate the natural defenses of the camels. Youssef once told her, "They can press their lips together keeping out most of the sand. They have two or three rows of thick eyelashes that protect their eyes, and they can close their nostrils completely. The thick coarse hairs that line their ears keep the sand out too." She also knew from unpleasant personal experience that if sand did get into their mouths, they were superior spitters, spewing their gooey sandy slobber several feet in the direction of anyone foolish enough to threaten or bother them.

"*Yella, yella!* Go! Go!" the man shouted. The huge black horse screamed in protest against the wind, and against the cruel man who yanked hard on the torturous pronged bit, which only a fool would have inflicted on such a wondrous animal. The muscles on the horse's neck bulged in anger, as the barbaric prong cut into the soft underside of its swollen tongue. Its eyes glazed with razor sharp metallic hate. Frothy pink foam blew from its flaring nostrils, and from the open black corners of its wounded mouth.

The stallion's mountainous body rose up to stand on its powerful hind legs. The sun behind him lit the silhouette of the horse. The blowing sand filtered the clarity of detail. Safina watched intently as the man beat the horse furiously with the stinging monkey-skin whip that he held with his clenched fist by its engraved silver handle. Blood ran down the neck of the horse in rivulets of shinny liquid, but the stallion refused to plant his front legs on the ground. Pawing the sky, he screamed in protest.

The curved blade of the rider's shabria was clamped between his teeth. The jewels embedded in the dagger's handle reflected the prism of the rainbow, throwing out surrealistic lines of brilliant color in all directions against the sun's red hazy glow in the sand-filled sky. The man crashed to the ground like a plump watermelon rolling off of a farmer's cart in the market. The shabria was still solidly locked between his cruel lips. A spray of blood from the sharp cuts it made when his body impacted the earth spattered the front of his white robe.

Safina smiled behind her veil. "*Allah hu akbar*," she whispered. The horse bolted, and her eyes followed it to the top of the ridge overlooking the encampment. The horse turned for a moment in the tangerine light, and looked at Safina sideways through one arrogant eye, seeming to beckon her with a sharp toss of its great head and blowing mane. Then it laid back its ears and, with its long thick tail arched in defiant superiority it was gone, disappearing over the sandy ridge. "May Allah lead you to water; may a thousand stars guide your way," Safina prayed.

Safina hastily drew water from the well, covering the goat stomach water bag with the folds of her robe, to prevent even more sandy clay from sticking to it. She retreated to her father's tent, hanging the bag carefully on a pole inside the opening.

Curiosity pulled her back to the entrance. *Who was he?* Safina stood at the opening of the tent, and pulled the veil to one side in order to see more clearly. Her foot protruded shyly from beneath the coarse black wool of her robe. A single narrow silver ring engraved with Arabic letters, encircled her naked toe. A delicate silver chain connected the ring to a braided band of tarnished silver filigree that wound tightly around her slim ankle and was secured with a small brass pin where the two halves of the anklet came together. She looked toward the mountain where the horse escaped. The sand storm subsided.

Safina felt the stranger's eyes upon her. Her face innocently turned toward him for a moment, as she tugged at the veil that lifted defiantly in the hot wind. Her silver green eyes, like those of a wild Lynx, looked into his being. A raven black widow's peak brazenly made mockery of the veil. Her golden nose ring flashed the trickles of sunlight that managed to penetrate the blowing sand. He moved closer. His eyes stared at her foot and traveled up her body. She saw beads of slimy white spit gathered on his thick lips. Safina shrank back into the tent in instinctive fear.

Khaliq pitched his tents in their camp. Each day he went out with the young men of the tribe to search for his angry horse, *Bedoui* (Nomad). Each day he returned without it, "*Bedoui, cous ochto bin cheleb,* (Nomad, your sister is a 'cunt', you son of a bitch)." He threatened and cursed the escaped animal with a slow and unmerciful death, describing in detail how he planned to castrate the stallion and roast its testicles over a fire where he would feast on them. The men listened to his tirades, and covered their mouths to muffle their laughter.

The tribe waited patiently, not only because it was the polite thing to do, but also because Khaliq was a source of entertainment and distraction during this long journey. Khaliq caught some of the boys mimicking him, "Hey, big horse, I will cut off your balls and sleep with your mother." The boys giggled and stomped their feet, shaking their fists. He sent them fleeing to their tents under the sting of his whip.

Soon after the caravan arrived the men of the tribe slaughtered and gutted a sheep. They marinated it for several hours in a mixture of sweet coffee, salt, a garlic rub, and olive oil. The women stuffed it with roasted pistachios, saffron yellow rice, and lemon-flavored honey-sweetened boiled quince. They cooked it over an open fire spit as it was turned on a skewer. They seasoned it with bright orange *hawaij* curry and sea salt. And the youngest girls dripped garlic-spiced olive oil over it as it roasted. They fed the man and his servants. Five times each day the men bowed together toward the holy city of Mecca in Saudi Arabia, the center of Islam and their holiest city, and performed *Salah*, the second pillar of Islam, a sacred prayer to Allah.

On the fifth night, Safina saw Youssef leave the camp. She assumed he went to relieve himself in the surrounding desert sand. She crawled away from the women's tent and made her way to the corral. She knew that Youssef would stop by Jamiilah's enclosure to check on her, as was his custom. As Youssef came near Jamiilah the gentle blowing of a horse could be heard. In the starlight he saw the great black stallion of Khaliq resting his neck against the soft golden brown mane of Jamiilah. The stallion was still wearing the saddle, blanket and bridle. The leather reins hung down on each side of his large head. "You are Nomad. I remember you," Youssef whispered. "Don't be afraid, I won't tell that fool."

The big horse stared at Youssef with his large round eyes. He neighed, lifted his head off the back of the mare, and took a few steps toward the young man. Youssef reached his hand into his pocket and produced a red apple. He stretched out his hand and waited, with his other arm hanging at his side. Nomad walked over to him and took the apple. He was having a hard time eating it because of the nasty pronged bit that was still digging into the underside of his tongue. Youssef could see the problem. He turned toward the shadows where Safina was hidden, "I want to remove the bit from his mouth, but I don't want to frighten him."

Safina stepped slowly out into the moonlight, "It will be alright Youssef. He knows you want to help him."

Youssef nodded at her and looked toward Nomad, "If you let me, I will remove that bridle and bit, and set you free."

Nomad dropped the apple and stood quite still in front of the youth. Youssef reached up as high as he could. Nomad was much taller and broader than any of his father's horses. He was able to unbuckle the bridle and slip the leather straps over the stallion's ears. The bridle fell away quite easily and Youssef pulled the bit out of the horse's mouth. Nomad nodded his head up and down and neighed, exhaling hot breath through his cavernous nostrils, looking as though he was thanking Allah for releasing him from that painful device. Youssef threw the bridle assembly over his shoulder.

Nomad pranced around Jamiilah, blowing and whinnying, showing off. She stood perfectly still and calm. Then he came over to Youssef, stretched his neck down to the ground and picked up the apple. When he finished eating it, he pawed at the ground and bent his head down again. It was clearly a gesture of gratitude and Youssef stroked the horse's neck. Nomad stood there in the light from the stars and waited for Youssef to remove the blanket and saddle as well.

"If the blanket, saddle or bridle are found anywhere around the encampment our father will disown me and exile me to the desert." Youssef said to Safina as he took the hobbles off of Jamiilah's front legs to free her. Youssef's narrow beard was braided at the end to keep it from blowing up into his face when he was riding. He was taller than his kinsmen and his hands were slender with long graceful fingers. He wore thick black boots with metal buckles at the tops. He spoke with authority and a degree of self-awareness that was uncommon among the tribesmen. While following all the Islamic traditions that his father mandated, Youssef was still his own man, unbroken by the totalitarian edicts of Islam.

"Hey big horse, give me a short ride and I will get rid of this stuff far from camp."

Nomad seemed to understand and he stood quietly as Youssef jumped up with his stomach on Nomad's saddle, and swung a leg over to the other side of the horse and sat up, taking hold of his mane. "Here, Safina, take my hand and come with me. No one will know."

Safina raised her arms and Youssef easily pulled her up to sit in front of him. The horse took off into the desert, Jamiilah galloping along side of them. Youssef and Safina were suddenly transformed into the most powerful and free people in their village. The gait was smooth and steady. The horse carried them far along the ridge and stopped about three kilometers from the encampment. Youssef slid off of his back, helped Safina down, and turned and released the saddle cinch around the horse's belly. He pulled the beautiful hand-tooled saddle off of the horse. The woven scarlet and gold colored blanket with its decorative tassels, fell onto the clean sand. Safina used her hands to help Youssef dig a hole in the warm desert floor, and put the blanket, saddle, and bridle into the shallow indentation. They covered it with sand and stomped it down. "There! It should not be exposed until we are far from the oasis and well on our way to Baghdad," Youssef said as he grinned with satisfaction.

Nomad stood quietly watching Youssef. The boy turned toward Nomad and stroked the horse's forehead and nose. "I will tether Jamiilah away from the campsite tomorrow night. She will be waiting for you. Now, *rouchi min hone* (run away from here)." Nomad neighed loudly, threw up his head and lifted his long tail high as he galloped away at full speed into the blue-blackness of the desert night.

Jamiilah started to follow him, but Youssef whistled her back. She returned to him. He lifted Safina on to the mare's back and jumped on behind her. They rode back to the encampment. Youssef patted Jamiilah on the side of her soft neck. "He's amazing! I think he will come back tomorrow night to visit you Jamiilah. Maybe thirteen months from now you will have a big black colt! *En shalla* (God willing)."

He slid off the mare and lifted Safina down to the ground. "Go back to your tent Safina, before someone sees us. Don't tell anyone about this." He put his finger against his lips and winked at her.

Resting comfortably on soft down pillows in the sheik's tent, Khaliq announced, "I must leave now and return to Basra to rejoin my Brethren, the Shia faithful. I cannot stay to look for that cursed animal any longer. It has been seven days. Your hospitality has been far beyond my expectations. If you find the stallion, you can keep him as a token of my gratitude for your generosity. But promise me that you will beat him and castrate him." He laughed long and hard.

One of the older wives of El Sighi put her hand over her mouth and chuckled into it. Then she turned toward Safina and Farka, "Your father has no hesitation about beating wives, concubines and servants, and even his children or the children of the tribe, but he will draw the line at beating horses, or his spoiled Saluki dogs that he is so proud of. He would protect their pedigrees with his life if necessary."

Her eldest son sat in the back of the tent listening to his father talk. His lip lifted in disgust as he whispered, "Castration is an impossible request, as it is stupid to castrate a magnificent stallion merely because the owner doesn't know how to ride him properly."

The boy's mother added, "However, the horse requires some type of correction."

El Sighi had perfectly trained horses because of the son of his first wife, Youssef. The villagers agreed that Youssef's ability was a gift from Allah. This was a matter of great pride in the village because visitors would come with their problematic horses from far away. Even Kurds would come down from their mountains bringing horses with behavioral problems. A particularly serious issue was any mountain horse that was afraid of heights. Not only was it impossible to keep such a horse in the mountains, it was also dangerous because these horses were unreliable on the narrow trails and icy paths along the high ridges. Youssef would take such a horse and show it that narrow trails and high rocky passes through the mountains are a refuge for their souls, and hold nothing ominous or threatening. He knew how to give them back their calm center of existence, and their confidence in the rider's judgment and trustworthiness to lead them only along safe paths and through secure passes.

The red mare that was tied outside the tent was just such a horse. She was traded for an angora goat. El Sighi would most likely sell or trade her in Baghdad and realize a profit.

Safina befriended the mare, sneaking some corn husks and fresh grasses into her pen. She called her *Quallil* (Little). Sometimes she would steal a handful of sugar and give it to the mare as a treat, "Quallil, I wish you could run with the black horse through the desert, free and filled with happiness that you have never known. He is a fine big stallion, as swift as the wind."

As Safina served the men their evening tea with sweet baklava honey pastries and *kiz memesi tel-katayif* ("young girl's breasts"),

18

which is shredded sweet pastry mounds topped with half a walnut. She listened to the conversation of her father and the guest, Khaliq.

Her father chanted from the Qur'an, "For those that fear the majesty of Allah there are two gardens, each planted with shady trees. Each is watered by a flowing spring. Each bears every kind of fruit in pairs. May you recline on couches lined with thick brocade, and within your reach hang the fruits of both gardens. May you dwell with bashful virgins whom men or jinnee demons have not touched before, virgins as fair as corals and rubies. Blessed be the name of Allah, the Lord of Majesty and Glory!" El-Sighi inserted the blessing of Allah, and politely left out the repetitive admonitions such as, "Which of your Lord's blessings would you deny?"

As Safina poured the sticky sweet tea from the sizzling finjan into delicate translucent porcelain cups she saw Abdul Khaliq eyeing her appreciatively and breathing through his mouth. *No, not me*, she thought. *Please Allah be merciful – not me.* She withdrew to the darkest and farthest corner of the tent. Her heart was instinctively gripped with fear. Her stomach churned as she tried not to think of what might happen to her.

"Farka, Farka!" She called out softly to her friend, the youngest of her father's wives. "I am so afraid. I feel that something terrible is going to happen to me." They clutched each other in the dark corner of the tent. Farka fell silent and would not talk about it with Safina.

Khaliq continued in his smooth, low voice, "May Allah bless you with strong sons and reward you with great wealth for your hospitality. May I inquire concerning the fair maiden, the one who so graciously served us these delicious pastries and this cinnamon tea, seemingly blended-in-paradise? What is she called, and is she a wife or a daughter promised in marriage to some fortunate prince?"

The man flattered Safina's father with his polite way of asking such a personal question.

El Sighi responded, "She is Safina. The daughter of Latifa, a temporary wife under the law of *muta'a,* who bore me three live sons. I refer to the children of my household by their mother's name. This helps to differentiate between the children of my wives. She is not promised."

Safina's father continued to explain, "We come from the most northern part of Iraq, very close to the land of the Kurds where Islam is tarnished and distorted by the Sunni. As you know, we are like you, of the Shia brethren, direct descendants of Ali, the cousin and son-in-law of Mohammad the Prophet. I would not give her unto the lowly Kurds to dwell in the reed and mud Sarifah huts and to practice the unorthodox and ungodly ways of the Sunni. I plan to make arrangements for her betrothal in Baghdad."

Now the bargaining could begin in earnest. Safina's heart beat faster. Clearly the man was intent upon completing his transaction, and Safina could detect no reluctance on the part of her father to part with his daughter, providing the price was adequate.

"I offer a strong, young, and obedient camel, five she-goats, and five gold South African Krugerrands, in exchange for one breeding mare, and the female, Safina." The man gestured toward Safina and then toward the feisty red mare that neighed nervously from outside the opening of the tent. He used the number five twice. Safina knew that the number five, *chamsa,* designated extreme fortune. It was very lucky, and strong medicine against the evil eye. To include it twice in one transaction denoted a high degree of probability that the negotiation would end favorably for both parties. As Khaliq spoke, he spread the five fingers of his right hand upon the small table, and moved his hand across the surface in a sweeping arch away from El Sighi to ward off *Al-Ayn* (the evil eye). El Sighi appeared to be flattered and pleased with Khaliq's clear understanding of bargaining etiquette.

"Two racing camels with full blankets and fittings, five wet she-goats with their kids, and five South African Krugerrands would be a modest barter for the magnificent red mare and the unblemished virgin female, Safina," her father replied with a broad smile as he extended the nargilla smoking pipe to Khaliq. He chuckled, perhaps in self-satisfaction at his obvious advantage in this bargaining process. Khaliq's hot blood would seem to outweigh his fiscal prudence. The opium smoke filtering through the water bottle in the base of the nargilla and sucked in greedily by Khaliq would make this negotiation "child's play" for the greedy Sheik.

"You are a clever and skillful negotiator, but Allah has been merciful and has granted us both of our wishes. *Allah hu akbar*," Khaliq inhaled deeply from the long umbilical tube of the nargilla. His eyes glazed noticeably in narcotic bliss, and then he passed it back to Safina's father to seal the transaction. El Sighi smiled, exposing his coffee-stained brown teeth as he shallowly inhaled the smoke from the pipe.

Safina's heart sunk in her chest. She was still a little girl. Her mother died before Safina could remember her. Her father had three wives. Two of the wives were old, in their twenties, with many bawling children. But his third wife, Farka, was only 12, a year older than Safina.

Farka whispered to Safina, "The doctor who visited my village before I came to live with your father put a needle into my arm to cause my blood to flow with the times of the moon, so that I could perform the duties of a wife. They will stick you with a needle too. It will make you grow a baby in your belly." Farka took Safina's hand in her own and laid it on her own belly. Safina could feel the tight ball that rounded out Farka's thin body where it was soft and flat before. "Now a baby is growing inside of me. Soon it will have to get out. It is already clawing at me from the inside, looking for the way out," Farka said. She held Safina's face in her two hands. "I will always remember you Safina. I will always think of our games in the courtyard and of the songs we made up together." She cried softly, burying her sobs into a scarf that was wrapped around her neck.

Safina could not answer Farka immediately because she was afraid that if she tried, the great hard lump in her throat would close off her breath and she would choke to death. Safina and Farka were more than sisters. They played five-rock games (a primitive form of "jacks", using small rocks) on the cool floor in the courtyard of their house in the village. Safina was pleased when her father brought Farka home. At last she had a friend. Now Safina would have to leave her only friend and go with this strange man, Khaliq. She reached over and wiped the tears from Farka's cheek, "Farka, I will come back to get you. I will! I promise that I won't forget you, and when I am able, I will come to save you. We will be together again. You have to believe me. I will find a way."

When Farka heard the news that her worst fears were confirmed, she cried loudly, taking handfuls of ashes from the burned-out fire ring, and pouring them on her head. She beat her chest with her fists, tore the edges of her clothes, and scratched deep cuts into her arms and legs to signify the act of mourning.

Safina was horrified at this behavior, for it meant that Farka believed Safina was dead to her, and that they would never see each other again. She sobbed, fearing the changes that were about to take place in her life. She observed how Farka was subdued and quiet after Safina's father would summon her to spend a night with him. It would be days before she would smile again or even speak to anyone. Farka was always in good spirits when Safina's father would go on a trip and leave their home for any length of time. Then she would laugh and play games with Safina. Safina knew that her father was doing something awful to Farka, but her friend would not tell Safina anything, no matter how many times Safina asked her what was wrong. She would only answer quietly, "I am his wife."

Visibly angered by Farka's outburst, El Sighi sent Farka sprawling outside the entrance of his sleeping tent, with one backhanded slap. "Go sleep with the donkeys and the dogs, and follow our caravan from afar. There has been no death in our camp, and there will be no mourning in our tents. We will celebrate the betrothal of my daughter, and then we will journey to Baghdad, City of Peace," he boomed in his most decisive voice.

The tribe celebrated with feasting and dancing that went on all night. The shrill high-pitched trills, "La-la-la-la-la-la-la" rang from the surrounding hills throughout the night. A betrothal was a welcome deviation from the desolate, arid, countryside they were about to traverse.

At sunrise the next day, as Safina left her father's tent, he handed her a small wooden chest, "Here are the belongings of Latifa, your mother. It is permitted that you take them with you as you go to the house of your betrothed. When you reach Basra, the Muktar will perform the marriage ceremony. You will be the wife of Abdul Khaliq Abu El Haj. You will do whatever he commands you to do. Give him many sons," her father commanded coldly.

The chest contained a piece of paper with Safina's birth date and the name of her mother and father, a small photograph of her mother, and a change of clothing. She could not read but her brother, Youssef read it to her. Then he touched her cheek, "Safina, someday you will learn to read and your life will be remarkable. Nomad, the big black horse who ran away, told me about you. You are important!"

Safina walked behind Quallil, the young red mare that strained under the grotesque weight of Khaliq. She easily balanced the small chest on her head. She wondered how far Basra was and how many days they would have to walk to reach it. She could not fathom what lay ahead for her.

CHAPTER 3

Escape

Safina was fleeing in a primal attempt to survive. There was no destination – only distance to be put between herself and a predator. The smell of cardamom and cinnamon rescued Safina from her tormented memories. Despite her desperation, the colorful sights and sounds of the ancient city stirred her senses, pulling her back into physical reality. Among the robed women, and the turbaned merchants of the market, there were tall, sinewy, ebony-black Ethiopians hocking peacock feathers and monkey skins; finely featured Yemenites with curly beards and long slender fingers, selling gold filigree bracelets of such exquisite delicacy that it was hard to believe they were merely man-made. Steaming pots of blended curries and roasted lamb stuffed with pistachios and almonds, and laced with exotic spices and pungent garlic, released their mouth-watering aroma on the early evening breeze. Safina's tongue moistened her lips, and her nose tilted upward, hungry for the wonderful smell.

She walked steadily on, unnoticed among the hordes of humanity in this Iraqi port city along the Persian Gulf. An old woman sat in the doorway of a shop, and smoked a *nargilla* under colorful loops of purple, gold and crimson strands of dyed woolen yarn. Her eyes were heavy in the seductive trance of opium. A naked baby whined as it pulled vainly on the old woman's empty breasts. Safina looked on with compassion, but she knew of no wet nurse in this strange place who could satisfy the crying infant. She sat next to them on the stone stoop for a while, so that she would blend with the scene. She feared that by now, it was probable that Khaliq had dispatched his men to find her. Then, as if conjured from thin air, two of them whom she recognized, walked by within a few meters of the steps. Her heart flattened itself against her ribs. Safina's breath turned heavy, trapped silently within her lungs. Unable to expel the sucked in air, she snatched up the baby and pretended to breast feed it by partially covering the child's head with her shawl and pulling her veil all the way across her face. As the breath finally came involuntarily from her blue lips, her heart resumed to beat hesitantly. Like a bird barely escaping a lair, a feather of her soul was left behind in that place to testify to the terror of the prey. She sat the baby on the step and cautiously moved on.

Night approached. She became more and more apprehensive, until hunger and fatigue forced her to stop at a community well. She was so afraid. No women were out after dark and she would draw attention to herself as an unaccompanied female; a violation of Islamic law that could be punishable by death.

Beneath a hanging oil lantern, she dug into her pocket and took out the yellowed photo. She pinched the paper between her thumb and index finger. But, it was the photograph of a stranger. Golden coins hung across the woman's forehead, and sparkling eyes stared at her over a veil of black, held at one corner by slender fingers adorned with enormous golden rings. She was obviously a lady of great wealth. Safina wondered how such a woman came to be her

26

father's temporary wife, for although he was not poor, none of his wives wore golden coins or golden rings. She alone wore a golden nose ring. She remembered her father's words when he gave her the photo, "This is an image of your mother, Latifa. She bore three sons. They all died young." As he spoke he reached out and stroked Safina's cheek affectionately. "You were her only female child." His voice was kind – almost regretful, - tinged with nostalgia. These were the only kind words she ever heard from her father, and they fell upon her ears like the sweet song of the desert finch.

Safina felt ashamed as she remembered her father's words. She knew she was not a good wife - she could never be a good wife to Khaliq. She wished she had died and gone to paradise where her mother dwelt.

She drew a bucket up from the communal well and dipped a ladle of water from it. Safina drank some of the cool water and then poured half of the ladle into her hand and splashed it on her face and neck. The water trickled down her chest and stomach, and she felt refreshed. She wiped at the salt-encrusted corners of her eyes, and promised herself that she would not cry. There was no one who would listen, not even herself.

An indentation about two feet wide in the wall surrounding a great white building looked like a possible refuge from the blackness of the night. Behind a Bird-of-Paradise plant she curled her body against the blocks of granite, and made herself a nesting place. She pulled the rag package from her pocket and ate the cheese, olives and pita, licking the olive oil from her fingers. Covering her feet under the skirt of her *abāya*, she tucked the edges of the robe around her, and wrapped her arms tightly inside her sleeves and shawl. No skin remained exposed. Scorpions, asps and centipedes dwell on the ground. She would be careful not to move too quickly if one of them should crawl onto her robe.

"*Allah hu akbar*," she whispered softly, and in moments she was released from the nightmare of reality to the freedom of her dreams. The huge horse galloped along the familiar hill tops that punctuated the horizon seen from her home, and Safina sat high on his broad, flat back, with her strong thighs gripping his smooth body, laughing as her veil was lifted boldly away by the rushing wind. Everything looked clear and precise to her unveiled eyes. The desert mice squeaked and scampered out of the way. The great white owl awakened from his slumber and blinked in concerned salutation. A coiled cobra raised her wicked head, and swayed back and forth with forked tongue twisting and twirling hypnotically, attempting to pick up their scent - but she quickly lost interest, and in self-preservation, moved from the path of the pounding hooves.

"I am Nomad," said the majestic horse. "What are you called?"

Even in her dream, Safina was not fooled by this illusion. "You are a horse. Allah did not give you speech. I am Safina, daughter of Latifa who dwells forever in Paradise."

"Latifa dwells on earth in the house of an infidel. She is descended from Fatima, the mother of Mohammad." His image gradually blurred and like dissipating mist he vanished, as Safina awoke, still curled behind the plant.

When the sun pushed its aura up into the emerging dawn sky, the flies awoke, abandoning their night roosting places to bite and harass living things. Safina, annoyed by their unwelcome buzz, moved slowly, checking her clothes and surroundings for venomous insects or snakes. She smoothed her dress and the hair beneath her shawl as best she could. She would search for a well nearby to temporarily fool her gnawing stomach. Relieving herself behind the plants, she kicked dirt over the area. The bleeding between her legs had stopped, and the burning sensation had subsided. Stepping from behind the plants she collided with a woman wearing tight clothing. Safina was surprised and embarrassed to see a woman outside wearing close fitting garments, showing the outline of her body, and without a veil; her thin face and graying hair shamelessly uncovered.

"Well child, where did you come from?" she grasped Safina firmly by her shoulders. Her fingers pressed Safina's bruises where they were finally starting to fade, causing the girl to flinch.

"I am sorry, I did not see you. Please forgive me, before Allah, I did not mean…" Safina could not seem to find an apology that the woman accepted, for she did not respond, and she held on tightly to Safina.

"What is your name?" the woman asked. She finally let go.

"I am Safina, daughter of Latifa."

"Why are you here at such an early hour? Where is your home, your family?"

"I am alone." Safina looked down at the ground. "I must go now."

"No, you must not go now. You must come with me. This is no place for a girl to be walking alone. I am Yasmine."

Safina did not argue. Now that she had made her escape from Khaliq she was relieved to have someone else making the decisions. She followed the woman through the gate and along the path to the building. The entry doors were twice the height of the tallest man she had ever seen. She thought the people who lived here must be giants. As they reached the closed door, Yasmine used a huge brass key to unlock it. As it opened, Safina's jaw dropped. She had never been inside such a big room. The ceilings seemed as high as the clouds, and the woman took her hand and led her up the marble stairs and into a foyer.

"Come child, follow me," Yasmine motioned to her. As they entered a large sitting room Safina could hardly believe that all the floors were completely covered with beautiful plush Persian rugs, woven in the most ornate designs, in the brightest colors of ruby red, indigo blue and luminescent gold. In the center of the room she saw a blue and white stripped satin couch, and in front of it there was a white marble table with gold lion's feet for legs. Brilliant green rubber-tree plants stood at each side of the couch, and brass pots hung from chains overflowing with all types of exotic flowering plants. Bright sky-blue walls protected all who entered from the dreaded "Al-Ayn". In Safina's tribe, most people could only afford a small symbolic square of blue on their white-washed walls to protect them from the evil eye. *This woman must belong to a very rich man. Where are his children and other wives?* Safina wondered.

"I will run a bath for you. You look like you need one. Follow me to the dressing room," Yasmine said with a kind smile, and her round brown eyes twinkled with amusement as Safina suddenly remembered to close her mouth.

Within a few minutes Yasmine helped Safina remove her clothing, and filled a black granite sunken pool in the center of the room, with foaming, churning water. Safina had never submerged her entire body in water before. As she descended the steps into the rose scented water, she thought this must be paradise or a trap to entice her into hell. As the warm water penetrated her sore and abused flesh, she ceased to ponder this, or to care. She felt a release of tension, and for the first time, a momentary surrender to fate. At least for now - for this moment in time, she was safe and protected.

Yasmine returned to find the child asleep in the small pool. Her head propped up on a thick folded bath towel at one end. The water was now silent and serene. The bubbles had burst. Black and blue marks on the child's body were magnified by the still water. She clenched her teeth and closed her eyes tightly for a moment. Gently she touched Safina's cheek, "Wake Safina, you must eat."

Helping her from the water, Yasmine enveloped the slender body in a thick ruby-red towel. Only Safina's face peeked out at an indifferent world.

A few hours later, clothed in a finely stitched white linen smock, Safina sat at the end of a long table in the kitchen of Yasmine's spacious house. Before her were *dolme bargehi* (small rolled grape leaves stuffed with ground lamb, parsley and rice). Slivers of translucent golden sautéed onion smothered in finely chopped grilled eggplant, mixed with cracked bulgar wheat, colored purple with beet juice, and spiced with pepper and curry, sat steaming in a delicate porcelain dish. Next to a stack of warm pita bread, wrapped in a hot moist towel, sat a bowl of bitter "*hilbe*" (fenugreek), flavored with fiery hot *schoug* (a spicy mixture of all types of peppers, garlic, and parsley, ground into a thick dipping sauce).

In the appropriate Islamic etiquette, dictating the use of the left hand for bodily hygiene functions and the use of the right hand for eating and handling food, she ate the delicious fixings, using only her right hand for tearing the pita and dipping the pieces into the spicy sauce.

Safina sucked her fingers loudly, and made numerous sounds of satisfied culinary pleasure, smacking her lips, and forcing gulps of air into her stomach that came back out as laudatory belches. She was signifying her gratitude for the hospitality and kindness bestowed upon her.

"My, my, child - you do enjoy your food, don't you! We'll have to address tribal manners versus urban etiquette, at a later time I suppose. Right now, let's get these dishes cleared away, and we'll enjoy some mint tea on the terrace."

Settled on a fat floor cushion, Safina sat at Yasmine's feet, looking up at the woman with the round penetrating eyes. Yasmine rested her bony hands in her lap, one over the other in a patient gesture,

"Now, tell me about yourself and how you came to be sleeping in my bushes," she said.

"I cannot go back to where I came from. Yet I do not know where I am going," she whispered, as she looked down. Yasmine saw that Safina was fighting back tears, unwilling to expose her pain.

"Are you running away from your parents?"

"No. Please don't send me back."

"Are you an orphan? Are you running away from an orphanage?"

Safina shook her head, "*La* (No)."

Yasmine reached down and cupped her warm palm under Safina's chin, lifting her face up. She looked deep into Safina's eyes. "Who has hurt you and made you run away? I promise I will not make you go back."

"My husband…"

A gasp escaped Yasmine's lips and tears welled up in her eyes. "Oh, Allah. No! No! A child bride," she winced. "A child bride! When will these barbarians stop molesting our children?"

She pulled Safina up, lifted her onto her lap. "Poor little girl," she whispered as she stroked Safina's brittle, dry, black hair, rocking her back and forth. "You are safe now. I won't let him hurt you again." Safina was as light as a bird. Her bones were visible under her skin. The girls face was gaunt and her sunken eyes stared vacantly at Yasmine.

Safina verbally cleansed herself as she told Yasmine about her marriage. The words pounded relentlessly on and on.

Long after the sun set and the chattering birds tucked their heads under their wings to dream their innocent dreams, Yasmine wiped tears from her clouded eyes. Now the child slept securely at last. She lay submerged in safe refuge, in a soft bed of fresh white comforters stuffed lavishly with the fluffy down of spring ducklings. Her long black lashes lay sweetly wet, glistening on her delicate, parchment-dry skin.

Yasmine breathed deeply. As she looked at Safina, something made her think about her own beginnings as a Muslim girl. Her father was an exceptional man; a man who traveled to foreign countries. He was a merchant who dealt in antiquities and ancient texts and scrolls. He owned many books which he treasured, and he was one of the few Muslim men of his generation who recorded the births of his children, including the females. He had one wife who he adored and revered, and he taught all of his children to read and write. Yasmine loved to climb the narrow stairs to the top of their villa and sit with her brothers and sisters on fat cushions on the floor. Her father sat on the plump sofa, surrounded by his botanical collection of plants, and read to his children from his favorite books. Yasmine found these literary escapes to far-away places exhilarating and, subsequently, she formed a life-long love of reading and learning.

When her father was killed by Taliban marauders, her Mother's uncle took over the patriarchy of their clan. He quickly arranged for the female children to be married off to the highest bidders.

Yasmine was torn from her sisters and shipped off to a man in Basra; he was nearly triple her age. She was considered "old" at sixteen, and her uncle told her she was lucky that he found a widower with children who needed a strong wife to care for his brood. But her fate turned out to be a blessing. Her husband was a kind and thoughtful physician and a friend of her father. He had come to her rescue. He married her to save her from the cruel fate that fell on most young Muslim girls. He did not consummate their union until Yasmine was well into her twenties and she had fallen hopelessly in love with him. Doctor Abussani trained her as well as any physician matriculating from medical school in Cairo or London. She was a skilled medical doctor despite the lack of any formal credentials.

Yasmine accompanied her husband to care for the ripped and bleeding bodies of physically immature young girls who couldn't give birth to the babies they carried to full term. The fatality rate was high, and unnecessary. Her husband did what he could for them, but the laws of Islam were very restrictive when it came to a male doctor administering to Muslim women. With Yasmine beside him, he could provide much better care and the mortality rate dropped drastically. The horrendous physical abuse was condoned by Sharia Law. Together the doctor and his wife set broken bones, sewed up deep lacerations, performed D&Cs on women with dead fetuses infecting their wombs, and extracted dead infants stuck in narrow birth canals and trapped in partial births. They saved as many girls as they could. Dr. Abussani had charitable sources of funding for medications and his traveling expenses. He had a private practice in Basra that supported his family.

Yasmine came to hate the Islamic culture of pedophilia being promoted throughout the Islamic world. She vowed to find a way to educate the women to fight back. Someday she planned to spark a revolution that would prohibit these barbaric practices.

When her elderly husband died, she continued his mission to the best of her ability. She had to be very cautious, because she no longer enjoyed the cloak of his medical credentials. She was suspect among the male population, but they were torn between getting medical care for their abused wives and children, who had cost them money or bartered goods, or dispensing with her services. There were no other doctors who would work in these rural villages outside of Basra.

She went to the kitchen and sat down across from her cook, Badrae, who was busy cleaning rice. As she removed each little piece of rice hull or stem Badrae quietly hummed.

Yasmine decided to call her dear friend, Vivian Von Stetton in Holland. She felt she needed to talk to someone about Safina. "You would not have believed it, Vivian. This poor girl released a torrent of pain. She described a bridal chamber of horrors, scenes orchestrated gleefully and sadistically by her husband with his power over females, granted by Sharia Law. She showed me the burns on the most intimate parts of her body, torn rectal tissues thickened in self-healing, a missing toe nail, and a patch of bare scalp cut away in the infliction of pain, which brought her husband to his 'manly' climax. She has a scarred and mangled breast with the nipple savagely bitten during his masculine ecstasy of ejaculation," Yasmine gagged as she retold the details.

She decided to hate Khaliq – to justify killing him at some time in the future. Yasmine had no doubt in her mind that she would kill Abdul Khaliq Abu-El-Haj. She had no choice. She was capable of killing. In the past she killed two Muslim men who were vile wife beaters and murderers. One killed his sixteen-year-old wife, as well as her new born baby, for giving birth to a third daughter. He had no sons. He would kill again and Yasmine knew it. The other man beat his wife almost to death for some minor household infraction and caused her to miscarry. Yasmine was barely able to save the girl from bleeding to death. She performed an emergency hysterectomy on the table of her small home clinic. The man had attacked Yasmine viciously when he was told that his wife would no longer be able to bear children. Yasmine had defended herself with her shabria. The older brother of the girl had helped Yasmine dispose of the body and had vowed to help Yasmine whenever she needed him. He was a good man who loved his sister and was disgusted with the cruel reality of barbaric Islamic law. In this manner, Yasmine had collected many allies along the way, men who would defend her and support an Islamic reformation.

She could hear Vivian crying over the telephone, "Dam them to hell, cursed promoters of child molesters and tormentors of women," Vivian sobbed.

Yasmine continued speaking quietly, "I wanted to cover my ears. I wanted to keep out the awful, horrible telling. But instead I held the child as she leached, by tears, the poisons of her husband. Release came in floods of words and curses that only a devil's victim might utter in seemingly unending repetition as learned from her tormentor's wicked lips. Words spewed from the blackened bowels of the girl's soul." Yasmine's jaws tightened as she told Vivian of her intense feelings of frustration. "I am filled with hate for this man. I want revenge!" She hung up with Vivian after saying her good byes.

The cook sat quietly and listened to Yasmine talking on the telephone for over an hour. The faithful servant and long-time friend sat in her chair and wiped her tears away with her apron. "*Imach Shemo (*may his name be erased)! I remember my own bridal chamber of horrors as a child bride," Badrae whispered. She told Yasmine how Dr. Abussani saved her when she was beaten and bleeding, and brought her to work in the kitchen of his house when she was just a young girl, long before Yasmine came to be his wife; how he had threatened to kill her husband, if he did not keep his hands off of her completely. "I slept in my husband's house for another decade, and I did my domestic chores, but my husband never touched me. Until the day he died he never spoke to me again. This is why I have no children of my own."

Yasmine went into the bedroom to make a last check on the thin girl curled into a ball. "Sleep my child, tomorrow we shall continue the healing of your heart and body." Yasmine shuddered as a chill passed through her. Some premonition lingered in the recesses of her mind. She felt as though Allah granted her some significant request that would come at a great cost. She didn't yet understand what her role would be.

She blew out the candles, and walked out of the room. Her feet were sure and solid, and her back was as straight as a date palm. She wondered: *Could this be the one? Could this be more than incidental? Was this beyond a random crossing of paths?*

CHAPTER 4

Birth

"Iy-y-y-y!" A human scream rent the frozen air, and slapped Yasmine into consciousness. Her eyes snapped open, her body jerked upright in a sudden flood of energy. She swung her legs over the side of the narrow bed and brought her feet to the cold stone floor. Quickly she found her slip-on house shoes, and threw her woolen shawl around her shoulders. She was out the door in seconds.

"Allah be merciful", she begged. It had been eight months since the homeless child, Safina, came to her. She knew, from the first week, that this day was inevitable. Yasmine was a knowledgeable midwife. Unfortunately she had extensive experience with very young girls giving birth to babies in Iraq. She entered Safina's room, turned on the lamp, and moved toward the screaming child. Yasmine fought the panic rising in her chest. She breathed in and out rhythmically, forcing herself to remain calm. The bedding was soaked in blood. Safina's baby was coming. From this young girl's tiny womb a life would be expelled, ripping and tearing its way into the world.

"*Amma, Amma* (Mother, Mother)," Safina sobbed. Her cold hand reached out, clawing at Yasmine, grabbing handfuls of the woman's nightdress.

"It's alright child, it's going to be alright. Listen to me," she said calmly as she stroked the girl's forehead with her steady hand. "You are going to give birth. You must do as I tell you, Safina." She called for the servant girl, Riya. "Fetch the basket under my bed, and bring me clean bedding and a basin of warm water." She began to remind Safina of her forgotten instincts, that all women possess, while she prepared a birthing place.

At the moment the first rays of the sun shot to earth, a female child was born from the seed of Khaliq, but its body was forced from the mother's womb, blue and cold. There were no signs of life. Yasmine severed the umbilical cord; and laid the cold lost life on the floor at the foot of the bed. She made the decision that it was more important to save Safina from massive hemorrhage, than to attempt resuscitation of a baby that was almost certainly dead.

"Take it away, Riya," Yasmine ordered the servant girl, as she turned back to take care of Safina.

Long distorted shadows of Yasmine working desperately over the bed loomed as an over-sized projection against the dim light of the lamp; Riya shivered and her hands shook. She looked tearfully at the bloody dead baby. She clutched her stomach and dry heaved several times.

"I can't take care of you too Riya, breathe girl..... breathe." Yasmine spared a brief glance towards her servant, one that brooked no indecision, and turned her attention back to Safina. Riya calmed herself enough to wrap her apron around "it", lifting the pitiful burden into her shaking arms. Tears dripped silently off the servant girl's chin. She withdrew quietly; her face was pale and she looked down at the floor as she played her part in this hideous sketch. As Riya walked toward the kitchen carrying the dead infant, it moved a hand. She laid the grisly bundle on the kitchen table. The baby's hand slipped from the folds of the apron and fell silently onto the table. Riya could not keep her eyes off of it. Then she saw a finger move. She needed help. In a panic, she raced to the kitchen and flung open the door. The fat old cook was snoring in a chair by the window.

"Badrae! It's dead, but it moved!" Riya cried out, rousing the old woman. "Safina's baby was born dead, but I think it moved," she repeated. "It's in the kitchen."

The cook hauled herself to her feet and quickly shuffled to the kitchen. All desire for sleep was banished from her mind. The soggy apron had fallen away from the baby. She placed her index finger on the skinny wrinkled neck. Her eyes opened wide. Her jaw set firmly, she put her finger in the baby's mouth and scooped out some mucus. Then she put her mouth over the mouth and nose of the baby and blew into them. She grabbed the baby's ankles tightly between her fingers, and began to swing the baby around and around her head.

Riya screamed. "Stop Badrae, have you gone mad?"

"Quick! Get the kettle of hot water hanging over the night coals," Badrae ordered. She speedily filled the sink with water from the single cold faucet. When Riya brought the hot kettle over, the cook poured most of it into a large empty pot on the drain board and then she cooled it by mixing cold water with it - but just enough so that it wouldn't burn the skin of the baby. All the while she was swinging the baby back and forth with one hand. The walls of the kitchen were splattered with flecks of slime and blood loosened from the baby's lungs and expelled by the spinning centrifuge that Badrae had created. She heaved and shivered. Her face gleamed with sweat. She plunged the still baby's body into the sink of cold water, while holding the baby's face just above the water so it wouldn't drown. After a few seconds, laying it face down over one of her fat forearms, she slapped its back several times. Flipping it back over on its back, she rubbed its feet and hands briskly, pinching the tiny nose repeatedly. Badrae put her ear near the baby's mouth and listened. Tears were streaming down her cheeks. Then she plunged it into the basin of hot water on the drain board: back and forth, back and forth, hot and cold, hot and cold. From the sink to the basin and back again. Every few seconds she stopped and put the baby's mouth to her ear, listening. She blew her own breath into the baby's mouth and nose, in small puffs by the mouthful, and then returned to the hot and cold, hot and cold plunging of the limp pale baby. Badrae was exhausted and panting hard, trying to catch her breath. Finally, she stood in the middle of the kitchen with the still baby in her hands, defeated and out-of-breath.

Slowly one of the baby's arms quivered. Then both arms began to move ever so slowly. Gradually they moved faster, and began flailing wildly.

"Wah-ah-ah-ah," the baby yelled in shocked pain as its tiny lungs inflated completely with the thick smelly air of the blood-spattered kitchen.

Badrae turned the baby upside-down, and smacked it aggressively on its rump, which produced another healthy, lung-filled scream from the baby. She wrapped it snuggly in a soft piece of lamb's skin chamois, and sat down to comfort the new life that she had snatched from the claws of death. A victor's smile hung crookedly on the cook's round and tired face and she panted. "You decided to leave us, didn't you? Just remember, princess, you can't go anywhere without Badrae's permission. Riya! Brew up some chamomile tea, and add a sprig of fresh mint. We've earned a treat tonight!"

Down the hallway, in Safina's sleeping chamber, Yasmine stuffed wads of clean "cotton wool" inside the unconscious girl trying to stop the hemorrhaging. Safina's color was bluish gray, her heart beat fluttered, skimming the sea of life as a flat stone flung across a pond that may sink beneath the water in a moment. The air stank of blood and sweat, and the memory of Safina's screams bouncing off the thick stones, still reverberated in Yasmine's mind. She massaged the girl's hands and feet. She grabbed some books from a shelf, and placed them under the foot of the bed to elevate Safina's legs. As Riya timidly entered the room, Yasmine straightened her back and wiped her bloody hands on a towel. She addressed the servant girl quietly and firmly, "Tell Badrae to prepare a brew of Tamar Hindi, very strong, and tell her to add two tablespoons of wild honey." She knew the thick Indian drink made from the shells of dates would help restore Safina's lost blood and fortify her devastated body.

Back in the kitchen, the cook dried the frail baby girl, fashioned a diaper from a clean towel, and fed her some warm goat's milk which the baby slowly sucked from a soft leather tit that the woman hastily devised. She placed the baby gently in a reed basket and covered the sleeping child in the warm pelt of a black, spring lamb. Badrae smiled in satisfaction seeing the baby's fresh bloom of its rosy cheeks framing miniature lips. Delicate black lashes rested peacefully against olive-bronze skin.

As the cook walked stiffly across the room she felt a sudden breeze from the open window, and heard the neigh of a horse. "Who could be riding at this early hour?" she mouthed. From the last light of the stars and moon and the first hint of sunrise, the shape of a huge unsaddled horse standing perfectly still on the top of a hill overlooking the sleeping city, was visible from the window. He stood staring at her, piercing the promise of this new day; his great head held high, and his long tail and mane dancing defiantly in the wind.

Riya walked into the kitchen clacking her wooden heels loudly against the floor. The cook turned to silence this rude interruption, and when she turned back toward the window the horse was gone.

"Mistress requires a brew of Tamar Hindi, very strong, and put two tablespoons of honey in it," Riya said.

"*Iawah* (yes)," Badrae acknowledged. "How is Safina?"

"Sleeping, I think. She is weak. Safina will be in Paradise before the sun rises, as her life pours from her in a river of blood," Riya stated plainly. Salty tears stained Riya's cheeks, and her eyes were red and swollen. "Poor orphan baby", she sighed as she reached into the basket to touch its hand that was curled tightly around strands of lamb's fur.

"This child is not an orphan yet!" Badrae said, as she rushed to brew the drink. "This is the traditional brew among the Yemenites, made to strengthen the faithful after a holy fast. A good choice. How clever of our mistress to remember its magical properties. Yasmine is a wise woman, with knowledge of medicines and cures. I have gone with her many times into the villages to help the poor women. She gives them medicine and teaches them to prepare food so that it would not make their families ill; showing them how to cleanse their bodies inside and out. Sometimes I think Yasmine is a sorceress. She teaches the women forbidden secrets to stop babies from growing in their wombs. Some of the men from the villages are beginning to suspect her of putting "*Al Ayn*" on their seeds, causing their wives to become barren." Cook looked at Riya, "Don't you repeat anything you heard here tonight. Swear it!"

Riya's eyes opened wildly, her exhaustion momentarily forgotten as she stammered, "I swear not to tell anyone."

Badrae took the *Tamar Hindi* to Safina's room.

"Oh, Badrae," Yasmine acknowledged the woman as she entered. "*Shukran*," she thanked her, as she took the tray with the steaming cup. "Did you bury the child?"

"No, I.......I didn't," the cook mumbled in surprise. "The baby is asleep in the kitchen."

"It isn't asleep, it's dead! We must bury it before the sun is risen," Yasmine croaked in frustration and despair.

"No, Mistress! The baby girl is alive, and I have fed her. She is safely asleep!" She spat three times on the floor to ward off the evil eye, and thereby protect the child. She also mumbled under her breath, "What an ugly and sickly baby."

Yasmine stared at Badrae, "There is no need to say bad things to protect this child from *Al Ayan*. Once a person has been saved from death no matter what is said about them, the evil eye cannot affect them. All the demons and devils lurking in the shadows cannot cancel Allah's protection. Whatever befalls them during their life here on earth is solely based on their own actions. *Allah hu akbar*! Praise be to Allah, and blessed be his faithful servants." Yasmine held her hands up in thanks to Allah.

CHAPTER 5

The Arrangement

The bleeding finally subsided, and Yasmine knew the crisis had passed. Yasmine's thoughts turned to protecting the girl and the baby. She began to form a plan.

Several days passed since the son of a friend was sent to her with a message. Abdul Khaliq was still searching for his runaway wife, even after nine months since her disappearance. He was offering a handsome reward for information that would lead him to his lost property. Yasmine must act swiftly if she were to save Safina and the baby. By Islamic law she could do nothing to stop Khaliq from torturing and terrorizing Safina or even killing her.

Yasmine called her servant girl into her room, "Riya, listen carefully. Take this note and this bag of coins. Go to the port, and find the captain of the Greek tanker, Hercules. Abraheem, son of the Silversmith, Farouq, awaits you on Salach-A-Din Street in the market place, by the central well. He will protect you. Do not speak to anyone except the Captain, and do not give him the money until you have his mark and seal on the note."

"Yes Mistress," she answered. "I will go at once."

Riya and Abraheem made their way to the port as the dawn glow tinted the sky. They hurried through the already bustling market. Merchants were arranging their goods, emptying bushels of crimson peppers and plump aromatic garlic bulbs into their woven baskets. Chickens squawked as they hung by their clawed feet from tent poles. Riya adjusted her veil snugly across her face, lest anyone recognize her. She gripped the small bag of gold coins close against her body.

Abraheem walked confidently in front of Riya, his right hand firmly on his shabria, alert to any suspicious movements in his peripheral vision as well as what lie directly ahead of him. From time to time Abraheem glanced back to make sure the servant girl followed safely. He was a tall man in his early twenties with finely chiseled features and square shoulders. His beard was full; and a long, straight nose gave his face the classical definition of masculine strength. He wore a stark white turban, and his mustache was carefully trimmed and neatly groomed. Abraheem did not have the unruly bushy brows of his clan. He was also taller, by a head, than anyone in his family.

His father swore him to secrecy; made him vow to protect the servant of Yasmine with his life if necessary. He was proud that his father entrusted this responsibility to him, for he was the third son of the Silversmith, and lived in the shadows of his elder brother. He thought to himself: *the task would be easier if Riya were allowed to walk in front of him, but this could arouse unwanted attention and curiosity.* Abraheem did not ask his father why he was ordered to protect Riya and take her to find the Captain of the Hercules, for it was not his place to question Farouq.

They turned into one of the alleys leading to the port. A beggar wrapped in dirty burlap sacks was hunched in a doorway. "*Ahalan ou Sa'alan* (Peace unto you)." Abraheem addressed the man, "I seek the captain of the Greek tanker, Hercules. For a sum, may it be that you can tell me where I might find this man?"

"For your kind generosity, I might have knowledge of the man you seek."

Abraheem slapped a small silver coin into the filthy outstretched hand.

"The Greeks like dancing girls and drinking. These things can be had by the infidels at the Golden Tents of Persia. Go west as you leave this alley. You may find the Greek Captain there. May Allah guide your path and protect you from harm," the beggar said through his broken-toothed grin.

"Abraheem, we must hurry - the sun is now high in the sky, and my mistress awaits my return," Riya said.

"Follow me to the end of this alley, but do not follow beyond that point. I know of this Golden Tents of Persia. It is a dangerous unholy refuge of thieves and unbelievers. It is no place for a virtuous woman. I will find the man we seek, and bring him here. Sit there in the darkness of that unused doorway and cover yourself with your shawl and veil. Speak to no one!" He slipped a silver dagger into her sweaty palm. "Here, take this. Use it swiftly and without warning if you are threatened. Remember the lessons I taught you and your sisters last year, when your mistress asked for my father's help in protecting your house from intruders. You were my best pupil, so I know that you can defend yourself. Do not be afraid."

Riya huddled against the cold stones of the arched door way. The rusty lock on the metal door, and the debris and smell of urine in the entrance way made it obvious that there was no chance that anyone would be leaving the ancient building from this unused exit.

Abraheem cautiously approached the brothel known as the Golden Tents of Persia. Dirty colored glass beads hung over the doorway, and the licorice smell of Arrack was strong. Abraheem walked with a straight solid step pushing aside the hanging beads. He settled himself on a broad sofa in the corner of the dark room and laid his silver shabria on the brass-topped table in front of him. He tossed two silver coins noisily onto the table. A fat man, wearing a stained red Fez and boasting a thick bushy mustache, hurried over to the table.

"*Salaam Ale chum* (Peace upon you). Perhaps I can be of some small service to you *Habib* (friend)?" He bowed at the waist, as he eyed the silver coins and the beautifully crafted shabria.

"Perhaps," Abraheem stroked his thick beard with his left hand, keeping his right hand very close to the dagger. "I have a message for the captain of the Greek tanker, Hercules".

The fat man beamed, showing some missing teeth. "I happen to be on friendly terms with this captain that you seek. He is an important man. It would take a great deal of persuasion from someone he trusts, like me, to convince him to receive a stranger."

Abraheem understood the bargaining of his world, and, given the luxury of time, he could have maneuvered this greedy idiot into giving him the information for practically nothing. However, he did not have the time. He was worried about Riya; and time was passing too quickly. He had to leave this dangerous area of the city before nightfall. He reached into the pouch tied to his belt and extracted a small gold coin. He stood up, grabbing his shabria. Grinning, he held the shabria to the man's throat; and thrust the coin into his open mouth. "You may swallow that coin, and retrieve it tomorrow with the help of nature; but now you will take me to the captain. *Yella* (Now)!"

The man gulped, swallowing the coin. His eyes were protruding from their sockets, and beads of moisture studded his forehead.

"If you try any tricks, or lead me into a trap, I swear by Allah that I will retrieve the coin myself, and I won't wait for nature to take its course." Abraheem stated with quiet, flat resolution, pushing the edge of the shabria into the folds of neck skin until a few drops of blood dripped onto the man's shirt.

"Y-Y-Yes. I will take you to Captain Demetrius. Please follow me, your humble servant. It just so happens that the Captain is asleep upstairs."

Abraheem withdrew the knife, and followed the man across the room, and up the ornate carpeted stairs. The man pointed toward one of the doors along the wide hallway. "He is in there with a whore, asleep no doubt, after a very rowdy and drunken night. These infidels are as animals."

As he pushed the man out of his way, Abraheem quietly opened the door. Captain Demetrius lay on a bed in the middle of the room. His hairy exposed belly was spilling onto the mattress in tiers of fat bulges. A naked young girl was asleep on the floor, black and blue marks were visible on her back and arms. Abraheem took a blanket from the foot of the bed and threw it over her. She murmured softly in her sleep. He stepped around the girl to the bedside. "Captain Demetrius! Captain! Wake up!" Abraheem said in English.

The man opened his eyes slowly, as he slid one hand under his pillow.

Abraheem held the tip of his shabria against the Captain's neck, "If you are reaching for your weapon, think again."

"Who are you? What do you want, you son-of-a-bitch?"

"Relax Captain. I come to transact some profitable business with you. I am sorry for this impolite intrusion, but the matter I wish to discuss with you cannot wait to accommodate the good manners to which we are both accustomed." He sheathed the knife at his waistband and stepped back from the bed. "Forgive me. I am Abraheem, son of the Silversmith, Farouq."

The cloudy eyes of the captain cleared somewhat upon hearing the word "profitable". "Very well, I forgive you. Wait for me downstairs."

Back in the alley, Riya looked exhausted from the terrible night that had passed. Lack of sleep and food made her legs tremble under her robe. As she took an unsteady step toward the end of the alley, Abraheem was coming around the corner accompanied by a stranger. His gait was sure and steady.

"I should not have doubted his success," she said to no one.

The captain was eager to conclude their business as quickly as possible. Riya listened carefully as the captain explained, "I am most willing to take a passenger on the Hercules. The ship will sail on the eve of the new moon - that will be in three weeks from today, before first light. We are bound for the Suez, and on through the Straits of Gibraltar, to bring oil to the refineries of Rotterdam in Holland. Tell your master the voyage will take at least a month." Captain Demetrius put his mark on the note, and sealed it with his captain's ring. He snatched the pouch of gold from Riya's fingers, "A boat will be waiting at the third hour after midnight. It will take the passengers from the pier to the ship. The passenger may bring one small trunk. It will be searched - no drugs or alcohol will be allowed. Do not be late! The Hercules waits for no one," the Captain stated.

CHAPTER 6

Preparation

Safina physically recuperated from the ravages of the pregnancy and birth. Yasmine carefully bound the girl's milk-swollen breasts, and applied cool compresses to relieve the pain. The milk was gradually reabsorbed and Safina's breasts returned to almost normal, despite scars from Khaliq's torture.

Yasmine had made a crucial decision on the morning after the birth. To protect the baby from Khaliq and from any claims to her, Yasmine swore Badrae and Riya to secrecy, "The child was stillborn. Not a whisper of her existence or identity will be breathed again in this house or elsewhere."

Yasmine told the cook to take the baby home at once, "Find a closed mouth wet nurse who will feed the baby without asking questions, in return for a generous payment."

She was surprised that Safina did not cry or visibly mourn for her lost baby, but Safina seemed almost oblivious to the explanation, "The baby is in Paradise, where birds with beautiful long feathers of every color, sing it to sleep, and the servants of Allah protect it from harm."

Yasmine discussed this with a psychiatrist friend in Baghdad, a man who was fighting the same battles against fundamental ignorance as she was. He was writing a research paper on the long-term affects of state condoned, and institutionalized, sexual abuse of children on society; specifically in a culture where they are unprotected by law, and where exploitation is promoted by that society.

He offered an explanation, "She is simply too young to understand what happened to her. She might associate her suffering with the child of Khaliq. In her mind, they may be the same entity, the same source of pain and brutality. You cannot judge her. She has dealt with things that no child should ever have to experience. I would not be surprised if she never finds love and never has more children. That may be for the best, if she is to survive," the doctor replied. "Relationships of trust and physical love would be difficult for a victim like Safina to pursue. They would, in most cases, embrace a solitary life style."

Yasmine accepted his explanation. They had worked together on the structure of the UFN (United Free Nations) Council and the charter of the future UFAS (United Federation of Arab States). In the many years they had toiled together Yasmine had learned he was an expert in his field, someone she trusted and respected, both academically and personally.

Several days later, as Yasmine sat on the veranda trying to find a solution to protect Safina and the baby, the cook approached timidly.

"Yes, Badrae? What is it?"

"Mistress, I have a story to tell. As you know, my youngest brother, Abdul, went to America to become a doctor. There, in a place called Philadelphia, he married an American woman. They have not been blessed with children. It is his and his wife's greatest sorrow that the laughter and joy that a child brings, is absent from their home. When he came to visit last year, he asked me to search for a baby that might be available for adoption. He specifically wanted a child who would be similar to him in complexion and features, so that no one would question its parentage. I think he and his wife would love our baby Assal as their own. Being a doctor, he could provide for her education; and afford her every opportunity in life, far away from here."

Yasmine smiled. "Assal? Yes, of course, as sweet as honey!" *Badrae must have named the child, and Allah has answered my prayers,* she thought. *How marvelous is his love. He has prepared a path for Assal even before she was conceived. How great is Allah's compassion. Assal is part of his plan.* "Yes, this is good news Badrae. Call your brother today."

Yasmine toyed with the green plant on the table. She noticed the narrow straight stripes on each leaf of the spider plant. They were like Assal's fingers, with perfectly formed delicate fingernails. She wondered what plan Allah had for the baby girl that had been snatched from death. As she looked up from her place on the veranda, she saw a black horse on the skyline above the city. Its long tail arched high, as it pranced and strutted back and forth across the backdrop of the city lights that were just beginning to flick on, as darkness descended. Then the horse was gone.

With the help of her friend from the hospital in Baghdad, Yasmine was able to obtain a birth certificate that listed her as the mother, and her friend as the father. Based on this original document and the subsequent signatures of her friend and herself, she knew the courts would issue a new birth certificate with the names of the adoptive parents, permanently sealing the original birth certificate, and hiding the connection between herself, Assal, and Safina. This way she would not have to reveal the truth to Safina. Khaliq would have no way of knowing about the child. The plan was bold but feasible.

During the following days, she saw unfamiliar men passing by her house and seeming to peer over the walls to see into the garden. She encountered a stranger on her front steps looking into the front windows. When she asked him what he wanted, he begged for a job washing her windows. But she noticed that he had no bucket, water, or rags for such a job. She sent him away and told him not to come near her house again. Yasmine knew that it was only a matter of time before Khaliq's spies would find Safina and drag her back to his chamber of horrors. She imagined that he was obsessed with getting Safina back; under Muslim law a wife is not viewed differently than chattel, and he would never be forced to give up his property.

Yasmine endeavored to strengthen Safina. She ordered fresh calf liver delivered daily, which she personally prepared. Her secret in retaining its blood-building capability was to roast it over white-hot coals, while slowly turning the skewered pieces without burning the liver, until it was just done, still soft and slightly pink in the middle. Slivers of sweet yellow onions, and precooked, heavily marbled, beef chunks marinated in wine were interspersed between the pieces of liver. She prepared a large wooden bowl that she rubbed with olive oil and crushed garlic. She cleared each skewer by pushing a fork against the pieces, sliding them all into the wooden bowl. She sprinkled the mixture with freshly ground black pepper, a pinch of salt, and a sprinkle of "*hawaige*" (a curry/pepper mixture of spices). Safina regained her appetite and her young body was Jasmine's ally in forcing a quick recovery.

Yasmine taught Safina all she could in the three weeks until the Hercules was scheduled to depart. Over the past eight months Safina had mastered elementary reading and writing skills. Yasmine had instilled a thirst for knowledge, and a love of literature in Safina. She was amazed at Safina's natural intelligence. Her fingers flew over the copybook's pages, leaving line after line of exquisite characters. Her memory was phenomenal. Yasmine had mentioned this to Vivian. There was something unusual and unique about her ability to recall events, people, news reports, and anything she heard or read in its entirety.

It was during this time that Yasmine began to wonder if this girl might turn out to be a person the UFN Council would consider for the future UFAS leadership. She called her close friend in the UFN, a retired French diplomat, Arnaud Fournier, to discuss Safina's future. Fournier was interested, "If you can get her to Holland in one piece, we can coordinate our efforts from there. I'm transmitting a list of operatives to you through our secured link. I think you are already familiar with most of them."

Yasmine contacted Luigi Morelli on the Hercules, who could get the girl into Amsterdam. He was a physician and research scientist. He said he knew someone in Holland who could help Safina, Vivian Von Stetton.

"I know Vivian well and have already spoken to her about Safina." she told him. "We became acquainted through her work with the UFN." Yasmine worried that the plan was too involved, too complex to work, but she had no choice. She could not take the girl to Holland herself. If anyone became suspicious about Safina and Yasmine traveling together that information might find its way to Khaliq.

There were already rumors flying that a strange girl was living in her house, and a neighbor came to tell her that one of the boys from the local school said that bulletins were posted at the school and at the mosque, asking all the boys and men to notify the *Mullah* (the local cleric) if they knew of any strange young girl appearing in the area. Yasmine armed her house servants with daggers, and let her big Kuvaz herding dog sleep in the house at night, outside of Safina's door, instead of sleeping with her flock of sheep.

As the time to leave drew near, Yasmine observed the sadness in Safina's eyes. She thought it must be the natural mourning over her lost baby that was finally rising to the surface. Several times she wanted to tell Safina that her baby was alive and safe, but she knew the girl would not want to leave her child. Yasmine was sure there was no possibility for Safina to escape Khaliq, and have any kind of future if she did not leave Iraq soon.

Badrae's brother and his wife were joyful at the prospect of adopting Assal, and they immediately flew to Iraq with their attorney to handle the legalities, and hopefully, take their new daughter home to Philadelphia. Yasmine insisted on meeting with them. She wanted to be sure they were suitable as responsible parents, and capable of loving the child as their own.

Dr. Zubayer was in his late 30's. His eyes were soft, dark brown, with thick lashes. Only his bushy mustache saved his masculine appearance. His wife, Christi, was from Atlanta, Georgia, and her Arabic was flavored with a charming unexpected southern drawl. Mrs. Zubayer was young, and full of energy. From the airport, they drove straight to Badrae's house. He gave his sister a big American bear hug when she opened the door of her modest house. It was a happy reunion, and Badrae hugged Christi and kissed both of her cheeks. They had not seen one another since Abdul and Christi's wedding. Badrae prepared all of Abdul's favorite Iraqi dishes. He licked his lips in satisfaction and smiled at his sister, "I had almost forgotten what a wonderful cook you are - truly an artist in the kitchen."

Christi laughed out loud when she saw Assal. She held the baby close to her heart and looked up at her husband over the infant's head, "Abe, can we take her home now?" she asked.

"I don't want you to be disappointed, so don't get your hopes up too high. Let's go meet with Mrs. Abussani before we fall hopelessly in love with this child." He took long strides toward the waiting car – and then remembered to wait for his wife who was carrying Assal wrapped in a colorful quilt. He held the rear door open for Christi while she secured the baby in the car carrier, and turned and hugged him around the chest. Towering over her, he pecked the top of her head affectionately. She settled into the back seat of the car fussing with the seat belts. Abe had insisted on bringing a baby carrier, but Christi was loath to give up holding the baby. He put his hand on her arm, "Christi, we must think of Assal's safety above all."

"All right, but as soon as we get there I am holding her again," Christi announced.

"Well, here goes," he said, as he closed the car door, ran around to the driver's side, and jumped in. Abe drove the rental car from Badrae's house in the village to Yasmine's villa on the edge of Basra. He held his wife's gaze in the mirror. "I love you, Christi. I hope this baby will be ours, but if for some reason it can't be arranged, I promise you we'll find a little girl to love and to share our happiness."

They walked up to the front door of the villa, and Abe lifted the big lion head door knocker, and let it fall upon the brass plate. Almost immediately the door opened. Riya was waiting for them. "This way, Sir," she whispered. She led them into a corridor from the right side of the large entrance hall, down a short flight of stone steps, and onto a private patio. A table was set with fine crystal, and antique bone china, hand painted in tiny ornate geometrical patterns with gold leaf edging. An engraved copper "*Finjan*" (metal pitcher) sat steaming over a small flame. The scent of cinnamon coffee permeated the air. Riya turned two small bowls over and poured the hot thick coffee into them. She placed a container of sugar and a small spoon between the bowls. "Please be comfortable. My mistress will come soon."

Abe seated his wife and then sat on the chair facing her. As he sipped the aromatic coffee, he watched his wife. Christi stared at the baby's face. Assal had fallen asleep in the car, and her long eyelashes, against her rosy cheeks, lent the baby's face an aura of blissful innocence. The carrier with the sleeping child rested on the carpet next to them. As he looked across the table at Christi his expression reflected the love he felt. She was a petite woman with deep brown eyes and luxurious auburn hair that curled around her cheerful face. Although no raving beauty, she radiated something that made her inner goodness obvious. She had no secrets and no guile about her. Everything she was could be read in the simple features of her face.

Yasmine watched the couple on the terrace. She wanted to see them alone, and if it meant spying through the lace curtains of the balcony window across the courtyard, so be it. She believed that before parents could love a child, they must love each other. After seeing all the suffering of women at the hands of their husbands and fathers, she had a low opinion of Iraqi men. She doubted that many of them were capable of loving anyone beside themselves. But when she saw Abdul rise, walk over to his wife, and squat down by her knees, she was surprised. He took Christi's hand in his, and leaned over to kiss her softly on the cheek. Then he reached up and cradled her face in his hands. He said something to her, but Yasmine couldn't hear it from her place behind the curtains. Christi smiled, and Yasmine knew that this man was no typical Muslim man. She knew he loved his wife, and she knew he would be able to hold Assal in his heart too. *He's a lucky man who found a good woman, and he knows it,* she thought.

She went down to meet them. They sat around the table and talked with Yasmine. She liked them. It was as though a weight were lifted from her heart. Allah had provided fine parents for Safina's daughter. Dr. and Mrs. Zubayer were dedicated proponents of Islamic reformation.

"Christi, would you be offended if I have a private talk with your husband? I have some procedural legal details for the doctor, and you look tired. I offer you the relaxation of my spa, and Riya has prepared a guest room for you to rest until dinnertime. Riya will take care of the baby. She has prepared some formula for her." Seeing the worried look on Christi's face she added, "Don't worry, after you have rested, Riya will bring the baby to you. Please feel at home, and your husband may join you shortly." She didn't wait for an answer. Riya appeared in the doorway, "This way Madam." She attempted to take Assal from Christi's arms. Christi wasn't having that.

She turned toward the door and shifted the baby to the other side of her body, away from Riya. "It's OK Riya. Show me where the guest room is. I'll change her while you warm the bottle."

Yasmine smiled as she watched Christi march down the hallway behind Riya. "She isn't going to be timid about protecting and caring for her daughter, is she?" She said to Abe.

"I think you are right about that," he answered.

With Christi out of the room, Yasmine stood up and began speaking in Arabic, "Dr. Zubayer, let us be candid. I am pleased that you and your wife want to adopt Assal, and I believe you will provide a loving home for the child. But I have some stipulations."

"Madam, what are these stipulations?"

"First of all, I want your written promise that you will provide for Assal equally as your legal heir, and that regardless of how many children you may father in the future, males and females, you will leave an equal percentage of your estate to Assal. Secondly, I want your promise that you will not enter into agreements regarding Assal's betrothal, and you will not seek monetary or personal benefit from any marriage arrangement made for her. You will set aside a trust fund for Assal's education. This money is to be given to a charity in the event that Assal does not seek higher education by the age of twenty-five. I am also setting up a trust fund for Assal, and will name you as the executor of this trust. She is not to be told about this money. It is to be given to her only if and when she should find herself in a situation that she wishes to leave, such as an unhappy marriage or political unrest in a country where she resides." Yasmine sat down to listen to Abe's reaction.

Abe looked pleased. "My sister has not shared much information over the telephone. I sense that there is more to this story. But, you are doing everything you can to protect the child, which is exactly what I want to do. You and I want the same opportunities for Assal. I can promise you, Madam, that all that you have requested and more will be provided."

Yasmine swore him to secrecy and then she told him the story of Safina. She told it quietly and in great detail. As the story unfolded Abe was listening with rapt attention. His eyebrows rose several times in surprise. But soon he was clenching his fists and becoming visibly angry. "I abhor the appalling disregard for basic human rights under Iraqi law," he said. "I wish there was something I could do to change that."

She appeared to ignore his last statement, "Khaliq can legally seize the baby as his property if he learns of her existence. You will receive a new birth certificate that lists you and your wife as the parents of Assal. This child will be free to find happiness, and purpose in her life, and you will be able to provide the father she deserves. Besides you, only your sister Badrae, Riya, and I, know the truth."

Abraheem hesitated for a moment as though he were deciding if he could trust Yasmine completely, "I watched my father beat my mother, as my grandfather beat my grandmother. I remember my mother's funeral, and the child bride my father brought home soon afterwards. I watched a young girl, not much older than myself at the time, turn into an old woman before her sixteenth birthday. I promised myself then that I would be different. That is why I couldn't return to Iraq after completing medical school. I couldn't stand by and watch silently as the Sharia Islamic laws protect pedophiles and wife beaters. Yes, I'm a Muslim, but I consider myself a reformed Muslim. I know there are many more just like me who pray daily for the Reformation of Islam."

"When Safina is safely out of Iraq and has a new identity, you will receive a safety deposit box key in the mail. I will give you the box number now, and its location in New York City. Please secure these items in a safe place where Assal can access them after her twenty-fifth birthday. If more information of importance should surface regarding Assal or Safina I will add that information to the safety deposit box. You may open it at any time."

They rose together, and embraced warmly. "Allah's blessings shall be upon you," Yasmine whispered in his ear. "Come, I will introduce you to Safina. But you must not tell her why you are here. She believes the child was stillborn. She must believe this to have any chance to escape Khaliq.

It will be emotionally difficult for all of us to see her interacting with Assal this evening. Please prepare Mrs. Zubayer for that. I told Safina that you would be bringing your infant daughter with you to dinner. This will be the first time Safina has ever seen this baby. It may bring the pain of loss to the surface when she observes Assal at the same age that her child would have been. I have decided to risk that possibility, because I want her to experience a few moments of joy in holding this child. We cannot know what the future may hold for Safina. Perhaps someday, far into the future, there will come a time when she will be told the truth. At that time she will also know that on this day, she held her daughter in her arms and looked into her eyes. She has been deprived of everything; she deserves this small gift."

Noises could be heard in the kitchen as Badrae and Riya prepared a feast. The smell of delicious food wafted throughout the villa. "I have made arrangements for a photograph to be taken of Safina holding Assal. I will take photographs of all of us this evening. These photos will be sent to you, and copies will be put into the safety deposit box for Assal," Yasmine said.

"It seems you have thought of everything. But, I suspect it will break our hearts to see Safina with Assal and not be able to tell her that this is her daughter," Abdul's eyes were shiny with unshed tears. "I'm not sure we can pull this one off."

"We must." Yasmine straightened her back resolutely. She stared at Abe long and hard, "Abe, there is a way for you to effect change in Iraq and throughout Islam. This is not the right time to discuss it."

Abe followed Yasmine to the kitchen. Safina was busy sorting rice. She was seated next to the window with a large hand-woven basket on her lap as she picked out discolored grains or small pieces of gravel or stems and put them on a rag that was spread on the table next to her. The setting sun behind her framed her raven black hair in a golden aura. Her skin was bronzed and smooth. Safina had delicate fingers and small ears that fit close to her head with ornate golden earrings that looped twice, hanging low at the level of her chin. The golden nose ring lent an exotic flavor to her persona.

Abe stood in the doorway, looking at her. She glanced up from the basket of rice. Her hazel-green eyes were sad, but her lips turned upward in a welcoming smile. "You must be Dr. Zubayer, Badrae's brother," she said. "Badrae told me you and your wife would be having supper with us tonight. I hope you enjoy your visit to Iraq."

They feasted on the cook's best Kurdish inspired menu: purple farina kubeh dumplings stuffed with roasted lamb, pistachio nuts, and sautéed chopped cracked, green, garlic-spiced olives, floating in spicy dark sweet and salty beet soup. Abe scooped out a plump olive and popped it into Christi's mouth. "Have you ever tasted an olive like that before?"

Golden almond-flavored long grain rice was heaped on a bed of lightly steamed cabbage leaves. Sprigs of fresh mint and paper-thin slices of oranges were strewn across the center. A dozen delicate small china bowls were filled with a variety of exotic salads made from ground sesame seeds, thick creamy yogurt from goat milk, and cucumber-tomato-scallion-parsley mixed with olive oil and lemon juice, were placed throughout the table setting.

Safina heaped her plate with roasted eggplant salad with tahina, and an adaptation of Greek Mousaka casserole made with melted feta cheese layered with ground curried beef and smothered in a creamy white sauce. Badrae beamed with pride over this wonderful meal.

They conversed in Arabic, a language in which Christi was surprisingly competent. "I met Abe in college when I took an Arabic class that he was teaching as a graduate student T.A. I was studying several dialects of Arabic because I was committed to supporting the liberation of women in Islamic countries. Abe was working on his doctorate and needed a competent native English writer to edit and polish his manuscript. I planned to finance my graduate Islamic studies with a grant from the State Department, by promising to work for them for a few years. It was a good match. I could master advanced Arabic and he would be assured that his doctorate dissertation was truly professional. He was so charming and easy to talk to, and we fell hopelessly in love by the time his dissertation was finished."

Riya brought the baby out after dinner. Safina was delighted to play with the infant, "Let me feed her." She was glad to be the one to feed the baby her bottle. She sat on the floor next to Assal, who was lying on a thick blanket cooing and looking irresistibly beautiful. Safina played with the baby, making funny faces and dangling toys above her. Assal wrapped her tiny hand tightly around her birth mother's fingers. The look on Safina's face was joyful. For the first time in months her eyes lit up with life. She was so focused on her connection with the baby that she did not see the pensive faces looking on at this bittersweet moment.

Christi and Safina laughed and talked together all evening, delighting Yasmine who had never heard Safina laugh before. Later, as they were leaving, Safina ran up to Christi and hugged her. "You remind me of my friend, Farka," Safina said. "I wish I could see her again. It was good to remember games we played and good times we had together."

Christi took a thin silver bracelet off her arm, and put it on Safina's wrist. "This is to remember me by, and to remember your friend, Farka," she said.

"*Shukran*," Safina said. "I will wear always," she spoke haltingly in English.

The next day Abe and Christi exchanged the notarized documents with Yasmine, who came to Badrae's house to bid them goodbye.

Yasmine lifted the baby from the sheepskin cradle, and kissed her on the forehead. "May Allah guide your way, and may your life be full of joy." She placed the child in Christi's arms. Abe and Christi got into the car and drove to the airport. In twenty two hours, they would be home in Philadelphia and Assal would begin her new life as an American.

Yasmine rose at midnight. She was unable to sleep. "*Allah hu akbar*. Guide this child, Safina, through a life of fulfillment and achievement. Through your love and mercy, give Assal great opportunity and purpose. Grant both mother and daughter strength and wisdom. Protect them from the demons of men," she prayed.

She returned to her bed and pulled the blanket up around her shoulders, and fell back to sleep. Later that night she dreamed of Nomad. He stood by the window outside of her bedroom as he spoke to her, "It will be twenty-five years before Assal returns to Iraq under very different circumstances, but she will return."

Yasmine arose in the morning refreshed and at peace. A sense of tranquility embraced her. It was as though a cloak of patience and trust had been given to her. For the first time in months she was not worried about the future.

CHAPTER 7

The Journey

The perigee full moon slid in and out, behind the ominous clouds of a black starless sky. The Hercules began her count-down to departure. The ship would be underway within the hour.

Yasmine, thorough as always, had asked a friend who worked at the Basra customs office to provide information about the tanker: the ship was a "T2" class vessel, small for a tanker yet well suited to her course through the Suez Canal. According to the data Yasmine found, the Suez was a world oil transit choke point; ships passing through the canal had to be significantly smaller than the typical behemoth transatlantic tankers going to sea. The Hercules weighed in at 16,000 DWT (dead weight tons); fully pregnant with the crude black gold of the Middle East, she rode deep in the water. The local Basra newspaper ran an article on recent piracy along the coast of Somalia. Yasmine was interested in the reporter's interviews of the Captain of the Hercules and several members of the 45-man crew. According to the article almost all of the ship's functions were manu-ally operated. The sailors claimed they were unafraid of pirates and, in any case, on this run to Rotterdam they would not be passing near Somalia. There was a photograph of the crew. They didn't look too bad. Most were neatly attired, and grinning for the photographer. Yasmine was satisfied that Safina would be safe.

As the Hercules' engines engaged, the sailors ran forward and aft pulling up anchors and hoisting her colors. She sailed under a Greek flag. Despite her advanced age, she was free of rust deposits, and her engines and nautical equipment were operationally sound. Abraheem, the son of Farouq, helped Safina into the long boat.

The day before, he told Riya, "I can't help wishing it were me instead of this strange girl, who is leaving. I want to sail on that ship. I want to see the world, and all its exotic places. It's a waste of money to send a girl on such a journey."

Abraheem helped Safina step into the Captain's Launch boat that would take them out to the Hercules, anchored just beyond the breakwater. He slipped a small silver shabria into her palm as he put one finger to his lips, cautioning her to be still. As she moved past him toward the back of the boat, he whispered into her ear, "Keep the dagger close always, for your safety."

"Are you sailing with us?" the sailor shouted at him.

"No," Abraheem answered. "I wish I were, though."

"If you mean it, we have need for strong man with taste for life. Angeleno, our cook's helper, got slashed in fight last night and won't make sailing. Are you ready to go on great adventure of life?" His Arabic was stilted, lacking the flow of someone fluent in a tongue that came easily to his lips. But, the offer he presented was clearly stated.

Abraheem's dark eyes sparkled in the lamplight, held high by the sailor. Impulsive and fearlessly decisive, Abraheem didn't hesitate for a second, "*Iawah!* Can I send a message to my father?"

The sailor nodded, "Come boy," he called to a waif on the pier. "Write note son," he looked at Abraheem, as he pulled a wrinkled handbill from his pocket. "You write it on back of this."

Abraheem raised his left foot onto the bottom railing that surrounded the pier. He smoothed the crinkled paper against his knee, extracted a silver pen from the side of his leather boot, and began to write:

Most honored father, I embark this day on a great adventure. As your youngest son, I hold no expectations in Basra. I sail on the Hercules bound for Rotterdam, and promise to protect the charge entrusted to me. Allah hu akbar,

Your Faithful Son, Abraheem.

He folded the paper in half and in the margin of the handbill he wrote: Farouq Abd al Aziiz - Silversmith, Salah A Din Street, Basra.

The sailor smiled; all of his front teeth were missing. In the dim moving light of the lamp he appeared grotesque. Abraheem shivered as his scalp contracted involuntarily. The sailor took the note and handed it to the boy. "Give to Silversmith on Salah A Din Street." He handed him a small piece of silver. "By Allah - swear it."

The boy swore, "By Allah, it will be done."

As the boat pulled away from the dock, its diesel engine spewed foul smelling fumes into the cold dawn. Soot blew back onto the shivering passengers stinging their eyes, and dusting them with black particles. The filth clung to their fog-dampened faces and clothing, but they accepted this without complaint or comment. There were just a few travelers: Abraheem shared a plank in the rear with the sailor who was manning the rudder; a few turbaned men with greasy beards sat in front of them; Safina and three other females squatted in the bow. Under their thick veils and dark shawls, they endured the choppy slap of the bow as it rose up and lurched back down, finding its jerky way through the wind-blown waves.

Abraheem's excitement and his impulsive mood quickly abated. "Where you go when we get to Rotterdam?" the sailor yelled above the "click clack" of the tired engine.

"As Allah wills my destiny so I accept it," Abraheem screamed his reply, more towards the heavens than to the Greek sailor. The boat reached the Hercules just as the eastern horizon began to brighten. The foggy mist was vanishing and glimmers of flying fish skimmed the waves every few minutes.

"*Yella, yella,*" barked the Greek sailor. "Quick, quick. The tide is changing." He herded them up the metal steps of the ladder. When they reached the deck they huddled together at the stern, and watched the chain disappear into the ship as the Hercules' anchor was secured. The three black smoke stacks coughed acrid smoke, building up steam that would push the huge pistons and turn the 1000 lb crankshaft to rotate the massive propeller. The Hercules shuddered, the grinding of her gears grating on the ears of the travelers; each one lost in his or her, own secret thoughts.

Safina held her fingers curled together for warmth and calmness in a world she had stopped trying to defend against. *Allah hu akbar,* she silently chanted in her mind, over and over, a mantra. But Allah seemed not to be concerned with the terrors of a girl.

"This way, this way," the Greek beckoned to them. The men shuffled behind him, and as always, the women followed several paces behind the men. Women were always last. They descended a narrow stairwell, and another, and another. Safina could smell the stale air and she thought they must be near the bottom of the ship by now.

The ship got underway and, as the bow lurched forward, the floor came up to meet her feet before she could plant them solidly on the metal floor. The others were having trouble staying upright, and soon sounds of gagging and retching could be heard. The stench was rapidly growing more putrid. Safina found a bench bolted along the oily wall of the ship's bowels, and she settled herself upon its hard yet welcome surface. Her stomach churned and her head ached; she waited for the nausea to pass, as her body adjusted to this different equilibrium. She nibbled upon a dried pita crust. This would help settle her stomach and avert losing her breakfast; another valuable remedy that Yasmine taught her during the pregnancy. *How I miss her,* Safina mused.

She awoke abruptly on the second night at sea, sensing some-one staring into her face. It was the same toothless sailor who brought them on board. He was grinning at her with wet lips and the lustful look she knew so well from her days with Khaliq. She smelled his sweat, and felt his breath on her. He grabbed her up off of the bench and threw her onto the floor on her back. He was immediately upon her, ripping her shawl from her body and expos-ing her flesh. His hand worked frantically to pull up her dress, and then to pull down her long pants under her skirts. She kicked at him but he was too tightly pushed against her to make it affective. Safina banged her head against his face, trying to break his nose. She attempted to bite him, but he grabbed her neck with his other hand and began to squeeze it in a suffocating grip. She felt her head spinning; the lack of oxygen was starting to dull her reflexes. Desperate for air, she fought to slide her hand into her pocket between his body and hers. Just as she thought she was going to pass out, she grasped the shabria handle and forcibly yanked it free of the sheath. With a sudden gasp, the sailor collapsed upon her. Slowly she withdrew the shabria's blade from his side. Blood gushed from the wound as she shoved the man's body off of her. He rolled over onto his back and lay still as his life's blood oozed from the deep slit, and finally the flow subsided as his breathing stopped. A red puddle was spreading beneath his body. Safina's clothes were not soiled. She had successfully avoided the blood.

A hand reached down to her, and she took hold of it. The hand was warm, and the grasp was strong and sure. As she was pulled to her feet, she looked into the face of Abraheem. Safina mechanically wiped the shabria off with her underskirt and put the sheath in place. She stiffly shoved it back into her pocket and set about mindlessly rearranging her clothes as quickly as possible. Her eyes were vacant and her breathing was shallow.

In the dim light of the small emergency bulb attached to the wall, Abraheem peered at her intently. "Safina, pay attention!" He grabbed an old canvas tarp from the corner of the corridor and rolled the body of the sailor onto it. He wrapped the body in the stiff fabric and tied some rope around it. He found some rags and a scrub brush among the stores at the end of the passage and brought them back to Safina. He was moving quickly and deliberately. He shoved them at her, but her hands didn't reach out to take them. "Safina - look at me." He touched her cheek and moved his hand under her chin and pulled her face up. "There is a bucket of water in the corner. Use it to clean the floor as best you can. I will throw this infidel overboard. Do not mention this to anyone no matter what they ask – you know nothing! I will come back to get the dirty rags and empty the bucket. Safina, what do you know about this?"

"Nothing," she replied. "I don't know anything about it."

"Good girl." Abraheem handed her a key to the bathroom, pointing to the locked door across from them. "That is the wash-room. Be sure not to leave any sign that you have been there. Wash your hands well when you have finished. Remember to lock the door behind you and give the key back to me when I return." He looked into her eyes, "It will be alright Safina.....trust me."

Safina was finally coming out of shock. Her hands trembled as she cleaned up the bloody floor. She took deep breaths and clenched her teeth tightly, despite the stinging bile rising in her throat. The smell of the fresh blood repulsed her.

The crew soon discovered that the sailor was missing. The Captain interrogated everyone. Safina was silent. She presented herself as an ignorant girl who could barely understand the Captain's questions. Finally the consensus was that the sailor was intoxicated the night they sailed from Basra – and probably fell overboard in a drunken stupor.

It was Abraheem who took over the duties of the missing sailor. It became his habit to check on Safina two or three times per day. He brought food for the passengers, and clean buckets of water for their personal hygiene, removing the dirty buckets and emptying them into the sea, being careful to rinse them well with salty sea-water and setting them on the deck to dry in the sun. Whenever he could, he would steal a piece of fruit or some vegetables from the galley for Safina and the other women.

On the fifth day of the journey, Safina found her "sea legs," becoming accustomed to the swaying and bobbing of the huge tanker, as though it were a cork afloat in the ocean. She paced back and forth down the short corridor, rubbing her hands, and taking them in and out of the folds of her robe. She reached under her veil and smoothed her thick black hair. Then she sat down on the bench, counting the number of rivets from the bench to the wall, noticing for the thousandth time each indentation, scratch or tiny imperfection in each section of the metal. She sang childhood songs in her mind, mentally walked through the house she grew up in, and remembered the games she played with Farka in the courtyard on the heavy blocks of stone. She was tired of being confined, tired of being surrounded by gray walls and gray floors, tired of eating the same tasteless watery soup each day.

She prayed silently as a way of calming herself - rocking back and forth on her knees during genuflection with covered head as she mouthed the words: *Allah have mercy upon me and command the winds and the waves to be calm during this voyage. Make thy servant strong and give me the faith to live each day believing there is a purpose.* Safina refused to repeat mindless admonitions from the Quran because she equated them to the religious practices of Khaliq and El Sighi. But even her prayers born of hope were transparently void of conviction. Safina suspected they were heard only by her own heart. She desperately needed Allah to be great and all-seeing, merciful and just, but her experiences had not born that out. Safina's brief childhood with its naturally endowed, translucent delicate weave of childish trust, had been fractured and rent; its fabric shredded almost beyond recovery.

Safina remembered the words of Yasmine: "The act of supplication in itself may strengthen your faith. This is the essence of repetitive prayers."

A few days later Abraheem found her in a depressed state of mind. She had no appetite and was clearly distraught. "What is wrong, Safina?"

"I cannot get the killing out of my mind," she answered, as she looked down at her feet.

"You are the bravest person I know, Safina. Don't be sorry. What you did was a righteous act. The killing of an infidel is the fulfillment of Allah's will," he spoke in a hushed voice as he handed her a small basket with fresh vegetables from the kitchen.

She continued to look at the floor, "I did not do it on purpose, or to honor Allah. I was afraid. I thought he would surely kill me," she whispered.

"It doesn't matter. You were victorious against evil. That is all that you should think about this."

A week later, she decided to sneak up to the deck at night. She craved a glimpse of the sea, and a breath of fresh air. Safina pulled her veil across her face and climbed the narrow stairs up to the next level. As she paused on the dark landing, she heard a step behind her. She felt her heart skip a beat, and suddenly she was hot and sticky under her thick woolen *abāya*. "Who is it?" she whispered. *Was she back in Khaliq's villa, hiding in the closet?* A sickening wrenching of her stomach was a warning too late. He came from behind her. A hand covered her mouth, and as he dragged her up the steps to the next level she fought to break lose. He was strong. He pulled her along the narrow passage from the second level, opened a door and effortlessly tossed her on the floor, as though she were a rag. He turned and latched the door behind him.

Safina screamed and crawled across the room into a corner. The room was much larger than the small space she had occupied below. A massive oak table stood in the middle of the room. A swinging lamp was suspended over the table by a black chain. Along one wall were many canisters with scrolls protruding from them. It was then that she realized this was the Captain's cabin. As she looked up, she saw his face staring back at her as his lips curled upward in smug self-congratulation. He had snagged a prize – one that he would amuse himself with during the voyage ahead.

The Captain came toward her. He was breathing hard through his nose. She could hear him sucking up snot from his nose and swallowing it, like one might do if they had no handkerchief or tissue to dispose of their mucous. She retreated to a mental survival place in her mind, one that protected her from the worst of the cruelty that she faced while captive by Khaliq. The Captain dropped his pants and lowered himself onto his hands and knees, grabbing her legs and dragging her out from the corner. He pushed up her skirt, pulled her pantaloons off of her, and forced her legs apart with his hands. His saliva dripped onto her face ....

Safina walked the sands of the desert and spied the great horse, Nomad on the top of a shifting sand dune. As her face tingled in the blowing sand, the horse effortlessly glided toward her, tossing his head in recognition. "You are with me, Safina. Let us race in the wind. I will show you the revelations of your future. You are strong and you will prevail." This became her proclamation: *I am strong and I will prevail. I am strong and I will prevail. I am strong and I will prevail. I am strong and I ...*

When it was over, she crawled back to the corner of the room. As she stared at the face of the Captain, he turned away. The Captain's eyes reflected physical fear. Safina's mind was powerful. The enormity of his crime, and the complete and absolute unforgivable evil state of his soul, was revealed in the lines of his face. "I am doomed," he later told the First Mate.

The Captain was hopelessly addicted to his perversion, and no matter how distraught he was at the end of each encounter, he did not stop the abuse of Safina. Holding her captive, he spiraled downward into a pit of deprivation.

The First Mate, Van Vleit, took note of the Captain's inability to focus, and command the ship with the expertise and dispatch he had previously exhibited. Days followed nights when the Captain would sit motionless on the floor, staring at his hands. Van Vleit was now responsible for the safety of the ship. It was a huge burden upon his shoulders. One of the cook's helpers by the name of Abraheem, approached him with questions about the disappearance of a young girl who was traveling on the ship. He appeared quite agitated and distraught. Van Vleit promised to launch a search for the girl, but he already knew where she must be hidden.

After several failed attempts to communicate with the Captain through the closed door, Van Vleit entered the Captain's quarters, gently helped Safina gather herself, and led her to a tiny cabin on the lower deck. He was visibly shaken by her condition. Anyone could have guessed what transpired, but there was nothing he could do about it.

He placed a sheet of paper and a small book in her hand, "Here, take this print'n of the Deutch alphabet, and a copybook and pencil. Practice the letters. I'll help ya with the sounds. When we get to Port, you'll have basics. When the ship docks in Rotterdam, I'll help ya get off and find a safe place." His Arabic was sufficient, but the Dutch accent was heavy. "I bring you some food."

Safina wondered: *How did he come to know my language? Can I trust this man? Is there a choice?* She was grateful to be away from the Captain's torture, and it would be good to have a plan and something to learn. As she washed her body with the cold salt water in the bucket, she held the rough cloth against the bruises on her neck. Because of the kindness of Van Vleit and the help of Abraheem, she could not hate all men. As Safina peeled back the prejudices she had against men, she realized they were not all the same. Good men, like Abraheem and Van Vleit, were strong enough to dispense kindness and mercy, without giving into their baser desires.

When Safina thought of the sailor that she killed, she could not resolve within herself an acceptable way of living with this fact. She had reacted to him in a state of panic, without thinking, without pre-meditation. The shabria was hidden in the pocket of her robe, and by the time she realized what her hand found there – she did not have time to threaten him or to slash his arm or face. Pinned under him, suffocating, she only managed to reach his side and force the blade into his body between the ribs. When she saw the blood drain from his body, she knew that she had taken his life. How should she think about that? It was something she never imagined or wished for in her short life. Abraheem was wrong, she thought, *killing infidels is not the will of Allah. If it were, I would not be in despair about it.*

Safina hid the knife in her small bag, and vowed not to keep it on her person for the remainder of the journey.

"Cap'n," said the First Mate as he entered the spacious quarters. "Doc Morelli's here, he's want'n to give ya a physical."

The ship's doctor walked over to where Captain Demetrius was seated with his hands on the table. "You haven't been seen on deck for some time. I think you should rejoin your crew." There was no response. He peered into the Captain's sunken eyes, and saw the shriveled skin on his hands and neck. "Oh, my God, he's comatose and severely dehydrated. What happened to him?" He looked at the First Mate, "Van Vleit, speak up man! How did this happen?"

The First Mate was visibly reluctant to disclose the details. "He's been keep'n company with a female passenger. I took her to her cabin last night. She's quite ill. He told me to go away. Sir, I didn't know what ta do – that's why I brought ya here."

"What is the girl's name?"

"I'm not sure Doc, I think it be something like Salina or Sabina. She don't speak no English or German, just Arabic."

"I wonder if she is the same girl that my friend Yasmine, asked me to put on a train to Amsterdam when we arrive in port? Her name is Safina."

"Ya, that's it, Safina. That's her name. Yes Sir."

Dr. Morelli's face fell. He ran his fingers through his hair and, removed his classes, placing them on the table. He bent over the table and put both palms down on it, holding his weight on his two arms. He looked worried. "Oh, my God, I was supposed to look out for her. I got so engrossed in my research that I put off looking her up, after we departed from Basra."

The doctor administered a stimulant and a Vitamin B shot to the Captain, and with the help of the First Mate he moved Captain Demetrius to his bed. "Bring the Captain a food tray from the galley." He drew a blood sample and examined the Captain's body completely. "It's gonorrhea," he said. "She probably has it too, although his case is quite advanced. When you have finished feeding the Captain, bring the girl to the infirmary for treatment."

It wasn't the first time Van Vleit had watched men's bodies being consumed by their own lust and excesses. "The Captain can wait for now. I'm going to get the girl. She needs treatment as quickly as possible. She is an innocent victim, the wicked can wait."

Van Vliet brought Safina to the infirmary. When the doctor examined Safina, he took cultures from various locations on her body. He tried to explain to her what he was doing and why, but language was a barrier. "I am fairly confident of my diagnosis but these cultures will show me for sure, in two days." He held up two fingers. "Then I will be able to see the bacteria, the sickness, under my microscope." The doctor doubted that she understood anything he was saying but he figured that a calming voice couldn't hurt. He went ahead and prepared an injection of Ceftriaxine. "If it is Gonorrhea, one dose will make you well." He held up the syringe to show her.

Safina objected to the needle vigorously, "La! No shots, no shots - no baby." She pointed at her stomach. He finally figured out what she was saying. He told her, "This will not make a baby grow inside of you! I promise - no baby in this needle!" She extended her arm and he gave her the injection. Before he left the exam room he told Safina to get dressed. As he closed the door behind him he spoke with Van

Vleit, "She's weak, and the gonorrhea has wrecked havoc on her due to her condition after child birth."

"Child birth!? She don't have no baby, Sir. She's travel'n alone. For sure, you must be wrong. This here girl is a religious one, one brought up in the Muslim way. I can't believe she would've gave up her baby." Van Vleit was distraught. "This girl is no more'n eleven or twelve!"

"I've seen this before. This girl was sold as a virgin to some wealthy older man who could afford her dowry. She was forced into sexual slavery. I found physical evidence that she delivered a baby within the last 2 or 3 months. How she managed to escape is a mystery. There are extensive signs of physical abuse on this girl. She may have several healed fractures, and her toes have all been broken and have healed crooked and misshapen. I'll know more when I see her x-rays. She has some missing and broken teeth, and deep scarring from lacerations. However, she is not malnourished, which is unusual in these cases. I think I know who took her in and fed her and cared for her until she gave birth. It had to be the same person who contacted me about her. It must have been the woman who asked me to help the girl get on a train to Amsterdam."

The doctor continued to speak his mind, "This penchant for child virgins......they are utterly obsessed with it. Mohammad, their prophet, married a six year old girl and consummated this "marriage" when she was only nine years old! He was fifty-two at the time! This is a powerful recruitment tool. Imagine millions of male followers of Islam who condone and venerate this practice throughout the world! One of the greatest taboos of Western culture ends up being the major force behind Islam."

Van Vleit sighed and exhaled a long slow breath through pursed lips. "He's no better than the bastard what bought her in the first place. He's not even a Muslim, for Christ's sake!" Van Vleit clenched his fists. The corners of his mouth turned down as he clamped his teeth together.

"Stop it Van Vleit, calm down. You best watch your tongue. Settle mate. I feel the same way, but if we want to keep our jobs and continue to help this girl we better keep our opinion of the Captain to ourselves."

The doctor pulled a thick wool naval blanket from his closet and opened the door to the examination room. He beckoned Safina to come out into his office. He unfolded the blanket and wrapped it gently around her shoulders, pulling it together and overlapping it in the front. He smiled kindly at her. In his quite rudimentary Arabic he struggled to make sure she understood him, "Take the medicine after meals – at least 3 – *talat* (three) times each day." He held up three fingers. He pointed at the First Mate, "*habib* (friend). He will bring you back in 5 days." He held up 5 fingers, "*Hamsa* (five)."

The first mate took her back to her cabin. Then he hurried to the kitchen to get some food for the Captain. "I should let him starve," he said out loud on his way to the kitchen. Van Vleit was angry, but the words of the doctor had made sense to him: "If we are to help this child, we have to maintain the charade of respect for the chain-of-command, and to continue to run the ship as best we can."

On the fourteenth day of the journey the Hercules, sailing under a Greek flag, traveled the length of the Persian Gulf on a southerly route out of Umm Qasr port, past Abu Dahbi of the U.A.E. (United Arab Emirates), past Masqat and Sur of Oman. She turned southwest along the coast of Yemen and turned again northwest into the Gulf of Aden well on her way to the Suez Canal. The crew members were a diverse group of men. The officers were mostly Greeks like the Captain, except for one Scandinavian navigator. The sailors were from Italy, Turkey, Ethiopia, Yemen, and a few very tall, ebony black men were Sudanese.

The smells from the cook's galley reflected the variety of cultures, as he was well versed in the preparation of all the ethnic dishes of the region. The Captain prided himself on having the best cook in the fleet - Prodromos the Greek, was a culinary magician in the galley. On any afternoon, the tantalizing aroma of exotic spices and curries wafting from the galley would seduce the crew into gravitating towards the mess hall. More than once the First Mate was forced to send sailors scuttling back to their duties as they congregated close to the kitchen. When mess call was sounded – the tables filled up immediately in anticipation of food prepared better than anything they had eaten in their boyhood homes. The Captain firmly believed that a well-run ship with a happy crew began in the galley, as he took the old adage: "The way to a man's heart is through his belly," quite seriously. This twist of his nature was in direct dichotomy with his treatment of Safina.

Dr. Morelli and Prodromos the Greek cook, were culinary aficionados. Both were educated, renaissance men with European sensibilities and tastes. They shared a unique hobby on board the Hercules - their collection of exotic recipes. Prodromos and the doctor sat sipping rich, freshly brewed hot foamy caramel macchiatos and discussing the foods of Kurdistan.

"The most succulent dishes are from Kurdistan. Do you know why Kurdish dishes are so delicious and interesting?" asked Prodromos.

"Because centuries of multinational, multilingual and transnational people of Turkey, Iran, Iraq and Syria came together in Kurdistan to create a cross culture, with a high degree of tolerance for ethnic diversity. The Sufi doctrine of *sulh-i-kul*, (peace with all) has also allowed the Kurdish palate to expand. The cultural richness of Kurdistan is reflected in the variety and scope of its cuisine – mouth-watering culinary works of art," Dr. Morelli answered in a slow deliberate voice.

The doctor was well aware of the cook's delight in the variations of *koobe* "dumplings" that Prodromos incorporated into his repertoire. He taught the doctor everything he knew about *koobe* because he had lots of time during the voyage when there was nothing better to do than play chess with Dr. Morelli, and talk about the world's cuisine. "These signature Kurdish dishes of *koobe*, are shaped into round balls, or flattened half-moons. The dumplings are filled with ground or chopped meat of lamb, beef or chicken, mixed with onions, garlic, turmeric, paprika, allspice, and pepper. They are served steaming hot. The dumplings are made with semolina, farina, cream-of-wheat, cracked wheat bulgar, or ground rice depending on how they are to be cooked; either deep fried, or simmered in a rich sauce or a pot of fresh vegetable soup." Prodromos shared his knowledge with the doctor.

Morelli looked amused as he held up one finger and pointed it at the cook: "Some dairy-based *koobe* dishes are stuffed with goat cheese, slowly cooked in heavy cream, and then served cold. You should try it for breakfast - it's indescribable. Bet you didn't know that!" He grinned triumphantly.

Over dinner the three of them, Morelli, Prodromos, and Van Vleit, talked about the food they had eaten at a restaurant in their last port of Basra. The First Mate raved about the deep purple variety of *koobe*, "It was float'n in beet juice with olive oil, cumin, wine vinegar and sugar; sweet and sour, spicy and tangy, all at the same time. The dumplings were purple in this wonderful spicy soup. You got to make some of that Prodromos..... it'd be a big hit with the crew."

Safina's favorite dish was *Yabrach* "stuffed grape leaves". She remembered how Yasmine had read the instructions to her from her cook book, when she was teaching her to read Arabic: "The original recipe for Yabrach was developed thousands of years ago in Western Asia and handed down through the Greeks and the Romans throughout their dominion, including Kurdistan. It was a natural by-product of grape cultivation for wine production." Yasmine would enter the kitchen to prepare it herself. Badrae would protest because Yasmine didn't want to share her recipe. As Safina picked up the dark green leaves rolled into small tubular lengths stuffed with seasoned rice, she dipped them in a spicy Yemenite *Hilbeh* "Fenugreek" and *Schug* "hot green chili chutney" mixture, and ate them with immense pleasure. She licked her fingers and savored the warm *Hilbeh*. *I wish I were sitting in Yasmine's kitchen being scolded by Badrae for stealing one of these*, she thought. Yasmine said that the Yemenite penchant for daily ingestion of Fenugreek was the secret to their unusual longevity: "Many Yemenites lived well over one hundred years," she told Safina.

After being rescued from the Captain, Safina's body healed. The increase in nutritious food, and the blankets provided by the ship's doctor made the difference. Despite the many visits by Dr. Morelli, whom she had grown quite close to, there were still long stretches of time where she had nothing to do except dream of a better existence.

During the nights she escaped the boredom of the journey by traveling with Nomad, riding the winds of the desert in her dreams, free from the scenes locked in her mind. The faces of Khaliq and

Demetrius blurred into one gray mass, without clearly defined features. The sailor that she killed receded from her thoughts, as she allowed the great horse to give her strength and take her away from this prolonged confinement on the ship. He transported her to the gardens of Yasmine. There she sat on the veranda and sipped Turkish coffee in a petite porcelain cup, sweetened with sugar and garnished with a slender sliver of orange peel.

Sometimes, in her dreams, Safina imagined that she returned unto her Creator, and she yearned for the peace that she believed death would bring to her. But in her vivid dreams of Nomad, the great black stallion spoke to her, "Safina, do not be fearful, do not hesitate, and do not turn from your mission. You are the one – the one who will lead Islam out of its darkest place, and you will prevail. Allah has ordained it."

When she awoke from these dreams she was refreshed and infused with hope. Safina pondered the words of Nomad, and could not comprehend the enormity of the task that lay ahead. She asked herself: *What could a girl do to change the world?*

CHAPTER 8

Hilversum

Dr. Morelli sent an encrypted e-mail to Vivian Von Stetton, in the Netherlands:

```
Please meet Safina as per Y's request.
She will arrive in Amsterdam on the
afternoon train from Rotterdam on
January 17th. Will confirm landing in
Rotterdam and boarding train #9339 at
17:03 to arrive Amsterdam at 17:43.
Please provide lodging/food. For
additional information contact Y.

Sincerely, L. M.
```

When the doctor returned to the infirmary from his quarters, he found the First Mate waiting for him. "What's go'n to happen to the girl?" Van Vleit asked.

Morelli trusted Van Vleit with his life because the First Mate had covered for him several times when the pharmaceutical corporate-hired thugs had come looking for him. Despite offers of money, and threats to his personal safety, Van Vleit had denied any knowledge of the doctor's whereabouts.

"I have arranged for a passport and identification through a contact of mine in Interpol, who owes me a favor. She will use my name and biographical data so that any inquiries would come directly to me for confirmation."

"I think you've become attached to this girl like a daughter." The First Mate smiled.

Dr. Morelli was quiet for a moment as he thought about this. "I have spent long hours on this voyage, getting to know this girl. We found ways to communicate. She is a special person. I think we must have known each other in a different life. She is part of me now. I can't tell you how I know this - because I don't have the answer to that myself, but Safina will literally change the world some day. My part in all of this is simply destiny. I know she is a person of significance. I have this strong premonition of commitment and purpose. I was somehow chosen to help her survive. That is why I have officially adopted her."

The doctor put his hand on Van Vleit's shoulder. "By the way, you should know that the Captain is not getting better. I must assume that the disease is too far advanced and has infected his brain and other vital organs. It is unlikely that he will survive. I am transferring him to the hospital in Rotterdam as soon as we arrive there, but I doubt he will live for more than a few months. You are the acting Captain until we reach the docks. We will notify the ship's owners, and they will assign a new Master Seaman to the Hercules."

Safina was gathering her meager belongings together in a cloth bag. Abraheem appeared in her doorway, "*Sabach Al Chere,* Good Morning," he smiled broadly.

She was glad that he came to say goodbye. It was the first time that Safina had smiled since she spent an evening with Christi, Badrae's sister-in-law. "*Shukran.* You were so kind to help me. May Allah bless you all the days of your life. I will never forget you Abraheem."

No longer hidden behind a veil, Safina's uncovered face made Abraheem blush. He extended a small kerchief knotted tightly by all four corners and tied together securely. As it dropped into her open palm she felt the weight of it. He was careful not to touch her hand with his. As her hand closed around it she knew it contained coins. "Keep these for an emergency. When all other means of negotiation and talking have failed and you are faced with disaster, silver has a convincing nature. My father taught me the power of money and how to wield it. If you are truly going to deny a man his power over you only money will soften his disappointment or dull his resolve." Abraheem told her.

"I'll remember your advice. Thank you for your protection and your help, and for all those many pieces of fruit that you were able to sneak out of the kitchen for me." Safina smiled. "I'll be alright Abraheem, after all that has happened to me, at least I know one thing. I know that I am a survivor."

"Convince men that you are a resourceful woman, one they would not want to have as an enemy. You must hint that you have other sources of riches which you might be willing to share with them. Drop a few coins into a man's hands and tell him you are going to get more for him if he will promise, before Allah, that he will wait for your return. Remember these words of wisdom that were handed down from my grandfather to my father, and to me."

Safina looked worried, "Abraheem, where will you go? Are you returning to Basra?"

"No, there is no life for me in Iraq. Now that we are parting ways I will tell you why I chose to leave. My mother is dead and I have no maternal siblings. My father was married to his first and second wives long before I was born. His oldest sons have divided the estate between them." He looked past her as if he were viewing a dismal future. Abraheem continued, "My mother was a lowly third wife, a child who was sold to my father as less than a donkey or a camel. She was a concubine; a servant. When she died at thirteen trying to give birth to my stillborn sister, she was cursed, and buried with her baby outside the gates of the cemetery, among the beggars and thieves. My status in the family is not unlike that of a slave. I was taught to do sums and to master languages, so that my brothers might race their horses and attend to their gaming schemes, while I worked long days in the business of my father. As it turns out this was an unintended gift. I never have to rely on family or clan to support myself. There is always a need for a man who speaks many languages, and can handle the calculations of running a business."

Abraheem inhaled deeply and he put his palms together, almost in prayer to Allah. "I will seek my fortune in the world; traveling and learning, and tasting what Allah has prepared for me. I am not a faithful Muslim in my heart. I see the suffering and the injustice in our country and my heart is wounded by it. To partake of the spoils that Islam reaps from the enslavement of women, and the poor, would be unacceptable to me. I believe that Allah has a plan for Islam. Before a river can change its course it has to overrun its banks and be diverted to a different path. Although that causes suffering to those who dwell along the river, in the end, the change of course and the fertile land that is left behind is an unexpected blessing for the inhabitants. I believe Islam will change its course.

You too, Safina, you deserve a life of meaning! Allah has an important destiny for you. I dreamed of it during this voyage. Believe, Safina. I know that I will see you again. I will stay connected with Yasmine in Basra. She will know where to find me if you need me," he said.

"*Enshala*, as Allah wills it," she replied. Safina's heart beat faster. *Abraheem must have seen Nomad in his dreams. He knows! Although he did not say it, I am certain.* Somehow this knowledge made it real. She felt empowered. She climbed slowly down the ladder and into the longboat that would take her from the Hercules to the landing.

She had a letter of introduction from Dr. Morelli, and a sign to hold with "Von Stetton" stenciled on it. When she got to Amsterdam she was to hold up the sign so that all would see that she was expected and was being met by someone. During the voyage she had developed a strong connection with Dr. Morelli. He had spent much time talking to her and advising her about the importance of education and knowledge. Luigi told her that she was the daughter that he had never had - and how glad he was that their paths had crossed. He made her promise to write to him.

"I will come to visit you and Vivian on our next voyage to Rotterdam. In the meantime I will send you letters and packages. This gives me something to look forward to, Safina." He pecked the top of her head and handed her a beautiful blue wool scarf as a farewell gift. "Off with you now, can't let you see a grown man weeping."

The short trip to the wharf was on choppy water; and an icy spray blew off the surface of the ocean. January in Rotterdam was a month of mean, subzero temperatures of unbearable cold. This was not the first time that Safina had seen snow, and layers of ice on everything. She had experienced this as a child, when her father took the clan high into the mountains of Kurdistan to trade there. She remembered that journey well; during the cold nights of that month-long trip she slept curled up next to a gentle she-goat and its kid. The kind goat herder let her wear some warm angora gloves, and a shawl made from the silky long hair of his goats. It was a time during her short life that she felt warm and safe. The memory of the snow-covered peaks of Kurdistan gave her a reassuring sense of calm, as she began her next journey. She touched her neck, as she remembered the soft Angora wool caressing her warmly. It had been hard to return the scarf and gloves the next morning, when it was time to leave. "Shukran, shukran," she remembered thanking the kind-hearted goat keeper. His eyes were big, and their gray blue-green pools contrasted sharply with his leathery brown skin, that was deeply wrinkled at the upturned outer corners of his eyes. He had constantly smiled at her. She saw his gentle handling of his goats, and she understood that he loved them, and she believed that his heart was good and unsoiled. She had felt no fear of that man.

Dr. Morelli paid one of the sailors to make sure she got on the train leaving Rotterdam for Amsterdam, and also to make arrangements for the porter on the train to help her get off at the correct station.

Stepping off of the long boat onto the wharf was strange. The icy wooden planks of the wharf remained solidly in place. Each step she took with hesitation but there was no shaking, rolling, or thumping from the ground. It just sat there, immovable, never coming up to meet her as her foot descended. She now had to trade her "sea legs" for "land legs".

The doctor provided a pair of sheepskin lined snow boots, and a long woolen sailor's pea coat in navy blue. In place of her traditional Muslim dress, she wore dark woolen pants, and a flannel shirt under the coat. A blue knitted scarf was wrapped around her head and neck, and a delicate gold bracelet adorned her slim wrist. They were both gifts from Dr. Morelli. Safina believed that the blue scarf would ward off *Al Ayn*.

Safina couldn't help thinking about all the things that she had shared with Dr. Morelli, First Mate Van Vleit, and of course, Abraheem Bin Farouq, son of the Silversmith. They found the courage to protect her from the Captain, teach her to read and write, and spend all of their spare time giving her the skills she would need to survive in this strange country of Holland. Despite the pain and suffering that she endured, she could not turn away from the truth. Safina began to open her mind to the possibility that her life's path and her purpose were unique and significant.

The train ride to Amsterdam was uneventful. She watched the lush countryside of Holland from her window, as the train climbed from almost seven feet below sea level in Rotterdam to sea level in Amsterdam. The city was protected from the sea by a system of ditches, canals, and dikes. She saw the massive windmills, with their towering monster silhouettes, against the Dutch skyline. Safina remembered the story that Van Vleit, the First Mate on the Hercules, read to her. It was the story of Don Quixote, a Spaniard, and his fight against the windmills. Now she understood the significance of that. It had been impossible to imagine a windmill, since she had never seen one, even in a photograph or drawing.

The thick vegetation and the unbelievable wide canals, brimming with water rushing by alongside the tracks, seemed decadent and sinful. To someone from an arid land where water is a precious commodity it was unsettling. She saw the fat cows with their thick stocky legs, digging under the deep snow of the Dutch pasture lands. They were a sharp contrast to the spindly goats and lanky camels of Iraq. Even the sheep of her village were never as fat as these Dutch cows.

The tall skinny two and three story houses, with sparkling clean windows and lace curtains hung only from the lower half of the panes, were like treasures lined up for inspection. Puffs of smoke were rising from each chimney, and she imagined warm cozy rooms with children playing in front of the fires, while mothers embroidered colorful designs onto new white blouses. She had seen a picture book at Yasmine's villa. It had pictures of red cheeked children sitting around a fireplace with long red stockings hanging from the top of the stone oven. Obviously they had been hung there to dry out. She had seen Yemenite embroidery in the markets of Baghdad; delicate golden and silvery threads stitched in circular patterns onto bodices of brightly dyed linen and silk, with such breath-taking precision and beauty. Maybe the two worlds were not as completely different as everyone had warned her they would be.

Somewhere along the way she slipped into a deep sleep. For the first time in many months, her mind rested peacefully. She could finally relax her vigilant protective posture. She released her fingers from around the shabria in her pocket. Safina didn't have to prepare for an attack on her body or have a plan for escape or a place to hide. This sense of peace and serenity was reminiscent of her days in the courtyard of her father's house when she played with Farka and was untouched and unblemished and could laugh out loud without the fear of reprisal or abuse, *"Oh sweet Farka, I miss you so. I never knew what he did to you. I never knew. You should have told me Farka. You should have told me." She plunged the shabria deep into her father's chest and blood squirted out and covered her arms and legs in red sticky goo.* She suddenly awoke and realized that she was dreaming. It was a nightmare; a dream of retribution.

Vivian Von Stetton drove through the icy rain and snow flurries from Hilversum to the Amsterdam train station. She knew who Safina Morelli was and why her dear friend, Dr. Morelli, wanted her to meet this girl and take care of her. Any request from Luigi was her pleasure to accommodate. He had cured Vivian's non-Hodgkin's Lymphoma using his own cancer research.

When she asked him about the process he explained it to her in great detail, but when she repeated it to the hospital investigators who came to her house, she purposely made it sound ridiculous and impossible to replicate. Morelli had created a process in which he married cellular/molecular memory with biotechnology, using designer nannites (micro robotics). He effectively "turned off" the cell replicating and regenerative subatomic cellular codes, and collected and expelled the cancerous cells, using an inorganic chelating process. It was brilliant and complex, and finally cancer was curable in all of its forms.

"The greatest breakthrough in medical history had occurred, yet I was forced to leave the hospital, Vivian. No one is interested in a cancer cure except dying cancer patients," Morelli wrote to her. "The development of a universal cancer cure is unacceptable to the corporations and universities around the world, who are involved in cancer research; a cure would effectively cut off their "unending" funding from private and government sources. Billions of dollars would dry up. This is an unspoken rule within the not-for-profit organizations, and the R&D departments of the "pharma" conglomerates and their lobbyists. There is an entire "feeding" network of parasitically dependent groups playing the "cancer" game - from corrupt government officials all the way to Wall Street. So I must go into hiding. All future messages between us must be encrypted. Talk to "Y" about this."

The request from Dr. Morelli to Vivian Von Stetton had such a high encryption rate that it took a full minute to decrypt the message. She smiled after she read the e-mail asking her to do this favor for Luigi. When she called Yasmine she told her, "Finally. When I think of all the times kindness has been extended to me from loved ones and from complete strangers, and now I have a chance to repay some of it."

Vivian had been cancer free for fifteen years. As she parked her Fiat and exited on the right side, she flipped open her umbrella and made her way to the arrival platform from Rotterdam. She was peering out through the drizzle when she saw the girl with the bright blue headscarf holding up a sign that said "**VON STETTON.**" She moved quickly toward the girl. "Hi! Are you Safina?"

The girl pulled her scarf down from over her mouth, "Yes, I am." Safina looked at Vivian through the gray fog. Her lips were blue from the cold and she kept changing hands to clutch the sign. Without gloves, she was having a hard time keeping her hands warm. She shoved one and then the other one into her coat pocket. Her small bag sat on the ground between her feet.

Vivian took the sign from her and tossed it into a nearby trash receptacle. "You won't be in need of that. I am Vivian Von Stetton. Come along now. Let us see if we can get you warm in my motor-car. Have you been waiting long? I drove slower because of the fog." She didn't wait for an answer. Vivian grabbed up the bag and walked toward the car.

Safina followed her, glad that someone she could trust was in charge. She recalled Dr. Morelli's words, "You can trust Vivian Von Stetton, she owes me her life, and she will protect you with hers." The woman reminded Safina of Yasmine, as she watched Vivian taking strong, competent strides toward the car, a woman of purpose. Safina didn't understand all of her words but she understood the gist of it.

Out of the corner of her eye, Safina saw a man watching them from across the street. She turned slightly to get a better look at him. His shape seemed familiar but it was too far away to make out his features except for his thick black mustache. She felt the muscles in her calves tense up. *Should I try to run? But where?* She spoke only rudimentary phrases in Dutch and English. She didn't know if this man was a threat to her or not. As she followed Vivian to the compact red car, she clenched the shabria in her coat pocket, and glanced back across the street. He was gone. She pushed her instinctive fear back down into the deepest vault of her mind, storing his image away to augment her survival in the future.

"I'll fling this satchel into the boot," Vivian said, as she popped the trunk open, and deposited it.

As they drove out of town, making their way to the countryside, Safina looked in the side mirror and saw that no one was following them. Cars entered the expressway and exited, but none stayed behind them consistently for any length of time. Soft music was playing on the radio, as a light drizzle was sporadically wiped away from the windshield by the short rubber blades of the car. She noticed that the passenger side blade skipped the same spot on the window shield each time it descended.

She studied this woman, Vivian: she was physically substantial, taller, by a head, than Safina, with muscle definition and a strong chin. She was probably in her mid forties. Safina had never seen eyes so sky blue. Brown and green eyes were common in Iraq and Kurdistan.

Less than an hour later they exited the Expressway and went through the town of Hilversum. Vivian turned into the driveway of a large country house on the edge of town. As they drove down the long plowed driveway through snow piled high on both sides, she saw smoke rising from a dark stone chimney, and when they reached the cobblestone courtyard, she saw the winter sparrows eating birdseed from a feeder on a pedestal protruding from the snow. The scene could have been taken from one of the art books in Yasmine's library in Basra. Safina had memorized all of those wonderful pictures.

The glow of soft lights flickered in the window panes, and the traditional Dutch lace curtains hung in every window. The house beckoned to her – it looked safe and warm – a refuge. A rope hung down from the upstairs window and on the bottom a tin bucket was tied. The bucket was about two feet short of reaching the ground. There didn't appear to be anything in the bucket. Safina couldn't figure out why an empty bucket would be hanging on a long rope out of an upstairs window. It wasn't until weeks later when she attempted to carry some packages up the narrow stairwell to the second floor that she understood this Dutch innovation. Later in Amsterdam she would see these "buckets" on almost every house.

Now Safina entered this old-money world of art and culture, history not taken for granted, and a philosophy unfettered by racial, religious, or political barriers. The Netherlands was known as a place of international diplomacy. This was a good setting for Safina to begin the preparation for her future role in the world. She was not yet thirteen years old. When she allowed herself to think about the possibility of some extraordinary destiny, it scared her. She felt small and insignificant.

CHAPTER 9

Dulcinea

Vivian lit a fire in the hearth, and the small country kitchen warmed up in a few minutes. Safina and Vivian settled down with mugs of thick, hot chocolate. Vivian spoke Arabic reasonably well, but it had been a while since she had exercised this skill. "Safina, I am going to tell you about Holland, and Hilversum, and about my family, the Von Stettons." As the hour grew late, they shared some Dutch pastries. Safina listened carefully. Later she would remember the story of the Von Stetton family, and how Vivian's German father had risked everything to save Jewish children during the holocaust. Safina knew so little about geography and history, so that Vivian had to briefly describe the major events of the 20th century to her as the story progressed.

"He was imprisoned by the Nazi's and selected for termination at one of the death camps, but he never gave up. In the end he was saved by some of the children he had managed to spare," Vivian told her.

Vivian shared information on Holland, and the city of Hilversum. It seemed to reassure Safina that she was safe in this new place. Vivian exuded strength, and promised protection against the unknown hazards that lie ahead. Safina slept undisturbed by dreams or nightmares.

Vivian contacted Yasmine the next day. Yasmine provided more information and reassurance, "Don't worry about the expense, she has ample financial support. There is no need to economize when it comes to selecting tutors and teachers to guide Safina."

Vivian walked to the library where she found her young charge timidly purveying the titles on the shelves.

"Safina, you will begin your studies immediately. You are far behind other students of your age." Vivian's Arabic was a slightly different dialect than the one that Safina spoke. She had mastered her Arabic while living in The Hashemite Kingdom of Jordan. But that wasn't an insurmountable obstacle to communication.

There was no opportunity for discussion, or any mention of a choice. It was clear to Safina that Vivian was going to provide strong leadership in this regard. "Yes, I want to study," Safina responded. "My teacher, Yasmine, said that my education should be first. She is sorry that she could not teach me all that I need to learn. There was not enough time before I was forced to leave Iraq."

"Well, she is a wise woman. Yasmine is right about learning – it is important. We will make sure that you learn that which is valuable and useful." Vivian ran her fingers over her thick blond hair with its interlaced strands of gray and white. She walked back and forth across the thick plush carpets. "It won't be easy! There will be times when you will not want to study. Even when you are uncomfortable and tired of learning you will not give up."

As Vivian wrote on a pad of paper and slid it across the table to Safina, she looked up at her with an enthusiastic smile, "You have a new name. Your name is Dulcinea Devorah Morelli, daughter of Dr.

Luigi Morelli who has legally adopted you. Safina died during child-birth, along with her baby daughter."

Safina stared at the English letters of her new name. It was another layer of protection and safety – a new name, a new path in life, a future she had never imagined – all these gifts bestowed upon her, just as Nomad had predicted. *How can I doubt him now?*

Dulcinea hadn't understood everything that first day she spent with Vivian, but even now, six years later, a knot settled in the pit of her stomach as she remembered the lost baby. She remembered the milk leaking out all over her bed sheets and the pain of the fullness of her breasts. Her arms tingled again, with nature's longing to hold her child. That was the first time that Safina learned that her baby was a girl. Perversely, the revelation had made the pain bearable – because a baby girl would have suffered so much in this world of vicious men. Someday she would change that, "*En shallah,* if Allah wills it."

Dulcinea put these memories back in a compartment of her mind where she could lock them away from her daily life. Yasmine told her over and over to concentrate on the positive things in life. She seized the opportunity to learn. For that she was grateful. Finding answers to so many unanswered questions exhilarated her.

Early on, in those first few years when Vivian spoke to Yasmine, and later to Dr. Morelli over secure telephone communications, she told them both, "She is an exceptional student with an uncommon ability to absorb vast amounts of information and recall it at will. I did some research on this. There are only a handful of people in the world who have this gift, and it is not photographic memory. It is total and complete recall of every event or occurrence they have experienced or heard or read about. I only found one study done in the United States, where there are a total of 5 documented people with this ability. They can recall any event by date, day of the week, and time. It is referred to as eidetic memory. They are not savants or autistic individuals. It is an amazing gift."

Yasmine has been hesitant to supply Dulcinea with too much information. She told Vivian, "I was reluctant to expose her to questions of science, biology, history or literature. If she should be forced to return to her old life, enslaved by Khaliq, educating her would only make the reversal of her fortunes less bearable. Once having eaten from the "tree of knowledge" it would be excruciating to live in ignorance and mental starvation. It could even be less acceptable than to be killed by Khaliq."

Vivian devoted herself to the academic and intellectual development of Dulcinea. As an accomplished linguist, she systematically took on the arduous task of developing language codes in Dulcinea's brain. These codes allowed her brain to grasp the nuances and flavors of each language, and to cultivate an appreciation of the cultures behind these languages.

Vivian started with English, "It's the most universal of communication tools, and rich in the shades and minute variations of a large and diverse vocabulary. A cultured person should be fluent in at least three languages – preferably English, French and Spanish. If one is also comfortable in German and Italian, one would qualify as a true cosmopolitan citizen of the world."

The teacher, Vivian, realized that she needed to shore up her own spoken Arabic, as she had to hesitate to find the correct words when she spoke to Safina. Mastering reading and writing of Arabic would give Dulcinea the full flavor, beauty and poetry of Arabic prose. "We'll work together. You help me with pronunciation and dialect in Arabic, and I will teach you basic Latin, and Germanic origins of the English language and the evolution of English. It is a fascinating linguistic journey filled with myths and unexpected discoveries that will delight your natural curiosity."

During their telephone conversations Yasmine asked Vivian, "Why do you believe it is so important for Dulcinea to learn multiple languages?

"Europeans hold a unique view of the mastery of languages. With short distances between countries, historically fluid borders subject to invasions and conquerors, and a diverse European wealth of literature – fluency in several languages is just another aspect of having a well-rounded education. Being unfettered by the need for translations is also a practical asset. If Dulcinea should become a successful participant in world events she will need to be accepted as an educated, and culturally knowledgeable person. It never hurts to keep your opponents off balance, because you understand every word. Nothing gets lost in translation."

Months later Dulcinea was smiling and even humming as she went through her daily routine. *This is the best time of my life. I could stay here forever, reading, studying, living in this storybook house surrounded by a garden and song birds. God willing.* She hugged herself and then threw out her arms and twirled several full turns. Stopping, she suddenly realized that she had mastered English, she was actually thinking in English.

Vivian was careful to ensure that physical activities were not sacrificed for the sake of mental exercises. Everyday they traveled to the gymnasium at the college in Hilversum. Vivian and Dulcinea played handball and, although it was incomprehensible to Dulci, she was required to put on a bathing suit and learn to swim. "It's too cold Vivian, and there is never going to be a need for me to know how to swim. Arab girls do not swim."

Vivian bent her head to one side and put up one finger in front of Dulci's face: "Arab girls usually do not read or write, or study history or mathematics either. Most Arab girls live in a very dark place behind a veil where swimming, reading, writing, and even thinking is unnecessary. I thought you were logical."

Dr. Morelli visited Dulcinea several times a year. When the Hercules came into Rotterdam, he discretely traveled to another small town in the opposite direction of Hilversum, and then hired a taxi to take him to the Von Stetton residence. He was careful not to be followed, or leave any trail that would lead to Dulcinea. During these visits he lavished her with gifts and constant praise, "You are a treasure my daughter. I am so proud of your progress." He beamed with satisfaction when Dulci spoke to him in flawless Italian with a distinctly Sicilian flavor.

"You are Papa to me. I cannot think of a way to show you how much I adore and respect you, and how grateful I feel in my heart," she told him in Italian. This made him blush.

It was visibly difficult for him to leave when the time came to return to the ship. "My heart is heavy. I hate it that I must leave you. But, I know that you are in a safe place and in good hands," Luigi gave her a bear hug and kissed her on top of the head. "*Ale viderchi* (until we meet again)."

On Dulcinea's nineteenth birthday Vivian woke her early, "*Fijne Verjaardag* (Happy Birthday)," she said in Dutch.

"It is my birthday Vivian; give me a break. At least let me sleep in on my birthday!"

"Get dressed sleepy head. Come down to the kitchen. I have a surprise for you!" Vivian eyes were overly cheerful, almost mischievous.

Dulci hurriedly dressed, throwing on the first thing that she found in the closet and running a brush quickly through her hair. She splashed some cold water on her face and ran a toothbrush back and forth twice. *It must be a new bicycle or the Ragamuffin kitten I have wanted for so long*, she thought. She loved surprises, and still barefoot, Dulci raced down the narrow stairway to the kitchen. She stopped on the last step, her bare toes gripping the wooden plank as she hung on to the railing to freeze her descent. This was not a kitten or a bicycle. A tall muscular young man, dressed in military fatigues, stood like a recruitment poster, in the middle of the kitchen. Dulci's face showed an unusual degree of emotion, surprise being the most obvious.

"Dulci. This is Brecken Petersen, your martial arts instructor. He is from the United States. Brecken will teach you how to defend yourself, and in return you will teach him how to converse in Arabic." Vivian "stacked" herself like a show dog, next to the smiling young man with the blue-gray eyes and short dark blond hair. As he grinned his white, even teeth sparkled, and his eyes crinkled downward at the outer and inner corners, slivered half moons turned on their sides. It was a reassuring, friendly smile. Dulci smiled back at him for only a moment until she covered her mouth with her delicate hand, "*As-salaamu alaykum* (Peace be unto you)," she said softly through her fingers. She stepped down from the step into the kitchen.

"I am happy to meet you Dulci," he said. "I can't wait to learn your language. *As-salaamu alaykum.*"

He's amazing! His accent was a perfect match to my greeting. Their eyes met for a brief moment and Dulci remembered to breath. "Are you going to teach me to defend myself with lethal force, or are you going to teach me to seek out and kill my enemies?" Her candor even surprised herself. *What is it about this man that makes me want to be myself, and not hide behind a made-up name or a made-up history?*

107

Brecken stood up straighter, and put his hands in his pockets. "I fear both are required," he said. His face looked quite serious; he closed his mouth, and his eyes stared back steadily into her's.

It was the right answer. Dulci was impatient to spill the blood of her enemies. In this moment of clarity she recognized her true heart. Somehow this stranger knew it too. For a second she wanted to tell him that her real name was Safina, but Vivian had instructed her on the importance of protecting her identity. Khaliq had the backing of his government and the Muslim Brethren to reach across the seas to recapture or kill her. *For now, I am Dulcinea, daughter of Dr. Luigi Morelli. Someday when I am a strong and formidable person of power – Khaliq will tremble in terror at the sound of my real name – Safina daughter of Latifa, wife of no man.* It was her first conscience admission that she wanted revenge. *I will use this Brecken Peterson to hone my lethal capabilities.*

Nomad the powerful black horse walked side by side with Safina in her dreams, and carried her forward in time to a place where veils, child brides, and male dominance no longer existed. He was the source of her strength, and awakened the confidence that was buried deep within her. "Revenge will be satisfied; your name will be restored; all of Islam and the world will know you as Safina, Daughter of Islam." Nomad told her.

Months of training had paid off. Dulci was as well-oiled a fighting machine as any Marine coming out of Special Forces' intensive training. "I would not hesitate to go into battle with you," Brecken said. "You are physically and mentally hardened, and your reflexes are honed to perfection. We have worked hard together, it's time for a break."

Brecken and Dulci ate together in the country garden of the picturesque stone house. They were surrounded by an explosive color profusion of tulips in all their flamboyant variations. Starched white Baby's Breath bordered all of the flowerbeds in this joyful garden in a seamless ribbon. The iris beds were purple blue splashes of intense beauty: tall Blue Suede Shoes German Iris, Blue Delft, Mariposa Skies Fragrant German, and the breath-stopping Bold Pretender Louisiana Iris.

Dulcinea had carefully covered the tender shoots of tulips and iris protectively when they first defiantly pushed their way out through the late Spring snow. She had brushed away the icy crystals, putting small soft blankets on them during the freezing nights to protect them so that they could provide this magnificent blanket of beautiful colors all through the Spring and into the Summer. She had mentioned it to Vivian: "Almost everything in life that is wonderful requires a degree of extra attention and care. Life doesn't explode into being from nothing. It is nurtured and cajoled into being exceptional. I think people are the same way; if we protect them with soft blankets during the darkest hours, they do eventually come out and gift us with their vibrant audacity."

Vivian was an accomplished cook and she introduced Dulci and the American, Brecken, to a wonderful variety of Dutch and German recipes, "These dishes have been handed down through generations of women in the Von Stetton family." She prepared the traditional *Poffertze*, a small yeast pancake, sprinkled with ample amounts of powdered sugar. They ate them with a bowl of chocolate flavored *Vla*, a thick sweet milk pudding. Dulci's favorite dish was the *Visal* pastry, an intricate sculpture of artfully latticed yeast pie crust.

Brecken complained, "Breakfast at the Von Stetton house will make me balloon to 300 pounds. Do you know how to cook, Dulci?"

"I have not cooked since I came here. I think Arabian food could be too spicy for Dutch taste. I don't know if I can find all the ingredients for the dishes I would remember. I wouldn't have the names of some ingredients in English, and I'm not sure how to make them," Dulci answered. "I was a child when I came to Holland."

"We'll have to look up the ingredient names and make a list .....then I can drive you into Amsterdam; we'll go to the Eastern Market Place and find what you need. Dulci, it'll be fun. I'm dying to taste some exotic dishes from the Middle East," Brecken said.

The weeks of spring and summer passed quickly; the days became shorter and the temperature began to drop. Whenever breakfast was blatantly rich, and high in calories, Brecken would work Dulcinea twice as hard on their martial arts exercises and strength training routines. When she was too exhausted to continue he would goad her into just one more set. Brecken pushed her to her limits, and worked right along next to her pushing himself. He was teaching her how to kill an opponent who might be bigger and stronger. One day, as they walked in the garden, he asked her outright, "Dulci, have you ever been attacked?"

"Yes, I have been attacked. Alright?"

"How'd you handle that? Can you tell me about it?"

"You ask me how I handled it. I'll tell you how I handled that. I killed him! I used my shabria. He was lying on top of me. I pushed the blade into his side between his ribs, as deep as I could push it. His blood ran out of his body. I'll teach you how to use a shabria," she looked at him with cold eyes. "The secret to killing with a knife is to know where to use the blade on the body, how deep it must be pushed and at what angle to insert the blade. You must have a good understanding of the placement of internal organs in the human body. Sometimes it's important to twist the blade as you pull it out so that the wound won't close upon itself and stem the flow of life's blood," Dulci spoke in a flat monotone.

Brecken was silent for a few moments. "You're serious aren't you! You actually killed someone? Wow, I never would've thought you've been through that at such a young age. Was it necessary to kill them?" He clapped a hand over his mouth briefly, "That sounded bad …….a stupid question. I'm sorry, I shouldn't have asked that." He looked at Dulci, and he saw the cold steel melt away from her eyes, and it was replaced with deep sadness. He reached out and took hold of her shoulders, and pulled her close to him as he enfolded her in his strong arms. She resisted slightly as intimacy was never her inclination, and her gut tried to push her into an offensive tact. But he put one hand at the back of her head, cradling it in his palm. He held her tight. "Dulci, I am going to be by your side for the rest of your journey. Look at me. As long as you want me near you, that is where I will be."

She was safe in Brecken's arms. He was strong and confidant. He reminded her of Nomad with that aura of justice, and the belief that "the right thing" was achievable; that he could make a difference. She thought some might call him naive, but she knew it wasn't that, not at all. Safina had thought about this for some time. She concluded that it was simply such a rare trait that too many people had forgotten it existed. When they glimpsed this quality in someone unselfish they tried to pull it down, belittle it, categorize it as blind ignorance, to make themselves more palatable in their own eyes and among their peers.

As she stood there, in that unfamiliar circle of safety, Dulcinea thought to herself: *He was born to champion justice, and he is willing to make the sacrifices necessary to put himself on the line for his convictions.* "Brecken, you are a throwback to the ancient codes of conduct and honor. That describes a patriot in the best sense."

"No, Dulci. That describes a United States Marine." His chest swelled a bit.

"Well, there you have it, you aren't perfect after all - you don't lack pride or vanity," Dulci said as she burst out laughing, and twisted free of his embrace.

Brecken laughed too. He cleared his throat and tried to look more serious. "We need to know each other better. We're going to spend many more months working together, maybe years." Brecken led her to a garden bench and motioned to her to sit down. He sat next to her. "We should be a seamless pair of warriors. Dulci, I'm a US Marine Lieutenant Colonel on special assignment. There are some things that I'm not allowed to share with you yet, but at least we can share our personal experiences." He hesitated as though he were searching for words he'd never even thought to himself.

"Dulci, I was born an orphan. My birth mother didn't even bother to wipe off my face, or to leave an imprint of lipstick on my brow. There was no "I'm sorry but....." note, no handmade quilt, and no little white bible tucked under a pillow beneath my head. I was wrapped in a dirty, bloody service station hand towel, and placed on the icy concrete steps of the local Fire Department. When they found me I was blue and almost dead from the cold."

Dulcinea stood up. "Let's go inside and I'll brew some of your gourmet coffee," she said. "I want to hear the whole story Brecken - all of it."

They settled down at the breakfast table with two cups of steaming "upside down" coffee (coffee beans brewed entirely with boiling hot milk). Brecken cradled the warm cup in both hands as he continued his story. "For the first years of my life I lived with the Fire Chief's family. His wife was overworked, and he was underpaid. The county provided some compensation to them for taking me in. Five years later, my foster father was killed while fighting a barn fire, trying to get the horses out. The family was disbursed among their relatives, and I was taken to an orphanage. It wasn't too terrible; there was plenty of food. And the orphans were taken care of pretty well. When I was six-years-old my adoptive parents finally showed up at the orphanage. I knew they were my true "forever" parents sent by my guardian angel."

He laughed out loud while he described his adoptive parents. "I loved them both from the moment I met them. My dad laughed all the time. He should have been a stand-up comic. He had permanent laugh lines on his face. My mother was quite plump, and smelled of apples. It was a wonderful life. I was loved. My father was a Viet Nam Veteran who had been wounded. When he returned from the war my parents could not have children. So they adopted me."

Brecken put his head in his hands and sighed. "Dulci, I got into some trouble as a teen, but my dad and mom took their life savings, and sent me to a military academy. My dad believed in me even when I didn't believe in myself. He said it was an investment in the future. My mother baked and cleaned, and prayed that I would turn my life around. It took a while, but in the end, with the help from a lot of wonderful people, I got back on track.

On my twenty-third birthday my parents made a trip to Washington D.C. It was their dream to see the Capitol. I was already a US Marine at the time, stationed at the Pentagon. We had a wonderful visit together. They even brought a birthday cake all the way from home. Mom held it on her lap on the plane so it wouldn't get crushed. When it was time for them to leave, I dropped them off at Dulles Airport early, for a flight to Los Angeles, where they planned to visit my mother's sister. They were passengers on American Airlines flight 77 on the morning of September 11th, 2001. I didn't go to work that day because it was the last day of my vacation." Dulci saw his eyes shinning with tears. She handed him a tissue and took his hand in hers. Brecken composed himself and cleared his throat. "Flight 77 slammed into the Pentagon in Washington D.C. It was hijacked by Muslim terrorists and used as a weapon to kill innocent people in the cause of Jihad. Until now I have never told anyone about this."

Dulcinea felt her throat closing as an immense wave of sympathy washed over her. She moved close to him and put her hand on his cheek, "I know Brecken, Nomad told me about you. I know, as no one else will ever know, the secrets of your heart. Your parents are fine. They know everything that you do, and they are proud. You will see them again, I promise."

Brecken seemed unnerved. He took her hand from his cheek and folded it into his, brought it to his lips, and kissed her finger tips. "Dulci. Who is Nomad? How could he know about my parents?

She sat with him at the kitchen table, sipping hot coffee. From the window they could see out into the garden. It was filled with colorful flowers, and carefree birds fluttering from tree to tree. The sun was shining and a pleasant breeze gently bent the flower stems. It made their sorrow blacker and heavier by contrast.

Dulcinea told him the awful story of her life. She told him about Nomad. It was also the first time she shared her source of strength with anyone. She knew he wouldn't doubt her. She knew she could trust him. "Allah sent you to me so that I would never be alone in my quest to save Islam. It is divine fate that you, who lost everything to the Islamic extremists, will play a major role in saving Islam from certain annihilation. The fate of over a billion and a half Muslims, throughout the world, rests on our success."

Brecken and Dulcinea hugged each other for a long time. Finally, it was Dulcinea who let go. "Nomad was right about you, Brecken. You and I are soul mates and we will always be together no matter what happens." Dulci looked at him, intensely focusing on his eyes.

He stood, and helped her to her feet. Dulci accepted the fact that she didn't mind the hug and the hand holding, or the brotherly kiss on the top of her head. It was the first time she didn't dislike physical contact.

When the pressure was too much, Brecken would get silly with Dulci, joking and laughing and telling her stories from his childhood in Nebraska.

Brecken was like a kid – plotting and planning a departure from the daily mundane tasks of Dulci's private preparatory program of education, culture and self-defense. "Of course, he's right, they really need a break now and then," Vivian told Yasmine.

The last few weeks were very intense. Dulcinea started from scratch in almost every field of study. She had no formal education until she arrived in Holland. This made the pace of her study program extremely accelerated beyond anything that Brecken had experienced. When Vivian and Brecken discussed Dulci's progress, Brecken remarked, "I'm amazed by the sheer breadth of Dulci's knowledge. It seems to be vastly superior to my own academic foundation, despite my degree from M.I.T."

"It's because of her remarkable recall ability," Vivian smiled. "Don't question it, just continue to feed her the information and facts that she needs. Dulci has studied continuously for the last five years; minus all the typical teenage distractions of boys, girlfriends, and pop culture in general."

When Vivian spoke with Dr. Morelli she commented about Dulcinea's difficult life ahead: "I hate it that world events are moving so quickly that there is no time for Dulcinea to be a young woman. From child bride to revolutionary leader..... there will be no hiatus between these two awful realities."

It was almost time for Dr. Morelli to pay another visit. Vivian read his letters out loud to Dulci and Brecken. He wrote them in English for the most part. The descriptions of all the places he visited were beautifully crafted. The ports of Africa sounded exotic and beckoning as they came alive on the pages of his letters. As always he included recipes from faraway lands; dishes that the marvelous cook, Prodromos, on board the Hercules, prepared after eating food at various establishments in the company of the doctor. It was their mutual hobby, finding new delicious culinary delights and attempt to re-create them in the ship's galley. When they perfected the recipe, the doctor would copy the ingredients and process, and mail it with a photograph of the finished dish, to Vivian at her Post Office Box. When he knew that she would not be able to obtain unique spices or exotic herbs called for in a recipe, he forwarded packages of them to her via the stationery store in Hilversum. It was Morelli's ploy to provide some distraction from the austerity of a life in preparation for sacrifice.

In his last e-mail Luigi added a postscript tucked neatly at the end of the message, telling them that the Captain of the Hercules died from complications of an advanced case of gonorrhea. It had only taken several years longer than the doctor had anticipated. "The world is well-rid of this monster. I never thought he would live this long. He has been hospitalized for years, I thought you should know."

Dulcinea wasn't ashamed that she felt glad that Captain Demetrius was dead at last.

The week before Dr. Morelli was due to arrive for a visit Vivian received an e-mail from Caspar Van Vleit, the First Mate on board the Hercules:

```
Dr. Morelli died this morning,
possible aneurysm. Death was
painless. Condolences to you and
Dulcinea. Letter to follow.

   Caspar Van Vliet, S.S. Hercules
```

The letter was delivered by messenger after a few days. The courier dispatched with the missive, also carried a wooden box with an intricate emblem of a falcon clutching a bag in its talon. The Falcon is the universal symbol of the Knights of Hospitaller founded in 1080. It was established to provide care for the poor and sick visiting Jerusalem. The image of a bag being carried by the falcon was something that Vivian did not understand. She thought that perhaps Dulcinea might have an explanation. Vivian signed the electronic tablet held by the courier, and without another word he left quietly, leaving them to their thoughts.

Dearest Dulcinea:

Luigi left everything to you. I'll forward the papers to sign and the information for his lawyer and bank. Several years ago he asked me to package up his personal belongings and ship them to you in the event of his death. I'll do that this week. Here's the key to his safety deposit box in Banka della Svizzera Italiana (BSI). This is a Swiss based bank and they have a Netherlands office in Amsterdam where his box is located. The password to that box is a combination of numbers that Luigi said he taught you, so you are the only person who would know that information.
He will be buried at sea tomorrow afternoon.
Sincerely, your friend,
Caspar Van Vliet

Vivian and Dulcinea cried quietly together as Brecken looked on, helpless to lessen their grief. Luigi's death was entirely unexpected, and Dulcinea was saddened that she did not have another opportunity to tell him how important he was in her life. She wanted one more chance to say good bye and to feel his strong fatherly arms hugging her. He was truly the only father she ever knew – and the kindest man she knew as well.

Dulcinea was surprised that he left everything to her. But she knew that he did not have any living relatives. Luigi's sizable estate would make it possible for Dulcinea to pursue her studies without financial barriers.

Something gnawed at the back of Dulci's mind. She couldn't put her finger on it. *There's something not right about Luigi's death. If he was the only doctor on board the ship, and they were at sea, how was the cause of death determined?* Dulci kept coming back to that question. There was no logical answer. *Why was it necessary to bury him at sea? They have huge refrigeration lockers on board – I saw them. The Hercules was due in Rotterdam in 8 days. They could have easily preserved the body until then.* It was nagging at her, she couldn't shake the feelings. *How do we even know that Luigi wasn't murdered? In fact, how do we know he is actually dead? I don't feel it. I don't believe he is actually gone. Something is going on…. but what?* Her thoughts were keeping her awake at night, and she was finding it difficult to concentrate on her studies. She didn't share her doubts with Vivian or Brecken. Dulci needed more answers before she could formulate any theories as to what really happened to Dr. Morelli. The symbol of the Falcon holding a bag that looked full, was yet another clue that she had yet to figure out. *Why did Luigi put that symbol on his box of personal belongings?*

CHAPTER 10

The Assassins

A week later Brecken decided they all needed a change of pace to get them out of the depression and doldrums after the loss of Luigi. He loaded up the car with cloth grocery bags and extra coats.

It was the end of a long winter. The snow was gone but the days were still chilly and an early spring snow storm wouldn't be unusual. Those were the worst; heavy sticky snow that quickly turned to mud and slush.

"We'll stop in Hilversum for petrol," he said to Vivian and Dulci as he helped them into the car. "I'll drive so that you two can relax and enjoy the scenery."

When they arrived in the city it was pristine. Dulcinea liked visiting Amsterdam, particularly because the canals and dikes interested her. Amsterdam was a port city that was below sea level and yet did not flood.

The International Market was well stocked with all the ingredients she needed to cook the basic cuisine of Iraq and Kurdistan. The merchants catered to a large Muslim population in Holland and Germany. While preparing for this trip, she located recipes on line, that she couldn't remember from childhood. When Dulci printed them out she smiled as she realized that even in her horrific past there were some good things. In Amsterdam she bought spices, grains, pungent seasoned oils, rendered butter, and a variety of wild rice that grew only in the Nile valley. She found specialty pans and utensils - everything she would need to prepare a succulent middle eastern meal. They left it all temporarily with a restaurant owner friend of Vivian, to be picked up on their way back to the car. Then they headed for the Main Station, Leidseplein, to board a canal cruise boat and see more of this cosmopolitan metropolis. She wanted to visit Rembrandt House and the Amsterdam Museum of Art.

As they were queuing up for boat tickets Dulci noticed a tall red headed man with odd-eyes, one deep blue and the other eye of jade green, joining the ticket line parallel to theirs. It was a startling contrasting feature and she couldn't help staring at him longer than a brief glimpse would warrant. A tiny filament of a connection was made. Embarrassed by her self-perceived rudeness, she looked away and quickly dismissed the encounter from her mind.

Vivian and Brecken were hanging over the deck railing toward the bow of the canal tour boat enjoying the crisp clear skies. Five minutes into the cruise, Dulcinea headed toward a bench about mid-deck to watch the people waving at other canal boats as they passed. "I'll get some hot spiced tea and bring it to you in a minute," Brecken called to her. There were only about two dozen other people on the boat. These tours were not that popular so early in the season, because few people decided to brave the chill.

She pulled her jacket up around her neck and pushed her hands into her pockets. Dulcinea could see the quaint narrow shops with their three story buildings all attached to each other in neat rows and adorned in lacy white curtains in the upstairs windows of the upper flats along the canal. Each stone or brick house had shutters and beams painted a different color: a delightful orange, then a red, a blue or a maroon – all with white moldings and white gingerbread trimming around the windows and doors. People were riding bicycles, walking dogs, or pushing baby carriages along the narrow pathways bordering the canal. She inhaled deeply, enjoying the air that was crisp enough to invigorate but not cold enough that she needed to cover her face and breathe through a scarf to protect her lungs. The sunlight reflected off the surface of the water relaxing her and finally she felt her worries fade.

She sat down on the bench that faced the port side, midway between the bow and the stern, and glanced toward the rear of the boat. Shock slammed into her gut, stopping her breathing. Seated on a bench, was the same man who had watched her in the Amsterdam train station parking lot on the day she arrived in Holland. That sense of familiarity she felt on the train was real. He was close enough that she could see his face and she did know him. Oh, yes, she knew him and why he was here. She turned to alert Vivian who was talking to someone at the front of the boat. Before she could get Vivian's attention two men came up behind her from both sides and grabbed her arms, dragging her toward the center aisle that divided the passenger seating areas into front and rear sections.

"Stop! Let go of me. Vivian! Brecken!" She twisted her body toward the man on her left, shin kicked him hard with her right boot, then leaned down and viciously bit his hand. He let go of her, screaming. Dulci ducked a backhand from the man on her right, who held her wrist in a vice grip with his left hand. She stepped back out of the reach of his right hand, and planted her right leg between his feet even as they faced the same direction. She was "lightening fast" grabbing her silver shabria with her left hand from her left pocket, unsheathing it with her teeth, and she immediately slashed the face of the man she had bitten. The blade cut diagonally cross his face from his left temple all the way to below his ear on his right, splaying open his face like a fillet. She plunged it all the way home when she reached his carotid artery, giving it a vicious twist before pulling it out. It took less than three seconds to neutralize him.

"*Cous Ochto*", he swore, a particularly nasty Arabic obscenity, as he fell to the deck gurgling and spouting pulses of blood from his neck. The grasp of the weapon in her hand helped her to focus. She spit the sheath of the shabria from between her teeth, and screamed at him in Arabic, "You filthy son of a bitch, no virgins are waiting for you in Hell, and that is where you are going!" His blood was spurting over everything, and he fell to the deck clutching his face with both hands and moaning.

The second attacker grabbed onto her upper arm in a painful bruising grip. She had her right leg wedged against the inside of his left leg. This effectively pushed him partially behind her and gave her the leverage she needed. She screamed vile obscenities at him as she leaned toward her right, plunging the curved shabria blade upward into his torso, twisting it as deep into his body as she could push it. When she could not shove it another millimeter she stared point blank into his sweaty face and their eyes locked. For a moment she saw the face of Khaliq in her mind. Dulcinea pulled and rotated the knife back out as the man screamed in agony. He let go of her and collapsed, crashing to the deck in silence, his body sprawled awkwardly between the seats. A great dark red pool of blood formed around him and ran in narrow rivulets toward the starboard side of the boat.

The man in the stern launched himself up and ran toward her while yelling at passengers in his way, "Get out of my way. Move! *Ruchi min hone* (Go away)!" Several passengers were seemingly paralyzed by fear and stood frozen in his path. He knocked them aside with his massive forearm. His coarse ugly face was dominated by a black, mustache that covered his mouth. Just as he reached her, she thrust the dagger toward his chest, but he saw the quick flash of metal in her hand, and he swung his right arm out, parrying Dulci's strike to his right – latching onto her wrist and twisting her hand. The pain wrenched a shriek from her as the wrist-lock forced her hand open and she released her grip on the shabria. She heard the dull thud of the dagger hitting the deck. He continued pulling her hand, spinning her around with her back to him and moving her arm up into a locked position with her hand brought up behind her back and pinning it against the back of her shoulder. He clamped his other hand over her mouth and dragged her over to the railing. Dulci caught the stare of the odd-eyed passenger sitting on the last seat next to the exit steps from the deck. He was the same man she encountered earlier while standing in line. She tried to ask for his help but she couldn't say anything coherent with the attacker's hand over her mouth. She beseeched him with pleading eyes: *Help me! Help me! Do something, move!*

But Dulci thought later that she should have remembered what her life taught her. When all doors are locked the unforeseen comes in through the window.

"Fuck," he said, his eyes wide. The passenger began to stand, but just as he moved, the attacker hit him with a quick kick to his torso. He pushed him overboard with his foot, through the opening in the railing, but in that second while his focus was elsewhere the attacker's hold on her arm loosened.

"Breck!" she shouted as the sweaty hand slipped off of her mouth. Her face was grabbed so tight she felt her jaw shift in its socket. But the grip was broken. She watched as Brecken glanced over his shoulder from the line at the kiosk in the bow of the boat. Scowling for a second Brecken sprinted toward her. Unexpectedly a fourth attacker was the first to intercept Brecken as he stuck his foot out in front of

Brecken's path down the center aisle, and at the same time he swung his right hand behind Brecken's feet while getting up beside him, and flipped Brecken over his hip, tossing him onto the passengers to their side. Passengers were screaming and shoving each other away as a number of them went down in the collision of bodies.

Brecken's attacker stumbled backward then fell straight onto his back as Vivian came up from the side and with her leg she swept his feet out from under him. As he fell back she landed a good fist into the man's face on his way down, breaking his nose, but the man sprang up from his back, paying no attention to his injuries, and threw a right cross into her kidney and brought her to her knees. He was just about to grab her head and break her neck when Brecken rushed forward again raising his left leg high in the air, catching the man in the left lower quadrant of his midriff with Brecken's boot. It knocked the air out of the assailant, and sent him twisting to his left. As he clutched his stomach with both hands, the momentum of his body being thrown back and to one side caused his head to snap forward, smashing his forehead down hard onto the metal corner of the bench back in front and to his left, cracking his skull. He collapsed on the deck, blood pouring out of his ears and mouth. Brecken took off sprinting toward Dulci, trying to get around the passengers and deck seats.

Dulci tried to break away to help her friends but the man holding her whispered into her ear, "Uh, Uh, Uh." She watched Brecken disappear in the chaos just a few rows ahead of where she was standing, as the passengers broke into a panic.

Brecken twisted and slid onto his back and swung his left leg behind a passenger's knee and his right leg in front of it and scissored them together to swing the person into Dulcinea and the man who was holding her. They both fell forcing the man to let go of Dulci. He immediately jumped back up, and was pushing people left and right screeching at them in Arabic. Just as he reached for Brecken he was shoved aside as the couple in front of him and to his left surged backward with the force of people scrambling away from the fight.

He rose up again and turned, reaching for Dulcinea with both hands, Brecken jumped into the air and slammed him hard in the chest with his right foot and at the same moment he came down onto his feet, he punched the attacker in the face with his left fist causing the man's head to snap sharply backwards. The momentum of both strikes propelled the man toward the waist high deck railing. Dulci saw Brecken spin 360 degrees in mid-air and hit the attacker for the last time with his right boot to the man's chest. This powerful blow knocked the man over the railing and his body splashed into the canal where it floated face down with no visible movement. A small speedboat came alongside of him and some men used a grappling hook to pull him into their boat and they throttled the boat at full speed, away from the cruise boat.

The Amsterdam police boat siren could be heard coming up from the north end of the canal and immediately gave chase to the small speedboat. Passengers huddled against the railing. During the fight some people had jumped overboard into the canal. Police boats were gathering them from the freezing water as quickly as possible. Dulci noticed the odd-eyed passenger being pulled to safety. He turned and waved at her with a big "glad to be alive" smile on his face. She returned the smile, although her whole body was shaking. His action, however brief, made the difference between life and death for her. She needed to sit down.

Vivian rushed over to Dulci, "Are you all right honey?" Blood was everywhere. She started to check Dulcinea all over for stab wounds. Dulcinea was shivering, holding the bloody shabria she recovered from the deck, and the knife's sheath in her other hand. The body of the man she stabbed was lying still on the deck.

As Vivian turned to look at him, the man who was clutching his slashed face, sitting in a pool of blood on the deck a few feet away from them, pulled an automatic Glock 9mm from his coat pocket and pointed it at Dulcinea, "Bitch, you will die, you will die you dirty infidel whore." Just before he fired it, Vivian threw her body in front of Dulcinea and grabbed her shoulders with both hands. Three shots rang out immediately as the Dutch police, who boarded the canal boat, fired into the attacker barely a few seconds too late. Vivian's body collapsed against Dulcinea, as she let go and slid down onto the deck twisting onto her back, unconscious.

Brecken rushed to Vivian and lifted her head up onto his arm, "Vivian! Vivian! Can you hear me? Open your eyes." He felt for her pulse, and slowly placed her head on the deck where he rolled her over onto her stomach. Blood was pouring out of the wound on her back. He grabbed a folded deck towel and pushed it hard against the wound. Just then a boat ambulance pulled up alongside their canal boat and two medics jumped onto the deck and lifted Vivian, face down, onto a stretcher and carried her to a ramp that had been positioned between the two boats. Another policeman led Dulcinea over the ramp and onto the ambulance. She was drenched in blood, bruised and gasping to catch her breath. Brecken was still applying pressure to Vivian's wound, sidestepping alongside the stretcher.

The medics took over from Brecken. The ambulance boat moved off at full speed with sirens blaring and blue lights flashing. Brecken was exhausted but hung on tightly to the railing along the outside of the ambulance boat cab. He made his way around the narrow outer ledge to where Dulcinea was seated on a bench just inside the cab cover. She was "white knuckling" a perpendicular handrail fastened to the inside wall of the cab. The cold salty spray from the boat cutting through the water was blowing back into her face, which was what kept her from keeling over. Her hair was plastered across her eyes.

Brecken hung from the outside of the boat next to her seat, grabbing the inside railing with one hand as he lifted his foot off the ledge along the bottom of the outside of the cab cover and placed it on the deck on the inside of the boat, followed by his other foot. As he eased his body into the seat next to her, Brecken dropped down and put his arm around her and she leaned hard into his chest. "You're shaking Dulci, let me get you a blanket," Brecken whispered into her ear.

"She may die because she saved me. Vivian is bleeding to death because of me." She said, her voice catching in her throat.

Brecken handed her some tissues from a box on the dispensary table inside, grabbed a blanket from the compartment under his seat, and wrapped it around her shoulders. Dulci wiped her eyes and blew her nose into the tissue. She began to shiver and her lips were turning blue around the edges. Pulling one arm out of his coat, he wrapped his wool jacket around both of them and shoved her hands inside of his shirt to warm them on his body. He flinched slightly from the sudden icy touch.

"No, Dulci. A bad man shot her. If she dies it will be because of him, not because of you. You haven't done anything wrong. Vivian loves you. She wouldn't want you to say that. If anyone is at fault it's me. I was supposed to protect you. I was sent to protect you and I screwed up."

Dulcinea sat up straight, "What are you talking about? What do you mean that you were sent to protect me? What does that mean?"

"They didn't want me to tell you. Yasmine thought it would make you nervous and afraid if you knew that I was a bodyguard sent to protect you," Brecken replied. He looked embarrassed and uncomfortable. "My job was to teach you self-defense and protect you from assassins and kidnappers. I didn't think about Amsterdam. I thought no one knew we were coming here today. They probably have someone watching the house. It's so obvious now, when I look back on it.

How could I have been such an idiot? I'm sorry Dulci.....I'm really sorry."

Dulci was exhausted, bruised, and cold. She could barely comprehend what had happened. Her jaw hurt like crazy and the marks on her arms were turning an ugly purple, yellow color. It was quickly becoming a bad dream that she would rather forget.

The canal boat ambulance cut the engines near a dock close to the hospital. The bow smacked against the large rubber tires suspended along the three sides of the dock, protecting the boat as its inertial momentum carried it into the slip. The smell of diesel fumes permeated the air. A Dutchman, actually wearing wooden shoes, threw a fat rope from the dock to a crew member. *It's true*, Dulci thought, *the workers along the canals wear wooden shoes because they will float if they fall off!*

As the boat was secured, Vivian was transferred to a waiting ambulance. On the way to the emergency room the medics hooked her up to I.V. fluids to avoid shock, and temporarily applied a pressure bandage to the wound. Twice they almost lost her during the transport as her blood pressure plummeted drastically. Her life fluttered precariously, sinking deeper into unconsciousness. After additional X-rays, she was sent up to the operating room for an attempted repair of her spleen and removal of the slug. The intern on duty in the radiography unit picked up the direct line to the surgeon standing by, "The bullet is lodged between her right subclavian artery and her brachiocephalic trunk."

The surgical team scrubbed in and before the surgeon made the first cut he described the way the surgery would proceed. "This situation is unlike most shooting victims, because this woman has been shot at point blank range in the back."

The surgeons and anesthesiologist discussed the options among themselves as soon as the damage was accessed. "I don't want to remove her spleen because she would be susceptible to all types of opportunistic infections throughout the rest of her life, and she has a history of cancer according to her government health record data base. This history further tends to compromise the immune system. "Let's get in, repair the spleen, stop the bleeding, and get out," the chief surgeon stated.

"Hang another bag of plasma. Her pulse is weak and sporadic and her pressure is dropping," the anesthesiologist barked at the O.R. surgical nurse.

"She's already been given a liter of "O" negative. That's gotta be at least thirty percent of her entire blood volume," she answered flatly.

"She'll die without it. Just keep it coming until her pressure comes back up," he answered. "I'll let you know when to close down."

Fifteen minutes went by with the surgeon wrist deep into the exposed cavity. "It's unusual to see the internal anatomy of a human being from this perspective. Most surgeries are performed coming in from the front of the body. The placement of the bullet and the angle of the entry wound give us no choice here, but to approach it from the back. It's like looking at a topographical map that was turned inside out. There it is," the doctor almost shouted it out. "There's the dam slug!" He pulled it out with his surgical tweezers. He saw the nicked blood vessel and sutured it. After suctioning away the last of the accumulation of blood, he said, "Close her up Hans. There are no more bleeders," pointing to the young intern standing across from him. "The bleeding has stopped and her pressure is back to normal. You can shut down the plasma," he looked at the nurse. After a short pause, he added, "Nice job all around. You all did great. Looking at the nurse he said, "It's up to Allah now," he grinned as he pulled his mask off at the exit door from the O.R. *Allah hu akkbar."

"Yes, Dr. El Khourey. We will leave the rest to Allah, but I will say a prayer to Jesus as well – just for added insurance," the nurse laughed.

It was a truce between them. The doctor was a Muslim from Lebanon and the surgical nurse was a Christian Arab from Jordan.

As Vivian's life "teeter-tottered" precariously between life and death, Brecken and Dulcinea were escorted to the "family only" lounge at the hospital. On the large TV screen attached to the wall of the waiting room, they watched local news footage of the police boat chasing the larger faster speedboat. Apparently, it got away because there was no follow-up story about the capture of the attackers.

They turned to see the doctor walk down the hallway toward them. They both rose to acknowledge him.

"Are you the family of Vivian Von Stetton?"

"Yes, we are," Brecken said without hesitation.

"The bullet has been removed. Ms. Von Stetton is a healthy, strong woman, and despite the loss of blood, she's holding her own. Her condition is stable, but guarded." He explained intricacies of the surgery and how critical it had been to get her into surgery so fast. "We're moving her from Post Op to Recovery. She'll be kept in I.C.U. here for several days to make sure there are no complications. You can visit her in the morning," the doctor announced.

"No," Brecken quickly responded. "She can't stay here.....she isn't safe here. Is there any way we can move her tonight? The men who hired the assassins are determined and resourceful. As long as she is here they can easily locate her. I believe they will try again."

Dulcinea raised her eyebrows in surprise. She didn't think the "bad guys" were after Vivian. She assumed that Vivian had just taken a bullet that was meant for her. She didn't think Vivian was in any danger at the hospital. *Brecken must be in shock; he isn't thinking clearly.* Dulci decided to let it go. If it made him feel better to be in charge, then that would be their plan. She knew when to assert herself and when it wasn't important.

"You'll need an ambulance or van to move her," said the doctor. "She must be kept horizontal with her feet elevated, and she needs the I.V. fluids through tomorrow; she'll be dehydrated from the surgery. and someone should monitor her temperature and heart rate. With her body in a weakened condition while her repaired spleen heals, her immune system will be less resilient. She could be susceptible to infection." He scribbled something on the back of his prescription pad and tore it off, handing it to Brecken. "Here is the address and phone number of a small private hospital where you can take her. They're discreet. I'll write a prescription for antibiotics when I sign her discharge papers. Good luck to you young man. Your quick thinking is what made the difference in this case. Without the immediate and constant pressure to the wound, she would have bled out before she made it into the ambulance boat. You did good; damn good! Do you have EMT training?"

"US Marine, B.T. Petersen at your service," Brecken smiled.

"No wonder! If you have to get shot, you couldn't pick a better person to be with," the doctor looked at Dulcinea.

The doctor reached out both of his hands and grabbed Dulcinea's hand, shaking it vigorously. "I'm told by the nurse that you have extensive bruising and lacerations. I'm surprised that you survived this attack. These guys each outweighed you by at least thirty kilos."

After the doctor left, Brecken contacted the private hospital. They were waiting for an ambulance to transport Vivian.

"Mr. Petersen and Ms. Morelli, I have a few questions for you," a stocky square man in a steel gray suit, navy blue tie, and white dress shirt, stepped in front of them as they emerged from the visitors' lounge. "I'm Investigator Schuyler with the Amsterdam Police Department." He offered his hand, and Brecken shook it firmly. Dulcinea ignored the inspector. "I took the liberty of getting your names from the hospital admitting record. I see that you're both friends of Vivian Von Stetton. Do you know why those men attacked you?"

"No. We don't," Brecken replied. "Can we see some identification, Inspector Schuyler?"

"Of course," he pulled out his badge and credentials and handed them to Brecken. The inspector looked at the small notebook he held in his other hand, and then focused his gaze on Dulci. "How about you, Ms. Morelli? Do you know why they attacked you?"

Brecken handed the badge and the laminated ID card back to the inspector.

"How would I know that?" Dulcinea asked a bit caustically. She didn't appreciate being grilled as though she were a suspect. "Shouldn't you be out chasing down the bad guys who got away?"

Inspector Schuyler ignored the question and continued in his measured voice. "The man you killed, Ms. Morelli, is a known terrorist from the Palestinian Liberation Army. Interpol has a long dossier on him. His name is Sayed al-Ataba and the Israeli authorities want him for bombings in Tel Aviv and Petach Tikva. Of course, we know from several eyewitness accounts, that you killed him in self-defense. However, I must ask you why you carry a lethal weapon on your person? Is there something you're not telling me?"

Dulcinea stared at him for a moment, "Inspector Schuyler, I am the daughter of Dr. Luigi Morelli, who was a research scientist. My father worked for the *Institut Scientific Romagnol Per La Studi E. La Cura Del Tumr* (IRST) in Rome. On his own, he developed a significant medical research breakthrough about fifteen years ago. There were threats on his life from large pharmaceutical corporations. The universities and philanthropic groups that benefit heavily from research grants and private funding, don't play well with others, if you get my inference. My father refused to hand over his research data and case studies to be destroyed. He had no choice but to go into hiding."

Dulcinea hesitated for a moment. Should she divulge anymore information or not? Vivian had told her: "When in doubt - be silent." She had to establish a happy medium between withholding relevant information and assisting the Dutch authorities in apprehending the assassins.

"Inspector, I am going to assume that you are a discreet professional and that any information I share with you will be kept confidential? Yes?"

"Yes, information that supports the investigation, but is not critical evidence in a potential prosecution, will be kept in strict confidence," Schuyler said.

"My father died unexpectedly about ten days ago." She bit her bottom lip as she fought back the overwhelming sadness. "He apparently died of natural causes while he was traveling. I am his sole heir. So it would be feasible to suspect that the same people who made threats on his life would now be anxious to silence me.

Second, the terrorist connection is unknown to me, except to say that it is not beyond reasonable deduction to believe that desperate corporate executives might hire "bad guys" to do this job."

Inspector Schuyler cleared his throat and looked directly into Dulcinea's eyes. "I have already read the preliminary autopsy report on the two dead men. The report on the first body states that the wounds indicate this was the work of a professional killer." The inspector looked down at his notes, flipping forward several pages, and began reading out loud. "The examination of the chest wound revealed that the knife entered the body........ Hmmm......... sorry, my notes are written in my own brand of short-hand.......ah yes, just below the sternum......... in an upward direction piercing the epicardium layer of the heart and on through the myocardium layer of tissue. What is most interesting to me is that apparently after the knife was thrust as far as possible into the right ventricle, it was twisted as it was withdrawn. It seems that this purposely prevented any chance of the wound closing on the blade and reducing the loss of blood. It was a lethal disruption of cardiovascular function."

He looked up from his notes and seemed to focus his attention on her reaction. "Toxicology and DNA testing are pending. The findings on the other body show a perfect knife slash from the upper right temple across the bridge of the nose all the way to the carotid artery on the left side of the man's neck, severing the artery as the knife was pressed hard at the end of the cut in the exact location to ensure death."

Inspector Schuyler touched his nose with the end of his pencil, closed his small spiral notebook and put the pencil and the notebook into his inside breast pocket. He looked at Brecken and then turned his head slightly in Dulcinea's direction. "If the police had not fired three rounds into him, he would have died from massive blood loss within minutes anyway."

Dulcinea put both of her hands into her jacket pockets and stepped closer to the Inspector. She looked up at him with a serious gaze. In a quiet, non-threatening tone of voice she said, "Regarding the knife - my father taught me how to use the shabria for self-defense." Dulci thought it would be prudent to interject Morelli as her lethal weapon instructor, instead of mentioning anything about Abraheem, who had actually taught her the art of killing with a shabria. " It's a good thing too, because if he hadn't I'd probably be dead right now. And, yes, he taught me to use it with lethal force. His comment to me was that if I needed to resort to the use of a dagger, I would need to resolve to kill the attacker as quickly as possible; otherwise, a knife wound just causes a rush of adrenalin and gives the attacker twice the power that he originally possessed. You cannot be suggesting that this was anything other than self defense?" She raised her eyebrows quizzically.

"No, of course not. We have dozens of witnesses to the fact that this was an unprovoked attack," Inspector Schuyler replied hurriedly. "I hope you appreciate a thorough investigation. Three people are dead and your friend was shot."

"OK, I understand that. When I left my father to come to Holland, he gave me the shabria to protect myself. It is a small weapon, easy to keep in a pocket or purse, legal in most countries, without a license. It doesn't require ammunition, and it is completely silent, yet quite deadly, even at a distance, if one has a steady hand and eye, as I do." Dulcinea was silent for a moment. She smiled at the inspector. "This one has a beautiful engraved design that most people would say is decorative – almost jewelry."

"Thank you, Ms. Morelli. Your knife - your *shabria* - will be returned to you later in the week, after we extract DNA blood and tissue samples from it. The second man, who was shot by the police, is unknown to us. Did you recognize that man?"

"No." Dulcinea wasn't happy with the information she was getting. None of it added up. Why wait over five years to attack her? If these attacks were made by men hired by Khaliq, they were long overdue. He could have found her much earlier. At this late date, they would simply have killed her on the spot. There was no point in trying to drag her away. After five years, she was damaged goods; and by Islamic standards she was too old for marriage, undesirable by age sixteen. She was convinced that by now Khaliq had purchased at least several girls to satisfy his lust for sex with children.

She believed what she told the inspector: this attack had to have originated in Italy or even on Wall Street. It just smelled like something other than revenge – something related to money or power. Dulcinea was beginning to develop insight into how the tiers of power and money were layered in the real world. Her analytical mind was working overtime to solve this puzzle. She needed to find a connection between the assassins on the boat and Luigi's cancer research.

"Mr. Petersen, did you recognize the men who attacked Ms. Morelli or the man you knocked overboard?"

"No, sorry. I didn't get a look at the faces of the two dead guys. I know that the man who attacked from the rear of the boat was a stranger to me. He had dark eyes, thick straight eyebrows, and a greasy mustache that covered his mouth. When I kicked him in the chest just before he fell back over the railing into the canal, the sleeve of his coat was torn away during the scuffle. I saw a strange tattoo on the lower inside part of his right arm. It looked like the head of a lion, the middle was the body and head of a goat, and the tail looked like a snake. It was unusual – something I have never seen before. It reminded me of a symbol I might expect to see in a Ninja movie." Brecken shoved his hands into his pockets and shifted his weight to one side. It was obvious that he was favoring his right foot.

Dulcinea's head bent back, her mouth opened slightly as she inhaled deeply, and pursed her lips as she blew out the breath through her mouth. Her arms were wrapped protectively around her body. For a moment her brow wrinkled as though she were trying to remember something important, "That sounds like the sign of a chimera, which is a being with two or more sets of DNA. Different cellular structures in their bodies can present completely different DNA strands because different cells came from different zygotes and fused together to form one being. That is a very rare occurrence. I read about it in my biology studies, and it came up again when I studied ancient mythologies in references to chimeras. They are painted or engraved on pottery and brass decorative items as having the head of a lion, body of a goat, and tail of a serpent. Some were depicted as having a lion's front, a goat's middle, with a second head that breathed fire, and a serpent's rear. I wonder, why someone would have such a tattoo? What would that signify?"

She was sure this was another clue to figuring out who attacked her and why. But so far, she couldn't understand its significance. Something was nagging and irritating her – something important. What was it? She closed her eyes for a moment and reached back in her mind to where she didn't wanted to remember anything until now.

Then she saw it in her mind: on the long trip with Khaliq from El Sighi's campsite to Basra, she saw this same tattoo on several of the men who were traveling with Khaliq's caravan. When they washed their hands before performing their daily prayers they rolled up their long black sleeves. She didn't remember their faces, but the tattoos were there – close to the elbow joint, on the inside lower right arm: A lion head, and a goat head on a goat body, slender sharp hooves, and the snake tail protruding from the rear with a diamond shaped snake head at the end of it. They were done in deep blue indigo ink. She could visualize the detail: there was something written in Arabic under the figure. She didn't know what it said because at that time in her life she could not read.

Inspector Schuyler asked them a few more administrative questions and he left. Brecken turned towards Dulcinea, "Dulci! What was that all about? What the hell is a chimera and what does that have to do with terrorists? The more information we get, the more questions remain unanswered."

"I can't tell you, Brecken. There are things that I can't tell you. I do trust you, but it isn't safe for you to know everything about me. This way, if they question you, you won't know. It's better that way ...... really....... you must believe me. It's better for both of us," she said. "And, I really don't know anything about chimeras. I think I saw it on the BBC last year...... something to do with double DNA sets in one person. Why it would be tattooed on someone's arm is just too much to figure out right now. I'm exhausted, cold, and starving. When can we get out of here?"

They went to the hospital's cafeteria and ordered big gooey Dutch pastries oozing with sugary frosting. They both needed some quick energy boost. After eating they returned to the waiting room until the ambulance arrived that would move Vivian to a safer location. They sunk into the soft leather sofa.

Brecken cradled her in his arms, and she rested her head on his chest. He didn't press her any more. She was so fragile, but when she slashed one attacker and plunged her dagger into the stomach of the second man right before his eyes without skipping a heartbeat, he must have understood that she wasn't frail or fragile or even vulnerable. As her arms went up around his neck, she hugged him tightly, as though she were reassuring him. It was then that he accepted the essence of this formidable woman. Her body was compact but strong and solid. Brecken relaxed and kissed the top of her head gently. She was supposed to feel safe with him, but the truth was that Brecken was safer with her around. He had witnessed the true capabilities of Dulcinea Devorah Morelli.

Brecken recalled a conversation he had with Vivian almost a year ago, as they stood by the window watching Dulci pick flowers in the garden. Brecken told her: "This woman is more important than anyone realizes. I have dreams of her standing in front of a great civilization. As I look up toward the hills behind her, I see a large black horse standing there with his mane and tail blowing in the breezes. I wake up with a feeling of renewed energy and purpose. But, honestly, I don't understand it."

"All will be revealed to you, Brecken. Be her friend and her protector for now. Soon she will be faced with the greatest of challenges, and she will need you to stand behind her, no matter what!" Vivian answered.

Vivian was transported to the private hospital, and guards were posted at the door to her room. She awoke for only a few minutes, and Dulcinea held her hand and told her she would be all right. After she slipped back into a deep sleep, Brecken drove Dulcinea to Hilversum. Despite her exhaustion she couldn't sleep. Rembrandt climbed up on the bed next to Dulci and laid his big black head in her lap. As she massaged the dog's neck and shoulders, she thought about what had happened and what might be in her future. Dulci knew the only way her life would have purpose was to prepare for the battles ahead. As she rose from the bed and sat at the small writing table in the corner of the room, with a pad and pen, she began listing the questions that would have to be answered before she could face her destiny.

At the end of the week Brecken and Dulcinea picked up Vivian from the hospital in Amsterdam. On the way out of Amsterdam they stopped by the grocery store where they stored Dulcinea's cooking ingredients before the attack. Brecken drove around in circles, made U-turns, and took side streets to make sure they were not followed. This would be the last time Dulcinea would see this city - and she knew it - and consciously treasured the sights, sounds, and textures of this Dutch masterpiece. For the rest of her life, she would remember these last precious days in Amsterdam; a city of remarkable cleanliness and crispness, and unique in its repertoire. No matter where Dulci traveled after that – no city would ever compare. Like a first lover, it would always be the benchmark for measuring any city she visited in the future.

CHAPTER II

Leaving Holland

Within a few weeks Vivian was back on her feet. With Dulcinea's help she was rebuilding her muscle tone and helping her body to heal quickly.

Vivian called Yasmine to tell her what happened. "We have to give Brecken the whole story, Yasmine. He can't protect her if he doesn't understand who she is and why this is the most important role he will have. He must come to terms with his feelings about Dulcinea. It is obvious that he has fallen in love with her. But, I believe he can put that aside if he knows it is in her best interests to do so."

"Yes, you are right, of course. You know him well enough to decide if he can be trusted. As far as his background check, it was impeccable and no discrepancies were found. It appears that he is exactly what he says he is – a man with no secrets and no political agenda," Yasmine assured her. "I will contact the Council and ask them to have his orders drawn up as soon as possible. I will have them delivered to you by my personal messenger. Abraheem carries a shabria identical to the one Safina carries. Ask him to show you his *persuasive secret'* – that is the password."

Within seventy-two hours the orders arrived, bearing the Presidential Seal of the United States. They were delivered by a tall handsome man who introduced himself as Abraheem, son of Farouq. When asked to provide proof of his identity by giving the password, he showed Vivian a shabria identical to the one that Dulci carried with her at all times. They were named *"Teounim"* (twins) because Abraheem had fashioned them with his own hands from the same piece of silver. Dulcinea was overjoyed to see him. They sat in the garden and talked for hours. At first, Dulci spoke with some hesitation in Arabic but within an hour she was talking freely and smiling at her guest. As Brecken watched from the window in the kitchen, his eyes narrowed and his jaw was grinding.

"Brecken, come into the sitting room. We need to talk," Vivian said to him from the doorway. He turned and followed her. " Please sit down." Brecken lowered himself into the overstuffed flowered armchair facing the sofa. Vivian sat across from him. "There are some things that you need to know about Dulcinea. I am assuming there is no need to remind you that this information is confidential. You cannot reveal this to anyone. Clear? Any questions about this?"

"No, I get it. Just tell me what's going on. I want to be in the loop. I can't do my job unless I understand what the threats are and where they're coming from." Brecken stood and walked to the window to watch Dulci and the visitor filling the bird feeders with millet and hanging suet cubes from the trees in the garden. There were many homemade cubes still on her tray, so he knew it would be a while before they would come back into the house. He observed Rembrandt protectively at her side, the dog was obviously aware that she was at risk. He never left her alone, always faithfully stationed strategically close by. Unless Brecken was in the room, the dog never slept . There seemed to be an agreement between Dulcinea and the dog. Brecken observed Rembrandt acting quite friendly with Abraheem, licking the man's hand and enthusiastically wagging his entire rear end.

Rising from the sofa, Vivian approached from behind and put a motherly hand on his shoulder, she whispered, "It will be alright. Dogs have good instincts about people."

Vivian told Brecken about Dulcinea's true identity. Everything she knew: the marriage to Khaliq, escaping to the house of Yasmine, the stillborn baby, leaving Iraq, the rape on board the Hercules, Dr. Luigi Morelli and Van Vliet.

"Keep her alive. Protect her at all cost. Dulcinea has a mission in life and if she isn't afforded the opportunity to pursue it, humanity will be the loser. You have been chosen by the leaders of the free world to follow her journey and put yourself between her and harm's way. She needs to be able to trust you no matter what transpires. Colonel Petersen, this mission is the most important mission ever assigned to a US Marine. You almost failed. If Dulcinea were not decisive and well trained with a dagger, she would be dead or kidnapped by now." Vivian's blue eyes cut through his boyish facade straight to his core. "I'm completely serious about this: there is no doubt in my mind that Dulcinea will change the course of history if she survives."

Vivian took a deep breath before continuing. "I also know that you have an emotional attachment to her, understandable, but it will cloud your judgment and deter you from focusing on the importance of her success. You might distract her from her mission, and you'll want to rescue her from her destiny. Brecken, we require your 100% unwavering commitment to this international plan, and to Dulcinea's path to becoming the most important world leader of the 21st Century."

Brecken sat still and listened quietly. He already knew some of the story, but after hearing all of it, he finally had something concrete to back-up his instincts. "Yes, I knew there was something monumental about Dulcinea.......... something that connects her to a universally significant singularity event."

" I have your orders directly from the President of the United States of America. As a US Marine, you will follow those orders without hesitation or reservation."

Brecken looked conflicted. He ran his fingers through his hair and paced back and forth. "Tell me something Vivian, will there ever be a time when Dulci will be free to pursue her own dreams and her own life? Do you think that day will come? Or is this all that we have between us, a mission and the camaraderie of two warriors?"

Vivian was silent for a several moments. She walked over to him, turning to face him. She reached up and took his face in her hands. She looked at Brecken with sympathy. "I know that you love her, and I suspect that she loves you as well. As to the future there is only one thing that I do know for sure. If you don't protect her and keep her alive there absolutely will never come a time when you can be together in this world of flesh and blood, and tears."

"Yes, I'll protect Dulcinea. I won't allow personal issues to interfere with my duty. I'm committed to the mission."

Vivian continued, "These orders are issued in perpetuity. In other words, they do not expire when this President steps down or if a new global government is established. We are living in uncertain times. We are putting our faith in your oath to protect the Constitution of the United States. The US Constitution parallels the charter of the UFN.

They heard the dog barking, and both of them turned to look out the window, as Dulci threw a ball for the old dog, Rembrandt. The dog was watching the ball but had not budged to go fetch it. "Go on Rembrandt, go get the ball, go get the ball Rem. Come on, you can do it," Ducli was calling to him.

"If she can teach that old dog new tricks, she can lead the world to peace and prosperity!" Vivian laughed out loud, relieving the tension in the room. Just then Rembrandt took off toward the ball, apparently intent upon retrieving it.

Brecken looked at Vivian, "I'll always do the right thing. If the White House is compromised, the US Marine Corps is not going to blindly follow."

"Yes....., but Brecken, we're counting on YOU – not on the entire Marine Corps. Your President is aware of the growing risks and dangers to freedom in the world. He's made the decision to provide support to the UFN. It has required courage and self-sacrifice for this President to risk everything. He's put the legacy of his presidency and the integrity of his reputation on the line to preserve America. Make him proud Brecken, justify his faith in your abilities and your dedication to your country.

You must understand that we are engaging in a battle. The struggle for world control of the banks and the military, nuclear armaments, and global energy resources is World War III. There can only be one victor: either the UFN coalition prevails or the New World Order regime usurps control. In the second scenario Islam and Israel will both perish, and the United States of America will be fundamentally torn down and reconstructed into something you would never recognize. They are incompatible with a New World Order run by William T. Monroe.

By now Dulcinea knew that she was gifted with unusual capabilities. She was smart enough to make comparisons between herself and those around her. As she worked on her plan, she was forced to make some difficult choices. It was clear to her that she needed to leave Hilversum and get out of Holland, it was too dangerous to stay.

But where would I go? She decided to discuss this with Brecken and Vivian. At least she knew why Brecken stayed so close to her. He was ordered to protect her. She smiled, *maybe it should be the other way around.* At first she was upset that he wasn't what he appeared to be. But working with him for two years brought them so close. They loved each other in a way that was hard to define. There was no day in her life that she didn't awake with Brecken on her mind. If he were there at the breakfast table, the meal tasted better. If he was reading a book to her, the story was more interesting, if he helped her in the garden the smell of the fresh earth was sweeter. They were simply best friends.

To embrace the closing of this chapter in her life, Dulcinea decided to prepare the most delicious Iraqi dishes that she could make. *Three different types of Koobe, and about ten different salad varieties and dips should be sufficient,* she thought. Freshly baked Saloufei bread, a delicacy in Yemen and the Sudan, would be a new experience for Vivian and Brecken. These were made with balls of yeast dough tossed like pizza into the air and stretched on a floured board until they were over twenty-five inches in diameter. It was traditionally brushed with rendered butter and sprinkled lightly with Caraway seeds and coarse sea salt as it came off the big hot bricks of clay that formed the interior sides of a domed oven. When the bread was ready it fell off the sides onto the waiting trays in the bottom of the oven. She improvised with a big field stone that she scraped and scrubbed, rubbed with olive oil, and baked in the oven overnight until it was uniformly seasoned and heated through. Then she spread the big flat slab of dough over the rock inside the oven. The only difference would be the rounded shape of the bread slab. Instead of being flat it would be concave because of the roundness of the stone.

Brecken said he had never tasted such delicious food in his life. Vivian was equally impressed with Dulci's culinary skills, "I should have let you cook years ago."

Dulcinea was pleased that her efforts had paid off. The food was appreciated and they feasted on it for several days. She finally understood the English word "succulent". She had read a book that Vivian kept near her bed, entitled Living a Bodacious Succulent Life. She had now mastered that concept. Learning to indulge herself in purely sensuous eating and decadent relaxation had brought a new dimension into her life.

The following days were spent getting Vivian back on her feet . Dulci nurtured Vivian as a loving daughter or sister would do. When Vivian couldn't sleep because of the pain, Dulci would rub her back and legs for hours until she fell asleep. Vivian knew Dulci was leaving. It hung heavy in the air between them, but neither of them spoke of it.

While they waited for Vivian to be strong enough to manage on her own, Dulci read *The Grapes of Wrath* by John Steinbeck, and *Uncle Tom's Cabin*, by Harriet Beechen Stowe. Vivian introduced her to James Michener and the amazing biographies by Irving Stone. Since the time when Dulcinea mastered reading, she became a voracious reader, thirsty for knowledge of the world. She was working her way through the classics.

Brecken purchased a copy of Tomas Paine's, *Common Sense*, and gave it to Dulcinea as a gift. They discussed the changes in perception regarding Muslims after the 9/11 terrorist attack in New York City. "Some political analysts believe that the free world is being intentionally pushed toward a financial catastrophe by the Muslim leadership around the world," Vivian commented.

Vivian insisted that, in addition to studying the Qur'an, Dulcinea read and study the Old and New Testaments of the Bible. Dulcinea often read to Brecken in Arabic to improve his accent and expand his vocabulary. "Listening to a language is a way to develop an accurate ear for that language. Later when you hear something incorrectly phrased or mispronounced it will "grate" on your ear, whether you know why it sounds wrong or not," Dulci explained to Brecken. "When I was trying to master English I would listen to the BBC radio station. Later when I felt more confident in my grasp of the language I would listen to The Voice of America, so that I could learn the American version of English."

In the evenings, the three of them sat around the soft light of the fire place, in the living room. Vivian and Dulcinea drank cinnamon/hazelnut coffee and discussed the ethical questions surrounding cloning and artificial intelligence. Dulci knew she was going to miss these mentally stimulating discussions. Brecken proved to be a constant resource to her, as he quoted philosophers and scientists, literary giants and the great scientific inventors of the 20th Century. Vicariously she was able to access his fine academic background through osmosis.

Dulcinea was intrigued by modern technology. She read the books of Ray Kurzweil and his views and predictions on a future full of wondrous advancements and how they might help humanity find its way in a world of complex problems that simple solutions couldn't solve. She didn't dwell on the "dark side": the use of advanced technology to wage war, or the potential of cloning technology to create slave races of soldiers and workers. These were questions that involved ethical considerations. *How could artificial intelligence and nano technology be used to bring about positive change within Islam?* This was the question that needed to be answered. Dulcinea had to find the balance between the establishment of law and order, the creation of collective opportunity, and the preservation of individual freedom, against the social justice that must exist in a humane society. She and Brecken argued about forms of government, and how ideology sometimes wins out over logic and results in unintended consequences. "Just look at what happened in Egypt," Brecken said. They should have prepared themselves for democracy. As soon as it started it was over - and now the Muslim Brethren owns it."

"The rebels were unsophisticated and disorganized. They sold out for personal glory and short term safety." Dulci looked disgusted. She spoke loud and forcefully, as her face became flushed, "The Egyptian rebels were manipulated by the Muslim Brethren to exchange one tyrannical dictator for one that is more toxic and destructive in the long run. America is blinded by their lack of "international street smarts". Here they are, playing with the big boys in running the world, yet orchestrating it with unsophisticated and inexperienced "newbies" and old fart *has beens* who have no understanding or insight into the Islamic trajectories." They argued these strategic and causality points, and formulated various scenarios.

Dulci presented her plan to modernize and educate women throughout the Muslim world. She thought the idea would be enthusiastically embraced by Brecken and Vivian, but she was wrong.

Brecken uncharacteristically raised his voice, "You can't just implant receivers or interactive AI devices into women's brains and start feeding them education as though they were lab rats! It's unethical. It makes the "good guys" as Machiavellian as those who abuse and deprive them. You're so arrogant Dulcinea. You think you always know best – but you don't – because you only see the world from your own distorted lens."

Dulci was surprised at his outburst. *Brecken is always so measured and steady. For some reason this hi-tech aspect of the reformation is not going to be easy for him,* she thought. She couldn't see it from his point of view.

149

"You're the one who is wrong!" Dulci said. "The women of Islam are deprived, uneducated and insulated from reality. The only way to reach them is by the use of technology."

"And who.....who decides what they should be told, what language they should speak, or how much they should be taught? Can they decide which technology they want downloaded or what classes they should take?" Brecken defended his position.

Dulci responded, "How can they decide if they want to know about the world around them, or if they want to stop having babies year after year, when they have no education and are barred access to information? I do not want to even attempt a revolution unless the women of Islam take an active role in it. In order to be truly freed, the victims must seize their liberty and fight for it. Anything given to them may also be taken away. The woman of all the Muslim countries must be set free from ignorance and seclusion. Then they will come out into the streets of the cities, the towns and the villages, by the millions, and take freedom and liberty for themselves, and never let go of it!" With that she almost threw herself onto the sofa. She reached out and grabbed up her water bottle that was heavily spiked with green tea, and guzzled it like a drunken sailor.

In the middle of this heated argument Rembrandt began growling in the back of the house. Brecken stood up and withdrew his gun from his shoulder holster, releasing the safety. He switched of the light and walked cautiously toward the kitchen in the rear of the house. Dulcinea motioned to Vivian to move to the space under the stairs. The back door slammed. She shoved her right hand into her pocket and felt for her shabria. Pulling it out slowly, she removed the sheath. Dulcinea held the dagger tightly in her right hand. One shot rang out, and the dog barked several times, and was silent. Nothing. The waiting went on and on. Dulcinea wasn't sure what to do. Brecken didn't return and they couldn't hear the dog. "We must get out of here," Dulcinea looked at Vivian and motioned towards the door.

Vivian was paralyzed with fear. It was an unfamiliar emotion for her. Before the shooting in Amsterdam she would have never been cowering, afraid, or fragile.

Dulcinea tried to look down the hallway but she couldn't see anything in the dark. "Come on, we're getting out of here now," she said, as she grabbed Vivian's hand and pulled her toward the door. When they got outside, she pushed Vivian toward the car, parked on the side of the house. "You have to get in and drive. I've never driven a car," she said.

"What happened to Brecken? Where is he?" Vivian whimpered. "Do you think they killed him? I can't do this, I just peed all over myself, Dulci, I'm too scared!" Her voice was shaky. She was still weak from her surgery. The effects of all the medications had dulled her "edge".

"Don't be such a wimp Vivian, I can't believe you!" Dulcinea spat back at her impatiently. Her voice was hard and authoritative. "Get in the car, *yella, yella* (quickly, quickly)."

Dulcinea hadn't driven before but she watched carefully whenever they went into Hilversum for groceries and when they went to the gym. "OK, scoot over to the other side, I'll drive. How hard can it be?" But, before she could manage to get into the car, someone grabbed her from behind, and she instinctively knew it wasn't Brecken. Her right hand was still grasping the dagger and she let her body go limp as though she passed out. The bear hug grasp from behind loosened and when she continued to slide down with her head limply resting on her chest, the attacker began to swear in Arabic under his breath, "*Ein al abuki,* you bitch – stand up straight!" He let go of her, and in that split second her whole body became taunt like a fully loaded spring. She rose and spun around on her right leg, landing a strong left knee to his groin, grabbing his neck at the same time with her left hand and with her right hand driving home the dagger into the left side of his chest where it slipped between his fourth and fifth rib, piercing his heart. Her foot went back down and she let go of his neck. In the low light of a half moonlit night Safina saw him staring at her in shock as he crumpled and fell away from the dagger she still held tightly, dripping with blood.

"Dulci, where are you?" Brecken screamed from the front of the house. "Dulci, Vivian, are you OK? Damn it, answer me. Dulci! Where the hell are you?" As he came around to the car, with his gun drawn and moving bent over, low to the ground, he saw Vivian sitting behind the wheel. Dulci was standing at the open driver's door of the Fiat. A body was lying on the ground next to her. "Are you OK?"

"Sure, I'm just great – no kidding. I kill someone almost daily. In fact I kill several guys whenever I hear a noise outside. I just kill and kill and kill. And it will never end. It is what I do best........... and..........its what I have to do........have to......" she was hysterical. Brecken holstered his gun and grabbed her shoulders and squeezed her tightly, "Stop it. You're fine – just shut up." He pulled Vivian out of the car and putting his arms around both of them, he led them quickly up the front steps. "Alright, get inside, just in case there was more than one creep out here. Come on Rembrandt," he called to the old dog to follow them.

Dulci turned to look back before going inside.

It was quiet. A soft wind blew the tree branches high above the house, and the porch light revealed a row of flattened spring Daffodils along the driveway where the car was parked. The body remained on the ground like a lump of something black and evil. She looked at her hand and saw her bloody shabria still gripped tightly.

The police were called, and the body was taken away. They were grilled by the local inspector. Brecken had fired at a second intruder but missed in the dark, and the man ran off. Finally, after everyone left, Dulci helped Vivian shower, and made her some chamomile tea. Within ten minutes Vivian collapsed on her bed from exhaustion. Dulci tucked her in and left the door slightly open.

Back in the living room, Dulci stood in front of the fireplace. She pushed back her hair with one hand while her other hand was held flat against her chest. She paced back and forth, "Brecken, I have to leave here before something terrible happens. I'm putting Vivian and you in danger. I can't stop every bad man who comes to kill me. One day they're going to succeed! Brecken, you can't protect me. You cannot!"

Brecken's shoulders drooped noticeably and his face was awash in an expression of surrender. The blue-gray eyes were somehow washed out as she never saw them before. He seemed defeated, gaunt, and brittle. "Hell, Dulci – you're right, I can't defend you like this." His eyes pierced her stare and his jaw set. He took a deep breath and deepened his voice assertively, "We're leaving here tonight. Make sure you get everything. If anyone searches this house they shouldn't find any trace that you ever lived here. That includes the exotic groceries that you purchased." His tone left no opportunity for discussion. They both understood it was time to go.

Dulcinea had mixed feelings. She couldn't help wanting to run away. It brought back the memory of her escape from Khaliq. At least this gave her a clear path. If she stayed she would be forced to take on whatever might be thrown at her, but by leaving now she could retreat and prepare herself for what was looming in her future. Nomad had visited her dreams, and he said that her mission was to save Islam. *But how will I do that? Millions of people depending on me to save them from death and destruction.* Sometimes she doubted the visions and prophesies of Nomad. *Are they just a young woman's fantasies?*

While packing up her clothing in the bedroom, she pulled out her mother's photo and held it between her thumb and index fingers.

What happened to you? Why did you leave me? I was just a baby. This time not even one lonely tear fell from her eyes. Dulcinea knew it wasn't true, but as she held the photo she felt that her mother was alive. "*I feel your presence, I feel you out there somewhere wondering about me as I wonder about you, Amma.*"

Putting distance between her and danger was a compelling need. And, staying with Vivian was becoming dangerous. Her nerves were raw since the last attack. She had killed four men – and she was still in her teens.

Dulcinea was saddened to leave Vivian Von Stetton. This kind woman had taught Dulcinea so many things that were beyond simple academics and languages. Their special friendship between two women was something rare for a Muslim woman. Vivian was a sister, mother, and a teacher. Yasmine had given Dulcinea refuge and safety, but Vivian had given her courage and purpose in her life. Vivian had ignited her imagination and nurtured her creativity. Vivian had taught her to feel valued, loved and respected. They were more than family.

She couldn't take the books with her, which was a painful realization. "Leaving them behind feels like I am cutting myself off from the knowledge and treasures of the world," she told Vivian.

Dulcinea had gained an understanding and appreciation of how the modern world functioned. She mastered English and French, and could converse fluently in German and Italian. She could read and write Arabic. Vivian opened a window upon a world that Dulcinea could never have imagined. Dulcinea longed for the day when all Muslim women would be taught to read and write, and pursue their dreams and aspirations without fear of reprisal or punishment. She vowed to pay this forward to the millions of enslaved women of Islam. She thought of them as the daughters of Hagar. In the biblical stories Hagar was the maidservant of Abraham's wife, Sarah. She gave birth to Ishmael, the first born son of Abraham, but was banished to the desert. Ishmael was the father of the Arab nations. Dulcinea thought of Hagar as an enslaved woman who was subjected to mistreatment and then discarded along with her child, left to die in the sands of the wilderness.

Vivian also gave Dulcinea music, art, and philosophy. They explored logic and deduction, and scientific analysis. Vivian provided Dulcinea with the road map to find her way in the world and prepare for the future. Above all she instilled a hope of all that Dulcinea would become. This core belief would give her the resolve that would sustain her on the difficult path she was about to embark upon.

"We're 'forever friends'. You're not leaving me. You're going to a place where you can prepare yourself. I'll see you in my dreams on the beaches of Lebanon before the wars of the past. We'll visit there and replenish ourselves." She winked at Dulci and blew her a kiss.

Brecken and Dulci said their good-byes to Vivian and they were on their way to France in Brecken's Peugeot. "I have a good connection in Paris," Brecken said. "This is a place where you can stay as long as you like. They'll welcome you, Dulci. These people are like parents to me. They have a son who attended university with me in the States, and they have never had a daughter. Monsieur Arnaud Fournier and his wife, Madeleine, will now be your Parisian family just as they're mine."

CHAPTER **12**

Gateway to Revolution

When they arrived in Paris the sun was melting on the horizon. The city took on a neon lavender glow behind a black iron silhouette of the Eiffel Tower. Dulcinea knew it would be lavender, and wondered how she was so right about that. She had watched hundreds of sunsets in Iraq, at sea, and in Holland, but none of them were lavender! Thousands of city lights gradually flicked on, like stardust flung about the city by giggling children on an early spring night. They seemed to land on the architectural wonders of Paris in big extravagant handfuls of luxurious diamonds from hearts aglow with expectations. This was a sky for the uninjured innocents: predictable, steady, joyous, and without a price to be paid. Yet its illusion of happiness and sparkle were balm for this very injured Iraqi girl.

Dulcinea could hear Vivian's voice replaying in her head as they had sat at the kitchen table in Amsterdam studying French and all things French: "Paris has a history of mixed signals. During WWII 10% of the French fought as partisans in the underground, and 80% managed somehow to survive the hardships of the war without any active participation or opposition. However, 10% of the population collaborated with the Nazi's and prospered. What of them?"

x

157

Most were dead by the time Dulcinea arrived in that famous city, but they left children and grandchildren and a legacy not to be held up to the light.

Vivian had given Dulci an important evaluation of modern day France as the once proud republic now lay almost gutted as an infestation of Islamofascists permeated all the socio-economic levels of the citizenry. They hated Jews. They hated Americans. They hated the English. The message of hate from infiltrating Muslims didn't have to inspire the Parisians much to engage them in the Islamification of Paris. The French were already filled with something transparently similar to sibling jealousy within the family of nations. Some said they were simply arrogant and filled with their own exaggerated importance among the European member countries. Regardless of the motivation behind it, many Frenchmen were rude and uncooperative with those who would save them.

On the drive to France Dulcinea and Brecken discussed the subject at length. Brecken told her about Monsieur Arnaud Fournier, his friend and mentor, and the father of his college friend.

"Arnaud says that France is terminally ill, buckling under the internal weight and pressure of Islamic forces. According to him there are entire Parisian sections where *gendarmes* are denied entry. French civil laws are subjugated to Sharia law throughout Muslim controlled areas of France. Britain isn't far behind on Islam's castration list of vulnerable countries, as hordes of Muslims immigrate and rapidly reproduce to repopulate Europe according to the Islamic Brethren's master plan."

Dulcinea commented, "The window of opportunity that will be opened for the Revolution and Reformation of Islam is not more than ten or fifteen years from now. If we fail - we won't get a second shot at it. No Muslims will survive the global backlash. The bloodshed will be devastating."

When Dulcinea arrived at the Fournier house it reminded her of the first time she entered Yasmine's villa in Basra. The huge wooden doors and the grandeur of the architecture, with its massive columns and ornate style, made her feel small again. Dulcinea's heart rate sped up as her mind raced ahead into the future. As she stood at the portal of this impressive mansion, she speculated that Paris might very well be the gateway to the revolution.

The butler who opened the front door was fully decked out in a black suit and white silk shirt with bow tie. He was gracious and courteous, "Hello Monsieur Petersen, it is a pleasure to see you again."

"Honoré, this is my friend, Mademoiselle Morelli. She'll be staying here for a while," Brecken said.

"Welcome Mademoiselle Morelli. Madam Fournier is waiting for you in the sitting room. May I take your coats?" The butler turned and handed the coats to a maid who stood just behind him. "Please follow me."

As they walked along behind the butler Brecken was smiling, "Honoré, how have you been? I have missed our chess games."

"*Oui*, Monsieur Petersen. I am superb. My chess table awaits you at your earliest opportunity," the butler replied in English with a decidedly Parisian accent. Dulcinea thought she spied a slight twinkle in the butler's eye and a subtle up-turn at the corners of his lips. She noticed how his shoes reflected the lights from the chandelier, and how the crease in his black pants was knife perfect.

When Brecken strode into the room a petite woman jumped off her chair and ran joyously to greet him. "*Oui*, Brecken, how wonderful to see you again in my house. We have missed you so." She reached up and pinched him hard on his cheek, "You naughty boy – why have you not come to visit us?" Black eyes sparkled against her white complexion; they locked onto Brecken's face. Her silver hair was gathered in a slick bun at the back of her head and fastened with an ornate barrette of silver and turquoise. The angora sweater was a luscious extravagant red and waist length, to show off her petite figure. Gray herringbone slacks and black patent leather shoes with stacked hardwood medium heels brought a studied elegant casualness to the whole look.

As Arnaud Fournier watched his wife from across the room he thought to himself: *She could be sauntering down the Runway at Fashion Week in New York or dropping in to talk "horses" with the Queen of England.* His chest swelled just a little, and his eyes crinkled ever so slightly at the corners.

Madeleine Fournier was 'old money' and 'blue blood' through and through. It was OK, not snobbery or decaying aristocracy, because her heart was large and everyone who came into contact with her was touched in some personal way. She lent her elegance and style to expand the horizons of each and every individual who passed through her life.

She noticed Dulcinea standing in the doorway. "Who is this lovely young lady?"

Brecken motioned to Dulcinea to enter the room, "This is Dulcinea Morelli, the daughter of Dr. Luigi Morelli, a renowned medical researcher. Dr. Morelli passed on recently. I asked Vivian Von Stetton to call you regarding Dulcinea. I hope she did so before our arrival?"

"*Ah, Oui.* We enjoyed a long conversation this morning and I am very happy to assist Dulcinea. Is it "Dulci"? May I call you "Dulci"? Dulcinea, although extraordinarily beautiful, is quite formal."

"Yes, of course. "Dulci" is fine," she replied.

Madeleine motioned towards Arnaud, "This is my husband, Arnaud Fournier."

"I am pleased to welcome you, Ms. Morelli." Arnaud stepped forward and took Dulci's hand in his, as he gallantly bent down and kissed it. As he looked up, Dulcinea's eyes intrigued him. He was curious about this young woman. A few seconds passed uncluttered with words.

Madeleine took charge of the silence, "We can all relax after dinner and get acquainted. For now, you can follow Honoré upstairs. He will show you to your rooms. Please make yourselves at home. Dinner will be at 7:00 pm and yes, we will dress for dinner tonight as it is a splendid occasion, meeting Dulci for the first time....... and, of course, having Brecken home again. *Tre magnifique!* " She clapped her hands together, her face aglow with joy.

"Dulci, if you need some fresh clothing, please feel free to borrow from the closet. My niece, Eloise, is away at University. She keeps some formal clothing in the guest room for her occasional visits. I am sure she would not mind at all. I believe you are the same size."

Inside the Fournier house in Paris, Dulcinea and Brecken followed Honoré down the corridor to the stairs. As they passed the open doors of the library, Dulcinea glimpsed the tall walls covered with books. She wished she could go there immediately. As they headed up the stairs two large deep brown colored English Mastiffs and a small white French Bulldog joined them. They were obviously familiar with Brecken and quite glad to see him.

"Hello boys. How you do'n? Are ya good dogs?" Brecken scratched behind their ears and when he put his arms out, the tenacious toy bulldog leaped directly into them, and then it was sloppy wet kisses all over Brecken's face. Dulcinea laughed; he looked silly trying to contain the feisty small dog without dropping him.

"This is Charlemagne," Brecken said, as he laughed at the dog and sat him on the floor. "The other two are brothers, Rémi and Gérard. Look Dulci, Rémi has a small black spot on the back of his ear. That is how you can tell them apart."

"Re—mee and Jer—ard," she repeated. "Yes, I will remember them – they are quite unforgettable." Dulci petted the dogs, and spoke to them softly in Arabic, "*Le sachbach assal metilchaso koo-lo*" (If your friend is honey – do not lick him until he is gone). For some reason she thought this was a wise quote for dogs. It was also a bit of middle-eastern wisdom meant to stop people from taking advantage of their friends. It had been a long time since Arabic rolled off of her tongue so easily. She smiled at the big dogs wagging their stubby thick tails in unison.

Dulci was not aware that the dogs were there to protect the inhabitants of the house. Brecken had trained them. They were a formidable security team. Rémi and Gérard suddenly rose from their position on the floor and quickly trotted off towards the back of the house. They appeared completely in sync – a matched set. As they neared the back staircase each one took a different exit door from the corridor. Dulci wondered where they were going in such a purposeful manner.

The previous year Vivian and Arnaud had reached an agreement as to what schooling and training should be provided for Dulcinea. Even if the kidnapping attempt had not occurred, it was prearranged for her to come to France for her advanced studies.

When it came time for Dulcinea to leave Holland, Arnaud had an in-depth conversation with Vivian Von Stetton in Amsterdam. She shared her assessment of Dulcinea, "She is well financed for education. Her mentor, our mutual friend Yasmine Abusanni, made more than adequate provisions for Dulci's college and beyond. Her adoptive father, Dr. Morelli, left everything to Dulcinea in his will. I see no reason not to afford her the best opportunities that are available. Dulci is smart and capable. She has a solid foundation on which to build her future," Ms. Von Stetton spoke with conviction.

"Vivian, during the past year radical political upheaval, and financial chaos has been spreading like a fungus. The UFN must accelerate their mission plans for reform in the Middle East. As the Muslim Brethren ratchets up its time line and swallows up more and more countries under their façade of democratic reform, the time-bomb for global Jihad is ticking away. If we don't act soon it will be too late to stop them!"

After meeting Dulcinea and learning about her background, I wonder if she is the person the Council has been seeking to take on the leadership of the revolution. Is it possible that the leader of the free world, the person who will bring radical reformation to Islam and stamp out the threat of Jihad, has miraculously landed on our doorstep?"

Vivian took a moment before she answered, "This is a young woman with years of education ahead of her. Arnaud, do we have the moral right to propose it? It will be so dangerous. It would seem that major pharmaceutical corporations are also set to destroy her by using the Muslim Brethren operatives as paid assassins."

"Dulcinea's role in that plan would be central to its success. I think it is time to sit down with her and share the plan with her; find out where she stands. Our window of opportunity is shrinking daily."

"No. Not yet Arnaud - wait until you have spent some time with her and get to know her. I respect your instincts." Vivian replied. "We must be sure that she has the fortitude and the will to commit to this. I am sure that Yasmine did not save this girl with any ulterior motive to sacrifice her for the Reformation of Islam. I've communicated with

Yasmine for five years now, and she has never suggested anything of the kind. We have always talked about who the man would be to lead the revolution – I never thought of it being a woman!"

Arnaud remembered his answer: "It should be a woman, Vivian. Who would be in a better position to understand the deplorable condition of Muslim women under Sharia Law? Who would be more committed, more able to lead Muslim women out of their bondage and misery – than someone who has experienced their plight – a true daughter of Islam! Don't you believe that the women of Islam would be more inspired to stand up for their liberation if one of their own were to lead them?"

Pulling his head out of reminiscence and back into the present, Arnaud invited Dulcinea to join him in the library. As Dulcinea entered the room she began to take a mental inventory of this French diplomat and surrogate father of Brecken. He was a distinguished gentleman in his mid 60's, taller than the typical Frenchman - close to 2 meters in height. He carried himself with a studied discipline and a trim vertical physique.

Brecken had already told Dulcinea about Arnaud on their way to Paris. She had remembered every detail: he was religious about his daily walk with Charlemagne, his dog. No one except his wife and best friend had seen Arnaud without a tie. His dress shirts were 100% Egyptian cotton 400 thread count, French cuffed, custom made by Charles Tyrwhitt on Jermyn Street in London. Brecken told Dulcinea that he knew this because he had gone with Arnaud once to pick up a new batch. Arnaud wore navy blue wool suits in the winter and gray or pewter silk blend suits in the summer. Italian hand-crafted soft leather shoes made up his ensemble. He wore classic black tuxedos to formal occasions.

When Arnaud spoke secondary languages to his mother tongue, he allowed a distinct hint of Parisian flavor to compliment his personal sophistication. He did not embrace the French penchant for self aggrandizing rhetoric. Arnaud did not slosh on a heavy French accent dripping from every word, which was customary among the typical Parisian political and diplomatic practitioners as they attempted to turn every language into a French bastardization.

Arnaud was standing next to the large Tudor style window with its antique glass triangular panes that reflected the light from the desk lamp near by. His dark hair with silvery sideburns and slightly receding hairline was impeccably groomed, as were his manicured nails. He took a few steps toward the middle of the room and settled into a wing backed armchair across from Dulcinea. "Tell me about you Dulci. Tell me what you see in your future." He leaned forward. With a monogrammed handkerchief procured from his breast pocket, he removed his gold rimmed glasses and wiped the lenses clean. Upon final inspection he put his glasses back on and returned his focus to Dulcinea. Then he sat back and placed his hands in his lap and listened attentively. His actions were slow and deliberate. Later Arnaud would teach Dulcinea to use this process to put the brakes on any important conversation. He demonstrated to her how this provided the speaker with an opportunity to gather their thoughts and to take their time. The conversation with Dulcinea was for the purpose of getting acquainted. He had to be sure that she was as worthwhile as her mentors represented to him.

"Ambassador Fournier, I have only just begun my preparations. But, I am clear about my purpose and the importance of the educational track I plan to undertake. Before we discuss that path - I need to know where you and Mrs. Fournier see yourselves in all of this. Since I trust Brecken and he has assured me that your intentions are noble - what remains to be discussed is how we will work together. I want to free Islamic women from their enslavement. I want to stop the Islamic practice of marrying off little girls and subjecting them to the atrocities of rape and murder. I was one of those children, a child bride sold to an evil old man."

Dulcinea could not have looked more sincere, more intense, or more determined. "Somehow I will find a way to expose these practices and institute changes in the Muslim culture. The women of Islam must be allowed to pursue education and self-determination in all the Muslim countries and communities of the world."

After an hour of talking with Dulcinea, Arnaud excused himself and went to join his wife. "This young woman is charming, articulate and surprisingly well read and knowledgeable for her years. I am not disappointed," he told her. "I think we finally have our man." He winked at her, pointing his index finger at her. "And, you, *mon Cheri*, do not seem surprised that he has turned out to be an amazing young woman."

When Brecken first met the Fourniers he asked their son, Julian, his roommate at college, how his father had become a diplomat. Julian told him the story: Julian's grandparents, Arnaud's father and mother, were descended from generations of aristocratic nobility with residences in Paris, London and Munich before the war. They were used to being wined and dined by European royalty and high society. They selected a career for Arnaud in the diplomatic core that was compatible with his social station in life and would afford him opportunities so important to a young man. As a result of that decision his formal education was dedicated to that calling, the promoting of peace and cooperation among world leaders. He was groomed to become a master international mediator.

When he completed his studies he traveled to America with a fellow graduate. They wanted to fly to the United States on the Concorde from Paris to New York City, see a Broadway show, and experience the excitement of returning home by crossing the Atlantic Ocean on a steamship before they began their diplomatic careers back in Europe. The cold war was grinding to an end. East and West Germany would once again be united, and the Soviet Union was on its way out as communism proved to be a dismal failure.

As fate ruled, they met a young American Jew in New York who was excited about the hotel linen market. He convinced them that there was a fabulous fortune to be made importing French linens and culinary supplies into the United States and exporting American jeans and pop music to Europe and into the Eastern European countries starving for Western culture.

Twenty years later, at the age of forty two, Arnaud retired a wealthy man, selling his financial interest in the hotel supply business to a major American corporation in Philadelphia, and profitably withdrawing his active participation in the export business, although he still held shares in the company. Not one to idle his days away sun bathing on a yacht or chasing women, he was recruited by President Valery Giscard D'Estaing as a diplomatic ambassador without portfolio (at large). Being an ambassador without portfolio was analogous to being the utility player on the New York Yankees baseball team or the closer, Goose Gossage, on the San Diego Padres. Arnaud served three successive presidents in the French government. He spent over two decades fostering and nurturing connections among the European rich and powerful politicians and industrialists. He negotiated mutually beneficial trade agreements with the kings and princes of Arabia.

It was no surprise that Arnaud was well equipped to understand what skills and base of knowledge Dulcinea needed so that she could achieve her full potential.

After hearing this story, Brecken made it his business to get to know Julian's father. He was a man that Brecken looked up to. Eventually Arnaud and Madeleine came to accept Brecken as a son. Julian was pleased as he could now pursue his playboy life-style without feeling guilty because of his parents. He had given them a surrogate son, the son they should have had - all noble and honest and ultra serious, hence Julian was "off the hook".

Arnaud quietly visited Yasmine in Iraq on several occasions. He avoided bringing attention to her. His friendship and connection to her and to Dr. Abusanni, prior to the doctor's death, were deep and long-standing. It was understood that this relationship was to remain private. Arnaud developed similar liaisons in diverse countries around the globe. He saw his mission as one of "insurance". He carefully cultivated a vast network of ethical and moral facilitators of intellect and reason, who he believed were capable of averting global disasters and thwarting the power hungry politicians and dictators that sprang up after the millennium like weeds in an untended garden.

When the new American President came to power, Arnaud expressed his concerns to Yasmine, "I know this man from my college days. We lived in the same building off campus. He was a frivolous, ungrounded, self-indulgent young man. This was not a typical American inaugural event. It was a cross between a Las Vegas circus and the crowning of a monarch. The guest list was bizarre and more because of who was not invited than for the scores of extreme liberal fringe supporters who apparently had complete access to the

President of the United States of America. Not surprisingly, William T. Monroe is a regular visitor to 1600 Pennsylvania Avenue. It is interesting to me to see this collection of left-wing progressives wrapped into a bed sheet with the big money wall-street crowd, paying public homage to this new conglomerate style American administration.

Bill Monroe is a vastly different animal than the old style political wheeler-dealers of the past. He is more like a 21st Century reincarnation of the world's worst tyrants rolled into one power-hungry narcissistic intellectual genius."

Yasmine looked surprised. "But, how do you know that? What personal indication do you have that he is truly this "master manipulator?"

" Monroe has attempted to buy my support just like he bought all the politicians and corporate CEO's in his political/financial bull pen. He didn't like it that I am not for sale. I live comfortably among the aristocracy of Europe. The "nouveau riche" have nothing to offer me. I am immune to these tyrants. They are afraid to come after me or my family - because if anything happens to me or my family - they will be exposed, and politically decimated on the international stage."

Yasmine wished that her husband were still alive. He told her once that Arnaud could be ruthless when necessary. "He has left enough political and financial corpses behind him over the years to demonstrate the dangers of dealing unjustly with him, or with people he considers to be his friends," her husband told her. "Don't worry about us. We are under his protection."

All of his professional life Arnaud was the diplomatic voice of reason, the measured advisor to the rulers of countries, and not just France. He also knew the limitations of diplomacy. During his battle scarred years in a cut-throat corporate business environment he had mastered the skills necessary to stand his ground and *make someone an offer they could not refuse.*

Bill Monroe had tried to neutralize Arnaud on several occasions by attempting to spread innuendo or rumors to undermine his credibility. Monroe set up financial traps, attempting to draw Arnaud into unethical and potentially illegal transactions. The sophistication and thoroughness of Arnaud's staff, his extensive network of supporters, and the loyalty of his long-time business associates had effectively thwarted Monroe's efforts.

When Bill Monroe resorted to threats of violence against Arnaud and his family he found that Arnaud's security systems were technically advanced and insulating. Despite all of his money and power Monroe could not get near Fournier. When weighing loyalty against money in a society of billionaires - loyalty is the valued commodity - because of its scarcity. No one would cooperate with Monroe to destroy Arnaud. He was insulated by a code that Monroe was not privy to - "old money" and ancestral lines of aristocracy. Americans didn't understand this - but European bloodlines were like a vast underground network - except it would have been more descriptive to call it an upper echelon network. It would be self-destructive to join ranks with the multi-billionaire Monroe. Those who knew Arnaud were not betting on Monroe's longevity.

Arnaud sent a messenger to William Monroe. "If another attempt to murder Arnaud Fournier or his family members is made, you will automatically be killed whether the attempt on Fournier is successful or not. The assassin has been contracted, paid, and is committed to fulfill his obligation," he said. Since Arnaud had never made an empty threat or bluffed anyone in his entire life - Monroe believed him. He decided to bide his time. And, despite his spies - he was not aware of Arnaud's role in the UFN.

Arnaud told Yasmine everything - she was his sounding board. Her cautious voice of reason and her unique analytical and logical approach to complex political dynamics vs. humanitarian considerations, gave him an important added dimension to his planning capabilities. Yasmine could help him avoid unintended consequences along the path to the revolution - she had the ability to see beyond the revolution and into the future society it was designed to create. That insight was what had helped her see past an eleven year old uneducated and unsophisticated rape victim of Islam to discover a potential world leader. Vivian had been wrong about Yasmine's intentions toward Dulcinea. Yasmine recognized the future revolutionary within a few months of taking her into her home. She had also had vivid dreams of Nomad that foreshadowed coming events.

The summer passed quickly as Brecken worked daily with Dulcinea to hone her martial arts skills to an even greater degree. She read books in French and immersed herself in French culture. Madeleine was delighted to teach Dulcinea the fine points of French cuisine and French fashion. She also schooled her in the etiquette of dining, manners, small talk, and art history - Madeleine's favorite subject.

They devised methods of hiding Dulcinea's ugly, mangled feet. Dulci told her about the torture by Khaliq to keep her from running away and how it had given her the inner strength to ignore the pain and escape anyway. This experience was an important lesson in her life. It was inflicted with the purpose of breaking and dominating her, but Dulcinea used it to provide the scaffolding to support her unshakable resolve in everything she did. That profound act of defiance had helped make her the perfect revolutionary leader.

It was difficult to find shoes that would fit over her deformed stubs. Although Madeleine tried never to let it show on her face or in her voice, Dulci could sense that it was painful for her to look at those hideous lumps. Dulcinea became self conscious about her feet. She found ways of sitting and walking that would minimize the exposure. The physical injuries healed long ago and except for some joint inflammation during cold weather, she did not suffer any serious pain from walking on those grotesque appendages. She wore low heels, loafers, flats, and sometimes a pair of sandals with closed toes. As a woman, she sometimes wondered how it would feel to have normal feet and wear beautiful sexy shoes. This was one of her few frivolous fantasies, and one which she rarely entertained.

Dulcinea settled comfortably into the Fournier household. The plan was to reside with them until she completed her education. It was time to buckle down and get on with the preparations that she mapped out for herself with the advice and counsel of Arnaud. Her French was improving by leaps and bounds. The daily usage was making the difference – and Dulcinea's ear for language gave her a significant advantage. She now spoke French like a true Parisian. No one could hear the slightest tinge of ethnicity in her voice.

It was close to a year since Dulcinea and Brecken had arrived in Paris, and the time had passed much too quickly for both of them. The muted colors of the flimsy dead leaves of autumn wafted in the chilly wind of September; it made the streets look ragged and anemic. There was no poetic way to describe the grayish, brown, untidy look of the city. Even the inhabitants seemed caught in its non-descriptive moodiness. Paris drifted into a lazy type of procrastination. Most of the tourists returned to their own countries, and the bright cheerfulness the vacationers with their cameras, colorful shopping bags, and stark white walking shoes was absent. It would be weeks before Oktoberfest celebrations would spill over from Germany into France.

Dulcinea could not let this lapse of enthusiasm pass unnoticed – undefeated.

Music, she thought. *They need the music of Paris in the fall.* But which collection was the one to infuse her newly acquired Parisian family and friends with joy? She loved *American in Paris* by George Gershwin. Dulci stopped at a music store and asked for Gershwin albums on CD. It took a few minutes to finally find them in the classical section, which surprised her because she did not consider Gershwin to be a classical composer. 'Vintage' was more descriptive. This was one of those subtle language and vocabulary questions that she wrestled with on occasion. She hummed the music on her way to the check out. She could hardly wait.

Across the promenade a man was seated on an ornate black iron bench. He was feeding the pigeons from a paper bag. As he threw out the small chunks of stale bread his eyes followed Dulcinea's exit from the music store. He took out a small hand-held recorder and spoke into it, then re-pocketed the device and rose to follow her. His steps were quick as he tried to keep up with her almost running gait. He had been maintaining surveillance on Dulci for weeks. She was a busy person, flitting from place to place as she learned the city of Paris.

Some days she lingered at the city *bibliotheca* where she immersed herself in a stack of books on some subjects that Arnaud mentioned at the dinner table or she heard someone refer to on the television the night before. Brecken had warned her to hold the Internet suspect when gleaning accurate information for research: "Confirm any facts you find on the Internet with other sources." Dulcinea was young and strong and preferred to walk rather than take a bus or a cab. The man resorted to cracking his knuckles and counting the number of Citroen Quatre Vouz and DS automobiles parked along the street; anything that would distract him from these childish excursions. But, he waited patiently for instructions from his superiors. His assignment was to record any connections she made, and document her favorite haunts.

He turned his face to a large storefront so that he could follow her reflection in the glass. He turned up his collar and yanked his hat down as far as he could. He should have worn a scarf. It was dam cold.

Brecken watched the man from a car parked at the end of the block. He exited the vehicle and walked slowly down the sidewalk. His long wool double-breasted black coat snuggly wrapped around his tall frame. As he reached the bench where the man sat, he bent down and shoved his hand under the collar and grabbed hold of the man's shoulder, pushing his fingers down under the man's clavicle bone, cutting off his arterial circulation. Only a few seconds of resistance from the man was noticeable as Brecken shoved him down hard into the bench, and then he slumped over as his brain was deprived of oxygen long enough to render him unconscious. It was an old combat trick Brecken had learned when he had trained briefly with the Israeli Red Barrett Airborne special forces in the Negev and Sinai deserts. Brecken smiled, *Mr. Spock would have approved*, he thought.

A van pulled up next to the bench. Two men got out and dragged the unconscious man into the vehicle. Brecken walked back to his car and resumed monitoring Dulcinea. She was still inside the book store - he could see the little blips on the GPS screen in his Peugeot.

The minute she got home she flew up the stairs to the electronic center that piped music throughout the house and inserted the Gershwin CD, setting the volume on low. As the music came over the speakers the house took on a different atmosphere. The servants were visibly cheerful, and Brecken actually found his smile when he entered the rear entrance a few minutes later, having dispatched the Chimera operative straight to hell (or Paradise, depending on one's viewpoint). UFN agents were tying up the loose ends, and the forensic evidence was being sent to the lab. Brecken wasn't going to tell Dulcinea. Paris was supposed to be a safe haven for her. He had handled it efficiently, and saw no reason to agitate her.

The music was having its desired affect. The entire household was uplifted by this one small gesture. It was an eye opener for Dulcinea. *Small, seemingly insignificant changes, can cascade into major shifts in attitude,* she thought. It was an important strategy that Dulcinea could apply in the future.

When Arnaud came through the front door smiling he greeted Dulcinea enthusiastically, "Dulci, we will visit the *Lycee Louis-le-Grand* preparatory school tomorrow. I have arranged for you to be tested in all of the major disciplines, so that we can find out where you are in your studies. Vivian supplied a curriculum overview so we can assess your strengths." Arnaud took hold of both of her hands and looked into her eyes, "Before that, I want you to tell me about your dreams for the future. What do you want to accomplish with your life? Tell me if the same goals you had a year ago still linger within your heart. What do you think you can contribute to the world? Come and sit with me in the library." He turned to Madeleine, "Will you join us?" he asked her.

Dulcinea followed him to her favorite room in the house, filled with volumes of the world's classical and contemporary literature. Arnaud motioned her to sit down across from him in one of the over-stuffed leather chairs, "I want you to think of this as your home and of us, as your family. We never had a daughter. When you came into our lives it was a gift. Isn't that true Madeleine?" He looked toward the door as his wife entered with a tray of fruit and crackers, and three cups of steaming French vanilla latte. She smiled and nodded her head.

Arnaud pulled his eyes off of his wife and refocused on Dulcinea. "You've been with us for a year now. If this is a "stepping stone" along your path in life, we want to make your time with us count. Madeleine and I have talked about this, and we both agree that your future is important to us." He took off his glasses and leaned back in his chair. He looked at Dulcinea intently, and then he extended his hands toward her with his palms up, signaling that it was her turn to talk.

"Monsieur Fournier, I am so grateful to you and Madam Fournier for welcoming me into your home. It is more than I ever hoped for. When Yasmine found me in her garden in Basra I was a scared and battered child. I was running away from a horrible nightmare, and I remember telling her that I couldn't go back but I didn't know where I was going. She saved me. At the time I didn't know why she did that.

Later when I was on the ship coming to Holland and another disaster befell me, two men on the Hercules also saved my life: Dr. Luigi Morelli, who adopted me, and the First mate Van Vleit who taught me the basics of reading. Then along came Vivian Von Stetton who opened the whole world to me through books and learning and her generous sharing of knowledge. She put herself in the path of a bullet that was meant for me. It seems that my life has become a series of events and people who are pointing me in one direction," she rose and walked back and forth, gathering her thoughts, trying to be careful to say exactly what was in her heart.

"I believe I am destined to fulfill an important mission in life. I know this probably sounds arrogant and self-important, but I know that my destiny is to save Islam from itself. I have a vision of the Islamic Revolution that will ignite the Islamic Reformation. What happened to me as a child should never happen to anyone. Pedophilia and the beating, raping, and murdering of girls and women must be stopped. The spread of intolerance and hatred through Jihad indoctrination must be eradicated from the earth. Muslims must live in peace with the nations of the world, side by side, in cooperation and good will." She stood up and kicked off both of her shoes, revealing the twisted ugly toes of her feet. She looked down at them and as she pointed to her feet she looked up at Arnaud and Madelyn. "This must never happen to another Muslim girl born into slavery without hope of deliverance."

She put her hand over her heart and making a fist, she thumped her chest twice. The gesture was explicit: she was taking on this mission - she was personally committing herself to make this happen. The look of hard determination on her face showed that she grasped the enormity of the task. " I understand that this commitment is irreversible - there will be no turning back once I set this plan in motion. My vision is of a reformation – an overhaul of the foundations of Islam. It will not occur over time or gradually. Although the planning for the revolution will take a number of years to put in place, the actual revolutionary takeover will move fast and be decisive. It will necessitate war and killing. I am going to lead the Islamic Revolution, and provide the lethal force necessary for reformation to take place. I am going to hold out justice and freedom as the prize. But I will face this evil with unrelenting ferocity. Extremist jihadist Muslims must be killed. They want to go to paradise and I will send them there. My vision of their paradise is a barren desert of scorching sand, without water, without trees, and without virgins, or women of any kind."

Dulcinea rested her hands on the arms of the chair as she spoke. Arnaud inhaled deeply as though he were about to comment. His face inexpressive. He watched her eyes as she spoke. There was no hesitation, no lip licking or jaw clenching. Dulcinea knew she had it right – It WAS her destiny to lead the Arab nations into the future. She slipped her shoes back onto her feet and stepped behind the winged chair, positioning her arms along the back of it and looked across the room at Arnaud.

Arnaud rose and stood facing her, "You will succeed. I know that. It will be a superhuman effort but your path is clear. You will save your people from ethnic cleansing of all Muslims from the face of the earth. If the jihadists continue with their plans, nations will tire of their attacks. Just one nuclear incident will cause the world to rise up and declare "ENOUGH". Without reformation there will be no hope for Islam's survival. The Islamic extremists vastly underestimate the backlash they will bring upon themselves. It will be a massive tidal wave of venom that they will not anticipate. They, as fanatics, believe that Allah is going to make them victorious. Sane people know this is not true. Fanaticism breeds madness. Hitler proved that to the world."

She was awash in the magnitude of Arnaud's proclamation. This was the first time she allowed herself to tell anyone except Brecken of her revolutionary goals. Knowing that it was said to a man who would support it and who would take her secret to his grave if necessary, infused her with certainty. Any minute thread of disbelief or hesitation that she harbored was wiped away.

Madeleine came across the room. She took hold of Dulcinea's hand, pulled her out from behind the chair, and wrapped her arms around Dulci. "Don't be fearful. We are here to prepare you, to give you strength, to champion you in every way that we are able. Arnaud has powerful allies and friends in high places who owe him great debts for his past services to them. These people are committed to helping you. He also has evil, selfish people in the palm of his hand, who cannot oppose you because you too will know their secrets and their weaknesses."

Madeleine excused herself and left the room.

Arnaud began bringing Dulcinea up-to-speed, equipping her with information she would need if something happened to him before completion of the mission. He revealed the existence of the United Free Nations Council, without disclosing the identity of the members. Arnaud showed Dulcinea how to open the doors to the safe room and central nerve center of the UFN Council. He made sure their conversations only took place in this room. "We call this room "the vault" because it is encased in lead and is electronically bug-proof. "

The discussion between Arnaud and Dulcinea continued for several hours. They talked of the future in broad terms. Arnaud gave her codes and passwords, and a list of safe houses and weapon/ammunition stashes throughout Europe and America. The information was stored in a memory stick as narrow and inconspicuous as the ink refill of a ballpoint pen. All she needed to retrieve the information was to push the point into the bottom of her cell phone. If the pen were misplaced or confiscated she was given additional instructions about what she could do to access the information. The data on this flash drive was encrypted. Her cell phone held the only key to decrypt the data. If her phone were lost - when the provider performed a remote wipe of the cell phone contents it would delete the access key as well. Arnaud was astounded by Dulcinea's unique ability to remember every detail that was fed to her. It transformed the flash drive into a back-up system in case she was incapacitated for any reason.

Arnaud described the Islamic Brethren and their agenda and goals for conquering the world. He surprised her with the names of well-known world leaders and celebrities in a dozen different countries who were members or agents of the Islamic Brethren or in a coalition with the Islamic Brethren. He carefully covered which people were willing pawns of Islam because of philosophical convictions and Islamic religious beliefs, and those who were engaged in infiltration and the destruction of democratic freedom purely for monetary benefits paid by Islamic extremists' backers. The deals made between Progressive world leaders and the Muslim Brethren were complex – akin to wolves negotiating which sheep would be slaughtered by which wolves.

Dulcinea left the library and walked to her room, Charlemagne trotted along beside her. When she came to her door, the dog put himself between her and the door, barked ferociously and jumped waist high to Dulcinea. He nipped at her arm when she outstretched it to grasp the knob. "Stop it Charlie, get away from my door. I'm fine – go away!" But Charlemagne would not stop and would not budge from between her and the door. She decided that he was just bluffing and would not bite her – so she reached out defiantly to grab the doorknob forcibly. To her complete shock, Charlemagne leaped into the air and bit her hand hard, drawing blood. She jerked her hand back and looked at it. The bite was deep and already beginning to bleed profusely. She couldn't believe that this dog would bite her. He sat back down on the floor in front of the door and growled. Dulci just kept saying, "I can't believe you did that, I can't believe it."

Arnaud came out of the library to see what was going on. Madeleine came racing up the stairs at the same time.

"What happened Dulci?" Brecken yelled from the end of the corridor. He was running out of his bedroom toward her.

"Charlie won't let me into my room and when I tried to open the door he bit me!"

"Get away from your door, NOW! Charlie is trained to detect intruders. He won't let anyone in the family enter a room where a stranger is hiding."

Dulci, Arnaud and Madeleine all moved to the end of the hallway. Brecken pulled his back-up gun from under his pants leg, and motioned them to go downstairs. Holding his thumb and little finger to his ear and lips as though making a telephone call, he nodded to them. They understood and moved quickly down the staircase. Arnaud already had his cell phone out and was dialing the IGS (*Inspection des Services – French Police)* to request that they dispatch gendarmes immediately.

Brecken gave Charlie a hand signal and the dog followed the others downstairs. Madeleine was wrapping Dulcinea's bloody hand in a handkerchief. Charlie's ears were down and he looked apologetic. "It's OK Charlie. I know you did it for my own protection. I forgive you." The dog perked up and his tail bounced hesitantly. He watched her. She couldn't help smiling at his sweet pushed-in face and big eyes. Charlie's corkscrew tail went into high speed. As far as the dog was concerned the whole thing was history.

"*Sortir!* Come out! Gendarmes have been summoned and my gun is aimed at this door," Brecken demanded loudly in French.

The door opened slowly. A slender black man emerged. He was dressed in a conservative dark suit with an almost uniform look to his white shirt, navy blue stripped tie, and well trimmed haircut "package". This visual picture was too readily identifiable as some type of "government" person. Brecken wrinkled his brow and pointed his gun at the man. "Put your weapons on the floor in front of you," he said.

"Of course," the man said with a clearly American accent. "I'm going to pull my ID from my left inside jacket pocket. Don't get nervous. OK?"

"Just take it slow. I won't hesitate to shoot." Brecken followed the man's movements with his eyes. The guy slowly reached inside of his jacket and pulled out a black, leather square, flipping it open to reveal an I.D. badge. Brecken took a step forward and took it from the man, but still held his gun aimed at the man's chest. He stepped back. "Put your weapons on the floor."

The man pulled a Glock 45 from a shoulder holster and placed it on the floor. Brecken motioned to his ankles, "All of them."

"OK, OK, don't shoot. Stay calm." He reached down and pulled up a pant leg. He was wearing a leather holster on his left calf half way between his knee and his ankle. He pulled out a small 9mm revolver and laid it on the floor next to the automatic. Then he stood up and smiled broadly. "Alright, what are you gonna do now …..shoot an undercover cop? I don't think so."

"Take off your jacket and throw it on the floor in front of you." Brecken demanded. Just then the two enormous Bull Mastiffs were coming down the hallway, one from each side of the doorway to Dulci's room. They were walking slowly just as Brecken had taught them. Their eyes were focused on the intruder. As they came closer, the hair on Rémi's neck stood straight up, and his lips curled up, exposing his powerful teeth. The muscles on the dog's rear thighs were tightly contracted under the skin, and then Brecken saw Rémi spreading his toes wide; a sure sign of impending attack. The dog was coiled and just about ready to launch.

As the intruder took off his jacket he suddenly spun around 180 degrees, pulling another gun from inside the jacket as he flung the garment toward the wrong dog, Gérard. Rémi's huge body was already airborne and his jaws clamped down on the man's gun hand, knocking the gun to the floor and pinning the man against the floor with all 250 pounds of angry canine coming to rest on top of him. Blood was gushing from the man's arm in rhythmic spurts that cascaded onto the polished cherry wood floor, but Rémi held on, waiting for Brecken's release command. The man's breathing was shallow and jagged. "Call off the dog, call off the dog, for God's sake mister, please... call him.... off......" his voice was weak and fading.

Brecken gave Gérard, the backup dog, a "down stay" hand signal and Gérard immediately dropped to the ground, effectively blocking any potential escape by the intruder. Brecken released Rémi, "*Maspeek* ("enough" in Hebrew). The dog let go and stood, stepping to one side of the man. Thick gooey lines of pink bloody slobber dripped on the man's face and neck. Remi's front paw was firmly planted next to the man's shoulder. There was no way the man could escape.

Brecken moved over to the man and squatted down next to him. The man's breathing was shallow and his eyes were closed. Brecken patted down the man's legs and arms, checking for more firearms, knives, or pepper spray. Using a handkerchief, he took two canisters of pepper spray from the pant pockets, and a dagger that was strapped to the man's right ankle. "*Tazooz atzida* (move over)," Brecken whispered to Rémi. The dog side-stepped another two feet to a position farther to the right of the injured man. Brecken removed the man's belt and fastened it around his injured arm as a tourniquet, effectively stopping the copious arterial bleeding. Police sirens could be heard in the background as they came closer to the house. Brecken flipped the man over onto his stomach and felt down the back of his shirt. Centered on the man's upper back, he found another knife secured with a piece of surgical tape. He yanked it off and threw it on the floor with the rest of the man's arsenal.

Brecken placed a call to the police dispatcher, "You have dispatched a police response team to 248565 Rue de Chartruise. Please send an ambulance as well. Someone is seriously injured."

While waiting for the police and ambulance to arrive Brecken had a chance to inspect the ID badge: Consulate Specialist of the United States of America Embassy, Paris France. Adjunct to the Military Attaché to the Deputy Chief of Mission, Charge D'Affaires. The name on the badge was Dwayne G. Edwards. There was a badge number and issue date. The Seal of the United States was embedded in the background. It looked authentic enough.

Brecken had Gérard and Rémi guarding the man so there was no way he could move an inch, and he appeared to be unconscious in any case. He grabbed his digital camera from his room and a canvas bag from his closet, and returned to the hallway. He turned the man onto his back and snapped photographs of him and the weapons, which he then deposited into the bag, being careful not to smudge any fingerprints or leave his own prints on the weapons.

There was no opportunity to interrogate him. Brecken doubted that he would divulge who he was working for anyway.

Brecken went downstairs to speak with Arnaud, Madeleine and Dulci. He brought the bag of weapons that he collected from the intruder with him, for the police. The oscillating sirens of the French police could be heard as they neared the residence.

"Arnaud, I have secured the intruder and Remé and Gérard are guarding him. He's badly bitten. I called for an EMT as well," Brecken said as he came into the foyer. The gendarmes were at the front door within minutes. Honoré opened the door and motioned to them to enter. As they came in they holstered their weapons. Brecken looked questioningly toward Arnaud, who nodded and held his palm open toward the officers in front of him. Brecken cleared his throat and spoke to them in French, "Messieurs, the intruder, he is detained by *notre chiens* (our dogs). *Venir l'escalier* (follow me upstairs) and I will release the dogs so you can take custody of him." He picked up the bag of weapons and handed it to a subordinate policeman, "Here, take these, *s'il vouz plait* – they are the weapons that I took off of *un vral salaud* (the bastard), and here is his identification." He handed the I.D. badge to the French Inspector.

"Merci messieurs. It seems you have everything under control here. I see that you requested an ambulance. Was someone injured?"

"The man who was hiding in the house was badly bitten by one of our dogs. He requires urgent medical attention." Arnaud spoke up in his "take charge" authoritative voice.

When the medics carried the man away on the stretcher, Dulci and Brecken both saw his arm where the EMTs cut off his shirt sleeve on his uninjured arm, and installed an I.V. On the inside of his left arm between his wrist and his elbow they saw the tattoo of the chimera. It was quite ornate with the head of a cobra on the end of its tail. Their eyes met and there was no need for a spoken confirmation of their mutual concern. The intruder was a Muslim Brethren operative. The question was who he was after; Arnaud or Dulcinea? At this early stage, it was more likely that he was trying to connect Arnaud to Dulcinea and Brecken. If he wanted to assassinate them, he could have blown up the mansion. For some reason the "Brethren" was either desperate for information or they were seeking links to the UFN Council so they could target their terrorist attacks more specifically.

While the French crime scene investigators swarmed over the second floor, taking pictures, swabbing all the door handles and collecting specimens of blood and dog hair, Inspector Delauney sat down in the dining room with the members of the household and questioned them. He recorded their statements one by one. No one offered any information as to why the man might have entered the residence or why he was hiding in Dulcinea's room.

Delauney reviewed and photographed all of Brecken's credentials and permits to carry a weapon, and the licensing and vaccinations of the dogs. All were in perfect order. "Please be available for more questions in the next few days. We'll interrogate the man if he survives. Here's my card. Call if you remember any pertinent details or if you have questions. I'll contact you tomorrow with an appointment time to come down to the station and file an official complaint."

As the French police cleared out, Arnaud asked them to remove all the yellow tape from the front of the house, and to dispatch a forensic team the next day if they needed additional items. He gave them 24 hours to complete the process. "I will have a cleaning crew in here in 24 hours - so your window of opportunity is limited," he informed them.

After the inspector departed Brecken told Arnaud that the intruder was a suspected Muslim Brethren operative and that he had probably infiltrated the American Embassy staff for purposes of espionage. "I think that tomorrow we need to do a thorough bug sweep of the mansion - and we need to distribute the photographs I took of him, to our own security network. I'll let you know what I find out about him."

As the weeks went by, the trauma of the attack faded. The man survived but was wanted in another jurisdiction and was handed over to the US authorities. Apparently the US State Department elected to extract him from France under diplomatic immunity. The fact that he was a Chimera (which is what Dulci and Brecken dubbed those with the tattoo on their arms) was disconcerting. "Do you think the State Department is protecting a terrorist operative? Maybe they didn't know he was a spy?" Brecken asked Dulcinea out loud. The puzzle pieces refused to fall into place. Like the death of Morelli at Sea which plagued her mind - Dulcinea still couldn't put it all together – there were too many unanswered questions.

Conversely, the whole thing made Dulcinea feel safer than in the past. She knew that the dogs were there to protect her. Gérard slept next to her bed with Charlemagne just outside her bedroom door. Brecken was dedicated to her survival. He shadowed her at school. The automatic 9 mm that she now carried on her person didn't exactly undermine her feeling of security either. She had weapons at hand, superior defensive training, and she knew that when necessary she was capable of taking care of herself. *I'm not that scared little girl that Yasmine found in her bushes in Iraq.* Dulci shut her eyes and thought about herself as Safina, she didn't feel like a coward. *It took courage to run from Khaliq, to travel to Holland surrounded by strange languages, and to face an unknown destination.* Dulcinea was proud of herself as Safina – she admired her own strength. This hadn't always been the case – but now she had been through enough life and death situations to give her faith in her own ability to handle almost anything that came her way.

Dulci immersed herself in her advanced studies at IEP (*Institute d'Etudes Politiques de Paris*) and she found it to be the most stimulating phase of her education so far. She had attended the *Lycee Louis-le-Grande* preparatory school for the first two semesters in France. Dulci was a superior student, graduating in the top of her class at age nineteen. At IEP she studied along side many of the future European leaders of the world. Her peers were young men and woman from around the globe. The exposure to cultural, theological, and philosophical diversity was as important to her mental development as were the studies of advanced military strategy, global economics, international relations, philosophy, international law and communications.

She held a fascination for science and when Arnaud offered her a post graduate intensive program at *Prepa Argos* in *Mathematiques Superleures* Dulcinea was enthusiastic about it – and looked forward to the chance to complete a highly touted scientific course of study there after graduation.

For her final undergraduate year she earned the equivalent of a Bachelor of Science degree at the Middle Eastern and Mediterranean Undergraduate Program at the satellite campus in Menton, a town on the French Rivera just minutes from Monaco and the Italian border. This program gathered students from North Africa, the Middle East, the Persian Gulf, Israel, and all of the European nations. Her classes were taught in French, English and Arabic. Dulci cultivated important relationships at IEP. Specifically she strengthened her ties with the Israeli intelligence, and Iranian dissidents under deep cover. It took a while but eventually opportunities arose to test code words and passwords to verify legitimate operatives. Some of the students who ridiculed her were actually maintaining her cover.

At Menton she met Claude Molyneau. He was a 26 year old brilliant and opinionated Parisian, the son of a wealthy French international banker. Dulcinea and Claude debated various political scenarios in working sessions of mock congresses as part of their International Communications studies. Dulcinea looked forward to these hotly debated forums. She found Claude Molyneau to be exciting and mentally stimulating. He wasn't hard to look at either: tall, muscular build, with thick wavy dark hair and hazel-green eyes. She attended all the basketball games, including away games and she loved to watch him on the court with the agility of a big cat. He was an accomplished athlete, and he moved like an athlete – purposeful, yet graceful. There was something about him that made her less focused at times. His slightly caustic arrogance was transparent to her because his eyes betrayed him. With all of his feigned confidence and self-assured tone of voice - she knew he was vulnerable. She could see through his charade. Once when they were exchanging notes on the next debate venue, she almost reached up to brush a lock of hair away from his eyes. She regained her composure just a few seconds before her hand rose up. She found herself having to recheck her debate notes more than once. With other debaters she rarely checked any notes because all of the facts were committed to her memory. It was more difficult to have immediate recall of the facts when her eyes tended to wander to Claude's anatomy.

Claude and Dulcinea were assigned to the same project group where they were given the task to design a theoretical revolutionary movement. The premise was that if one designed a revolution – one would be better equipped to thwart or defeat a revolutionary dissident movement. Claude was the team leader and Dulcinea was his second in command. She didn't like being second, and she made no secret about it. Claude didn't care. He controlled the project, meticulously researched and documented everything he did, and impressed her with his "take charge" attitude and disregard for gender when it came to getting the job done. The team was large - over 20 members. Each member had expertise in a particular field. Claude was a master of delegation - perfectly matching individuals into seamless sub-groups designed to fortify each other's strengths and minimize their weaknesses.

Dulcinea's natural project management ability facilitated the building of flawless time lines and extraordinary workable building blocks which put the Molyneau/Morelli project out in front of the competing teams. No one could match their smooth transitions, and multi-task verifications. Dulcinea exhibited superior anticipatory leadership skills with her attention to technical details, and her analytical sequential logic.

Molyneau's team excelled. Nothing fell between the cracks. Dulcinea's primary emphasis was on developing unique and effective international communications systems to organize and sustain a revolutionary movement. "I'm reluctant to do this too well," she told Arnaud during their nightly communications. "I don't want some of these students to master all of the technical communication skills that could be beneficial to this project. They might end up as combatants fighting against the Islamic revolution."

Claude's focus was on the financial requirements and the generation of capital to ensure that the infrastructure of the revolution was sound and that post revolutionary long-term plans were fiscally prudent and achievable. Together they were a formidable two-pronged team.

Dulci developed a decidedly assertive degree of self esteem and confidence which sometimes bordered on arrogance. Because it wasn't safe or desirable to share her background and experiences with any of her peers, her demeanor was sometimes viewed as "snobbery" and fostered the dismissal of her opinions as coming from a spoiled rich girl who had no real-life experiences to back up her smugness. Being astute and aware of these attitudes, Dulci often avoided these encounters. She went about her business as usual and rarely found it beneficial to interact with her fellow students. There were only a few exceptions - and those were individuals whom she felt warranted a closer relationship because she either admired their abilities, or she felt they had perspective on their countries of origin that she lacked.

In the late afternoons some of the team members would assemble in small groups in the garden. Generally they sat on the grass and talked about the project they were working on. It was not only an informal exchange of ideas but also an opportunity to socialize and get to know the other students. They all realized that they might be networking together in the future as their diplomatic careers advanced after graduation. Some of them were far from their homes and families and longed for companionship.

As they sat on the lawn at the end of the week making plans for their Saturday excursions and rendezvous, Dulcinea walked by on her way to the dorms. She pretended not to notice them. She had been particularly demanding that morning - pressing her team hard for completion of a complex logistical report that she needed for her weekend project. She was determined to beat all the other teams by producing the most comprehensive and superior project - thereby earning an "A" for all the team members.

"She is so pig-headed and stubborn. No one on the team is allowed to have any ideas of their own. I am so sick of her attitude. Who the hell does she think she is?" the daughter of the Turkish Ambassador to the United States flipped her straight ironed hair back to punctuate her statements. She was exotic looking and gave off an air of wisdom that did not prove to be a valid assumption. Like most Turkish females she preferred a*u natur-al* for her personal grooming. In Turkey she was extremely popular with young men, but here she couldn't understand why she was shunned when it came to social interaction with either gender. *It is a clear example of cultural bias,* she wrote to her sister in Turkey.

"No one knows anything about her family. That whole story about being the daughter of a famous medical researcher is so phony. I *"googled"* her name and nothing comes up. I think she is some diplomat's love child by a mistress," a young Spanish woman spat out venomously.

"She's rather vogue, don't you think?.....quite a nice ass for someone not from African descent. Those feet are disgusting, for sure. She had to have been born feet first, kicking and screaming the whole way out. Don't you just love her voice though – so commanding! She could be a dominatrix quite easily. Whenever she talks I just want to comply immediately," said the risqué young man from Los Angeles as he pursed his Botox injected pink lips, and rose gracefully from the grass. Anthony Dickerson turned and sauntered away from the group with one hand caressing his hip and the other one wrapped around the back of his own neck affectionately.

What Dulcinea knew about Anthony was the fact that he was being prepared by the CIA as a deep-cover operative. She had read the report on Dickerson because Arnaud had asked her to cultivate this young man's friendship, "His homosexual orientation and "attitude" qualify as a commodity in the intelligence community. Not much has changed since the sixteenth century in Queen Elizabeth's court . Some of her best operatives were "boy-toys" to the powerful men in the Royal Court and the Vatican, who plotted to assassinate the Queen. Sex is a useful tool in the world of espionage and counterespionage in the modern world as well. Men of great influence often harbor powerful animal lust both in their political lives and in their personal lives. Their tendency for duality is not always confined to power grabbing lapses of integrity – it may extend quite naturally to their sexuality."

The other students covered their mouths with their hands or looked away. They nodded silently as they watched Dulcinea in animated conversation with Claude Molyneau, as the pair conversed across the university mall. Claude rested his hand on Dulci's shoulder. Claude was the unofficial leader on campus. His chiseled face towered above the other students in his "basketball player" physique. Tall and muscular as he was, it was easy to ignore anyone around him. But Dulcinea Morelli was the exception. She was not breathtakingly beautiful or statuesque. Her dress was conservative, and nothing about her screamed of trendy fashion, but she stood out in a crowd no matter who was gathered around. Her understated elegance, unusual "widow's peak" hairline, and beautiful green eyes and flawless skin, set her apart from other women; there was something unique and confidant in the way she carried herself. Her voice was masterful and edgy but there was an undercurrent of enticing sexuality to it. Dulci had a "presence" about her, and she commanded attention.

Her intellect was sharply honed. She held strong convictions based on her own research and discovery. One did not question her facts without having done one's homework on the subject in discussion, or they would find themselves verbally skewered and castrated by her almost clinical observations, dissections, and unadulterated logic. She never discussed anything she had not studied and conquered. She would listen and gather information and opinions – and then she would "do the work" required to develop her own soundly anchored position. The next time the subject surfaced she was fully prepared to support her premise.

When Dulcinea made her preliminary presentation to her team before commencing the project she had laid out her premise: "Contrary to the popular contemporary views that quick thinking and shooting from the hip abilities demonstrate leadership qualities and a high level of intelligence - it is a measured long-term and thoughtful approach that will sustain any campaign or project such as a revolution. This approach ensures that the initial plan is a sound and workable strategic blueprint. We must proverbially close and lock all the windows before we can open a door and confront the enemy threat. We must come to the game to win. Leave no room for any other outcome. Anticipate your enemy and always prepare for worst case scenario by having a counter punch prepared."

Gyasi Moubarik, the son of the Director of the Cairo Oncology Research Center, spoke up, "She's brilliant. I find myself fascinated by the processing of her conclusions, and so-o-o articulate. I think she "nails" almost every debate with outstanding clarity. I gotta tell you – if I'm confronted with serious dilemmas in the future regarding diplomatic negotiations or analytical strategies I hope I can call on her for advice! You know she is making us all look good on this project. I think we could do worse than to cultivate a friendship with Dulcinea Morelli." He was tall and willowy with large brown eyes and thick black lashes, and a captivating toothy white smile.

A German student, Hendrick Krüger from Berlin added, "She has a way of making me want to do my best; to give that extra 10%

above and beyond what I thought was a good effort. I never expected to be so engaged in a theoretical exercise. I think that Molynaeu chose well."

Gyasi got up and grabbed his backpack, "I gotta hit the books this evening or "smarty pants miss-know-it-all" is going to cream me in Global Economic Theory."

When Gyasi spoke it was with deliberation and in a measured voice of reason that was impossible to dismiss. The other students appeared to rely on his "closing comments" to set the tone, for there was usually little discussion following his statements. Gyasi had a way of getting to the core of a matter and extracting the important substantive conclusions from the rhetoric and "spin" surrounding the subject. Dulci had said as much to Brecken, "If all the Muslim leaders possessed Gyasi's insight – there would be peace and prosperity in the Middle East overnight. When the UFAS is established I must recruit him."

A few weeks later Dulcinea was returning to her campus quarters late at night, having been at the library for hours. She saw Anthony Dickerson being attacked behind one of the darkened campus buildings. She knew it was him from his slender, slightly bent silhouette. Dulci watched as they knocked him to the ground and the three of them were kicking him. She sprinted to his aid pulling her shabria from its holder around her thigh. The drunken bullies were pounding him and yelling "fagot" and "butt fucker".

They never saw her coming. Dulci savagely slashed one of them across his face, spun around 90 degrees and cut a second one from his shoulder to his elbow, slicing his jacket and shirt as the razor sharp blade severed the flesh of his lower arm almost to the bone. She leaped at the third boy and shallowly gashed his chest. But she did not push the blade home to finish the job. She intended to wound them as they were never a threat to her. Bleeding profusely, and probably fearing for their lives, they took off running into the night. The whole thing was over in a few seconds.

Dulcinea turned around and saw that Anthony was curled in a ball on the ground. His pants and underwear were pulled down around his ankles and his body was bruised and scraped. She wiped her blade on a tissue from her pocket and returned it to its holder. Without saying a word she helped Anthony to his feet and pulled his shorts and trousers up, tucking his shirt in for him. He looked away from her in shame. She fastened his belt and pulled his sweatshirt up around his shoulders and zipped the front of it up. She pulled the hood up over his head and pulled the draw strings. She helped him walk to his dorm on campus pushing her shoulder under his armpit to support him; opened the door and pushed him inside of the foyer. In the dim light she looked into his eyes, "They are cowards and fools. Remember my words, Anthony. When you're ready, find me and I'll teach you how to defend yourself in all circumstances. If you want revenge on them, I'll help you find it." She stood up as tall as she could and brushed his cheek with a gentle kiss, squeezed his hand and turned and exited the foyer.

She walked away and never spoke of it to anyone. Months later, Anthony came to her to learn the art of wielding a shabria with perfect surgical precision. She ordered a silver shabria from a friend of hers and she had the relief of a horse rearing up on two legs, engraved on the sheath. She presented it to Anthony as a gift, "The horse is Nomad and he will protect you."

Anthony became Dulcinea's lifetime ally. Over the years ahead he would supply her with useful intelligence. He would also enlist supporters for her cause and quietly neutralize those who would create obstacles for her. He was a loyal friend, and he never told anyone where his confidence and self esteem originated. Anthony, like others whom Dulcinea had reached out to help, would gladly put himself in jeopardy to assist her.

It was the beginning of the new fall semester and Dulcinea stood before the podium, preparing to represent the position of the United States in the matter of the Iraqi invasion.

As introductions were being made by her professor, she took a deep breath, letting it fill her body. She loved debating in front of large audiences. It was almost as if she was going through a stage rehearsal, in preparation for her life's performance.

The moderator sat at a table between the two podiums. "The subject of this debate is the US policy in Iraq, Afghanistan and Pakistan between 2002-2014." He introduced the two opposing debaters: Dulcinea Morelli and Claude Molyneau. Dulcinea represented the American objectives, and Claude debated the legitimacy of the American actions.

She began her presentation standing in front of a large video screen. "Regardless of popular opinion within the United States or the political right or political left, there was no alternative to going into Iraq and taking down a compulsive unstable dictator. Saddam's assertion that he had weapons of mass destruction, and his declaration that he would use them, sealed his fate.

To remove him was the only reasonable course of action. The American mistake was not broadcasting his atrocities before they invaded Iraq. If they would have systematically and fully publicized and communicated his actions, the world would have viewed the Americans as rescuers of the Iraqi people. They should have gone in, destroyed him, and gotten out. The conflict between the Shia and the Sunni sects would have continued just as it always has. Millions of dollars in wasted efforts to democratize a nation that is founded on Islamic concepts of theological fascism and dictatorship could have been better spent in developing Pakistan. That country could have been "bought" and run by American entrepreneurs and corporate ingenuity. The Taliban could never have competed with capitalism in Pakistan – the Pakistani military that runs that country is too greedy and too smart."

Her arguments were cold and deliberate. She didn't give a damn about "political correctness". She delivered her message unemotionally, while standing in front of a large screen that was showing filmed atrocities carried out by Saddam Hussein, which he had filmed so that he could threaten and intimidate the citizens of Iraq. It was a compelling presentation.

"America could deal with Iraq, and the objectives were defined and achievable. In Pakistan there is a government within a government. The Pakistani military operates autonomously inside Pakistan. The army has its own agenda, its own internal power structure and is not controlled by the official Pakistani government. They have an independent treasury and pay their own soldiers. This is not widely known in the West. Agreements and treaties made with the Pakistani civilian government have no serious weight or significance in practical terms. Al Qaeda operates in Pakistan under the protection and support of the Pakistani military.

Going into Afghanistan to eradicate al Qaeda would be like trying to kill the fleas on a dog with a fly swatter. At some point it might have been possible to form a loose coalition between the tribal groups of Afghanistan and establish a long-term educational program to bring them out of the dark ages. This will never happen. Afghanistan is, unfortunately, expendable within the larger picture. Their general population is not only ignorant but they lack the potential to evolve into anything more than a loosely connected tribal conglomerate."

Dulcinea stopped a moment to take a drink of water. She looked out at her audience – they were still attentive. She did not want to miss this chance to state her case for revolution to the future leaders of the world, without presenting it as such. She wanted to make these men and women dig down into the subject and really think about it from a different perspective.

"Add the central obstacle to resolving the issues in Afghanistan – the cultivation of poppy seeds for heroin production which is protected and advanced by the U.N.'s Interpol police force. This is how they make it possible for Interpol to team up with the drug lords to produce and distribute 90% of the heroin sold in the United States. The use of U.N. vehicles to transport it and ship it to the US is well known and protected by diplomatic immunity and exempt from inspections. To think for even a minute that US Homeland Security, the FBI and the New York Port Authority are not aware of these "Interpol" activities is simply naive. Not only are they aware of it - they facilitate it."

The room was so silent that one could hear the ticking of the debate clock on the podium between the team desks on the stage. People were staring at each other with open mouths.

"If you thought I was going to present a moral justification for the American presence in Afghanistan – you were wrong. It is not a moral conflict – it is about money and greed. American soldiers are there for the protection of America's heroin resource."

Her professor was waiting for her as she came down the steps from the stage, "Good God, Dulcinea, you could get us all killed!" He looked pale and agitated. I think you should take off for a few days - go to Paris. Visit your family. Go hide somewhere! Let's hope this doesn't get publicized."

It was only at that moment that Dulcinea felt a knot forming in the pit of her stomach as she realized she had committed a grave error in judgment. She had broken a basic diplomatic rule: Provide information on a "need-to-know" basis. She had egotistically allowed herself to indulge in a grandiose public disclosure of classified information in order to shock the audience and get a lot of unnecessary attention focused on herself. Not only could this compromise her deep cover, but it had the potential to disconnect her from her sources in a way that could be fatal to the revolutionary plans of the UFN council. From now on it wouldn't just be the Muslim Brethren who was after her.

Claude Molyneau stepped up to the podium where he unleashed a scalding verbal assault against Dulcinea's premise. Attempting damage control for her unforgivable blunder, he aggressively dismissed her disclosure as a childish conspiracy theory and ridiculed her lack of sophistication and understanding of the serious and complex factors for the US continued presence in Afghanistan. "US heroin resource? That's just a lot of bullshit. Does anyone here believe for a second that this fabrication has any merit? This is a wild accusation made by a desperate debater. Ms. Morelli is obviously suffering from mental fatigue. One thing I have to say about her mythical explanation is that it was quite entertaining."

He was using the tools of a professional debater (the unofficial job description of a politician) - one of the most important ways to discredit a public disclosure that was unfavorable, or to dismiss an argument that was credible, but conflicted with the debater's position, was to belittle and insult the opposition with personal attacks.

When Claude was finished ripping her up one side and down the other, the audience gave him a standing ovation. They were visibly relieved that the shocking premise Dulcinea had presented was nothing more than a cheap debater fabrication - and they could once more choose to believe that free countries had altruistic motivations - and that it wasn't really an international gang war that was being militarily and financially waged around the globe.

For the second time this semester, Claude wasn't sure that he won the debate. No matter how prepared he was or how compelling his position - Dulcinea had trumped him on her revelations of America's objectives and why there was no option but to stay in Afghanistan. He had prepared for a debate about the morality of the invasion and the morality of the long drawn out presence in Afghanistan. Claude had not been prepared for Dulcinea's expose' on the American heroin trade. He doubted that he would ever trust Dulcinea Morelli again. He wasn't sure he could forgive her major error in judgment either.

Within the hour Dulcinea left the campus and went home to Paris for spring break. She was glad that she didn't need to remain there after her debacle. Arnaud had called her on her way home and told her not to speak with anyone and to come directly home. Apparently he had his own sources at the university who had contacted him immediately. It was streamed into the UFN "vault" of the Fournier mansion, on a live feed.

Arnaud had already instituted appropriate protocols, and activated selected operatives on campus who were destroying any record of the debate. Substitute video of old debates were being spliced into the electronic feeds that recorded the speeches from the podium. They would obliterate any record of it. The professor handling the debate series was extremely cooperative. Sophisticated electronic devices were scanning the audience members as they exited the lecture hall and wiping their digital cameras and cell phones of any recordings made during those critical 10 minutes while Dulcinea had chosen to jeopardize the future of the UFN and the revolution. Arnaud was thankful that the University had strict rules about turning off cell phones during all debates. There were only a few phones left on and only one that had recorded the incident. "It could have been much worse," he told Madeleine. He looked angry and distraught.

"I am positive that Dulci feels terrible about this," Madeleine said. "She made a mistake - and I don' t think you should reprimand her any more than she is already doing to herself. Arnaud, promise me that you will not be excessively harsh with her. She has given up so much - and remember how few mistakes she has made. Remember yourself at her age - flying across the world, getting drunk, refusing to follow the path your parents laid out for you........ Need I continue?!" She uncharacteristically reached over and pinched his cheek - hard! "She's a wonderful girl. I will not allow you to be mean to her!"

Weeks later the debate incident had blown over, and Arnaud had successfully neutralized the potential damage. Dulcinea had suffered her first major fiasco, and the lesson had been a memorable one. She finally put the episode behind her and embraced the important lesson she had learned.

Dulcinea addressed the UFN Council before returning to campus. After admitting her error to the participants and asking them to restore their faith in her commitment and ability, she briefed them on the factual information that she possessed. Dulcinea's statistics were verifiable as she laid out the intelligence in chronological sequence, day by day as it all came together. Of course she couldn't share all of her sources. She gave the members just enough to establish her credibility. She was building her international network for the future.

She had better connections with CIA unit commanders than the current Secretary of Defense of the United States. She already worked with them individually on intricate code breaking and the evaluation of highly sensitive documents coming out of Iran, Iraq and Pakistan. Arnaud called on her dozens of times to analyze various situations, and to provide insight into the motivations behind certain clandestine alliances between highly placed American politicians and known supporters of the Taliban and al Qaeda, in Pakistan and Afghanistan. Her sources were unaware of her "lapse" on campus.

The CIA solicited Arnaud's assistance, and he simply deferred to Dulcinea who was the mind behind the analytical data. He knew full-well that these projects would hatch the highly beneficial relationships between Dulcinea, select US Senators, and the CIA. "Why go through me as a third party when I can introduce you to the author of these theoretical scenarios? You can inquire with her directly and collaborate as needed," Arnaud told them.

Arnaud and Dulcinea intentionally never included FBI or American HS operatives in any communications or sharing of intelligence. "They are compromised institutions – to be kept outside of the loop. Internally the FBI is hemorrhaging from a lack of leadership. Operatives do not put their lives on the line for good pay or extra benefits – they do it because they buy in. They are patriots – soldiers standing to post," Dulcinea wrote in her report to the UFN Council.

Her intelligence sources within both of these organizations indicated extensive turmoil and major dissatisfaction among the established rank and file. Recruitment of unqualified and politically selected new agents was undermining the effectiveness and integrity of the FBI. Reliable and experienced agents were taking early retirement; mid-career FBI and HS key players were resigning and moving their game to other security operations, both international and private. Among the beneficiaries of their expertise and training were UFN sponsored operations, and special forces within US Naval operations.

"The CIA is an entirely unique organization," Brecken explained to Arnaud and Dulcinea. "The CIA is not a tiered structure. It is intentionally organized into insulated units with firewalls separating various operational aspects of the CIA. It is structured in this fashion because of the sensitivity of intelligence data collected and analyzed by the CIA. There is only a handful of men and women who can access more than 3 or 4 segments of the whole at any given time. When a project requires cooperative activity between the units - a liaison request is initiated; a special agent is assigned by the CIA director to breach the firewall and allow a cooperative mission to proceed. Details of any mission in total can only be accessed by the liaison agent assigned to that mission. Not even the Director can obtain detailed information - with locations, field operative I.D., and safe house protocols. At the completion of a mission the unit commander activates a "swipe" code that reseals the firewall and terminates access to the encrypted files." Brecken grinned, "Slick, isn't it?"

Dulci knew that she was building bridges for the future, but she also loved solving these intricate strategic puzzles. The dynamics of world finance and politics were exciting and mentally stimulating. Dulcinea was the first person to correctly measure the progress of the Monroe/Muslim Brethren plan to divide world power between them, and to identify who the "ringer" would ultimately turn out to be. That speculation was incomprehensible to both FBI and CIA operatives.

Even the Mousad which was quite adept at rooting out the sources and the pivotal players in the international arena were taken aback when she turned out to have "nailed this one" five years before anyone else realized the truth. Of course, she had an insider working within the congressional system; Anthony Dickerson was a source she would not now, or ever, share.

Complex analysis would prove to be the most valuable ingredient in the efforts to foil and disrupt the progression of the Islamic Brethren's ultimate goal. Dulcinea was among a handful of political analysts working for the UFN to understand that the revolution would only be successful by using all of the most current technological and scientific tools available.

This was not a war to be waged strictly with the literal sword, and not with pen and ink. It might end up being the world's first digital political revolution - sparked in a virtual world and electronically bled into the homes and streets of the towns and villages and cities of the real world. Social media would effectively be commandeered and redirected to circumvent the physical world of concrete and steel barriers, of bullets and currency. Weaponry and bloodshed would be the reinforcement and backup system to prevent slippage and to provide containment in cases of flare ups and opposition, to prevent all attempts to recoup and re-organize and mount any counter attacks or effective response. Star Wars communication networks would replace jammed CIA backup systems.

At her UFN briefing in July of the same year she spoke out clearly: "This war will be won with a combination of education, technical innovation, ground breaking scientific hi-tech surveillance hardware, and state-of-the-art software applications," This is where her lifelong fascination with scientific innovation and applications would give her the edge over pure military power, psychological rhetoric, and philosophy. Dulcinea's edge was that she was not a politician by nature or by machination or indoctrination. She could best be described as a prototypical next-generation warrior tech nerd with both virtual and hardware weaponry, and real-time verification systems. This describes a failsafe operation with multiple redundancies locked in.

"We won't have the luxury of decades of education of our Muslim sisters. They have lingered in the shadows of ignorance and dismissal far too long." She pounded her fist once upon the podium as she swept the faces of the audience from left to right and back again. "The only way we can extract them from the cement of one thousand and four hundred years of ignorance, and recruit them for the revolution - is to use artificial intelligence linked with their human brains to download vast data bites of information that have been withheld from them. We only have 4 or 5 years at the most to rescue them. If we procrastinate and become bogged down in political correctness and civil rights issues – it will be too late. The Islamic people will be slaughtered.

I know – you might think this is science fiction. But it isn't. It is feasible and doable right now. We can do it. By utilizing this technology we will leap forward from 700 AD to 2020, in the blink of an eye. Five hundred million educated women will emerge to take their rightful place in the world! No one can deny them their right to enlightenment."

There was a heavy silence in the room. Some people stopped breathing for a moment in time. *Was it true! Could that be done? Really? Would doing it make them worse than those who enslaved Islamic women? How could it be ethical to manipulate a person's brain?*

The revolution was no longer an intangible dream – it was going to happen just as they planned. Until that moment it was an idea, a pleasant fictional and unsupported hope for the future. Dulcinea divulged the technological resources at her disposal and the method of delivery to the recipients. Yes, it would happen. Dulcinea and her group of dedicated scientists were ready to implement the delivery system. It would be done over a five year period. It would be incremental with a simultaneous intimidation program meant to paralyze Muslim males and retrain them, using negative reinforcement and behavioral modification methodology.

She delivered the first primary message that would be spread throughout all the Islamic nations, "The molestation of children, the taking of a child bride under the age of 18, the beating of women, the rape of women and the stoning of women will no longer be tolerated. Men who do these things will suffer punishment and even death."

CHAPTER 13

A Mother's Pain

Dulci was tingling with anticipation. The Fournieres were planning a huge party at their residence. Arnaud felt it was time to introduce Dulcinea to the political and diplomatic circles of Europe. He gave his wife a list of at least two dozen mandatory participants, and she was told to fill out the remainder of the one hundred invitations in any way that she saw fit. Madeleine pored over the invitation list, reviewing her selections with Arnaud. This was not just a social event. The plan was to introduce Dulcinea into a world of involvement, and concern with issues that were larger than the individual, the local politics or one's country of origin.

After eighteen months of immersion in history, language, geopolitical science, and cultural protocols, Arnaud felt that Dulci was ready to be launched into the fray. "I think she can hold her own." he argued with Madeleine. "And, if we don't try we will never know how she stands up under pressure."

"Oh, Arnaud – you are over confident. These "barracudas" will devour her. There will be a "feeding frenzy" as soon as they realize that she has a brain. It will become a contest: Who can destroy Arnaud's protégé?" she said indignantly. "What are you thinking? She simply is not ready for this!" Her voice quivered as it rose higher in tone and intensity. Madeleine held her arms stiffly at her sides, with clenched fists.

Arnaud would not budge – so despite her apprehensions Madeleine tried to arrange the seating and the entertainment in a way that would mute the focus on Dulcinea. Their marriage had always been one of mutual respect and shared decision making, but in the end it was Arnaud who held the tie vote on important issues. He very rarely exercised this vote. He fully utilized this prerogative with regard to Dulcinea's readiness for public exposure.

Madeleine involved Dulcinea in all of the arrangements. It was an opportunity to teach her from start to finish how one orchestrates a large important event. As Madeleine watched, Dulci took over each task with finesse and competency. From catering to invitations, from appetizers to desserts, and even the wine list, she was superbly qualified. Not only did she infuse the occasion with her own personality regarding the color schemes, flowers, music and ambiance, she did it all with a smile and good nature.

Dulcinea assembled the staff and solicited their help with all of the arrangements, "I want to thank all of you for the generosity shown to me since I joined this household. You have extended yourselves beyond your employment obligations to become my mentors, my friends, and my corner stone as I transitioned from a very different world to this one of opulence, culture, and myriad levels of detailed protocols. Now, I must ask you once again to support my humble efforts to orchestrate a major social and diplomatic event here at the House of Fournier. I know that I cannot accomplish this task without the help of each and every one of you." Dulci smiled at the group of household staff members she asked to attend this meeting. "But let it be fun and let it be memorable – not just for the guests but also for you and for me!"

As she sat at the breakfast table, Madeleine began to cry. She daubed at her tears with a lace handkerchief. "Late in life, God has granted my lifelong wish for a daughter. Enough – let's have a cup of tea together on the veranda and Honoré can bring up samples of the dinnerware and cutlery that we have in-house. I want to use our own china instead of having the caterer supply something that we find less appealing or lower quality."

As the two women sat together and sipped their strong black afternoon tea, Dulcinea thought about her journey to this point. *I am almost ready*, she thought. They chose a dignified traditional pattern for the dishes and Dulci was adamant about pairing it with very heavy, ornate cutlery. As she held the heavy knife in her hand with the ornate monogram "F" engraved upon it, she remembered the weight of the silver shabria that gave her focus during the fight in Amsterdam. It was as though the vivid memory of that moment was embedded in the palm of her hand. It suddenly came to her as clear as the crisp clean air of a stark winter morning after the long night of a raging blizzard: *This is who I am. This is my place in the Universe. There is no choice, no decision to agonize over. I am the person who is meant to bring freedom and choice to Islam. I am the leader who will lead the Islamic nation out of darkness and into the light........ My life means something important.*

As the guests began to arrive, Honoré greeted each one. He knew most of the guests by name but was careful to address them by title and without banter. Those who attempted to interact with him were answered with a polite nod of his head. As he handed over the coats and hats to the maids standing nearby, most of the guests ignored him completely. As they dismissed the presence of a servant so casually as though he were some innate object, Honoré listened carefully to their comments among themselves. It was his task to gather this "mundane" information and later he would transcribe it from his pocket recorder and add the information to his weekly reports to Arnaud.

Mr. and Mrs. Yehiye Shmaiya of London England were announced, and as they stood in the foyer, it was difficult for all the guests not to stare at the beautiful wife of one of London's top jewelry designers. She was breathtakingly exquisite. Her hypnotic green eyes, slender long nose and lush lips, were accented by a perfect widow's peak of raven black hair pulled straight back and coiled in shiny black loops of thick braids. Her long neck and perfect posture accentuated her statuesque voluptuous body. Madam Shmaiya's complexion glowed in a warm coppery hue which perfectly complimented the deep purple silk of her full length evening gown. Everyone's eyes were captured by her emerald and topaz jewels set in heavy opulent gold earrings, stunning necklace and matching bracelet. Not many women could have carried it off without looking "over-the-top". But Madam Shmaiya had the carriage, and the sophistication to bring it all into perfect cohesive balance. By contrast her husband was short with close cut curly gray hair, and he was as dark skinned as the blackest Ethiopian – although everyone knew he was a Jew from Yemen. It was said that his jewelry was actually designed by Egyptian gods and that he made some pact with the devil in exchange for his beautiful wife. By all accounts, she adored Yehiye and was devoted to him. The speculation surrounding this oddly matched couple was notorious among the diplomatic core in embassies throughout the major cities of Europe.

"Latifa, let's go find Madeleine. I know you can't wait to meet Dulcinea. Then I must find Arnaud as I have something to discuss wih him," Yehiye whispered to his wife.

"*Bonsoir, madam,*" Latifa greeted Madeleine. "It is so wonderful to see you again. Why do we not get together more often? Must it always be some stately occasion? I would prefer to have you and Arnaud visit us at our summer beach house on the coast. Madeleine, please do come in June. You don't have to swim. *Oui?* You will come? We can watch the big boys play with their sailing boats while we catch up! It has been too long *mon ami.*"

"*Oui,* Latifa. It has been too long. I would love to come in June. I have to see what Arnaud has planned though. He has been quite busy lately. The world is in some kind of monetary crisis – so Arnaud is running around holding hands and spreading his own private brand of diplomacy. Everyone knows he is retired except him!" Madeleine looked around the large room until she spotted Dulci, "*Bon magnifique* – now you must meet my lovely "almost" daughter, Dulcinea. You may call her "Dulci". She is remarkable, and you must be told – she has arranged this entire event almost single-handedly." She took Latifa's hand and conspiratorially pulled her across the room.

As their eyes met, Dulci felt light-headed. She knew this woman – but how? As far as she could recall they had never been in the same room together. The woman was from London and Dulci had never visited London.

Latifa was visibly shaken. She was reeling inside; the blood drained from her face, and her heart was almost jumping out of her chest. Tiny beads of perspiration were accumulating on her upper lip.

As they approached the dark-haired girl, Madeleine announced, "This is Dulci, my star pupil. As I told you, she arranged this entire event." Madeleine looked from Latifa to Dulci. "What's wrong?" she asked.

"Nothing. I guess I'm tired from all the preparations. I was going to get some punch and sit down for a few minutes. Will you both excuse me?" Dulci asked.

"Of course *Mon cheri*. You look a little wilted. Go take a break in the music room. I'll take over for a while," Madeleine touched her on the cheek, and then turned to Latifa. "Shall we go get some hot Danish Julegløgg. It's the only time I can get a good stiff Brandy and not have rumors flying around about my pending rehab at the Betty Ford Clinic!" she laughed.

Latifa looked relieved, "Yes, that sounds good. I don't know why I forgot my manners when you introduced me to Dulcinea. She's delightful and beautiful. Doing all of this is quite amazing at her age! Tell me more about her, Madeleine. Wherever did you find her?" Her color was returning to her face, and her voice was steady again.

They got their drinks and sat down in a corner of the room. People were milling all around them, talking and laughing and of course, eating. Madeleine looked at Latifa straight in the eye, "I can't tell you about her Latifa. It's all top secret and hush, hush. Her father was the research scientist, Luigi Morelli. He died and left her a fortune. Maybe it has something to do with his research," she leaned over close to Latifa. "Someone has tried to kidnap her. She ended up here in Paris, under the protection of Arnaud. That is already more than I am supposed to say. If anyone asks, she is with us temporarily until she completes her studies. To be honest with you Latifa, Arnaud and I are not looking forward to her leaving. She is an unexpected gift at this stage of our lives.

Arnaud has not been the same since she arrived. He walks with a spring in his step. The servants are all smiles too. Even the dogs adore her. And, of course, best of all, Brecken is home. He is the one who brought her to us. It's amazing what that young woman can accomplish. She completed her undergraduate work in less than two years! And not just '*foo foo*' courses either! She took on some very heavy subjects. She has a fascination with technology; knows more about robots and artificial intelligence than anyone I know." They sipped their drinks and watched the other guests. Latifa remained quiet and pensive.

"I need to lie down. I'm so sorry, I just got a little dizzy for a minute."

"Of course, rest in Dulci's room. The guest room is full of coats." Madeleine answered as she opened a door and motioned Latifa inside. "I would stay with you but I have to get back to my guests. I'll ask Honoré to send up a cup of tea. Are you going to be OK?"

"Yes, fine – just need a few minutes to compose myself. I'm sorry Madelyn. Thank you for being so gracious and understanding." As Madeleine closed the door to Dulci's room, Latifa lie on top of the bed spread with a thin coverlet that Madeleine had given her. Her head was propped on a large pillow. She looked around the room. There were no personal items, no photographs of friends or family; no keepsakes from childhood – teddy bears or dolls. Then she saw it. On the top of a high mahogany chest of drawers she saw the edge of a bracelet. Without thinking about what she was doing, she threw off the coverlet and rose from the bed. Latifa walked slowly over to the chest. She could almost feel a physical magnetic pull coming from the top of the highboy. She reached up and took the bracelet down. It was instantly at home in the palm of her hand, and very familiar. As she cradled it in her hands, tears began to course down her cheeks. The anklet was perfectly hand crafted of delicate silver filigree. There was a fine silver chain attached to it and at the other end of the chain was a silver toe ring. The toe ring was decorated with beautiful scroll work in Arabic letters all around it. The inscription read: *Beloved.* The ankle bracelet was made in two parts hinged together with a tiny brass pin on one side and a silver clasp on the other. It was a beautiful piece of unique handmade jewelry. It seemed as though it were from another world, from another time line. She held it up to her lips and kissed it. She knew now why her heart beat so quickly and why she reacted so strongly to seeing Dulcinea. Standing close to the girl evoked an almost chemical reaction in her body.

A mother's heart knows her child, Latifa said to herself.

The bracelet had been crafted by Latifa's first husband, the man who died so long ago. He made it for Latifa as a wedding gift. Dulcinea was her daughter. Dulcinea was Safina, the baby that she had nursed and nurtured and loved above everything. She walked back to the bed and sat down.

When Madeleine returned to check on Latifa she found her sitting on the bed clutching the jewelry and rocking back and forth. "My dear friend, what has upset you so much?" She rushed to her and enfolded her in her strong arms. "There, there, *mon cheri,* whatever it is, you can tell me. I will help you. I promise you Latifa, I promise you *cheri.* I have never betrayed a secret of anyone. What is it – tell me so I can comfort you."

Latifa looked up at Madeleine with tears bouncing off of her open palms. "Who is Dulcinea? Who is she – really? You must tell me. I must know for sure."

"*Attendez!* Latifa.,wait! I will fetch Arnaud. It is Arnaud who will decide."

Latifa's heart was beating as if she were running a marathon. Her mind skipped jaggedly trying to understand how her daughter could be here in Paris. *My lost baby living right here? In this house!* It was too much to fathom. She looked about the room and all she could see were rows of books. There were books in French, English, Arabic and Spanish. Expensively bound editions, and jacketed new releases in glossy Madison Avenue, attention-grabbing, covers. There were fat laborious volumes in Italian and German. At the end of the farthest shelf she saw a leather-bound copy of the Qur'an in Arabic. The beautiful Arabic script on the cover, "*The Qur'an*", was inlaid with Gold. As she rose and pulled it off the shelf, she began to leaf through the delicate thin illuminated pages, with gold leaf edges. Many sections of the text were highlighted, and notations were scribbled in tiny letters between the paragraphs and in the margins. She found a piece of paper folded and placed between the pages. As she opened it, she was surprised to see beautifully scripted Arabic, written in a delicate artistic hand:

I hereby swear before Allah my creator, that I will abolish the enslavement of women in all the Islamic countries of the world. I will cause punishment and death to Muslims who would defile girls and rape women under the cloak of the Qur'an. I swear by my own life that I will not rest or stop or withdraw from my mission on earth to free the Muslim world. I will reform Islam to reflect compassion, tolerance, and justice. I will save Islam from annihilation and from ethnic cleansing from the face of the earth forever.

As Latifa read the signature her legs could no longer hold her weight. It was signed in Arabic: *"Safina, daughter of Latifa".*

When Madeleine returned with Arnaud in tow, they found Latifa sitting on the side of the bed. Her face streaked with tears. She was holding the ankle bracelet in her hands, and the Qur'an was on her lap. "Latifa, tell me why you think you know Dulcinea." Arnaud said.

"Because this is my ankle bracelet, made by the hand of my first husband."

She began telling them her story. "I was the wife of a successful jeweler and silversmith. We were on a long journey across the desert. Usually he didn't travel with wives or children, but on this trip he wanted his eldest son to fulfill his obligation of a pilgrimage to Mecca as a devout Muslim, and thereby earn the *Haj* designation.

My husband became deathly ill after we departed from Mecca, and our caravan stopped at one of the villages along the way to get some help for him. But it was too late, and he died in horrible pain. His eldest son was eighteen, not ready to lead a caravan. I was forced to take over. At the time I was barely twenty years old. I had several young children as well. At each village or town where we stopped, the son of my husband was foolish, and gambled his father's money away. I was scared because all I wanted was to get back to our home as quickly as possible. As a woman I had no authority to stop this foolish boy. After several days he gambled away all of the gold that my husband had brought on the trip, but he still wanted to gamble. That is when he offered me as his stake. Men flocked to the village as news of this game spread quickly. He told everyone that I was 15 years-of-age, and beautiful.

Of course he lost his bet, and that is how I came to belong to Sheik El Sighi. The sheik never formalized the marriage, so I remained a temporary wife under the Sharia law.

El Sighi took me and my youngest son back to his village in Iraq, where I was treated as a slave and concubine. I gave birth to several children, but the only one who survived was a daughter, Safina. Even my young son, Fahid, died shortly after we arrived in the village. This baby girl, Safina, was loved from the minute I held her in my arms."

Madeleine sat down on the bed next to Latifa, offering her a glass of water, and a handkerchief. "It will be alright, Latifa. I don't know how - but I just know."

Latifa took a sip of the water and wiped her face. Her breathing was more even now, and her hands had stopped shaking.

"When Safina was two years old, a caravan came by the village. El Sighi invited the merchant to join him for food and smoking. The merchant turned out to be a Jew, who collected all types of jewelry from around the region. He resold it in European markets, or incorporated the designs as part of his collection, and sold them worldwide under the Shmaiya hallmark. Later Yehiye told me that as a Jew, he had never been invited into a Muslim home, and certainly not to dinner. He said that he thought he should comply so as not to insult

El Sighi unnecessarily. Despite the non-kosher food and drinks that would certainly be offered, Jews are allowed to break dietary and even sabbath laws, if not breaking them was physically dangerous or life threatening. After hours of eating and drinking – including alcohol forbidden by Islamic Law, El Sighi fell into a drunken state. He commanded me to disrobe in front of his guest, and in front of his own grown male children, and to have intercourse with him in front of everyone. I refused and he beat me into unconsciousness. Yehiye said that El Sighi told him that he was going to beat me to death for disobeying him. Yehiye, was horrified and offered to take me, the unruly woman, off of El Sighi's hands for a lot of gold. The offer was accepted and Yehiye Shmaiya gave the Sheik an exorbitant amount of gold in exchange for the "filthy" disobedient wife - me.

I was barely alive when Yehiye carried me to his encampment. He told me that I was trying to say something about my baby, but I don't remember any of this. He says that when he sat me on a blanket in his tent I managed to ask him to remove my silver ankle bracelet and my gold nose ring, and go back to El Sighi and give them to him for my baby girl. He returned to the Sheik's house and asked to purchase the baby as well, but El Sighi refused to let him take my daughter, saying he would keep her to sell later as a virgin. There was nothing Yehiye could do to change his mind, and El Sighi's sons were becoming more and more threatening. No amount of money would persuade him to let the daughter go. El Sighi passed out on his satin couch and Yehiye wisely withdrew.

When Yehiye left he spread the word about how angry he was that he had paid all that money for a worthless woman who then died within a few hours after the deal was done. I remember that we camped at some tiny Oasis off the regular caravan route for several weeks, while Yehiye nursed me back to health so that I would be able to travel. He made no demands on me whatsoever.

During the rest of our journey home to London, I traveled disguised as a male servant wrapped in layers of baggy galabias and wearing a turban and scarf."

Arnaud was called back to the party by Honoré because they had been gone too long. He was just digesting Latifa's story in his own mind. *It explains a lot of unanswered questions regarding Safina.* He went to find Yehiye. He saw that Dulcinea was entertaining the guests and making sure everyone was properly taken care of. They had begun to depart the mansion: a few guests at a time begged their leave and thanked Dulcinea for a wonderful party. Honoré was retrieving coats and ushering them to the door; the valets were fetching their cars and limos. Everything was moving smoothly. It appeared that the evening had been a success. Dulcinea looked pleased with herself and it was obvious to Arnaud that she had "charmed the pants" off of everyone!

Back in the bedroom, Latifa continued to tell Madeleine her story. "I was nearly dead when Yahiye rescued me by giving that *kelev* "dog" every last piece of gold that he had with him, to secure my release. He did everything he could to rescue my daughter but there was no way to convince El Sighi. Yehiye went back to the camp later that night and he gave my bracelet and nose ring to another wife of El Sighi, and begged her to keep it for my daughter, Safina, and to give it to her when she was older so that she would remember her dead mother."

Arnaud knocked on the door and Madeleine told him to enter. He looked very upset. He was rubbing his hands together and began pacing up and down the bedroom. "I asked Yehiye to wait outside until I could talk with you, Latifa. He is anxious to comfort you - but I need to have a conversation with you alone."

Latifa interrupted him, as her voice cracked from pain, "Dulcinea is my daughter. My heart knew it the minute I met her, and almost leaped out of my chest as it pounded in joy. She too, felt it – I know it.

She knew me. Ask her! I know she will tell you that something powerful tugged at her soul when our eyes met," Latifa spoke through her tears of joy and tears of loss. "All those years – gone... Years I could have devoted to my child. There were no more children after the beating by El Sighi. He literally ruptured my uterus and cracked my pelvis, and if it hadn't been for Yehiye's compassion, and his connections in London – I would probably have died soon after."

"I believe you Latifa. What is your daughter's Arabic name?" he asked.

"Safina." That is the name I gave her at the moment I felt her stirring inside of me. I don't know why I chose that name – but it was preordained. There was never any other choice. Look here at her declaration written in her own hand and signed with her name: Safina, daughter of Latifa." She handed him the piece of paper she had found in the Qur'an.

Arnaud was somber. He sent Madeleine back to attend to their departing guests as he pushed the door closed behind her. As he turned to face Latifa he said, "You cannot tell Dulcinea any of this. She is the key to unlocking the chains of slavery that hold the Nation of Islam in a virtual vice, and threaten the survival of the world. Something like this would tear her apart. She would lose her focus and her self image.

Do you understand Latifa? She would become someone else. She needs her pain and vengeance to give her power to accomplish her goals. This is a long and difficult mission for her, and she is at the threshold. Yehiye and you have been associated with the Council for years - you know what is at stake here. If you reveal yourself it will be a "happy ever after" ending to her ordeal. Nothing will matter as much once she has her Mother back. No, no you cannot embrace this reunion. I know it will be a huge sacrifice for you – but you have already made that sacrifice and now you can be at peace because you know that you and your daughter went through this horrible chain of events for a very specific and very important reason. The certainty of this is absolute." As he spoke Arnaud watched Latifa's face turn very pale and contorted. Tears gushed like rivers from her eyes and her hands clawed at her hair, pulling and pulling on the shiny black strands.

"Iye, iye, iye....." Latifa wailed. "No, do not ask this of me. It is too much. No, Allah be merciful, do not withhold my daughter from me. Do not expect me to understand or to have any concerns for the fate of Islam or the world. I want only to hold my daughter in my arms where I will keep her forever." She wrapped her arms around her body and rocked backwards and forwards, shaking her head from side to side. "No! Do not ask this of me," she wailed in Arabic.

"Latifa, you have to understand. You cannot reclaim your right as her mother. You will support her from afar, from behind the scenes. You cannot breathe another word of this to anyone. If you pursue this you will be putting her life in danger. Already there are forces at work trying to kill her. We can protect her as Dulcinea Morelli – but we cannot keep "Safina" safe until the day that she will be ready to proclaim freedom for Islam, for herself, and for all Muslim women in the world.

Latifa's coppery skin took on a translucent grayish pallor, as tears dropped onto her silk evening gown, leaving long dark stains on the rich fabric. She rolled herself up into a ball on the bed, tucking her knees up against her stomach, sobbing.

Arnaud tried to comfort her and to put the situation in perspective, " Latifa, you could be such a support and help to her because you know so many key people in Europe and in America. Between us we could smooth the road for her in important ways. Join me, and talk to Yehiye about working together to help Dulci literally save the world! As fantastic as that sounds, as exaggerated as you may think that statement is – it is my firm belief that your daughter will be the most powerful and influential world leader of all time.

We are on the brink of a disaster for Islam. If the community of nations in the throes of a global financial crisis, combine forces to destroy Islam because fanatical extremists push them to the wall, all Muslims will suffer. The ethnic cleansing in Sarajevo will look like child's play compared to the slaughter of millions of Muslims in every country. Islam will cease to exist. You know this, Latifa - you have seen the evidence in the Council documents. Muslims will be effectively wiped off the face of the earth. This will be an act of survival for all the non-Muslim nations. We will have no alternative option - no choice! Even you and your daughter will not be spared!

With the help and backing of the Council and powerful allies dedicated to stopping this coming holocaust, Dulcinea will launch the reformation of Islam, bringing it into the 21st Century. She will establish a new nation – The United Federation of Arab States. The UFAS will be a member of the UFN (United Free Nations) that will replace the now defunct UN as a global alliance for freedom and prosperity. Latifa, we have a feasible, workable plan.

As members of the Council of United Free Nations. We have labored long and hard to build a global network that will support the reformation/revolution. Bring Yehiye back here on the 27th. I am inviting some key people to discuss our options and solidify our strategy. Dulcinea is ready. Your presence will be an important asset."

Arnaud closed the door softly as he left the room. Yehiye was waiting, and Arnaud put his arm around him and guided him stiffly down the hallway toward the stairs. "Let's go have a drink, old friend. Latifa told me the whole story. We have some things to talk about." He smiled as he came down the steps into the foyer. His eyes and his lips were at odds with each other. His eyes were not crinkled at the outer corners, and his voice did not have the friendly solicitous tone that endeared him to his friends and family. He was functioning mechanically, "Hello, how are you this evening?" He shook hands and reached out to touch shoulders and arms, he feigned great interest in whatever was being said, nodding his head up and down and stroking his chin while making eye contact with the guests. These were the stragglers - the people who linger on after the party is over, reluctant to give it up. Every so often he would look up toward the top of the stairs expectantly – as though something important and significant should occur soon.

Latifa lay on the bed crying. She listened to every word he said. She had been forced to give up her child so long ago, but today she had a choice, "How can I give her up again?" she whispered between sobs.

She fell asleep and dreamed of a black horse. Latifa was lifted off of the ground and placed upon Nomad's back, and just as her daughter had experienced it, she too felt the salty breezes from the ocean caressing her bare skin as Nomad raced along the wide beaches of the Mediterranean, kicking up millions of years of ground up sea shells that fell back to earth and lay stranded on the smooth wet surface of the sand. As he ran his hoof prints were covered by the tide and swept out to sea. Latifa opened her mouth wide, and eagerly breathed in the fresh unfiltered sea air. Her thick black hair glittered as the sun dropped deeper and deeper into the sea. She held onto the horse's thick mane, wrapping the strands of his hair around her fingers. She could feel his powerful lungs expanding and contracting under her legs as he ran full out, and the wind rushed against her face and through her hair. Her pain subsided. The big horse slowed to a trot as they moved along the seashore.

When Madeleine returned to check on Latifa, she wisely decided to let her sleep as long as she wanted to. She covered the grieving mother with a soft afghan, and dimmed the lights. Madeleine withdrew from this sad chamber of sorrow.

When she found Dulcinea in the kitchen she addressed her immediately, "Dulci, one of our guests, Mrs. Shmaiya, was overcome with fatigue, and she has fallen asleep on your bed because the guest room was full of coats at the time. Could you please spend the night in Janai's quarters? She is gone for the weekend to visit her relatives in London."

"Of course I will. It is no *problème.* I thought she looked pale when I met her early this evening. It is nothing serious? Oui? Mama, have I ever met her before? She seemed so familiar to me – in fact I was trying to remember all evening, where our paths may have crossed. My biological mother was named Latifa, but she is dead."

Madeleine controlled her emotions. Using her most authoritative voice she said, "No *Cheri,* I cannot recall any event that you would have attended when Latifa was present. She and her husband have not visited us for a very long time. I think the last time I spoke with Latifa was at her husband's charity jewelry show in London when he was commissioned to create a piece of jewelry for Princess Diana a few months before her death.

I also wanted to tell you, Dulci, that I'm delighted with your management of this event. You have far exceeded my expectations. In fact, I think you've approached this task with outstanding thoughtfulness and foresight," Madeleine praised her.

"Only because you have taught me so well; everything I did is a result of your tutoring and encouragement. Oh, Madam Fournier, you are truly my dearest Ma ma!" They hugged each other and Madeleine turned and walked toward the library where she knew she would find Arnaud and Yehiye.

The guests had left, and Arnaud and Yehiye were still talking outside the door of the library. Madeleine walked up and tucked her arm under her husband's arm, "Yehiye, Latifa has fallen asleep and I think it best that we allow her to sleep on through the night. As you can imagine she was quite upset. You can make yourself comfortable in the guest room, or we can book a room for you at the Hotel Vernet or Hotel Le Champs Elysees Plaza on Rue Berri. They are both fabulous. They will usually accommodate our guests even without reservations. If you prefer to stay here – you are most welcome. Honoré will set that up for you comfortably. I know that Arnaud has explained the situation regarding Latifa and Dulcinea, so I'm not going to say anything else about it. Just inform Honoré of your decision. Good night." She let go of Arnaud and walked toward the master suite.

"Well, my friend, I suppose you have no choice. Once Madeleine has taken command of a situation – there is no diplomatic negotiation. She is quite adamant about her decisions. I have to say that in this incidence I agree with her. Go off to bed Yehiye, we can talk again in the morning. Whatever you decide – just have Honoré handle it. Now I must join my wife or she will not be pleased to have to come and look for me."

When he was alone with Madeleine in their bedroom he sat down on the edge of their bed. Arnaud looked at his wife with tears in his eyes. Madeleine had never seen him so emotional. She immediately went over to him and sat down, taking his hand in hers.

Arnaud began to speak in a hushed voice as though he were telling her a secret, "I am amazed at the bravery and courage of Yehiye Shmaiya. This Jewish man put his life in danger to save a Muslim woman, who he didn't know, from almost certain death. He even went back and at great risk to himself he attempted to save the daughter. If he had been successful in saving Safina - it could have affected the future of the entire world. Madeleine, do you realize that one seemingly insignificant man choosing to do the right thing, yet not succeeding, could end up saving the world? A Catholic nun, at my primary school once said to me that God works in mysterious ways. It's an old, tired, cliché – but...... there is no other plausible explanation."

Latifa opened her eyes slowly and immediately was pulled back to the events of last night. When she looked at the clock on the table next to the bed she was surprised to have slept more than twelve hours continuously. She pulled herself up to a sitting position and let her legs slip across the slippery coverlet that she had slept on. The plush angora shawl fell away from her shoulders. Seated on the side of the bed with her feet touching the floor she looked out the window at the cold dark clouds gathering over Paris. Her hand uncurled and there was the anklet and toe ring that had pressed against her palm so strongly that an angry red imprint was temporarily embossed into her flesh as she dropped it into her other hand.

As Latifa reached up to smooth her hair she felt something between her fingers. She pulled her hand down and looked. There were two long black thick strands of coarse hair, caught on the prongs of her ring and wound around her little finger. Then she remembered how she had held onto the horse in her dream, by grasping his flowing mane with her right hand. Could it be.......her eyebrows rose in surprise. A feeling of resolution and peace came over her. "Yes, I know what to do now," she said with quiet resolve. Latifa rose, walked to the highboy and returned the ankle bracelet and toe ring to the place she had found them.

a Leader is Chosen

The revolutionary plan awaited the right person to lead it and the UFN was strongly committed to an agenda which paralleled the goals of the Islamic revolution.

Arnaud was seated in the Presidential office of Andre Laurent, discussing the selection of a revolutionary leader with the French President, "The time has come to select a leader. It should no longer be delayed or debated. I'm issuing a request for names. The candidates being considered are justifiably concerned with security. We know the risk is high even before the AJGA (Anti Jihadist Global Alliance) gets the reformation off the ground," Arnaud stated.

"Everything the revolution stands for is in direct opposition to the tenets of fundamental Islamic doctrine which is: subjugation of women, intolerance of other cultures and religions, and the killing of nonbelievers. Jihadist Muslims will fight hard to preserve these practices. Democratic forms of government are incompatible with the totalitarian and static culture of Islam. Think of it Arnaud, this is huge, gigantic, and volatile. My God, this mission represents the greatest overthrow of an entrenched theocracy in the recorded history of mankind. We are about to engage a toxic enemy who will wage war in a massive suicidal hysteria!" Andre looked pale as he stood up, walked over to a side table where an ornate silver tray sat with several bottles of Scotch Whiskey and some shot glasses. He poured two shots and carried them back to the long yellow sofa where Arnaud sat. Handing one of the drinks to Arnaud, he raised his glass, "Viva La Islamique Rèvolution!"

President Laurent rubbed his chin, sat down and crossed and uncrossed his legs, and finally cleared his throat. He was a seasoned politician, born and bred to embrace compromise and prided himself on being a master of negotiation and mediation. "You are so correct, Arnaud. It is.....how should we say it ...... impossible to achieve any of these..... *aspirer à faire*. The subjugation of females, no matter how incomprehensible to civilized society, is a cornerstone of Islamic culture. These Muslim women are so oppressed that they suffer from the *Stockholm Syndrome*. Enslaved like animals all of their lives, they cannot comprehend freedom. Significant numbers of Islamic women are so terrified by the idea of making their own choices in life, and so brainwashed by centuries of oppression that they would fight alongside their tormentors to sustain their own bondage." The skepticism in his voice was hard to miss. "I do not relish the thought of rushing into battle to save them, and possibly having our men shot by the supposed victims."

Arnaud smiled at him. "Courage Andre, courage my friend. The fight for a secular democratic government is a battle that will require audacity AND daring, typically French attributes, I'm told. But Andrea, you would also be saving France - already dangerously infected, and the rest of Europe as well. There is really no choice - we can't do it without you, and if you elect to sit by and straddle the fence, you will later be forced into joining the rest of the world in genocide in order to stop this Islamic expansion spreading like a plague across Europe.

Come on Andre, we only have a few hours to join the others. Let's make this an historic day. Let's go elect a leader and get this show rolling." Arnaud put his arm around the French President, almost protectively. It was a gesture of a brotherly solidarity in a fight for survival.

President Laurent told his aid to call an undercover ride for them - a nondescript, unmarked car without an escort or driver, and of no obvious importance. They drove out of a concealed automatic gate at the rear of the palace, through a well disguised garden and onto the road. Arnaud was surprised to see that Andre Laurent was a competent driver and that he wore plain black-rimmed eyeglasses and leather gloves to drive. Arnaud had never learned to drive - he had always had a personal driver or a friend who drove.

The room was subdued – the atmosphere was heavy with serious apprehension. The participants were facing the spectrum of dire consequences under an uncertain outcome to these deliberations. Each man and woman sitting here had so much to lose; their faces reflected their internal struggles. Beads of sweat trickled down some brows even though the temperature was a mild 24°C (75°F). Ultimately they also had much to protect. The selection today required a unanimous vote with all members physically present. No proxy votes or electronic voting was allowed. It had taken months of careful planning to get all of the UFN Council in one place at the same time without detection, and without compromising their mission and their identities. Arnaud doubted there would be another such assembly until after the revolution was achieved.

The alternative threat of worldwide ethnic cleansing resulting in the end of all Muslim existence was a strong motivating factor. The problem was finding the right combination in a candidate: intellect, commitment, leadership ability, "street smarts", and the willingness to make a lifelong commitment to the preservation of the foundation that would be established. The individual had to be decisive, pragmatic, and well prepared. He or she would need to be armed with a vast knowledge of history, theology, and military strategies all the while building consensus among competing egos in the UFN community of nations. They also must be emerging from nowhere – in other words – without any history of allegiance or vested interests outside of preventing the annihilation of the entire Muslim population of the world. The description of the perfect leader seemed to describe an individual who was impossible to find. But they knew the answer. Everyone there had already made a wise decision.

Dulcinea rose from her chair, and looked out at the individuals seated in row after row of polished mahogany tables. Their perspiring palms would leave their imprints on that virgin surface, free of dust particles and devoid of any traces of past decisions made here. There were no sharpened pencils, or clean papers, and no pitchers full of ice water or carafes of rich steamy coffee. It was pristine.

One hundred and seven senior delegates were in attendance. Arnaud was responsible for orchestrating this meeting of the UFN members; all of the nations in the UFN were represented.

Dulcinea stood at the podium and delivered her opening address, "Ladies and gentlemen, of all the states of being that exist for mankind and that compete in this world, freedom is the easiest to give up and the most difficult to obtain." She waited for that statement to sink in. "We have one agenda at this time - to stop the spread of Islamic fundamentalism throughout the world. By instituting a massive reformation of this fanatical religious doctrine of jihad, and by pulling all the Islamic nations under one secular umbrella we can accomplish our goal of creating the United Federation of Arab States, the UFAS."

She walked around behind her chair and stood with her hands on the top of the chair back. They were strong, well-manicured hands, steady hands. Dulcinea looked at the map on the wall to the right of her. She moved easily, with shoulders back and head held high.

Dulcinea began speaking in a clear and controlled voice, "When the Islamic Brethren makes their final move to devour the free world, this will create a powerful backlash of non-Muslims capable of destroying all people of the Islamic faith, perhaps even targeting anyone of Arabian or Persian descent." She paused to let this statement sink in. When the nations of the world are forced to unite against Islam, fundamentalist Muslims will underestimate the power and resolve of those nations acting together to survive.

Muslims are 1.5 billion people or 22% of the world's population! If Muslims are left unrestrained their population will reach 50% of the world's human inhabitants by the end of this century." There was a collective intake of oxygen in the room. The quiet that followed was heavy with dread.

Someone said, "Almost a quarter of the world's population would be wiped out!"

Arnaud interjected, "The leaders of Islam believe that by dying in holy war they will be *"raptured"* into Paradise as a reward for killing all infidels, and causing ruination and cataclysmic destruction around the globe."

Dulci continued, "There are two options before us: the first one is an ideological marketing approach, using appeasement and intense long term educational campaigns. I have already explained in previous analyses why this approach would not work. We must discard the notion that Muslim males, steeped in centuries of extreme doctrine, are candidates for educational reform. The other option requires two phases. The first phase is to prepare now for a full-fledged military confrontation across the board, and to put in place a plan for unilateral suspension of international alliances that do not support the revolution and the Islamic reformation. The second phase of this option is to utilize hi-tech scientific developments to mobilize the women of Islam, recruiting them to stand up and fight in their own defense. Before we can take one step, we must have a consensus, here and now, on how we will proceed from this point forward."

She sat down slowly, putting both hands on the arms of her chair to support her descent. She motioned to Arnaud by pointing her index finger at the wall behind him.

Arnaud rose and turned toward a wooden panel mounted on the wall, and with a remote control he activated both side panels to slide open. A projection device was revealed. Arnaud clicked the remote again. After a brief flicker a holographic power point presentation was launched. Images of 3-D life-size men and women scholars, scientists, and archaeologists appeared out of thin air and walked back and forth in front of the audience, using visual aids with charts and graphs, and photographic materials, they presented their information. The rapt audience watched and listened. If anyone there had doubted the technical expertise of the UFN Council, their doubts dissipated rapidly.

With a seamless integration of the holographic presentation, Arnaud built his case for the Islamic reformation piece by piece, supporting it with clear cut evidence and facts. Archaeological excavated materials proving multiple and conflicting versions of the Qur'an written over hundreds of years: analytical dissection and exposure of redundancies in the text; hi-lighted changes in literary style that indicated multiple authors; references from other historical sources of the same time period exposed the band of Mohammad's ancient followers as merciless marauders. "They hacked off the heads of anyone who did not accept Mohammad as the prophet of Allah and who refused to pay tribute in gold, merchandise, or female slaves.

Islam remains intact and unchanged only because of the manner it is enforced to this day: without mercy, without recourse, without any thread of empathy or humanitarian considerations. Islam is a quasi cult/religion of the sword - 'comply or die'. That philosophy stopped the evolution of Islamic society in its tracks. There is no hope of any natural or gradual reformation of archaic primitive beliefs under this constant threat of death to any Muslim who doesn't swear allegiance to the Prophet and his laws without deviation.

Then he presented the proof of global contingency plans to wipe out Islam and all traces of Islamic influence around the world simultaneously. The highly classified covert plan was titled: "Sarajevo Cleansed". The name was telling - Sarajevo had become 100% Muslim, infested with al Qaeda terrorists.

As he surveyed the room he spoke just above a whisper. "The documentation is meticulous – these are the dates, locations, and names. Islam, without a doubt, is targeted for complete destruction. The plan is to be executed over a 72 hour window, and carried out brutally in every corner of the world. Operatives are in place and waiting for activation. Over a hundred countries are listed as having ratified the coalition documents." Arnaud took a break and sipped a glass of ice water brought to him by his assistant. He coughed nervously, wiped his lips with his handkerchief and returned it to his pocket. "There is even a detailed disposal plan supported by sophisticated technical equipment standing by," he stated quietly.

As he sat down, Dulcinea spoke, "The catalyst for 'Sarajevo Cleansed' going operational is another major catastrophic attack on US soil or, against a nation allied with America. Detonation of a nuclear bomb by Muslim terrorists will put the rest of the world on a swift and lethal warpath against Islam.

High ranking US, and British Intelligence, along with Military High Command in the NATO countries, stand apart from the political posturing of Washington D.C., London, Paris, and other parliamentary bodies of politicians. For the most part, their political leaders have been excluded from this mission. The UFN is concerned only with preserving the sovereignty and freedom of UFN member nations upon the earth – and we are sworn to neutralize and destroy any global nuclear or biological threat to human existence. The men and women in this room are each charged with representing the independent councils in each UFN member nation - set aside from the existing governments to preserve humanity in a state of freedom and liberty. Like it or not – if our mission of Islamic Revolution and the reformation isn't implemented or doesn't succeed, everyone here will become participants in Sarajevo Cleansed. We won't have a choice."

They took a break at this point. Arnaud ushered them into another large room, and they were served a nutritious meal of ethnic variety. This was another opportunity to demonstrate cooperation and goodwill between the UFN members, and to celebrate their cultural diversity.

Most of the members were acquainted with Dulcinea, and they understood the important role she would play. Some of them had consulted with her in the past when questions arose as to strategy or time lines. They realized that the vote would be taken soon - and a revolutionary leader would be selected or rejected.

She wore a plain dark blue silk dress with a white, tailored wool jacket, practical low heeled black pumps and a wide black belt. The hemline was just above her knees, and the fit was not too snug. There was just enough room to hide her 45 in a side holster, and as always she kept her shabria handy, tucked into the inside lower sleeve pocket of her custom designed jacket.

Brecken stood nearby, while other armed guards were strategically positioned throughout the building.

None of the delegates knew where the building was located except for President Andre Laurent, Arnaud, Dulcinea, and Brecken's team. The members had been brought to the location in closed, sound proof vehicles, and were only escorted from those vehicles after entering an underground series of tunnels.

Paris has a vast network of underground passages and caverns known as *"les carrieres de Paris."* A large portion of it is an underground ossuary located south of the city at *Place Denfert-Rochereau*, (Paris' stone mines). A subterranean city bustles beneath the modern streets of Paris, France. Much of it consists of abandoned quarries, cisterns, and aqueducts dating back centuries ago. "Off-the-grid" communities of fringe Parisians reside in these ancient caverns, and travel these subterranean corridors on a daily basis. This particular cavern was said to have been the meeting place of the Knights Templar, and was located not far from the vast underground graveyards of the 1700's, on the outskirts of Paris.

A short distance from Arnaud's mansion in an elite neighborhood of stately homes, not far from the Presidential Palace, an access tunnel was dug with a sharp descent from inside what appeared to be an historical, now defunct, emporium building. The tunnel twisted and turned over 25 kilometers until it reached the newly excavated quadrant. The UFN rebuilt a section of it to serve as an operational bunker for the revolution. The "vault" in the basement of Arnaud's mansion was too small to house the full voting membership, and the consensus was that there should be a "back-up" HQ option in case of an emergency. It was well-equipped and could house the full membership for an extended period of time if that should be necessary.

The outer doors of the room were closed and sealed for the duration of the meeting. The low hum of the ventilation system purred softly, supplying fresh cool air and dehumidifying the naturally dank underground facility.

As the members returned and were seated, Dulcinea began speaking, "The Islamic Brethren has developed a master plan for the establishment of the Third Caliphate which they are implementing. Their ultimate goal is to install Islam as a totalitarian theocracy worldwide. The plan is being followed to the letter and is currently on track." The time line that Dulci presented to the Council was absolutely accurate – and the corresponding "completed or in progress bar" was nearly half way across the time line!

She raised her voice to emphasize the point, "We paid over ten million Euros for a copy of the Islamic Brethren's original blueprint and time line for the Third Caliphate. The items hi-lighted on this graph are more than shocking. Even though many intelligent people suspected the causes and source of financial upheavals in the global economy, it is horrifying to see the proof of what, until this point, has been primarily speculation and conspiracy theories. We can see from the evidence that the financial collapse of American currency and the bond markets was orchestrated behind the scenes by a partnership between The Muslim Brethren and William T. Monroe. I am not going to cover all the details of this diabolical scheme - but outlines and time lines will be transmitted to you via secure communications. You can review them yourselves.

She stepped out from behind the podium and clasped her hands together in front of her, with fully extended arms resting against her body. "Today I stand here as a Muslim woman, as a previous child bride, as a victim of enslavement, and rape. I offer myself as a survivor, and as a soldier and leader in the UFN army. I am well prepared for this battle," she walked briskly across the low stage as she looked out into the faces before her. When she got to the side, she pivoted suddenly, looking straight ahead into the audience.

Dulcinea stood quite still for a moment, measuring the impact she was having on the delegates. "I am educated, intelligent, globally connected, and I am brave and committed to the mission. This is not a job for the timid, or the hesitant. It is no job for small egos, or men or women of compromise and diplomacy." She was silent for a moment – letting her words sink in. "I am a warrior! I have killed assassins and confronted evil without mercy. I stand before you to tell you that if you give me your mandate to lead this revolution, I will carry out this mission. For me, failure is not an option. I will succeed, and I will reform Islam and save my people from annihilation, thereby stabilizing the world economy and launching a long period of peace and global prosperity. Give me your mandate!"

The vote was unanimous. Dulcinea was chosen to lead the revolution and to establish the United Federation of Arab States. She was also asked to establish the Theological Council for Islamic Reformation – to assist in the selection of the panel, and to address the members individually and collectively. She was then introduced to her new command, the revolutionary military leaders and advisors from every country via secure satellite feed. She was pleased to see female officers among them, who had been secretly training in Israel and the United States.

As she walked around the room, shaking hands, smiling, whispering in a few ears, and generally basking in this peaceful moment before the storm. She saw Yehiye and Latifa Shmaiya across the room, recognizing them from the party that she had organized at the Fournier mansion. They were old friends of Arnaud and Madeleine, who apparently used to vacation together on the French Riviera and in Monaco. She had seen their photos in the family album, taken at the shoreline and on their yacht. She made her way over to them, grasped Latifa by the arm and leaned over to whisper in her ear, "Have you seen Madeleine? I wish she were here - it seems like an historic moment. I wish my Mother were alive to see this - I think she would have been pleased."

Latifa looked as though a chill had passed through her body. "I'm sorry.... I don't know where Madeleine is, we arrived late..... it's nice to see you again Dulci.... I'm sure your mother would have been very proud of you. We all are........"

It was only seconds until they were calling Dulcinea back to the podium for a toast. She hadn't had a chance to respond to Latifa. She thought her heart was racing because of the occasion and the election. *I thought I was ready for this - I have to control my emotions - this is crazy to be this jittery. Get a grip girl - that's what Vivian would tell me.*

As she raised her glass and smiled, the applause from everyone in the room was deafening – the task had begun. The members stood in deference and respect as the leader of the revolution and the future President of the UFAS walked away from the podium, toward the door. She was a formidable world leader and she carried herself as such.

Brecken stood by the doorway in full Marine parade dress uniform. He snapped to attention and saluted her as she passed him. Under his breath he prayed, "Nomad, wherever you are - help me to keep her safe." He watched her walking confidently down the hallway toward the exit.

Dulcinea was filled with optimism and fueled with a great surging energy. She was very cognizant of the potential for failure – but equally enthused with the specter of success. At this point, all things were possible. She allowed her fear and anticipation to reach a crescendo and then she mentally turned that wave of raw emotion and energy, narrowed it, condensed it into a mental stream of thought, and focused it to fuel her resolve. It was a mind trick that Brecken had taught her.

CHAPTER 15

Global Positioning

Arnaud Fournier, Claude Molyneau and his father, Jon Pierre Molyneau (President of the European Market), President Andre Laureat of France, and US Senator Sean Thibault of Texas sat with the UFN revolutionary leader and future UFAS President, Dulcinea Morelli, around the conference table at UFN headquarters in Paris. Although these individuals were the key players in structuring the Islamic Revolution, there were other representatives of UFN member countries in attendance as well. They had come together as a planning committee to discuss and debate the funding of the UFN as it positioned itself in the current global arena. The revolution was the center piece of the UFN agenda, and it required major financial resources. This committee had an important job to do - find the money to make it happen! They didn't want to create a crippling debt for the newly created UFAS - even before it was officially born.

They were in the middle of a working session and the walls were lined with charts and graphs. Each one was viewing their own electronic screens. "This changes everything," President Laureat said. "The Japanese debt accumulation after the quake and tsunami has altered the dynamics, and as a result I believe we will see new alliances with the Muslim Brethren. Japan will not be in a position to go forward with the Brethren's global strategy. The coup in Venezuela which overthrew the Marxist dictator, and their fragile new government scrambling to resuscitate and rebuild a democracy, puts Venezuela in a precarious position. That is certainly not in step with the 3-party pact they made with the US Administration and the Brethren. The Venezuelan democratic coup has far reaching ramifications for the global banking networks. Venezuela has applied for membership in the UFN. These issues are all up for discussion at the next UFN Council meeting."

Arnaud joined in the discussion: "The disintegration of the UN, and the subsequent alliances of the socialist democracies consolidating into their own global organization of the APN (Alliance of Progressive Nations) has destabilized the emerging economic foundations of developing countries. It has also shifted the priorities and hierarchy of the major world powers. The United States is in flux, and appears to be headed toward domestic upheaval as a forceful and vocal segment of American conservatives resist efforts to transition willingly into a socialist progressive form of government – this division creates a potential security problem for the UFN because the United States of America possesses the greatest military might in the world. We really can't wait and see which side of that coin comes up. Domestic instability within the United States is a concern to all UFN members. Senator Thibault, what can you tell us about this situation?"

"It's true. Despite media rhetoric diminishing the strength and sophistication of US strategic power – the sheer size and technological superiority of the US Military is far advanced beyond anything that any rival superpower could fathom or match. The Governor of my State of Texas has created a covert task force to allocate resources and make logistical plans to dig in for the long haul. If the current

White House Administration continues to usurp the power of the Congress and to make repeated end runs around the Constitution, I believe that a US revolution is inevitable. He took a deep breath and stood up, pushing his chair back and leaning on the table with both hands. He looked around the table. "We have one last opportunity to thwart Bill Monroe's plans, and restore the Republic's integrity. If we can stop the Islamic Brethren from creating a major terrorist event, such as the detonation of a dirty bomb on US soil - which the administration will use as an excuse to declare martial law and suspend the elections - we would still have the ballot box to defeat their plans. We believe that we have a 50/50 probability of success." Senator Thibault sat back down in his chair and ran his hand over his bald head. He looked tired and the furrow between his eyes had deepened since the last time Dulcinea had seen him.

She had not met one American Senator or Congressman who wanted to go through an American revolution. There were a handful of left wing rhetorical socialist die hards who were working hard to dump the Constitution and establish a socialist regime. They didn't have the conviction or personal experience living under communism to pull it off. Dulcinea doubted they would be able to push the country into anarchy or any kind of Marxist revolution. All they could do was wreck havoc with the US economy.

Dulcinea cleared her throat and took a drink of water. Then she began to speak, "The UFN Council's primary mission at this juncture is to enlist the backing of the Guardians in support of the Islamic Reformation. The Guardians are the key to world stability – but they will not intervene unless they jointly concur that US existence is threatened. From their perspective, 9/11 was a mosquito bite – troublesome, irritating, policy changing – but not a lethal threat to the existence of the Republic. Their charter is to protect the Republic from fatal corrosive internal and external attacks on the principles of liberty and justice in America, to preserve constitutional protections, and to destroy confirmed threats to the Republic with decisive, extreme actions. Monetary or military threats are equally subject to intervention. The Guardians were established and chartered by an inner group of the founding fathers of the United States at the Constitutional Congress during their final deliberations. Senator Thibault is our UFN liaison with the Guardians."

The discussion was lively and as usual Dulcinea had some astute observations, "The developments in Venezuela are of primary interest because we can glean important perspective on what to anticipate after the Islamic Revolution. This gives us valuable time to formulate counter measures to avoid the sink holes that are plaguing the revolutionaries in Venezuela.

As I listened to the description of the Guardians' charter - it occurred to me that we should also create a similar organization to preserve the work that we are doing here." She tried to read the faces around the table - who were silent and frozen. Then one by one she saw expressions of comprehension spread from person to person - and heads began to nod as a collective agreement was reached.

Dulci had recruited Claude Molyneau to work with the UFN to provide a comprehensive financial assessment and concrete recommendations to the Council. He was a world class banker and astute economist, with a genius for seeing "the big picture" and accurately forecasting financial outcomes. He and his father were currently heavily engaged in a financial rescue plan for the European Market.

Claude stood up and walked to the side wall as the chairs swiveled to watch him. He pushed a button on the wall and a screen appeared. A map of the European Market countries was revealed. "German economic support has held up the European Market despite their threatening rhetoric to "go it alone". A list of German investments and loans flashed onto the screen. "The Germans decided it was in their best interests to shore up the financial dikes and hold back the floods until the "member" countries could combine forces and create a financial "phoenix-like" rise from the ashes of the failed global banking community. Their conservative philosophy serves them well. Germany stands tall as an example of fiscal prudence."

The German representative at the table grinned.

Claude's father, Jon Pierre, approached the screen and faced the members. He was slightly bent for a tall man and his full head of stark white hair sharply contrasted with his dark complexion - still a striking figure even at the age of eighty two. "The Germans stood alone in their resolve to spare Europe another dismal decade of recession followed by astronomical monetary deflation. It was with a sure hand that they reached out to their fellow Europeans to shore up the weak elements of the Common Market." Jon Pierre pointed at Arnaud and smiled. He walked stiffly back to his chair and sat down. The meeting continued for a few more hours until they broke for dinner.

Later that night Claude and Dulci talked about the meeting and how intricately the political and financial trends were grafted into any successful society. "You have to concede, Claude - money and power have been the catalyst for change throughout history. It seems to me that disasters and uprisings, oppression and subsequent rebellion eventually led to the advancement of humans to the next higher level of civilization. The end product is ultimately the creation of a better world than existed before major conflicts and catastrophes," Dulcinea said.

"Yes, you're correct, in theory. But, it is important to note that digression from principles can plague revolutionary objectives. There's no reason to repeat bad history. Let's be prepared to ward off undesired consequences. To do this we need to be proactive, and to stay one step ahead of anarchy, terrorism, and tribal mentality. And not just financially!"

Dulcinea knew that Arnaud had something to do with the German change of heart. He worked long and vigilantly behind the scenes to convince Germany to stand fast. Arnaud knew of the alliance between Japan and Turkey that plotted against the United States, against the European Common Market and against America's steadfast friend, Poland. He had reliable intelligence information from Israeli Mousad operatives, who trusted him, and from "friends" inside the Turkish inner circle. Since the "domino" revolutions of the individual Arab dictatorships, the rulers of Turkey were on a quest to emerge as the Islamic Superpower that replaces all other Muslim options dominating the Islamic World. Gyasi Moubarick had supplied verified intelligence reports. His wife was the daughter of the Turkish Ambassador to the United States.

Turkey was the real enemy, and no one saw that as clearly as Dulcinea. They all thought it was the Muslim Brethren, but that was too obvious, and ultimately too easy to defeat. Turkey was sneaky and America did not get that. They looked back to a time when Turkey was secular, modern, still trying to be accepted in the family of nations. The Turks were rapidly reverting to Islamic dreams of world domination as they were sucked deeper and deeper into religious fanaticism.

It wasn't yet confirmed that the Muslim Brethren was in league with the Turkish leadership, and some speculation was voiced that there may be a conflict between those two extremist groups. What was obvious is that the fall of dictatorships throughout the Middle East was not part of some drive for democracy or secularism, but rather it was carefully nurtured and orchestrated by the organized Muslim Brethren master plan for the Third Caliphate. Dulcinea didn't believe that Turkey was going to embrace that concept – and she was already figuring out how she would take advantage of that conflict between Turkey's Muslim Clerical leaders and the Muslim

Brethren. Arnaud had given Dulcinea his intelligence report from his last visit to Germany:

At a luncheon in Unterturkheim near Stuttgart Germany, at the Daimler-Chrysler Factory, Arnaud shared selective pieces of intelligence with a top German intelligence director, "Satellite codes for the American Space defense grid are compromised. The CIA has backed off all collection of intelligence data under the Presidential amended guidelines. The Turks' confidence that their Japanese co-conspirator's will knock out the "eyes" and "ears" of the American satellites at the correct time, is the key to delivering the final blow to US world domination as a Superpower. Their goal is to rebuild the Turkish Empire and establish Turkey as the world's strategic and financial center of power. Apparently visions of the Ottoman Empire are still alive in the breasts of the audacious Turks."

The German intelligence director spoke in a measured, staccato pace, "Yes, we have our sources. The Japanese proposed a clandestine pact with Germany. It circumvents the Turks. It deals a fatal blow to the Polish/American alliance. Germany is evaluating their proposal."

Arnaud wasn't comfortable with the intricate and complex backroom deals that were being struck. He observed the shallow G20 meetings in London and in Mexico that appeared to make headway for a while and then suddenly stalled. "The old adage that "nature abhors a vacuum" will play out here," Arnaud told the German director. "If America continues to increase its massive debt service obligations, it will commit financial suicide. There will be plenty of wolves to join in the feeding frenzy. These Internet orchestrated, plastic mini-revolutions playing out like so many virtual video games by Arab adolescents across the Middle East are basically 'children playing with fire.' The dangerous consequence of this fanatical, juvenile activity is that it plays into the hands of the Muslim Brethren. They create chaos by the agitation of disorganized, largely uneducated and unsophisticated 'twenty-somethings'. When the dust settles they fill the void with their organized infiltration of these activities. It's genius and insidious."

The German director spoke with conviction, "The dollar is shaky as the monetary standard. American banking systems and manufacturing were effectively nationalized since the last election. If the administration leads the country into default now or in 18 months, the end result is the same. They are intentionally escalating a financial crisis. Combined with terrorist attacks on US soil, America would be ready for the transition that will be presented as the only solution to put the people back to work and restore civil order. They will be pushed to give up their democratic form of government through a bloodless coup, and to abolish democracy in exchange for a totalitarian regime that promises to restore law and order, and economic stability.

"That's exactly what the Muslim Brethren anticipates. The Muslim Brethren is waiting in the wings," Arnaud nodded his head in agreement.

His reputation for being closed mouth and reflective stood Arnaud in good stead, as various long-time diplomatic and political relationships brought up-to-the-minute information to him, and solicited his interpretation and analysis, "We must convene the Council as soon as possible, Arnaud. The disastrous component of this whole global "twitter" are the Islamofascists. They could drastically affect the world economy with just one fanatical nuclear attack in the US or Europe," the Director of the *Deutch* equivalent of the CIA for the Bonn Government commented.

"It is only a matter of time before the American position in the global economy will deteriorate sufficiently to cause noticeable shifts in global power coalitions," Arnaud responded. "We need to get together with the insiders at the top of the European Common Market finance committee. And, I know just the man who can arrange that." He pulled out his UFN communication device and tapped in a code that would establish a satellite link to a unique relay system that would send his call millions of miles into space, bouncing it off of a remote sub-station that only a select few people on earth knew of its existence. He waited for the delayed encryption to activate. "Hello Jon Pierre, this is......well, you know who this is. I need a meeting. You, me, and the German who we talked about before. I'm thinking tonight, thinking contingency plan, iron out the options and get this done before a melt-down in December would proceed the Senatorial transition in the US. Can you do it?" He waited a moment and looked at his German friend across the table from him. "Ah, yes - but not later than tomorrow evening, I have to get back to Paris." Another break as he listened to the other side of the conversation. "Oui, that is an acceptable location - then.... *au revoir.*" Arnaud looked up at the German director. "We're on for tomorrow evening. I will send my driver for you. Be ready by 7:00 pm."

China had developed new technology and tactics targeting US aircraft carriers. This was not a secret – yet Washington DC had not responded to this threat. The US military resources were so explicitly superior to any other world power that realistically the "top brass" was not alarmed by a major threat to American sovereignty. It was the threat of small insurgencies, and "dirty bombs" that might make it through US security grids that were more worrisome and potentially politically destabilizing.

The CIA and US military leadership were now firmly committed to supporting the UFN Council because they saw it as the optimum tool to save the free world from the Islamic takeover and also defend against the Chinese aspirations of world domination. These two powers thought to crush the rest of the world in their vice-like grip. Like typical thieves and snakes, they would then turn on each other and the survivor would rule supreme.

Dulcinea was discussing this evaluation with Gyasi Moubarik, her Egyptian friend from IEP (Institute d'Etudes Politiques de Paris). After graduation they had co-authored two books: *The Power Structure of the Persian Gulf Nations*, an in-depth academic study of the make-up and psychology of modern day Middle Eastern rulers and dictators; and a more popular analytical volume: *When Ideology Supersedes Logic in World Conflicts*. They were well received among diplomatic circles and within the CIA. Dulcinea and Gyasi were regarded as experts in this field. They coined the term: "Political Socio-pathology"

Several of the high level CIA undercover operatives worked with Dulcinea on analysis of intelligence data collected in the Middle East. Counter intelligence officer Ronen Kyson contacted Dulcinea directly, "Listen Morelli, we're well aware of the UFN operations, and we want in! Let's lock in a partnership with the UFN Council – at least until we're in a political climate which allows the US to join. The situation is critical here. The intelligence community is doing a "high-wire act". Really, Dulci, our guys were the last of the "warriors" that came up through the ranks; not the new crop of Harvard Law progressives or political appointees. We're in a sticky situation here. We don't think it's in the best interests of the US to go through a military coup. Some of the generals currently in place are not the strategic giants of the past. The "watering down" of the US Military has reached the top echelon of the US Marines and the US Army. Solid ground prevails only within the Naval and Air Force operational branches of the military. You must realize that the Marine Corp is very much a stand-alone arm of the US Military at this point. It remains the "question mark" if a confrontation should arise between the Administration and the pentagon. Frankly, we don't know how that would play out.

"I will take your proposals to the Council." Dulcinea answered him honestly. When she called Arnaud with a direct link-up to the Paris Council HQ vault, where several prominent members of the UFN were gathered, she brought this request up. She reminded them that the operatives who were begging to participate were not briefed on the Guardians. Dulci and the other members were sworn to secrecy, and would never reveal their identity or their mission. How would they walk this fine line between full cooperation and only partial disclosure? Dulcinea felt conflicted and unwilling to make a decision about their inclusion. "I think that it may better support the revolution, at this time, if the CIA operatives are contained within their roles, and are not briefed on all of the components of the UFN."

The President of the United States delivered a series of speeches. His proposal to split Israel into two countries and to award Jerusalem as the Palestinian capitol under Hamas was enthusiastically received by the Islamic Brethren. Their time line toward the takeover progressed rapidly.

The Iranians wished to preempt the Turkish grandiose plans to be the center of Islam. They pursued their own objectives, impatient to become the leader of the Muslim world by escalating their planned operation. Just a few years after the proposal of a Palestinian State was announced, the world was shocked when Iran launched a nuclear attack on Tel Aviv wiping out at least half of the city's population, killing a quarter of a million inhabitants and paralyzing the Israeli economy. Iran simultaneously launched 4 nuclear missiles intended to annihilate the Jewish state. Only one of them managed to avoid Israeli counter measures, and to hit the intended target and detonate. The UFN Council held an emergency session. There was no comment from the White House - the President and his family were on vacation again. The American liberal media played it down, and after only a week of broadcasting the story, it was eased off the press agenda.

Oil commodity prices soared and the world scrambled to secure their crude oil sources. The price of crude quadrupled. The retail price of gasoline went ballistic – up to $10.00 a gallon.

The US Administration was silent. Some posturing took place on the floor of the US Senate but nothing was actually accomplished. Without a leader in the White House there was no one at the helm.

Texas and Oklahoma opened up their reserve fields and Standard Oil activated their emergency contract clause and disengaged from OPEC. They began harvesting their off-shore fields. Oil crews headed for the massive underground oil deposits in South Dakota – it was time to stop playing the game, and bring out the massive energy reserves held by the United States of America for decades. Enough oil to fuel America for 300 years was a conservative estimate. Stock in Standard Oil was off the charts as each oil giant arose from slumber and began the process of finally ridding America of its dependence on foreign oil. Years of oil field banking had finally paid off. Iran had killed off their own resource. They would fade into history as having committed national suicide. No country would ever purchase Iranian oil again. But it wasn't done by choice.

When the US President objected, and his female mouth piece, the top White House presidential advisor, threatened that the President would issue an Executive Order prohibiting domestic oil production, "......because we will never touch our reserves," a respected senior Senator within the President's own party told her, "Sit down and shut the fuck up, you bitch, or the President will be impeached and tried for treason."

Israel hunkered down like a wounded wolverine, ready to launch her nuclear arsenal and unleash her formidable conventional weaponry upon any Arab country or terrorist organization that sneezed in their direction. They lost the ports of Tel Aviv and Yaffa in the Iranian attack; in addition to the dead and dying, nearly two million people were displaced, half of their population. Deaths from fallout radiation would continue far into the future. Most of the Baka valley which produced 90% of Israel's food was contaminated by radiation. The resilience of the Israelis was phenomenal. In the face of atrocious evil they survived, and began rebuilding their small, yet historically significant, country. No longer able to rely on their American allies, they formed a coalition with several moderate Islamic countries. Jordan and Lebanon who had barely survived an attempted takeover of their countries by the Muslim Brethren, were still actively engaged in that struggle.

The Egyptian military that had ignored the rigged elections, had realized that without Israel they would be invaded by Syria and Iran, and possibly suffer the same fate as Israel. Even Iraq was sending emissaries to talk with the Israeli's to try to work out some kind of military coalition. They knew it was only a matter of time before Iranian forces would slither into Iraq and enslave the population. Iran had done more to dissolve the Muslim Brethren's power base and dreams of Islamic Jihad than any of their enemies could have hoped for. It was their blind fanaticism that would destroy them.

The attack was meant to be "the final solution" for dealing with the Jewish State. If all four missiles had been delivered as planned it would have succeeded. Israel was strangely silent. "Licking their wounds I suspect," was the remark by Brecken.

But Israel was by no means "finished" and in reality it was clear to Dulcinea that the attack had sealed the fate of Iran. She knew what many others did not - that Israel was more than well prepared to retaliate, and when they made that move it wouldn't be just a "slap on the hand."

The second Jewish Holocaust had happened and the world reacted pretty much the same as they had the first time. The American government stood by and spouted rhetoric but did nothing, the French secretly celebrated, and Britain was ruled by Islamic Sharia law by then. There were no other military powers that would intervene. China disengaged from the fray, standing by waiting for the whole house, built on sand, to sink so that they could swoop in and assume the position as The Super Power in the world.

The Iranians would either overthrow their government within the next few weeks or Israel would retaliate with a vengeance, and deprive the entire world of Persian Gulf oil indefinitely. The UFN would not chastise them, but Dulcinea had a better plan. She contacted an allied operative in Metsada, a small effective assassination unit of Mousad, and gave them a list of those directly responsible in Iran: the hands-on technicians and pilots who had implemented the strike. The list included their physical location, known family members, associates, photographs and pertinent affiliations. Her advice to Israel was to surgically remove the offenders, and wait for retaliation on the regime when the timing was appropriate.

Arnaud and Dulcinea sent a message via Mousad channels to the Israeli Prime Minister, "We are close to implementing our plans as previously conveyed to you. The attack on Israel is unforgivable. Those responsible must be killed. Please hold fast until we can launch our offensive. When we succeed, and reason prevails. We will live side by side in peace." They signed it in Hebrew: *Elohim yivarech otchem ve yeshmor otchem* (God bless you and protect you).

A month had passed since the attack. Israel's wounds were raw and the opposition parties in Israel were screaming for retribution. The Israeli parliamentary coalition of the conservative and labor factions was fragile. A call for a "no confidence" vote in the Knesset was inevitable. It was the last thing that Israel could withstand in this crisis situation. The prime minister of Israel had no options.

"Turn on the news reports coming out of AP right now," Brecken almost screamed into the phone. He was speaking with Arnaud and Dulcinea from Washington D.C. where he had been attending a pentagon debriefing.

Arnaud flicked a switch on his console in the "vault" and Dulcinea rolled her chair over to his desk and sat down. The reporter was talking as background video was streaming showing chaos and rioting in the streets of the major middle eastern cities: Baghdad, Teheran, Cairo, Amman, and Saana in Yemen." At 0500 hours today, three IAF squadrons, 150 Sqn, 199 Sqn and 248 Sqn, based at Sedot Mikha Israeli airbase, the command post for Israel's nuclear strike force, launched 30 air-to-surface Jericho I and II medium-range ballistic missiles armed with 100 kiloton warheads. They successfully targeted the main nuclear facility and the oil fields of Iran. A Jericho III SLBM, submarine long-range ballistic missile, was launched simultaneously from the Israeli submarine, Sharone, hitting an al Qaeda stronghold in southern Pakistan along the Afghanistan border.

Interestingly, the American troops were pulled out of that region of Afghanistan only a few days ago. A fortunate coincidence for them. At least that is the official statement released by Admiral Taylor on the USS Nimitz, standing by in the Indian Ocean."

The TV screen went to a commercial and then was interrupted by a special bulletin. It showed the Israeli Prime Minister, Itzhak Tsurieli standing at a makeshift podium in front of the Knesset building in Jerusalem.

"Israel was forced to remove the threat of more attacks by Iran because we would not survive. Our intelligence revealed that the Iranians were preparing to launch a second nuclear strike against us. We do not apologize for collateral damage, nor do we request the approval of other nations. We take full responsibility for our defensive and preemptive actions."

As the UFN members watched and listened to the broadcast it became clear that the retaliation by the Israelis had obliterated the oil fields of Iran. There were mixed emotions about this within the UFN. Dulcinea was especially torn between understanding the necessity to respond to Iranian jihad, and how this event would have far reaching ramifications for the new UFAS after the revolution. The oil resources had been factored in as an economic vehicle for establishing the democracies of the member states. With the oil resources gone, it would be doubly important to recover the vast amounts of money that had been drained off by the Iranian, Iraqi and Saudi governments, and hidden in secret accounts around the world.

A week had passed, and the chaos was beginning to subside. Rioters had receded back into the countryside, and refugee camps were being established throughout the region. The UFN had already dispatched its secret operatives to circulate the words of freedom among the Islamic female population in the camps.

Brecken was debriefing the UFN Council, "American intelligence organizations expressed shock at the size of the Israeli arsenal, and their sophisticated delivery capability. Somehow Israel had managed to move their launch vessel within striking range of Iran. Their submarine stealth technology was unknown to most of the intelligence community of the world and unknown specifically to the United

States prior to this attack. The pentagon was aggressively pursuing answers to their questions.

Admiral Taylor looked out on the ocean from his command station high in the tower of the gargantuan aircraft carrier. He smiled. This room was off-limits to all personnel except the Admiral and the Captain. "Thank God the founding fathers had the foresight to establish a parallel failsafe to the US Constitution. They were insightful and wise far beyond their time. John, we are privileged to serve." He poured some whiskey into two shot glasses on the table, shoving one across to the Captain sitting across from him. He raised his glass toward the Captain, "Here's to the Guardians."

The Captain looked pensive and then he downed the whiskey in one gulp, "It was a surgical attack. They didn't randomly hit cities or villages inside Iran – only the oil fields and nuclear facilities. Iran brought this counterattack upon itself." He reached over and poured another shot in each glass, "To the United States Navy who rules the breadth and depth of all the Oceans of the world."

The American President issued a recorded statement condemning the use of nuclear weaponry, and warned Israel not to proceed with further strikes against her neighbors.

The President gave a press conference where he described the retaliation by Israel as a nuclear attack on Iran and her neighbors. He referred to it as "an unfortunate escalation of hostilities by the State of Israel". He issued an executive order that shut down humanitarian aid going from the US to Israel. Jewish aid organizations routed food, blankets, clothing, and medicine through Mexico and Canada to Israel. It was pouring into Ports of New York and Florida, loaded onto ships, and then running the US blockade to get sorely needed supplies into Haifa port in Northern Israel.

Arnaud received a coded message from the American Admiral of the Sixth Fleet, "The Presidential order to blockade the straits of Gibraltar and the coast of Israel, and not to allow humanitarian aid into Israel is not compatible with the spirit and philosophy of the United States of America. Please inform the UFN Council and your sources in the Israeli government that as an Admiral of the United States Navy, with a long history of rendering aid and assistance to victims of disasters around the world, the blockade will be in place for executive confirmation only, but will not deprive the Israeli nation of the assistance they require. We will also provide safe passage across the Atlantic Ocean, through the Straits of Gibraltar and protective convoy in the Mediterranean Sea through the 200 mile sovereignty zone of Israel. God bless Israel and keep her safe." Admiral Taylor, US Navy.

.

CHAPTER 16

The Brethren

During the turmoil of the second decade of the millennium, Dulcinea completed all of her advanced studies, and set in motion the necessary mechanisms to launch the Islamic Reformation.

She provided the UFN Council with documented proof of the sterilization of "infidels". Muslim extremist doctors and nurses volunteered at abortion clinics and worked in the obstetrics and gynecological departments of hospitals where they sterilized non-believers without their patients' knowledge or permission whenever the opportunity arose. The Brethren calculated that by the time anyone discovered what was happening it would be too late. Whenever they were questioned they would utilize the Islamic edict of *Taqiyya* (the commandment to lie and mislead any infidel in order to achieve the goals of Islamic jihad). They would threaten less enthusiastic Muslims with death if they exposed them or even if they did not take part in the process. The sterilization and abortion of infidels was holy jihad implementation. When a generation of child bearing age non-Muslim women and men were sterilized, that would end non-Muslim resistance. The plan would then focus on the coercion of moderate

Muslims who did not adhere to strict fundamentalist practices. It was simplistic and effective.

In Europe the time was right to reassert democratic leadership. The British natives were sick and tired of the Islamic take-over of their country. Open physical attacks by Muslims on British women and on female tourists visiting London became common place. Stones and mud were hurled at them and "dirty infidel whore" was yelled out repeatedly. Muslim neighborhoods in all European cities looked like the slums of many Muslim cities - dirty, unkempt, neglected, while full-grown men sat around smoking and playing backgammon and cursing infidels. Women were enslaved in these enclaves of Islam - persecuted without the protection of civil law.

Vigilante style reprisals were sporadically increasing in number and scope. Several mosques in London and Paris burned to the ground. Rallies were organized to oppose the rule of Sharia Law condoned and protected by the British Parliament. British lawmakers were bombarded by complaints and demands to address the invasion by Muslims. Whole sections of Prague that were strongholds of Muslim extremists were being targeted by Czechs who had fought for freedom from Soviet domination only to see the Muslims taking over their city.

The bodies of Islamic women, who displeased their families, were found dumped in alleys and gutters.

Civil unrest surfaced in France and in the Baltic countries of Eastern Europe. The cry escalated for the annihilation of all Muslims in a final effort to complete ethnic cleansing. A vigilante group calling itself The Soldiers of Charlemagne beheaded a Muslim rapist in Paris after the Sharia courts found him not guilty by reason of his right to Muta'a *(temporary marriage for sex with or without a woman's consent).*

It was becoming more dangerous for Muslim males to venture onto the streets after dark, and women's activist groups called for the castration of Muslim clerics who preached enslavement of women. The demonstrators carried banners in English that read: "FREE THE WOMEN OF ISLAM NOW", along the streets of Paris where five thousand angry women marched with their children. Long lines of Christian, Jewish and Muslim women marched together arm in arm – sisters linked mind-to-mind, heart-to-heart, by their shared belief that women were not created as slaves for men.

Well known prominent male and female politicians from America and Europe were strangely silent and non-responsive to these cries for freedom. The American Secretary of State laughed at American conservatives and their values, with Muslim heads of state, ridiculing them openly. She demonstrated her disdain for democratic discourse and cooperation. This did not go unnoticed in America, as she threw back her head and laughed out loud at American patriots. The liberal cause was losing ground and esteem. Each time that she revealed her disregard for the fate of Islamic women everywhere, the American public withdrew their support of the current regime in Washington.

It was evidence that the "seed" that Arnaud and the CFN had hoped would take root and grow, had taken hold. They had supported it in the press, on T.V., on talk radio, in popular songs and in rap music that depicted the evil servitude and subjugation of women and encouraged open opposition. Non-Muslims throughout Europe and Eastern Europe were actively protecting and giving sanctuary to Muslim women fleeing the wrath and retribution of their husbands, fathers, brothers – and even from their sons.

While all of these "pots" simmered around the world, the Council finalized their plans. Arnaud trembled at the scope of the mission. If the execution of the plan was not absolutely synchronized it would fail miserably, and those who were involved in it would be slaughtered.

Arnaud went over the list, briefing the members on each item in chronological order.

The time was swiftly approaching when the powerful Islamofascists could not be destroyed. Arnaud began having weekly meetings with Dulcinea and Brecken, including Latifa and Yehiye whenever it was convenient for them to attend. He became the liaison between the Council and Dulcinea and her supporters. Brecken beefed up Dulcinea's security with a dozen operatives assigned to that task around the clock.

In the midst of this monumental operation, Dulcinea decided it was important to pursue the publication of Dr. Morelli's cancer cure. She timed its worldwide release with the launching of the Islamic coup that would ignite the waiting revolutionary forces. Having acknowledged that she might not survive the revolution, Dulcinea prioritized her goals so that she would be able to achieve maximum results along a predetermined time line. This would allow a "Plan B" operation to seamlessly be interjected in the event of her death.

Dulcinea contacted her Egyptian friend, Gyasi Mobarik who made arrangements for her to meet with his father, the Chairman of the Egyptian National Cancer Institute in Cairo.

"This is absolutely unacceptable," Brecken said. "It'll be impossible to provide security through the airports, on the plane, and afterwards in Cairo."

"I'll be OK. It's best that I travel by myself. It'll draw less attention. I'll dress inconspicuously to blend in. If you can manage to carry on a facade here that indicates I'm busy studying and corresponding with my peers around the world – that should do the trick. They won't be looking for me inside an Arab country," Dulci reasoned.

"Oh ya! Sure! They'll arrest you the minute you step foot on their soil. They'll know it. One glance at your French passport will confirm it."

" I'll travel under an American passport that my friends at the State Department have arranged for me. My American name is Maria Fernando de la Silva. I'm zzza Hispanic Ameri-can! *Ole!* I'm on vacation from my job at the Mexico City American Embassy where I work as a translator. Si?"

"Oh my God," Brecken was laughing so loud that his coffee came spurting out of his nose. "Jesus Christ, Dulci. You crack me up. I have seen, what I thought was all sides of you, but MARIA FERNANDO – OLE!? Are you kidding me? You better tone that one down. Sounds like you need a fruit hat with bananas and a parrot! Gosh Dulci........ aren't we having enough fun around here?"

Dulci was on her way back to Paris less than a week later. She had made arrangements for the publication of Dr. Morelli's research, and successfully brokered an agreement between the Egyptian and Israeli researchers to complete the refinements, and establish safe protocols to validate the research. They would present the world with a genuine cure for cancer; without destroying the patient's immune system, and without toxic chemicals or radiation. This accomplishment alone was a monumental achievement. Dulcinea knew in her heart that whether the revolution succeeded or failed, this was something that only she could have pulled off. No one else had the perfect combination of intellect, negotiating skills, scientific knowledge, and the iron resolve to make this happen. She utilized this opportunity to cement important connections between the Minster of the Interior in Israel, and his Egyptian counterpart without the knowledge of the corrupt Egyptian President.

On her return to Paris she took her seat near the back of the plane. She laid her head against the backrest and rested her open right palm on her chest. She could feel her heart warmly thumping away within her breast as she took a deep satisfying breath. *You did good Safina,* she thought. She had almost forgotten *Safina* as she became immersed in her Dulcinea alias. She opened her left hand and with her right index finger she traced the Arabic letters of her true name, S a f i n a, onto her palm. She remembered who she was, where she was going in her life, and most importantly she rededicated herself to why she was going there. Feeling the letters spelled out on the palm of her hand was one of the tools she had adapted whenever she needed to lock something into her mind.

Dulcinea had made them an offer they could not refuse: rid the world of cancer, lock in a binding scientific research coalition of the oncology research teams of the Egyptian Institute for Cancer Research in Cairo and the Hadassah Cancer Research Department of the Hebrew University in Jerusalem.

She shared her vision with them and inspired them to come together for something greater than themselves and their national politics. Here was real justification for throwing down the offensive shams of international power struggles, and snatching up the opportunity to restore life and happiness to millions of cancer victims and their families. But most importantly she gave them the combined capability of funding research in the future. The revenues generated from the cure of cancer and subsequent vaccinations and nutrient supplements would enhance their capabilities. Israel and Egypt were uniquely equipped to provide these medicinal products to the entire world. She had supplied an International Patent that would not revert to the public domain. The Foundation would provide treatment for patients who could not pay. There would be plenty of revenue to support the prevention programs because the disease itself would be almost eradicated from the world. Being pragmatic, she had also ensured that each coalition member had control over one half of the process - and one could not go forward without the cooperation of the other.

Dulcinea picked up a magazine from the back pocket of the airplane seat in front of her. She hadn't seen a real paper magazine for years. She was surprised that in this age of electronic reading devices someone was still printing anything. It felt nice in her hands as she ran her fingers over the glossy paper of its colorful pages. She brought it up to her nose and smelled the combination of paper and ink. She turned the pages slowly. It was one of those free travel magazines with ads in the back for luggage and e-books. As she flipped through it to pass the time, her eye caught the title of a short story: JERUSA-LEM. She began to read it:

JERUSALEM

The road from Tel Aviv curves upwards, twisting this way and that way and doubling back on itself to reach its divine destination, the "Holy City". Jerusalem (*Yer u Shalom – they will see peace"*) is drenched in gold. As you ascend to the city the sunlight reflects on the ancient and the newly quarried, blocks of reddish pink granite and bright sandstone. They conspire to deck her out in gilded finery. It will stop your breath for a moment as you come around the curve in the road, and glimpse this spectacle - as though flinging open a window exposing a feast of visual decadence. She is a solid and reliable old lady, perched among the mountain tops, with her unique skyline of mosques, towers, balconies, electric lines, and television antennas. She almost always begins her day with fresh linens drying in her breezes, and puffy down comforters hanging over balconies and poking out over her windowsills, breathing the mountains' delicate brisk air. On overcast days the dark moisture filled clouds rest precariously on her roofs, charged with ions and heavy with the exciting scent of rain soon to be unleashed. Electric lights and candles can be seen glowing in her windows waiting for the torrential burst.

As the spring, and then summer come to pass, the sounds of the busy women who awaken the city each morning are heard. Pulling and pushing the children out of beds, and opening the wooden shutters to the chatter of the sparrows, the women hum throughout the city. Carts and donkeys, automobiles and their piercing horns build their volume gradually as Jerusalem stretches and yawns, and shakes out her cramped limbs from a night of slumber.

Jerusalem is a fat, but hardy old "broad" with good bones and tacky makeup. She is still there, in gaudy trappings with her dirty petticoats, which she tries to conceal.

When I was a child I labored up and down the hills of Jerusalem on my gear-less bicycle. Every downhill free ride that Jerusalem offered was extorted in twice the normal toll on its upward side. She tricks you with her pleasant breezes, and her evergreen trees into thinking it is, after all, not a hot Middle-Eastern sun beating down. She will suck the moisture from your hair and skin, drying you out, shriveling your body, and sapping your strength. Jerusalem, like Delilah, sneaks up on you unexpectedly, laying you low with her dry thin mountain air. If you survive, you learn her naughty tricks, and you come prepared.

Jerusalem, with all her golden stories, and international acclaim, is secretly a slovenly housekeeper. But she hides the dirt, and flaunts her new buildings and her fine public gardens with all types of roses and tulips, and designer horticulture, imported from Holland, along wide boulevards. If you know her well, you know where she hides her garbage, and in what massive heaps of disregard for the poor. She was more charming when she was uniformly dirty, like an old mountain woman should be – because she is old and doesn't have running water. It seemed more "fair". She is still beautiful, and so we forgive her, and remember her before the Six-Day War. The remnants of lost Jewish children remember the Western side of her, where they came to rest after the horrors of the death camps. She was more real then.

Jerusalem was smaller to us, because we lived in only half of the city. When we walked her streets we knew the vendors, and the bus drivers, and the beggars and the idiots who lived on her pot-holed streets, and sat on her crumbling curbs. We knew them all by name. There was Zazi who blew the harmonica in and out all day on just two notes. He did math problems in his head faster than any calculator, and we gave him coins for the entertainment. Someone said he was a camp survivor. A ragged man and his ragged lady lived somewhere by the open market, and one icy cold winter dawn they were found huddled together in death, and we mourned them, and came together to bury them with respect. The city is indifferent to us. No one kept track of how many thousands of beggars have quietly died on Jerusalem's ancient stone paths or on the hard concrete sidewalks of modern times. They are like the yellow hi-lights that we mark on our exceptionally good books, thinking what a wonderful turn of a phrase or what a superb painting with words, but then we never return to those pages again – not ever. We ate hot corn-on-the-cob from huge steaming vats along King David Street. We stopped at Zion Square in front of the old movie house, at the corner of Ben Yehuda Street (that isn't there anymore), where we bought cubes of cactus candy dipped in white powdered sugar, and we drank cold spring water out of brass cups attached to copper spigots with thin brass chains, and no one caught a disease from the cup – perhaps we all had the same germs – or because we didn't obsess about catching diseases from cups in those days. We didn't worry about cigarette smoke or cholesterol. We drank hot mint tea with three teaspoons of sugar, and dipped our jelly donuts in unpasteurized honey. We didn't drain the oil off of our meat, or remove the skin from savory spiced chicken, and we cooked over open fires to roast lamb until it was succulent and delicious without any fear of carcinogens. The wars and the terrorists' bombs made living immediate and void of analyses. We kissed passionately, and held back no portion of our hearts. Those sweet peaceful days between wars were cherished. We knew they were to be valued and remembered. We knew they were fleeting. We embraced them while they were in our grasp, and did not have later regrets that we let them pass without knowing, without noticing, without laughing out loud. We never had to say: "I wish I had paid more attention." Every minute of every day was grasped and squeezed, and every single drop of joy and laughter, love and friendship, was extracted from the passing time in full measure. Never has anyone truly lived life if they have not lived it after war.

Jerusalem was raped and plundered in ancient times, bombed and looted in modern times. Jerusalem endures those indecencies, and she resists and succeeds. Neon doesn't fit, and plastic domes are out of place. Somehow we know she is her own. We debate her fate, and we argue and kill for the sake of Jerusalem, She is not ours.

Jerusalem lifts her golden face to the clouds and to the stars, and we are allowed to stay a little while, and we are gone. Jerusalem will "be" as long as the earth "is". Only mortal mothers remember their dead children, and we are the children of the Holy City – the immortal Jerusalem…*"They will see peace."*

When Dulcinea finished reading the story she leaned back, closing the pages of the magazine and her eyes at the same time. She could see the streets of Jerusalem through the imagery of the writer. It was a different perspective. She tasted the sweet cactus candy and watched as the women of Jerusalem hung their fluffy comforters over the windowsills of the stone buildings. She thought of the truth of living to the fullest in the face of war and not dismissing any moment of friendship or love because it may be the last kiss or the last hug or the last glance from the eyes of someone you hold dear.

Dulcinea remembered her escape through the open market of Basra and the smell of freshly roasted lamb, and the squawking of the chickens cruelly tied upside down to sticks as their cries were not simply ignored – they were not heard. She often felt as though she were one of those pitiful unheard chickens that was intended for the slaughter but had by some miracle escaped from the market place and run into the fields where it lay low and hid, gathering an army of chickens that would storm the market and kill the beastly humans. The women of Islam were not heard – but she would make their voices unbearably loud!

"Mademoiselle, you must put your seat in an upright position and buckle your seatbelt. We are on approach to Charles De Gaul International Airport. Do you have anything to declare for customs? I have the forms if you need one."

"No, I have nothing to declare."

She pulled her seat upright and tightened her seatbelt. Running fingers through her hair she realized that she had been dreaming. The magazine was still on her lap and she deposited it back into the seat pocket in front of her. Then she pulled it back out, found the story JERUSALEM and did something she had never done before. She tore the two sheets of the story out of the magazine and quickly folded them in half and then in quarters and slipped them into her purse. She would share the story with Vivian. She remembered that Vivian told her she worked in Jerusalem at a summer job while she was on sabbatical from teaching in Holland. Vivian actually had a friend in the United States whom she had met in Jerusalem working at the same Hotel Services Office. *She will enjoy this story,* Dulcinea thought. She put the mutilated magazine back into the pocket of the seat.

The airplane landed with a small bounce and taxied a short distance to the terminal. It rolled to a jerky stop and the passengers began to prepare to disembark. Always on alert, Dulcinea grasped her tiny decorative shabria that hung as jewelry from a cord around her neck. Looking around at the passengers in her vicinity she did not detect anything suspicious. It was good to be home in Paris. She hadn't realized until that moment that she actually felt "at home" in Paris. She missed Brecken – he was her "rock" and the person she could count on no matter what happened.

Brecken was waiting for her in Terminal I, the International Terminal at CDG Airport. She came through customs from the baggage claim area. She ran to him and threw her arms around his neck. She was so happy to see him. He hugged her tightly and kissed the top of her head. "Hey girl. I guess you had a stressful trip huh? I can't remember the last time someone was that happy to see me!"

"I had a great trip; a successful trip. I am happy to see you because you are my best friend." She grasped his hand as they walked to the baggage carousel. When she looked over at him their eyes met. For a moment she wanted to turn and kiss him.

Suddenly she was almost knocked to the ground by a large man in a dark blue shirt and pants, pushing a luggage cart like the ones the skycaps use, piled high with a dozen large brown identical suitcases. His bald head glistened with sweat and she noticed that his eyes kept moving back and forth.

"Oh, my God! Are you OK? I am sorry. I never saw you. I was trying to keep all these suitcases balanced on the cart and ………"

"*Qui s'excuse, s'accuse*………(he who excuses himself, accuses himself)," Brecken shouted.

The man's eyes almost leaped out of their sockets as he looked past Dulcinea. She turned to follow his gaze and there was Brecken standing with his gun drawn and aimed at the man. He stood with his feet apart and both hands on the 45 automatic aimed at the man's chest. His face was set in stone and his blue gray eyes drilled into the man. They were as cold as Siberian crystals.

"Do not shoot! Do not shoot Monsieur! I did not mean to hurt any persons. My childrens are waiting for me on the other side of the security. I was trying to go to them as fast as I could. There is no one to watch them. See! Look, back of you – those two childrens on the other side of the glass. Go ahead Monsieur – look back of you." His Arabic accent hung awkwardly on his sketchy French.

Brecken's eyes peered into Dulcinea's. She made a very slight negative side to side movement of her eyes. There were two kids, a small boy about 2 years old and a girl around 5, but a woman joined them and picked up the small boy. She took the girl's hand and led her away from the security glass. Some woman a few meters behind Safina started screaming when she saw Brecken holding the gun, and then everyone was running away from them.

"Lie down on the floor and spread out your arms and your legs now! I'll count to three and then I'm going to shoot you. One, Two, Thr............."

The big man dropped to the ground and spread himself wide on his stomach. Brecken made a loud whistle and out of nowhere there was Rémi trotting toward the man and then stopping with his huge jowls hanging over the back of the man's exposed neck. "Hold him." Brecken commanded the dog. Brecken released the trigger and returned the automatic to the leather shoulder holster under his jacket. He walked over to the spread-eagled fat man, and removed a number of weapons from the man's pockets, and from a calf holster. He laid them gently on the floor, careful not to smear any prints on the guns. "If you make any moves, the dog will bite through your neck and you will bleed to death."

Dulcinea only now released her death grip on the small shabria hanging from her neck. "Who are you?" She forced the question from between her clenched teeth.

"The wrath of Allah. I am the slayer of infidels on Earth – a martyr of the holy cause, Jihad!" he replied in Arabic.

"Well Mr. Jihad, where is your bomb? Because you son of a bitch, if you have a bomb, you are going to die as dog food pâté." Brecken said in perfect sophisticated Egyptian dialect.

There was silence as a few by-standers watched from afar. Half a dozen French policemen cautiously approached, with their silly emasculating non-lethal stun guns drawn. Brecken flashed his badge at them. He spoke loudly and clearly in French, "I am a licensed body guard. This man attacked my client. He is a terrorist in the Islamic Brethren, taking Sharia revenge against a victimized woman who escaped her rapist husband. The dog is a licensed guard dog, fully trained and certified. He will not attack without my command. Stand down."

The gendarme leading the group relaxed, and motioned to the others. They put their stun guns away. The French policeman walked over to the dog and said, "Good job Rémi, we trained you well!" He patted the big dog's head. "I recognized him from the black spot on the back of his ear." He grinned at Brecken.

"Yes, Jacque Montegue, the police-dog trainer. I remember you well. Yes, he is a wonderful dog, even better than we hoped for."

The terrorist groaned and Rémi snarled in response. Perspiration dripped off the fat man's neck forming a small circular pool on the cool concrete floor. "Roll over slowly when I command the dog to back off." Brecken ordered.

The man slowly rolled over as Rémi backed up a few feet. The dog was clearly distrustful, and did not seem to readily agree that this threat was contained. As the man rolled toward his left side he slowly moved his right hand across his exposed chest and into the left inside of his jacket. As he continued to roll more quickly, his hand came out of the inside breast pocket holding a small black cell phone. Before he could flip it open, Rémi bit down hard on his arm causing him to drop the cell phone. At the same time the French gendarme pulled his 9 mm SP-2022 out of his holster and fired one round into the man's head. The terrorist died immediately.

"Why would he risk death to retrieve a cell phone? His mission was not completed," Jacque Montegue said. As he peered at the dead man he noticed the cell phone lying next to the body. Brecken saw it at the same time and yelled out loud. "Wait a minute, careful Jacque! Call your bomb squad in here, and clear out this building immediately!" Brecken grabbed Dulcinea's hand and dragged her out of the building as fast as humanly possible. Rémi followed closely at their heels. He seemed glad to rid himself of this place. The French gendarmes were herding some stragglers out of the building and shouting "*Bombe! Bombe!*" People were running in all directions, almost reaching the exits.

When they moved through the doors of the terminal building Brecken glanced back through the double doors, as he tugged on Dulcinea's arm trying to pull her along faster. A deafening explosion sent them flying across the walkway through the air like rag dolls. Brecken landed on top of Dulcinea in the middle of the street. He was knocked out from the blast for a few minutes. He awoke coughing as he attempted to clear his throat and mouth of the acrid black dust. "Dulci, where are you?" Then he realized he was partially lying on top of her body. He tried to crawl off of her but he wasn't able to get his legs to work. *Am I paralyzed? Is she even alive?* Tears ran through the soot on his face. He felt nauseous and afraid. Without his legs, his physical strength, his mental stamina, he was no good to Dulcinea or himself. He closed his eyes and cleared his mind of the fear that gripped his heart. *Dear God, I have nothing more here – I need your help. I need to get on my feet and move Dulci.* He pulled his body forward slowly, inch by inch.

As Brecken raised his body up on one elbow and looked out through the haze of smoke and dust he could make out what appeared to be bodies, strewn in a grotesque twisted manner as though they were part of a choreographed futuristic dance decrying the end of all things beautiful. Bloody body parts were haphazardly scattered among the carnage. A baby was screaming in the clutched arms of its mother lying on the ground just 10 meters from where Brecken and Safina had been deposited by the blast. A tall thin woman was shuffling around in the smoke as though sleepwalking, holding her severed left hand in her right hand that was still attached to her arm. She kept calling out, "Andre, Andre, where did you go? Andre, come to Mama." She was covered with blood.

Sirens blared and alarms went off all over the airport and sur- rounding area. Smoke poured out the now-glassless doors and escaped up through a gigantic gapping hole near the ceiling on one side of the partially collapsed terminal building. The chaos was worse than unimaginable – it seemed the people were locked into a collec- tive nightmare. Then ominous, loud "crunching and popping" sounds could be heard all around them as layer upon layer of the 7 tiered cake-like terminal imploded upon itself. Great black clouds of dust and smoke rose high into the air, bellowing up and out into the street. One huge crash after another shook the ground as each layer gave way and came crushing down on the one below it. Acrid dust–laden smoke rapidly engulfed the scene.

Brecken felt a surge of energy throughout his body. Maybe it was adrenaline or maybe it was an answer to his prayer. He managed to pull himself up to his feet and to drag Dulci, who was unconscious. He wrapped his one good arm around her under her arms, tugging her dead weight all the way across the street to the parking structure before the final layers of the terminal collapsed. He got both of them into one of the exit ticket booths and closed the narrow door and glass window behind them just as a second blast hit. He was barely inside with her when a wall of thick sooty gray air pummeled the booth, shaking it so hard that he was almost positive it would be ripped from its cement pad. The yellow barrier arm that kept people from exiting before paying, came flying from in front of them almost skewering the booth's window. It missed them by a hair. Brecken had covered his face while he dropped Dulcinea down onto the floor and used his own body as a protective shield.

As soon as the explosions stopped Brecken lifted her onto his shoulder and carried Dulci to the grassy area between the terminal and the hanger as far from the bellowing smoke as possible. Triage appeared to be setting up there. So far it was just a row of survivors and someone had put some coats and blankets over the injured to keep them warm until the paramedics could attend to them.

Brecken took off his jacket and put it over Dulci, tucking the edge of it under her chin. He grabbed a loose singed cushion that was lying near by and shoved it under her feet, and put her head flat on the ground. She looked "shocky" to him. He checked her pulse. Her gums were white, and he pulled down her lower lid and the color was also too pale. Her breathing was shallow. She was probably bleeding internally. Dulcinea's condition was fast becoming critical. Brecken was scared. He thought she might die in front of his eyes. How would he bear such a loss? He tried to focus on what he could do to get help for her.

Dulcinea opened her eyes and looked into Brecken's face. He was covered in soot. A gaping laceration on his forehead oozed blood that slid down the ridge between his eyes. It dripped off the end of his nose in muddy red drops. Ambulances, medics, and firemen were all around them. Someone bandaged Dulcinea's leg; she felt no pain, as long as she focused on Brecken's eyes she was able to hang on to consciousness. It was strangely quiet – and she realized that she could hear nothing – not even her own breathing! "Brecken, I can't hear anything." She clawed frantically at his arm. "I can't hear, I can't hear – Nothing, nothing at all!" She watched his lips moving and he stroked her cheek and forehead, his lips were moving, but no sound came out of his mouth.

Brecken's demeanor was that of strength and focus. His intensive Marine training held him together, and allowed him to prioritize in the face of disaster. He gently squeezed her hand. She was possibly the most important individual in the world but all he could think of was how important she was to him. He lifted her up into his arms. Dulcinea was wounded and broken. She couldn't hear him. Brecken looked up into the smoke filled sky, "Thank you God, thank you for saving us."

There were bodies lying on the cement in front of what was left of the terminal. Airport ambulances were being shuttled from the terminal to the hanger. Two EC145 medi-vac helicopters of the *Gendarmerie Nationale* aerial units could be seen on approach to the scene. Their festive red and yellow markings lent a carnival atmosphere to the wreckage that was out of place with the horror on the ground. Emergency personnel and equipment were being diverted from the other parts of the airport to Terminal I. Brecken sneered as the helicopters approached, "They sent two mosquitoes to handle a hemorrhage. They have no clue as to what happened here today."

As the helicopters neared the Terminal, one of them circled the area briefly. "*Oui Capitaine, le dommage - extensif.*" The helicopter pilot was describing the scene in detail via radio to the Airport Security

Officer. "There is a collapse throughout terminal 1, and the entire structure has slid to one side of the site pad. As it collapsed the upper levels of the terminal spilled onto the Eastern apron crushing at least two DC10's and a Jumbo 747 that were positioned on the eastern ramps. They were fully fueled and ready for departure just minutes before the blast. It looks like they exploded upon impact. The second 747 that was positioned parallel to the other gates on the Eastern apron, but father down the ramp line from the initial collapse, taxied away from the terminal. I can see it almost at the central runway now. That plane must be locked onto the automated evacuation sequence. A number of service vehicles in the vicinity of the blast are over-turned. I must speculate that passengers on board the DC10 planes, and the affected Jumbo Jet, were incinerated. There is no chance that anyone in or near those planes could have survived. This is a large chaotic crime scene *Captaine*."

Brecken held Dulci tight against his body trying to keep her warm. He wrapped her in his jacket as best he could. She was turn-ing blue and drifting in and out of consciousness. He began to rock Dulcinea in his arms. He was caught up in a reflexive survival mode. "You'll be alright honey, you're going to be alright. Just be still and wait for an ambulance. I'm going with you to the hospital." Brecken mouthed the words slowly to her – until he saw comprehension in her eyes, "I am not leaving you. Understand? I am never leaving you."

Huge black vans pulled up to the terminal and deposited armed policemen equipped with guns this time – not the toy stun guns that were politically correct – this time they had the real thing.

"*Messieurs*, she is going to need an MRI to rule out internal bleeding. Her blood pressure is low and respiration is shallow. What-ever you do, keep her awake until we can transport her. *Oui?*" The EMT said, his voice carying above the din of their surroundings. He motioned to the airport personnel who were moving wounded victims on stretchers to the transport area, pointed at Dulcinea, and he made a large circular motion with his arm over his head that obviously meant she was to be "*medi-vaced*" by helicopter to the hospital as soon as possible. He slapped an oxygen mask on her face and handed Brecken the small canister attached to it. Just keep this on her until you are inside the helicopter!

"*Merci,*" Brecken mouthed as he cradled Dulcinea. He watched the young man close his medical bag and run to the next victim lying nearby. He swallowed hard as the burning bitterness of bile rose into his throat.

Terminal 1 was the International Terminal of the airport. It was built to resemble the layers of a round cake. The upper levels of the multi level circular terminal had collapsed upon the bottom level where baggage claim, restaurants, and shopping were housed. Only a third of the circle had come down but the surviving structure was compromised, and could collapse at any moment. With over 50,000 people per day coming and going from the Charles De Gaulle Airport, it was the worst terrorist attack since the Twin Towers in New York City.

Planes damaged by the blast were checked for victims and towed to a holding area near the maintenance terminal. Their fuel was siphoned into empty undamaged tankers. Dozens of airport ground crews were called in by emergency pager, and took their positions quickly. Processed damaged aircraft were towed to the aprons surrounding the maintenance terminal, and parked there. Huge billowing clouds of flame retardant foam shot out of numerous cannons enveloping the damaged aircraft before they might burst into flames. The Paris airport was remarkably well-prepared and the workers were properly trained in emergency procedures. Their equipment was superior and over-all they were dealing with the disaster much better than anyone could have anticipated.

As each undamaged plane was refueled it was instructed to take off, and await further instructions when airborne. The pilots were unaware of their diversionary destinations until they were actually in the air. Communication devices designated for emergency use were activated on all airplanes worldwide with the exception of planes serving Islamic states.

The devices were installed in all planes during their manufacturing process, but those designated for, or sold to, Islamic airlines were not operational without UFN authorized activation signals from Satellite link-ups. They were located in a hidden panel of the cockpit and only opened by remote command from the ENCT (Emergency Nerve Center Transmission). Pilots and ENCT were able to communicate directly through an ocular implant in the pilots' ear. The pilots themselves were unaware of this feature. When they received their implants they were told that it was designed to accelerate their training. Each pilot had a unique code that was randomly assigned to him by computer on each flight and transmitted to his ocular implant immediately after takeoff. The advantage of this system was that no terrorist could commandeer the aircraft.

If the pilot were disabled or killed the airplane would revert to automatic pilot mode and there was no device to return it to manual control without ENCT command. Only the personal code of the live pilot could access the ENCT channel. The pilot could activate it or a certified airport controller could activate it under the direction of the Airport Security Officer. Islamic pilots were excluded from this feature in the program due to the security risks involved. The consensus at the highest security levels was that Islamic pilots were loyal to the Islamic principles of jihad. The top echelon CIA's ENCT program was disclosed on a "need-to-know basis".

The signals back and forth from aircraft were satellite based relays bounced off signal amplifiers on the lunar surface. The ENCT stations were far out in space, beyond enemy detection. Unsung American Astronauts/Marines had given their lives on one-way missions to build the Star Wars Network. The ENCT stations and missile defense system were well protected by massive galactic laser cannons on the moon, and strategically placed clusters of more conventional space nuclear missile launchers. Some people believed that JFK wanted to go to the moon merely to boast that Americans made it there first! That was an excellent cover story. The territorial disputes on the lunar surface were primarily between the Americans and the Japanese. Japan was delusional if they thought for a moment that the US would acquiesce.

"Those who control the moon, control the earth."

NASA Internal Command Memorandum

While the world watched the dramatic "one great step for mankind" played out on worldwide TV media, major construction was going on out of camera shot.

Airports in Hamburg, Los Angeles, Montreal, Mexico City, Las Vegas, and Prague all blew up at precisely the same time as the Charles de Gaulle airport. Their encounter with the fat terrorist in the airport terminal was a coincidence, and not a targeted attack on Dulcinea. The time table for the world launch of Sarajevo II had just been drastically accelerated.

Brecken was finally able to get Dulcinea onto a stretcher and carried over to a waiting helicopter for evacuation to a hospital. Her face was pale gray and her lips were blue. He wiped at his eyes with the back of his sleeve. His jaw had been clenched so tightly that his teeth hurt.

"*Monsieur*, take this and drink. You look like you may collapse," said the nurse on board the helicopter. "Don't *vorry* so much *Monsieur*, she *vill* be fine. See – I give her glucose and at *l'hôspital* they do MRI and stop bleeding. They give plasma and *voila*! -- she is all better! You are strong now – *Oui? N'est-ce pas?*" She gave him a small bottle of orange juice, cleaned his head wound with some disinfectant, and put a temporary bandage around his head. "You *vill* need some stitches Monsieur. *Arriver à l'hôspital* in 5 minute. What is her name?"

Brecken knew that she was traveling under an American passport issued to Maria Fernando de la Silva. But he was reluctant to use that name – because he could not find any passport, purse, briefcase or shred of evidence to support that. "She is Dulcinea Morelli. She is a guest of Ambassador Arnaud Fournier and his family. I am her personal assistant, Brecken Petersen."

"You *vill* complete more papers at *l'hospital* . Do you know her blood type?"

"Yes. That I know. We were just talking about that last week and she told me she is type O positive."

The French nurse filled out a plastic band and fastened it to Dulcinea's wrist. "Is she allergic to anything?"

"No. I don't think she is. Anyway, she never told me and I've known her for several years." His cell phone began to ring and he reached into his pocket to retrieve it. For some reason he was surprised that it still worked. His head was pounding and the swelling of his face made it difficult to speak.

The man on the other end of the line was an official of some sort at the airport. "We have found a very large dog lying on the ground near the collapsed terminal. He is critically injured. When we scanned him, your name and number came up from his micro chip. Do you want us to go ahead and put him down, or do you want to have him transferred to a veterinarian hospital? He is most probably fatally injured."

Brecken clutched at his chest as though his heart had turned over. He had forgotten about Rémi. "Please transfer him to the emergency veterinarian hospital in the area. I'll come there as soon as I can. I'm in route to the Saint-Antoene University Hospital in Paris with a seriously injured friend. *Merci monsieur* for attending to my dog. He is *en famille* (a family member) and we will spare no expense to attend to his wounds."

Arnaud, Madelyn, and Brecken waited outside the surgery wing of Saint-Antoene Hospital. Brecken had called the Fourniers as soon as the ambulance arrived there.

The surgeon came out to speak with them. He was pessimistic about her prognosis, "She has lost a tremendous amount of blood, and it was over an hour before she was transported to the hospital and another forty-five minutes before she was sent to the O.R. There is a large wound from a metal fragment that entered from her lower back in an upward trajectory. The MRI shows that it lodged in her left lung causing it to collapse. The fragment passed through her spleen, almost slicing it in half resulting in massive bleeding into her abdominal cavity. There are several broken ribs and her left arm and left leg are fractured. Ms. Morelli has suffered a severe concussion and an auditory disruption. This is just what we know about so far - and we will not be able to ascertain the full extent of her injuries until after the surgery, and not until she regains full consciousness. She is being prepped right now."

"She couldn't hear anything when she regained consciousness at the airport. It didn't look like she couldn't understand – it looked like she was stone deaf. I heard her say that she couldn't hear anything. If her ear drums aren't broken, why can't she hear?" Brecken asked.

The surgeon reached out and grasped Brecken's arm. "We believe she can physically hear but her brain may be unable to register or decipher the auditory input. We hope that if Ms. Morelli survives the surgery, her hearing loss will be temporary. We have not detected any swelling of her brain and we know she received adequate oxygen at the site of the explosion, it is possible that there is no permanent brain damage. Her ear drums are not broken, however there could be damage to the nerves, which is difficult to assess at this point." The surgeon spoke quickly, " I'm sorry but I have to get back to the OR and scrub in." He turned and almost ran down the corridor and through the automatic doors of the OR.

Madeleine was teary eyed as she leaned into Arnaud for support, "*Mon Dieu*, I do not believe I shall stand this much longer. It seems to me that we have been waiting here for days. That poor sweet child! How could such a thing happen? We should have never let her go off to Rome by herself. Oh, Arnaud, why did we do that? Why?" She wrung her hands repeatedly until they were red and tender from her administrations.

"Settle down Madeleine, *mon cheri*, she will be alright. Dulci is a fighter *extraordinaire*. I know of no one else with more resolve, more perseverance, or more dedication to her mission. You need to have faith." He took out his handkerchief and gently dabbed her cheek, then handed it to her. "Wipe your tears, and let's see your courageous smile. Dulci would want you to be strong and fearless – for her sake."

Brecken paced up and down the long corridor. He vacillated between cursing God to pleading with God: *I don't care if you're Allah, God, Buddha, or Elohim. Just make sure she lives, and has all of her faculties.*

Time passed painfully slow in the waiting room and the three of them paced, and cried, and prayed. The heart-piercing question, the one they dare not let escape from their lips, hung in the air in the void created by "not knowing" how to ask the question. Would Dulcinea survive?

Hundreds of patients were steadily being fed into the ER system, and yet the staff maintained their systematic approach and patience. Every doctor and physician's assistant in Paris had been recalled to the hospitals in the area. The parking lots and the corridors were filled with families and friends waiting for word of their loved ones or trying to locate those who were still unaccounted for.

Brecken paced up and down the hospital corridor with his cell phone pressed against his ear, "*Oui*. He is a large brown Mastiff with a black dot on the back of his right ear. His micro chip number is 20709A4638. " There was a pause and Brecken stopped pacing and stood perfectly still. "Are you sure? I will be there as soon as I can – probably in a few days, to make arrangements. *Merci, Merci*." Brecken's eyes were wet and glossy, and his voice quivered in his throat as he turned to speak with Arnaud and Madeleine. "I have sad news that I wish I didn't have to tell you. But, I have no choice. You need to know that Rémi passed away on the operating table 15 minutes ago. The veterinarian surgeons were unable to save him."

Brecken sat down and held his face in his hands. He was exhausted, drained emotionally and physically. He had trained Rémi from a pup of six months. They had worked so closely together that a unique bond had developed between them. The dog was more than a security measure. He was Brecken's friend and a loyal protector. Brecken's mind raced: *Is this a prelude to Dulci's fate? Will I lose both of them?*

Madeleine stood up and walked over to Brecken, sitting down next to him on the sofa. She put her arms around him and hugged him closely. She seemed to need this physical comforting as much as Brecken. "He was a fine dog and brave to the end. Rémi's life was filled with purpose and love. We will miss him," she said quietly. Brecken sobbed into his hands as his despair reached an unsustainable level, and he could no longer contain it within himself.

They waited. They waited to hear if Dulcinea would join Rémi or stay with them in this life. The hours crept on into the night; far longer than the doctors had anticipated. Finally the surgeon came out. His look was guarded and reserved, "Dulcinea has survived the surgery. She received massive amounts of blood. We were forced to remove her spleen and a section of her liver. We found more metal fragments in the pelvic area and we had no choice but to perform a partial hysterectomy. I left the ovaries.......she's a young woman, and they were undamaged. We set the fractures, putting several pins in her leg which was badly shattered. The ribs will heal on their own. We did manage to save the collapsed lung which is holding together quite well. I hope we got everything but there was no time to recheck or explore. I needed to get out before her vital organs began to shut down. Her blood pressure was "thready" and unstable. She also had some difficulty maintaining consistent body temperature.

I must warn you that this is one of the most extensive and surgically challenging operations we have performed in this hospital. I chose not to ventilate her because in her weakened condition intubation carries more risk for infection than she could tolerate. We won't know the outcome for at least a few days, if she survives that long. There is nothing more we can do. Although we will monitor her, and provide necessary support, she is now in God's hands, and her prognosis also rests on the strength of Dulcinea's innate will to live."

Exhausted by the stress of the day's events and emotionally devastated by the strong possibility of Dulcinea's impending death, and the loss of Rémi, Brecken's knees almost gave out on him. As he struggled to stay upright he felt the hands of Arnaud supporting him from behind. Arnaud placed his arms under each of Brecken's elbows and gently pulled him toward an armchair, Brecken swayed slightly to one side and found Madeleine catching him on that side and helping Arnaud lower him into the chair. These were his surrogate parents. Their compassion enveloped him. He closed his eyes and slept in the chair - a silent stoic slumber where his body retreated because the tangible world of consciousness was far too difficult to comprehend.

Granules of sea salt lightly grazed Safina's cheeks, and her eyes squinted from the brightness of the orange sun ball which perched expectantly upon the vast blueness of the sea. Here, in this reality she was Safina – not her assumed identity of Dulcinea.

The black horse trotted next to her. Nomad's big shiny hooves cut into the wet sand at the edge of the froth, as the water receded back into the icy coldness of its beginning. He ran back and forth and circled around her as she moved along the beach. He came to stand in front of her, blocking her path, and blowing his hot breath above her head. Safina raised one palm with her fingers stretched upward to brush away the splatters of wet sand from his long coal black mane that spilled onto his forehead. Her fingers combed the thick black strands. She smelled his aroma of pine mixed with the damp saltiness of the Mediterranean. The wild phantom horse, and a young woman of exceptional valor, who must decide to live in real time, or in this pleasant alternate existence of what might be – something? What? They stood together this way, with Nomad's head slightly cocked to one side. His great black eyes looked through her and into her heart. *Is it a vivid dream or a parallel universe?* She didn't have the answer. Nomad shook his head, spraying a shower of salt water over her, and she felt his power infusing her with energy.

This was the famous "Lebanese Riviera" of Lebanon's coast before the wars, before the destruction of that country. Safina didn't know how she recognized this place that she had never visited – but she was sure about it. As she peered ahead to the empty expanse of rocky beach hundreds of meters in front of her, she saw a large dog frolicking with a man along the water line. The man was throwing a piece of drift wood which the dog retrieved again and again. They seemed oddly familiar to her, yet she couldn't see the man's features from this distance. He moved in a comfortable easy way that made the game appear effortless for him. The dog was more cumbersome and lumbering in its gait. She thought the dog must be a more serious creature than this game of "fetch" represented.

"Rémi, Come back Rémi, bring the stick here!" Brecken called to the big brown dog. Safina could barely make out his words.

She grinned. It was Brecken and Rémi! She was so glad to see them both again. Safina ran toward them, but no matter how hard or fast she ran they remained a set distance from her. Before long she was gasping for air and her muscles were sore. She had no choice but to stop. *Why do they move away from me?* She thought to herself. She sat down on the beach and cried. It wasn't fair. She just wanted to be with them. As she turned to call Nomad to her she saw his long thick tail flowing in the wind as he ran high up on a ridge looking down on the beach. The big dog stood next to Nomad, regally surveying the beach front. Safina could see a child perched upon the horse's back and clinging to his thick mane as her bare legs clutched the sides of the stallion. She had long black hair falling off of her shoulders and reaching down to her waist. She was laughing and calling out to Remi, "Yella, yella, let's go now, let's go quickly."

Nomad ignored Safina's beckoning. He turned and trotted the length of the ridge with the young girl on his back and the dog running along beside them. Safina wanted to feel Brecken's strong arms around her, and to have the reassurance of Rémi's constant vigilance. She had never become close to Rémi, but she knew he would give his life to protect her. Rémi was a soldier in the Revolutionary Army. When he wasn't eating or sleeping, he stood to post. "He knows what he is," she had told Brecken on more than one occasion, "....and he is not merely a dog."

"Come back to me, Dulcinea. Come back to me." She could hear Brecken screaming at her from far behind, as she walked in the opposite direction, toward a bright glowing sphere of illumination that she could see far down the shoreline. The brightness of it had a magnetic quality. She was compelled to keep moving in that direction. But, the unrelenting and demanding screams from behind her began to annoy her and distract her from her progress toward something she knew would take away her pain and indecision. She saw Nomad far down the beach, drawing her along with him to that harmonious, soothing destination. The girl was nowhere to be seen – no longer seated on the horse's back. Brecken would not be quiet, "Come back to me Dulci, I love you."

I wish he would just go away and leave me here. I need to get to that place where the light is waiting for me. Why is he calling me over and over? Why doesn't he just go back without me? I don't want to be there anymore..........It's peaceful here. She kept walking, and then she heard the voice of a child crying out to her, "Mama, Mama, come back........don't leave me. I'm so afraid.....Mama, Mama." Remi stood in front of her and would not let her move farther down the beach.

As Dulcinea turned around to see why the child was calling her "Mama", and to tell Brecken to leave, she opened her eyes and found herself lying in a bed, and Brecken was sprawled in a chair next to the bed, asleep.

It was the third day of the bedside vigil, Brecken was slumped in a chair by Dulcinea's bed, sound asleep. They had been through half a dozen code blues, and his hand was stuck inside his wrinkled coat jacket clutching his automatic just in case........ and his other hand lay placid upon his thigh in easy reach of his leg holster firearm if he needed more gun power. Despite repetitive admonitions by Arnaud and Madeleine, he had refused to leave the hospital. Madeleine brought some personal items to him from home, "You need to keep your strength, and I know you don't want Dulci to wake up and see a scary wretch standing over her bed. She has suffered enough." He cleaned himself up in the small bathroom connected to her room – and then fell asleep again in the chair.

Dulcinea laid there contemplating this unusual image of Brecken. He was curled to one side with his head resting awkwardly on his shoulder. His breathing was rough and shallow. Brecken, the "stepped-out-of-a-band-box" parade-field Marine, looked disheveled, vulnerable and exhausted. She took it all in while she watched him intently. Then she called to him, "Colonel Petersen, what's up with you?"

Brecken's eyes opened and it took a moment for them to focus on her face. He grinned, "You're back! You're back! Thank God."

"How long have I been here?" she smiled weakly at him.

Brecken moved close to her. He reached down and took her hand in his. He leaned over her and brought his face close to her face, "Three days." His eyes showed his immense relief. He kissed her forehead before he sat down on the side of the bed, and pulled her hand up to his lips and kissed each finger tip, "Hey there sleepy head. Where did you go? I think I dreamed of you on the beach. Rémi was there, and a big black horse walked around you. Did you invade my dreams? Did you and your horse come to see Rémi and me?"

Dulcinea felt the wave of his love passing through her, around her, saturating every fiber of her being. She knew the absolute unbending safe haven he offered to her, without chains attached. Brecken's soul was simple, and flat open for her to see all of its creases and wrinkles and the flaws that made it genuine. His bond with her was sharply in focus, with nothing imagined or hoped for; no frayed or tattered margins, muted or diffused. There were no questions to ask, no confirmations to extract. His love was not anchored in physical fulfillment or chemical attraction. Brecken was bound to her with all of his heart and mind, and she was alive because he had willed her to live if she chose to come back to him or not. Only a soul mate could have retrieved her from the Lebanese beach of another Universe, and convinced the powerful spirit of Nomad to walk away from her and to allow her safe passage through the barriers of that existence to complete her mission in this one. Only Brecken could have commanded Remi to force her back to him from across the galaxies.

She looked directly into his eyes and straight into his being as no one else would ever do. "Listen to my heart Brecken, as I will only say this once to you. I dream without analysis. I dream without explanations. I dream of all that is improbable, impossible, and unbelievable. We will dream and we will awake, and this world is improved because of it. You and I must believe in our dreams. Without the dreams of sentient beings there is no physical existence throughout all the Universes we inhabit. It is our belief that endows us with substance and purpose – nothing more."

Dulcinea whispered into Brecken's ear, "I love you. That is where I was, looking for you and wanting you to be with me on that beach. What I have told you is true and you should accept it as truth. Rémi has passed. I saw him there with Nomad by the sea, where he left your side. When I couldn't hold onto your image – and I was being pulled into another portal, Remi stood in my path and forced me back to you. He is happy and free. He was a good soldier of the revolution. I shall miss him and I shall cry that he is gone from my existence here." Her salty tears traveled from the outward corners of her eyes and down each side of her head as she lie flat on her back. She smiled because her tears were the gift of her creator, and she was released from her vow made in Basra, to never cry again because no one was listening, not even herself. She cried for Safina, the tormented child bride, and for all the daughters of Islam. She was ready for the battle; ready to lead them through the ages and into a brighter future.

Despite the IV hook-ups and heart monitoring wires, and the dangling oxygen tube, Brecken scooped her up into his arms and held her tightly against his chest where his heart beat. "You and I are a force upon this world, in this time, in THIS Universe. We'll command the tides of revolution and one day we'll fall weary, and we shall lie down together. I'll wait for that day, no matter how far into the future. Until that time we can't rest. You have your mission and I have my solemn oath to protect you. Keep our love safe within the recesses of your heart Dulci."

Dulcinea summoned all of her strength as she reached up around his neck and placed a kiss upon his lips.

CHAPTER 17

The Reformation

Three months after the airport disaster, Dulcinea had recovered from her surgery and regained her energy enough to go home. Brecken was her physical therapy/trainer for the rehabilitation routine. The doctors estimated a six-month recovery period to regain full strength and stamina. During this time she wrote two books.

With Arnaud's recommendations Dulcinea set up a Board of Directors for the Luigi Morelli Foundation. It was comprised of people who she knew to be ethical. There were key international scientists, and retired CEO's of major corporations and financial institutions. Some members had been besmirched and displaced by the current batch of world dictators, and pseudo-dictators who functioned under questionable legitimacy. They were committed to the success of the Luigi Morelli Foundation Project.

"It is done." she declared to Vivian. "This stage of my plan is complete. Now we will advance to the next level."

Dulci had been on the phone all morning, working out the intricate details of the revolutionary project. She paced back and forth from one end of the library to the other, clutching the cell phone in her hand. Dulci stopped at the large table where books could be spread out for research. She laid the "smart phone" in the middle of the cleared surface of the table and pushed the speaker button. "The carnage of retribution has begun – how can the UFN Council delay the revolution any longer?" She leaned over the tiny phone – and studied it carefully. It was a universal symbol of modern technology. "Disconnect!" The red LCD light was extinguished by the voice activated command.

Vivian hung up on her end. She held her breath as long as she could, then she exhaled in one long breath through pursed lips. Vivian knew that it wasn't unusual for Dulcinea to be hostile toward the telephone. She had smashed several telephones within earshot of Vivian. Dulci had thrown them at the wall – and Gerard had retrieved them and calmly brought them back to her – sitting very straight and dignified in front of her with the cracked telephone held firmly between his teeth. Even Dulci had laughed when she told Vivian about the dogs' reaction to her outbursts, "Rémi is such an anchor of sanity – he's the 'straight man', and Gerárd always plays the comic. He assumes that if I'm flinging something across the room – it is all in good fun and he joins in to please me – while in reality he hasn't a clue about playfulness. I think he has completely forgotten puppy-hood, if he even had one."

Dulcinea was nearing the end of her patience. She had failed to convey the urgency that she knew was critical to the plan's success. *"Nomad, where are you? I have not ridden upon your warm broad back in months, and I have not whispered the secrets of my heart into your velvety ear through the rushing wind. Nomad, come to me in my dreams and inspire me,"* she begged.

Her frustration regarding the snail's pace leading to the revolution, was the cause of her "temper tantrum". She knew it was childish, and didn't support her mission goals, but she couldn't stop herself.

Her anger and impatience bubbled up and flooded over onto those who were closest to her; upon those who least deserved her wrath!

Muslims were being targeted all over the globe, and she anticipated the activation of the Sarajevo II directive to be sooner than anyone thought. Blowing up airports around the world was a stupid move by the Muslim terrorists. She wondered if they were actually this blinded by their own rhetoric. Until now she had never underestimated the cunning and the commitment of the Muslim Brethren leadership. Now she began to suspect that they were being manipulated and channeled for some sinister cause. *God, how I wish I could discuss this with Luigi. He would have figured this out. Arnaud is too close to see beyond the obvious.....but I know there is more to this than just fanatical clerics and raging masses of ignorant suicidal followers. But, who and what, is it?* Her internal monologue kept grinding away, looking for the answers.

Arnaud opened the thick cold metal door for Dulcinea. It glided easily across the thresh hold but was heavy enough to stop at the point where he quit pushing it. She took in a deep breath of cool lemon scented air. *This is it, the trigger, the starting point,* she thought. *I am initiating the launch point – the irreversible step that can never be reversed.*

Dulcinea sat down at the head of a table, and she took some time to look at the individuals sitting around it. Behind her confidant demeanor she was questioning the validity of this group of participants: *Were they, despite the careful screening and investigation, "not for reformation?"*

Each person sat still as if cast in granite created a million years ago. They were attentive, bathed in the soft indirect lighting from above. The steel gray walls and mahogany woodwork lent the scene a highly polished, sophisticated ambiance. It was staged by Arnaud, to illicit feelings of reverence and respect.

She spoke to them in Arabic, "This is the critical point.... the first stage of implementation of the revolutionary plan." She continued in a clear voice, resonating across the expanse of the long smooth table, "This is a monumental undertaking and one that will sustain Islam. You will bring lasting peace and prosperity to the weary embattled inhabitants of the world!" Looking from face to face, she saw hope behind doubtful eyes. *This will be a long session,* she thought.

Dulcinea wanted to encourage the council in a positive direction, with clear guidelines, but she did not wish to dictate the New Qur'an, or the accompanying New Book of Islamic Law that would replace Sharia Law. The religious reformation process had to be separated from the governing policies and legislature of the UFAS. She believed that these men and women were religiously and ethically pure in heart. They had been selected by the UFN because of their history of adhering to documented accuracy, and also because of their humanitarian core beliefs. They were moderate Muslims who did not embrace jihad or adherence to mid-evil, archaic Sharia Law.

"The Council of the Islamic Reformation is right here, at this table! This is a world-changing body." Safina spoke forcefully. The significance of her words was not lost upon the faces looking back at her. "You know why you were selected. You understand what you must do. This is the most significant task you will perform in your lives. Nothing will ever be as important. Nothing has ever, or will ever, alter humanity's path as drastically. Well, maybe with the exception of Jesus Christ and the birth of Christianity.

I believe that your work on this council will save Islam from global ethnic cleansing, and from the most violent retribution for the acts of Islamic terrorism being perpetrated upon the inhabitants of the earth. Your scholarly efforts will bring Muslim women out of the darkness of slavery. For the rest of the world your work will bring long awaited peace, prosperity, and enlightenment. You will break the sword of hatred and retaliation against Muslims that is inevitable if Islam is left unreformed and unrestrained.

You were taught to consider anything conflicting with the words of the prophet to be blasphemous. That is an unsustainable position. The time has come to lift the blinders from the eyes of Muslims.

If we do not reform Islam, worldwide violent ethnic cleansing will destroy it. Millions of Muslims, regardless of the degree of extremism they embrace, will be exterminated around the globe. That is a fact. I'm going to show you the proof of that plan today, so that there will be no doubt left in your mind that your task is just and necessary. The rest of the world is not going to convert to Islam, and they are not going to allow Muslims to slaughter them. Despite extremist misconceptions and blind faith that Allah will spare the faithful and defeat the infidels, those of us with logic know that it is simply not true!

Think of the reformation as the salvation of Islam. The murdering of infidels; the promise of virgin girls as enticements into paradise; *taqiyya* (admonition to lie and steal to achieve Islamic power over infidels) must be stopped. Honor killings and stoning must be outlawed and those who engage in them must be punished."

One of the security stipulations of the project was that members would remain anonymous - to protect them from reprisals and harassment by radical Islamic extremists. Dulcinea gave a brief introduction of the areas of expertise they would be addressing, and a general description of each of the panel member's qualifications. She went around the table and asked each individual to give an overview of their position, expertise and a synopsis of what they believed must be accomplished through reformation.

The first presentation came from a scholar on ancient texts, and addressed the anthropology and the forensic authentication of documents, "It will be an unprecedented feat to preserve a religion without the central figure of a divine prophet. Once the myth of the Qur'an's authenticity is exposed through verifiable documentation, what will the anchor of Islam become? The questions that will be paramount are as follows: can Islam be reformed into a religion of peace and love, a belief in Allah as a supreme entity? Could the surgical removal of the edicts of the Qur'an kill the religion of Islam? We have to believe that the core of the Muslim people long for the love and the mercy of Allah, for equality of the children of Islam, and for peace and prosperity for Muslims around the world. We must have faith that Muslims are weary of hatred, revenge, subjugation of the weak, and the exclusion of half of its population from the enjoyment of life itself. Those negative descriptions of Islam are documented, and we have the scrolls and narratives to support those facts." The dignified, soft-spoken scholar sat down, and sighed as he settled into his chair. He stroked his beard nervously, twirling some wayward strands of gray and black whiskers between his fingers.

The next panel member asked to speak was a well-known Islamic religious leader who had drawn the wrath of the traditional theocracy leadership when he dared to reveal his opinion that Islam was in dire need of reformation. "Like the UFN members, I am convinced that without reformation there is no future for the Islamic nations. We will be decimated by the reprisals from those who were targeted by Islamic extremists." He began his talk with a prayer, "May Allah bless the participants of this forum, and make our steps straight and just."

He stood tall and proud with his hands resting on the smooth table, "In monotheistic Islam, which is what defines the whole of Islamic totalitarianism, Allah is one, and unique without partners, wife, or children. This is a strange description of Allah because according to the Qur'an Allah has no gender and no similar shape to any creature or human being, but then it is deemed necessary in Islamic writings to make mention of his lack of a wife or children; not the lack of a soul mate or the lack of a husband. This would indicate that Muslims believe Allah has to be masculine in gender, and hence all of the writings of Islam refer to Allah as 'he or him'.

According to the *Shahadah* Allah is defined by our behavior as Muslims: affirming the unity (uniformity) and uniqueness of the *worship* of Allah, and does not actually define Allah as any particular entity. Throughout the teachings and writings of Islam Allah is defined by the adjectives that followers attribute to his nature or his behavior, such as merciful, forgiving, magnificent, all-knowing, to be feared, etc; they are flowering adjectives without focus or justification of any kind. It demonstrates the perfect reflection of a barbarian mind, defining the source of creation by the barbarian's acts of worship instead of attempting to understand the substance or essence of the deity.

Although this may seem like a pointless exercise in time traveling back 1,400 years to the birth of Islam, it has significant ramifications to the reformation of Islam, and the possibility that reformation may not be a feasible project in itself. How can we reform something that was born out of ignorance and the absence of any reference point other than violence and the subjugation of the weakest members of a tribal society? Take away logic, compassion, all scientific explanations of the Universe, and create a theology fabricated from the mind of a primitive, illiterate and violent man. Then seal the entire concept in an ironclad edict that commands the believer, under the threat of death, never to alter, amend or delete even one word or one letter of that doctrine forever!"

Dulcinea had seen evil. She had experienced the devil incarnate when Khaliq tortured and abused her as a child. She was willing to die just to have a chance at defeating Islam and freeing the enslaved daughters of Islam. She didn't really want to be the champion of men. Her focus was on the women, the true victims of Islamic fanaticism. But she could see the moral obligation to save all the members of Islamic society.

"When you consider punishments and admonitions be cautious. We want to create an open society that is conducive to asking questions, challenging legislation, and ensures civil rights and freedoms."

As they began to work on the detailed commentary and the foundations of the new Islamic theology they became animated and enthused with the importance of the mission. Dulcinea left the chamber and told Arnaud that she felt the task was in good hands. She had reminded them that in the end it had to be a living, useful, practical document that could inspire millions of followers.

The arguments among the council participants exploded a few days into the deliberations. The participants battled among themselves, and rebelled against the ideas of reformation. They were steeped in generation after generation of core beliefs about the inferiority of women, and the undisputed law that made questions and doubt regarding the prophet blasphemous.

At times Safina and her colleagues on the UFN Council despaired that this important aspect of the success of the revolution could be achieved. "I think I spoke too soon and was overly optimistic that these individuals were capable of overcoming their biases and brainwashed minds."

The scholars and theologians fought on, day after day, night after night. They debated every sentence, every word, every tenet of their faith. Letting go of their ingrained doctrines and mindless adherence to the elements of militant jihad, and realizing that the plausible possibility that 25 million Muslims would be killed if they did not reach a consensus was real, won out in the end.

The panel worked tirelessly, line by line, page by page - proposing, discussing, and verbally battling. These were honest men and women, who were willing to sacrifice everything to save Islam. They had opened their minds and their hearts to the task at hand. After loud yelling, fist shaking and even a few who walked out of the room in anger and protest – but with Dulcinea's mediation, later returned - they successfully created a scholarly body of work of near perfection.

They had been given the opportunity to take the hind-sight of 1,400 years and use it to structure a theology of tolerance, and a way of life that would enhance the Islamic traditions of arts and science. It allowed for the worship of Allah in an atmosphere of hope, and celebration of life. Most importantly it would free the women of Islam to pursue their individualism, realize their personal talents, and become masters of their own bodies and lives, as equal members of Islamic society. Remarkably, the new Qur'an was uniquely Islamic – with a huge difference in its inherent core of tolerance – something that had been dormant within Islamic culture, and was only practiced within the Kurdish Muslim community - *"sulh-i-kul"* (Peace with all). The practice of *sulh-i-kul* became a foundational tenet of the reformation of Islam.

When the task was finally completed, Dulcinea held a celebratory dinner to commemorate their achievement. "Today I speak to you as Safina Abousanni, daughter of Latifa, my true name. The next time you hear that name it will be the day that I go to battle to preserve the work you have completed. It has taken eight long months – almost the same time that it takes to create a child of Allah.

You have retained all that you could that is beautiful and good within Islam. The New Qur'an and the New Laws of Islam, will allow our people to bask in the righteousness of Islam. They will be able to live side by side with all the other nations of the world."

Dulcinea stopped to take a drink of water and a deep breath. She spread her arms wide as she faced the listeners: "You cannot fathom how pleased and proud I am of this body of men and women. This is a powerful example of cooperation, dedication, and noble accomplishment. You are blessed by Allah, and you honor humanity with your achievement." The room exploded with applause and tears. Everyone felt and understood the significance of this day.

Arnaud sat nearby and took it all in. Later in his life he would write about this day in his memoirs: "It was one of the greatest turning points in the history of mankind – and there was no media coverage, no fanfare, no long-winded speeches, no hype or commercial hoopla. Almost like the birth of Christ. It would be decades before the world would know who had saved Islam from the abyss, and why the Reformation Council members were hunted down and murdered by the Muslim Brotherhood by the end of the Islamic Revolution."

Dulcinea addressed the scholars and theologians, "I am going to give you a file with a brief description of the foundation for the Constitution of the UFAS. This important document is still in its preparatory state, but we expect completion to be swiftly accomplished post revolution when the delegates of all the Arab states will come together in a Constitutional Congress to work out the details democratically.

When the revolution is launched you will see significant blood shed. Those who stand militantly in the way of the Islamic Reformation will be impossible to persuade, and we don't have the luxury of time for a gradual educational process. If they choose to die for the preservation of pedophilia and murder, then we will facilitate that wish. You will have times when you will abhor the loss of life, but know this: if they are not removed as obstacles to the freedom and liberty of our people, we will be destroyed along with the fanatics. Some of you, here today, may not survive the revolutionary battle that will soon commence. I can only promise you that your sacrifice will never be forgotten – and we will fight hard to make sure that your passing is not in vain.

Winston Churchill gave a speech in 1899 about the reality of Islam. I am handing out a copy of that speech for you to read. Churchill was a wise man who many believe saved the world from Nazi Germany. He warned the West about Islamic Jihad – but they ignored his warnings and allowed Islam to grow and flourish."

The River War, first edition, Vol II, pages 248-250

"Muhammadanism lays on its votaries! Besides the fanatical frenzy, which is as dangerous in a man as hydrophobia in a dog, there is this fearful fatalistic apathy. The effects are apparent in many countries. Improvident habits, slovenly systems of agriculture, sluggish methods of commerce, and insecurity of property exist wherever the followers of the Prophet rule or live.

A degraded sensualism deprives this life of its grace and refinement, the next of its dignity and sanctity. The fact that in Muhammadan law every woman must belong to some man as his absolute property either as a child, a wife, or a concubine, must delay the final extinction of slavery until the faith of Islam has ceased to be a great power among men.

Individual Muslims may show splendid qualities, but the influence of the religion paralyzes the social development of those who follow it.

No stronger retrograde force exists in the world. Far from being moribund, Muhammadanism is a militant and proselytizing faith. It has already spread throughout Central Africa, raising fearless warriors at every step; and were it not that Christianity is sheltered in the strong arms of science, the science against which it had vainly struggled, the civilization of modern Europe might fall, as fell the civilization of ancient Rome."

Winston Churchill, 1899

Dulcinea continued, "When we officially establish the UFAS and uniformly organize each State in the Federation with its own constitution we will establish true representation of the people, including women and non-Muslims, to participate in the drafting of secular laws and setting up secular judicial courts. There will be no recognized separation between Sunni and Shia sects of Islam.

We want Muslims around the world to understand that they are members of the modern world community and cannot hold themselves apart and isolated, locked in an ancient time capsule. Islamic extremists recruited the ignorant and the defective rejects of society. Mohammad and his followers were aware of the true purpose of their blunder and conquests. But I cannot believe that even they could have fathomed the spread of toxic isolationism and its perpetual enslavement of the nation of Islam locked into a culture of violence and slavery.

I am asking you to select an Islamic Theological Council from among you, that will handle disputes relating to religious matters and will oversee any changes or amendments in the future. We need a clear and definitive separation of secular and religious jurisdiction. I assure you that your names will remain anonymous until after the successful Revolution."

Yes, she thought – *finally I believe. Finally I embrace it. Finally I am filled with the convictions that were so hard won and so hard digested."*

Dulcinea's religious experience was a unique theosophy anchored in her dreams and visions of Nomad; the prophetic and mind expanding insight into what is, what could be, and what would be. Nomad was a literal and a virtual representation of her inner strength and conviction. He was an antidote against her conscious inhibitions and doubts, and a conduit to her driven purpose on earth. It took Safina years of meditation, and self examination to understand the significance of Nomad. For a long time she had accepted the black horse as simply a vivid memory of the real animal who escaped Khaliq and ran free in the deserts of Arabia. She reasoned that Nomad's escape represented her own desire to be free.

The reappearance of Nomad in her dreams and occasionally "in the flesh" atop hills and mountains, or standing on the horizon, convinced Safina that the veil between universes was fragile and traversable. Perhaps the original flesh and blood horse came into her life, not through a random occurrence, but by design. She had even considered the possibility that she, herself, sent him from another universe into her existence to correct the errors that occurred in this time line. Might there be some all powerful centric force in the cosmos that would work to balance the co-existence of universes still in their evolving stages? Could that be the definition of Allah, God, Elohim? Jews had defined God in the simplistic prayer: *Adonai Elohenu, Adonai, Ahad* (The Lord Our God, the Lord is One). But Dulcinea considered the questions: "One" as in the only one? "One" as in the first of many? "One" as in one with humanity? "One" as in one interpretation of existence? Or was it "one" as in the chosen one?

She felt the heat coming from her old scars, and the memories of the old life of Safina playing as though DVR'd sequentially on HD video loop. Closing her eyes for a moment, she saw Nomad racing up the sand dune from their encampment in the oasis, and Khaliq cursing and swearing at the horse as it fled. Safina prayed, "May you find sweet cool water and may the stars lead you safely through this vast desert." She had reached that moment where one presses "play", except in this universe there was no "reverse" button. From now on it was "fast forward" all the way.

A secret executive meeting of the UFN Council was called in Paris, and finally the next stage in the revolutionary plan was put in play. It was obvious to all concerned that time was of the essence. The clock was counting down to a point where all would be lost, and it would be impossible to restore sanity and order in the world. All the members agreed on moving up the time table due to the ratcheting up of the Muslim Brethren's timetable. For security reasons it was actually a good plan to go forward now. The longer they waited, the higher the risk of exposure. Dulcinea would accept a position in the US Embassy in Baghdad as US Cultural Attaché to Iraq.

Arnaud made the call to the US State Department, "Yes, Steve, it's time. We can't wait any longer. We may not have another opportunity to install her." Arnaud nodded his head as he paced back and forth at the end of the conference room. "Use all of your resources on this one, it is imperative that she have time to establish her credentials in D.C. Yes, right…. the name I gave you when we met in Germany, Dulcinea Devorah Morelli. That is the name on her Birth Certificate and on her American naturalization documents. Just bury that second alias, the Hispanic one she used for her trip to Cairo. It won't make any difference anyway, after the completion of the 'project'." He listened carefully to the other end of the line. It was an encrypted communication so there was an almost imperceptible delay. Arnaud identified it because he had used the encrypted communication programs in the past. "Yes…..she does, she has US naturalization papers filed with the State Department. She is an American citizen and has been for several years. We have never disclosed that to anyone outside of the family except to our Dutch connection and Colonel Petersen, the bodyguard." He looked across the table at Dulcinea and Brecken.

When he hung up Arnaud addressed Brecken, "I hope you have taught Dulci everything American. It will be difficult to pull this off without having visited America. We have just two weeks before she must leave for Washington." He turned toward Dulcinea, " I think we should spend it preparing you for American culture. Let's see, there's cuisine, slang, music trends, celebrities, various organizations, media celebrities, TV programs, etc., etc. Do you think we can do this?" Dulci winked at him uncharacteristically.

Brecken smiled, "First we'll teach you to use contractions consistently. I know we've worked on this. You've improved, but if you want to sound American you'll have to own this. Your accent is excellent but your cadence will have to come more naturally. This'll only happen when you begin to think in English and stop translating from Arabic in your mind. The way to conquer that habit is to speak faster. Your brain will kick into the English language code and filter out your Arabic codes. My best advice to you Dulci, is to talk faster."

CHAPTER 18

~Night Before the Dawn

Muslim women in Baghdad, Cairo, Tehran, and Jerusalem tucked their children into bed for the night, with brushed kisses upon the foreheads of their babies, their eyes watering with emotion. Under their veils and robes they hid pieces of paper found among their children's belongings. Some papers were discovered pushed inside of paper diapers sealed in plastic, some were hidden among the grains of their infant's cereal inside what appeared to be sealed canisters. A few were quickly thrust into their palms as they walked through the market places toting their heavy cloth bags of vegetables and baskets of trussed-up squawking chickens.

"Can you read?" was the question whispered into their ears by other women passing them along the paths or waiting in line at the neighborhood grocery store. Some of the notes were encapsulated in dried corn husks baked in the center of a loaf of bread. When they cut apart the fresh fish from the markets in Basra and Yaffa along the Persian Gulf or the Mediterranean Sea, they found small transparent plastic bags that held their message of hope. "Can you read?" The whispering of their sisters roared in their ears. Something was happening. Something wonderful and great was coming. "Ask the nurses, ask the doctors, ask your young sons to teach you the letters." Their sisters whispered. Women covered in their big tent-like *Burkas* with mesh windows to see out – were not locals. They were brave emissaries from the UFAS! They roamed the market places following the male operatives who worked for the UFN. The hard physical preparation to lay the foundation for the revolution had begun.

Yasmine and Latifa had co-authored the message:

"Allah has heard the lamentations of women. He has heard the curses made under their breath, and deep within their hearts. Allah is merciful, Allah will avenge the cold gray sisters whose still bodies lie mutilated and bloody in the alleys of Indonesia, in the gutters of London, in the dark stairwells and catacombs of Paris, and those innocent sisters strewn naked in the deserts of Saudi Arabia and buried in shallow cold graves in the oil fields of Kuwait, and those dumped in the open sewers of Iran and Iraq. The tears of the motherless children of Islam have flooded the hearts of the righteous. Allah will dispense justice; unrepentant Muslim men will become sterile and impotent, and many of them will die painful deaths of retribution."

It started with small sound bites dispersed between radio commercials for washing powder, or placed discretely at the end of a stanza by a famous Arabic female singer: "Allah will avenge the women."

Dulcinea had told the UFN Council what she knew would happen and why, "Men won't hear it – they won't notice – they won't heed its importance – because most of all they'll be complacent in their self image of superiority.

Muslim men are universally absolute in their belief that women are vessels to be used as one would utilize a utensil or a tool. They believed that females have no souls, no secret desires, no personal agenda. In their belief system Paradise is filled with a renewable resource of beautiful ignorant and selfless virgins provided by Allah to endlessly satisfy a man's physical desires. Who would question the wisdom of the Prophet?"

"This is why we must carefully prepare the women of Islam. 'Can you read?' has to be the core question - the one that will spark curiosity and eventually spread across Islam initially as a female quest for knowledge," Latifa said.

Brecken laughed out loud and then put a hand over his mouth.

"Why do you think this could possibly be funny?" Dulci yelled at him.

"I can't help it Dulci – I keep wondering how they will react if they arrive in Paradise after a day of murdering infidels – and they find out that all the heavenly virgins – are men?"

There was dead silence as Arnaud, Latifa, Yehiye and Dulci stared at him in shock. And then, like a floodgate, they could not contain their laughter. Latifa was obviously embarrassed that she found this statement to be hilarious – but in the end the hard laughter was, as usual, exactly what Brecken had hoped for. Everyone needed something lighter to focus on at this point. It was all so tense and scary as they came closer and closer to the battle ahead of them. The mental picture of Holy Jihad warriors arriving in Paradise to gain possession of their 97 virgins, only to see a long line of bearded, swarthy male suicide bombers waiting for them, was just too funny.

The messages to the women became something to seek out. The women anxiously awaited new pieces of this puzzle as the notes appeared magically in every conceivable place that only women would access. They picked up their son's copy books and began to trace Arabic letters, "Come, Yousef" or "Come, Ahmed. Teach me this reading. Teach me what you are learning in school. Teach me and I will prepare your favorite dishes with honey and pastries and sweet dates and red stained pistachios and *escadanias* (tiny orange sweet fruits to be sucked from thick tough skins), that only Kings are served, and I will watch the goats today while you visit your friends. I will even brush those hateful spitting and biting camels and collect their apples of dung for the fires. Just teach me one letter each day."

As sons sat down to teach their mothers to read they relished their mothers' thirst for knowledge. "*Iyawah Amma* (Yes Mother). You are a quick student. You are reading now, but don't tell my father about this, he would not like it." They joined in the shared pride of learning, and the progression from understanding the letters and then the words. The sons' hearts softened. They taught their mothers and sisters the letters and the words, and they were profoundly changed in a way that no one, not even Dulcinea, could have anticipated. The joy of learning and discovery is a balm for the human soul. These sons were different from their fathers, because now they were exposed to the pleasures of teaching and watching the seeds of knowledge grow within the hearts and minds of another human being. They questioned the unquestionable. They challenged the heretofore unchallengeable laws of Islam.

The medicinal magic of knowledge dissolved the barbarism of 1,400 years of female enslavement and degradation. In a culture where the brutal practice of stoning people to death was practiced with enthusiasm, they could never again think and act like their fathers without suffering unbearable remorse and guilt. They were not genetic psychopaths, they were simply brainwashed by generations of ignorant barbarians.

Son's warned their fathers, "If you strike my mother once you will face the wrath of Allah and be denied entry into paradise. If you strike my mother again, you will never see Allah. I will cut your body into a million tiny pieces and feed them to the ravens and the buzzards. You will be nothing but bird droppings cast across the land. No one will remember your name. Your sons will take their mother's name and glorify the house of their mother. Your family name will cease to exist and nothing of you will be remembered. It will be as if you and your ancestors had never been born. This is the curse of sons upon their fathers who would strike women. No longer will you be allowed to vent your importance upon my mother. This is not a threat. this is the law of this house from this day and forever. Islam will be avenged and you and your kind will hold back your whips and your curses. You will swallow your bile and burn your throat as its evil fire turns back upon you."

Fights broke out and fathers and sons were at war with one another. The sons were dedicated to change. They were fast becoming protectors, mentors, guardians. They stood strong against the ignorance and the corruption of Islam. There were a few brave clerics whom Allah had touched with clarity of thought and a logical mind. They were learned men, who knew the world beyond the confines of Islam, beyond the myopic vision of the prophet.

The humiliation going on in the lives of Muslim women within the Islamic communities in towns and villages, in cities and even in nomadic campsites was horrific. There were compassionate sons who welcomed the inclusion of their mothers as individuals with rights and protection under just laws.

There were young Muslim men who had glimpsed Western civilization, and who realized that women were free in other countries while being held in slavery in the Islamic world. As they traveled abroad and were educated as doctors, scientists, and engineers, they were exposed to 21st century reality.

Rami Ahed Sadam, Abu El Haj rose early on this holy day of the holy month of Ramadan. He had eaten heartily the night before in preparation for the month-long fast during the daytime. His second wife, Jamillah had been slow to bring the newspaper to him this morning, and he reprimanded her with a vile curse and a hard slap across her face. She stood defiantly before him with her piercing black eyes staring shamelessly at his face, instead of looking down at the floor as was her place. She did not even put her hand up to her face or wipe the stinging tears from her eyes. She was silent as her cheek turned an angry red and began to swell. This enraged him, and he knocked her down with a fist to her jaw. "I dare you stare at me you filthy "*Kalba*" (bitch)." She laid still on the floor and then turned her face toward him and continued to stare at him in silence. His son, Abdullah, was standing behind him at the entrance to the dining room.

The boy was well developed for his age of fourteen years. He was not angular and lanky as his father. Abdullah was short and stocky, and he fancied himself to be a body builder. He lifted weights in the cool stone courtyard of their villa in the suburbs of Tehran. He worked out every day preparing for the time when he would travel to the United States and compete in body building competitions. His room was filled with Western Body Builder magazines and photos of famous body builders posing in their shiny oiled bodies.

Abdullah loved his mother with all of his heart. She was kind and gentle and as lovely as her name, Jamillah (*Ja-mil´-lah, beautiful*). In his entire life she had never raised her voice or her hand against him. All good things came to him from his mother's love for him. He was her firstborn and he held a special place in her heart. When he looked into her eyes he could see his own reflection and the pride that his mother felt for him.

When Rami Ahed Sadam pulled his foot back to kick Jamillah in the stomach, Abdullah could not stand by and watch as he had in the past. This time his desire to protect his mother was too strong to ignore. He drew his shabria from his belt and ripped the metal sheath from it a split second before he plunged the blade deep into his father's neck. Rami's body crumpled to the ground and lie still, never knowing that his own son had killed him. Jamillah rose from the ground and ran to her son. He threw the blood drenched shabria on the floor and sank to his knees. He was OK. He knew he had done the right thing. His mother would never suffer again from the rage of his father. His father's evil cruelty was ended.

Jamillah and her son Abdullah dragged Rami's body out into the alley and rolled it into the sewer trough where it disappeared beneath the deep vile sludge. They returned to the villa to wash down the floor and walls, and to comfort each other. As they threw their bloody clothes and cleaning brushes into the raging fire beneath the clay ovens in the courtyard, Jamillah pulled a piece of paper from her son's breast pocket and said, "Abdullah, what is this? Read this to me, my son."

He took the folded paper and slowly opened it, studying it carefully: "It says: No man shall beat or rape his wife without severe punishment. There will be an eye-for-an-eye, and a-tooth-for-a-tooth, from this day forward." Abdullah pulled his mother into his strong embrace, "He will never hurt you again, and no man shall ever beat you again, I promise." Abdullah stroked her head scarf as he pulled the veil away from her face. He put his hand gently on her soft brown swollen cheek, "Inside this house you will not wear a veil that covers your sweet face and hides your smile. When I take a wife she will not be mistreated or live in fear as you have been forced to do. My sons will never watch their father beat their mother. I promise you this, *Uma.*"

Jamillah wept. For the first time in her life she was safe; utterly and completely safe. She had never experienced this state before. Her entire life had been lived in fear and silence: her opinions unsolicited, her needs inconsequential, her desires pointless, and according to the Prophet, she was not allowed to question her status.

In Pakistan a man who was known to beat his three wives almost daily, was found decapitated. His bearded head was discovered on the steps of the nearby mosque. A piece of paper was stuck between his front teeth. A policeman removed it and began to read: "No man shall beat or rape his wife without severe punishment to his person. There will be an eye-for-an-eye and a-tooth-for-a-tooth, from this day forward. Allah has heard the lamentations of the women."

In Eastern Jerusalem, in the old part of the city, a 42 year old Muslim man had taken a willow branch from a tree in his garden and whipped his 12 year old bride until red swollen welts covered every inch of her shoulders and back, while he screamed obscenities at her.

Two shots rang out, and the child bride uncovered her face and turned to see the older wife with a rifle in her hands and her children gathered around her skirts crying. "Come child, come here and be safe from that demon," the older wife motioned to the child bride. She lowered the rifle and lay it on the ground. "Don't touch it!" she told the children. As she pulled the young bride close to her, she wrapped her scared arms around the girl, and hugged her tightly, "We are sisters, we are sisters! He cannot hurt you again. I have killed him." She took her inside the house and cleansed her wounds with cool soda water. She called the police, "A man has been killed for beating his child bride. We need the Israeli police here or the man's male relatives will murder all of the women in this house. Please come quickly." Sirens could be heard as they entered this section of the old city.

Jerusalem had seen worse, but this was unique. In the bigger picture of this incident one might see the irony of calling upon the Jews to facilitate the saving of Islam for all time. They gave asylum to these women and saved them from feudal revenge. The message was clear:

sisters of Islam are also sisters of the world; no effort shall be spared in saving them.

Muslim clerics and their followers began to reconsider the consequences of their rage and violent behaviors. "Honor killings" did not seem so "honorable" and appropriate to Islamic men. The Qur'an's admonition to beat women who disobeyed their husbands did not seem such a clear cut commandment. In their hearts they knew it to be wrong. They had been duped for 1,400 years into following this man-made religion. With all of the accomplishments of Arabia, including science and art, architecture and poetry, advanced mathematics and astronomy, how could they have been so deceived by the threat of the sword that they would have succumbed to this cult leader who could neither read nor write?

Throughout the Muslim world things were rapidly evolving. Whenever a man lost his temper and unleashed his rage upon his wife he could be sure of retaliation. He might be waylaid coming home from prayers, or sometimes he was pulled forcibly from his bed in the middle of the night and beaten almost to death. If a man raped his wife and she told her neighbor or she told someone at the clinic about it, her husband was found castrated and thrown in an alley in his neighborhood. Some men bled out and died. Occasionally the castration was so poorly done that he remained permanently dysfunctional. The men began to carry shabria's strapped to their waists, and they feared to venture out after dark.

These events were becoming more and more common. Men who married child brides and consummated these marriages were attacked by mobs of women and beaten to death. When babies were born to young girls, relatives and neighbors would visit the household and leave desserts and savory dishes as gifts. They would caution the women of the house not to partake of those dishes. The husbands who ate this food would die painful deaths or fall ill for long periods of time.

If a child bride died giving birth, as is common among Muslim populations, their husbands were caught and murdered within a few weeks of the tragedy. The Princes of Saudi Arabia had their operatives investigate these killings but they could find no information. Muslim men who cooperated with the authorities were often beaten severely a few days later.

There had been no justice in Arabia in over a millennium, so there was no expectation of due process or any criminal prosecution of the men who had oppressed over half of the Muslim population century after century. It was Dulcinea's logical conclusion that the courts were unjust, and women had no voice in them. Vigilante justice was all that was available to them so she would make sure it was swift and targeted.

While the master plan was progressing gradually throughout the world, all the measures that the Council had taken were coming to fruition. Gradually a new awakening was happening among the Muslim populations of the more progressive Arab countries. Islamic women took notice, learned to read and write, and they began teaching their daughters. They raised their sons differently as well, demanding respect and teaching them the importance of kindness and civility.

Women began to walk taller and to initiate conversations with their children, particularly with their sons. They were brave and many of them were victimized for their courage and still they stood fast, and they longed for freedom, something they could only imagine.

CHAPTER 19

The American Back Door

Dulcinea was ready for America. She was respected in intelligence circles and in diplomatic circles. Her keen mind and
awareness of the internal structures of governments were considered a valuable resource among the hands-on operatives working
in the European political and financial spheres of power. The West
was the logical next step.

Arnaud had made the necessary arrangements through his friends
in the US State Department. Dulcinea would travel to the United
States as a guest of an important Senator. Her citizenship had been
established several years before, and an American passport was issued
in her name. Her friends in the CIA were delighted to know that she
would be in DC, readily available to assist their evaluation of options
in dealing with the Middle East and terrorist threats. She knew how
to massage egos and manipulate zeal. She had quietly negotiated the
release of a number of non-combatant detainees.

Dulcinea and Brecken entered Arnaud's study at the same time.
They sat on the plush yellow sofa near the center of the room. Honoré
brought in a tray of scones and marmalade with hot lemony tea, and
withdrew, closing the ornate doors of the study behind him. Arnaud

cleared his throat as he stood near the window looking out on the distant view of the Seine River as it wound its way through Paris. He considered how its flow was uninterrupted and unchanged for generations of Parisians. Despite the pollution, the building, the wars, and the "rejuvenation projects" the river continued to flow. Nothing seemed to stop it. He thought how appropriate it would be if freedom were like a river – unending and constantly renewed.

"It is time for you to go to America," Arnaud said.

"Is the international plan going forward smoothly?" Dulci questioned. "I don't want to start anything until all the pieces are in place and we have a high success probability when we go operational."

Arnaud went over to the inside wall of his study and removed a book from a lower shelf. The entire bookcase moved about six inches forward and then slid horizontally to the right, exposing a large steel vault. He punched in some numbers on the front keyboard and they heard a metallic "clunk" as the locking mechanism disengaged. Arnaud then pulled open the vault door and motioned them inside. A week earlier, Arnaud had given Dulcinea a code on her cell phone that would supply new combinations for the vault each month. "Just in case something should happen to me Dulci – you should not delay the revolution. You would go on to complete our mission and the reformation," he had insisted.

They followed Arnaud down a narrow hallway that opened into a large control room. There were streaming digital video monitors all along the walls – at least thirty or forty of them. They appeared to all be coming from similar control rooms around the world. Arnaud touched a numerical keypad on a screen and immediately they could hear audio signals coming in. At first Dulci had to adjust her hearing, as the voices were in various Arabic dialects which she had not been prepared for, but she quickly came up to speed. They were giving coordinates and troop movements. Arnaud looked at the digital read-out on the wall above them. Paris time was 10:00 pm. - there were digital time readouts for all the monitors.

Brecken was incredulous, "Holy cow, this is impressive. I don't think the Pentagon has anything comparable, except maybe at NORAD in the Rockies."

Arnaud was mildly amused: "Failure has never been an option. This will succeed, and yes, everything has gone even better than anticipated. I have confirmation from every corner of the globe. I was amazed that our top mathematicians' projections indicate over 100 million moderate Muslims will join the cause, eager to shed the bonds of the extremists and the atrocities promoted by them. They are ready to embrace the reformation.

They understand the consequences of doing nothing. Even more astounding is the number of educated, articulate Muslim women who have joined our ranks to save their sisters in Iraq, Kuwait, Saudi Arabia, Afghanistan, Pakistan, throughout Africa - Egypt, Libya, Nigeria, Uganda, Yemen, Ethiopia, Tunis, Lebanon, Jordan, and most of all from Iran. The percentage of Arabs among Muslim populations is small – perhaps less than 2% of the world's Muslims are Arabs. The Muslim sisters have awakened throughout the world – and they are hungry to be free." Arnaud was smiling.

"OK, I am ready to leave – ready to become an American. Do you have my destination?" Dulcinea said.

"Of course, you will travel with Brecken to Washington D.C. where you will be working in the offices of the CIA with some friends of yours from college. The State Department will prepare your diplomatic credentials for the US Embassy in Baghdad. Your title will be Cultural Attaché. This assignment is primarily a social function to promote cordial relationships with Iraqi officials and dignitaries, but it will give you access to the dinners, parties, and upper crust functions in D.C, which you will attend. It will also be an opportunity to interact with the operatives who have been working on behalf of the revolution. These "operatives" will be your liaison between you and the UFN Council members in each country."

Dulci yawned. She was exhausted. It was time to unwind and recharge. "I'm so tired Arnaud, may I just leave you now and take some time to digest all of this information? By the way, when am I leaving for America?"

"In forty-eight hours you will be on a plane."

"Come on Brecken, let's get out of here," Dulcinea said.

CHAPTER 20

Secret Child of Hope

Christi held Assal's hand firmly as they walked under the color-ful umbrella of dying leaves. Nature's brashly painted notes of autumn floated down from above, twittering and twisting in the air. The mavericks among them swirled in tight circles, feigning disinterest in the mother/daughter pair, and landing ahead of them on the pavement like desperate handwritten requests for amnesty from naughty angels. It was cold in Philadelphia at this time of the year.

Some people were already lighting their fireplaces, and the scent of burning wood lingered expectantly in the sweet damp air. Christi relished this season because it captured the promise of soon-to-come holidays and festivities, yet the hustle and bustle had not yet begun. The excuse to bundle up and meander about the city was too won-derful to resist; going nowhere and doing nothing important. Christi savored the word "meander", it gave license to taking a break, to sim-ply living and feeling her body stretch, watching her warm breath materialize in miniature clouds in front of her face, and knowing that the planets spun around in circular and elliptical revolutions in the Universe without destinations. It was at times like this that she embraced her life, and felt the power of God shielding her and those she held dear.

The child pulled on her mother's arm as she bent to scoop up red and gold leaves with her free hand and stuff them into her pocket. "Mom, they're so beautiful. I wish they'd stay like this forever. Why do they insist on jumping off the tree branches and falling upon the sidewalk? I think they'd be happier stuck on the branches where they can see the world and know they're safe." Assal's questioning hazel green eyes looked into Christi's brown ones. Mother and daughter, so different, yet their hearts connected inseparably.

Christi spoke in her soft southern drawl, "Bein' safe isn't always the most important part of liv'n. Sometimes it's worth the risk to experience someth'n new. We can be brave and leap into life, take'n chances without bein' fools." Christi answered honestly. Her voice was husky yet soothing. She never lied to her daughter about anything. "It's OK to take risks and reach for what ya want, as long as someone else isn't hurt in the process." She wanted her daughter to be fearless. Long ago she decided not to deceive Assal. When Abe and Christi brought their adopted baby girl home to Philadelphia more than a decade ago, they made decisions about how she would be raised. She knew she was adopted and she knew she was born in Iraq.

Christi clearly recalled the day they arrived in Philadelphia and made their way home from the airport. When they finally settled into their bedroom and the baby slept soundly in the cradle at the end of their bed, Abe took his wife's hands in his own and pulled her to him, tightly holding her within his arms, "One day this child will be an influential woman. We must make sure that she has the tools to become the person she is destined to be. But the purpose of her life must come to her on its own.

"Mom, Mom, look at that big dog on the other side of the street! He's my dog." she exclaimed loudly!"

"No dear, you don't have a dog."

"Yes I do Mom. He lives in my dreams and he plays with me on the sand by the sea. He's my dog – he is! Now he can come home and live with me. He can sleep next to my bed and we can be together all the time. His name is Remé. I remember his name from my dream. Remé, Remé, come here doggy, come here!"

Christie looked across the street, down one side and up the other. They even crossed the street and looked into the alley. But she never saw a dog. Apparently he had slipped out of sight or else Assal's imagination was working overtime. It wouldn't be the first incidence. Six months ago Assal had been going on about a black horse named Nomad. Assal claimed to ride this big horse in her dreams.

The pediatrician told them it was just a phase that bright and imaginative youngsters go through. The doctor assured Abe and Christi that the best thing to do was to ignore these revelations. Christi wasn't sure about the dreams. When she went to cover Assal during the early morning she pried Assal's fist open and found her clutching a strand of coarse black hair that did not come from any-where that Christi could identify. She was highly suspicious.

When they returned home Christi left Assal with her tutor while she went to meet her husband for lunch. She took the hair to the hospital to show it to him.

"I'm here to pick up Dr. Zubayer. Can you page him please?"

"Yes, of course Mrs. Zubayer. I will get him here right away. The nurse smiled at her.

As Christi waited she saw a lab technician that she knew from Abe's staff, "Hi Joel, how are ya?"

"I'm fine, Mrs. Zubayer. Is there anything I can do for you?"

"Yes, ya can. Could'ya check out this hair and tell me what it's from? I think it's from some animal, but I'm not sure."

"Of course, I'm on a break right now. If you have a minute I'll run down to the lab and look at it under a microscope. If it's something common, I can probably identify it."

Christi smiled, "Tha'd be great. You're always helpful Joel. Thank ya."

Joel ran down the hallway. He was only gone for a few minutes and she saw him running back toward her, "I have to get back to work now, but this was easy. This is a horse hair – from the mane, judging by the length of it.

She caught her breath and then quickly recomposed herself, "Thank ya Joel. I appreciate your help."

When Abe joined her he was wearing his long black overcoat and a huge grin at seeing his favorite person waiting for him. He moved quickly toward her, reached out and lifted her off of her feet and spun her around twice before putting her back down. He never failed to take her breath away. He kissed her on top of her head while everyone in the corridor and at the nurses' station stood and grinned as they watched this serious doctor turn into an adolescent boy whenever he saw his wife! He gave her a bear hug and waited for her response. She had ceased to become embarrassed by these public proclamations of his love. In fact, she was slightly boastful in her heart, because this lovely man could still be so infatuated with her after all these years. Two decades had passed and his love was even greater than when they had married. They were soul mates, so inextricably locked together that it was impossible to find the tiniest seed of marital discontent in either one of them.

"How has your morning gone Christi? Anything exciting happen this morning?" Abe asked.

"You'll not believe what I 'm about to tell ya over lunch," Christie beamed at him. "I found this hair squeezed tight in Assal's hand ...."

"We're supposed to be at the reception by 6:00 pm. Abe," Christi said. "It's a long drive into D.C. from Philly. We need to get going."

"Why go early? It's only for some Cultural Attaché, not even the Ambassador. I'm not in the mood to meet some Iraqi snob who will go around all night quoting from Omar Qiyam or reciting parables from Kahil Gibran, trying to impress Westerners with Muslim literature. These academicians with doctorates in Islamic Culture hardly differentiate between the primitive Arab Bedouin usurpers who masquerade as Egyptians, or the true Persian descendant's of Babylonian Kings with their rich cultural history in the arts and science. They believe that an Arab is an Arab, is an Arab....... I've heard it all before and it is boring as hell."

Abe was quickly souring on the whole idea of the evening even before he had donned his dinner jacket. "No one speaks of the unspeakable. No one stands up for injustice and the plight of Muslim women. As a doctor I am enraged by their hypocrisy." His demeanor was menacing and his dark eyes looked back at him in the mirror in rebuke. He slumped slightly when he realized that Christi had fallen completely silent. He turned and his face softened radically when he saw her put one hand to her mouth as she slowly sat down on the end of the bed behind him. His lips spread into a big toothy grin. "Alright, OK......I will behave myself. Don't worry."

When they walked out the front door, Christi eyed her husband appreciatively. *He looks so handsome tonight,* Christi thought. *I should keep my arm in his the entire night or some wicked enchantress will steal him away.* She was never really jealous, and she didn't actually worry about Abe wandering away from her. He was devoted to her and Assal, and virtually blind to his own charm, and the sultry gazes of other women.

The limo driver glowed with admiration as they entered the vehicle. Dr. Zubayer was not blind to his wife's beauty. He stared at her tailored satin gown of ivory that accentuated her beautiful petite figure (she had shed her baby fat after the adoption of Assal), yet somehow the cut of the dress imparted a false impression of height that was merely an optical illusion. It was the long satin inset from her plunging bust line to the narrow hem that just barely skirted the top of her silver sandals that made the whole look so beautiful. Her thick auburn locks were piled high upon her head and long white gold earrings with diamond drops were not inconsequential as they framed her face and complimented her soft brown eyes. Abe had personally selected the earrings as a birthday present. *I knew they would be perfect on her,* he bragged to himself.

"You look gorgeous," Abe whispered in Christi's ear. "Maybe we can leave the party early."

Christi's soft peachy complexion and pale silvery nails were exquisite, and perfectly in sync with the entire ensemble. She flashed her crooked smile at him. That magical grin lent a unique charm to her otherwise symmetrical face. The imperfection was obvious but it did not detract from the whole. Abe had thought about that smile and why it was such a treasure. Then one day it came to him: *the master painter Picasso knew that trick too. One can see it in many of his paintings. But in his case it was reverse trickery. Everything was skewed grotesquely in his paintings, and only one or two elements were perfectly balanced and synchronized. That was the key to his brilliance – and Christi was definitely a work of art to be appreciated.*

They stepped out of the limousine and walked up the few marble steps to the Ambassador's residence. An ebony black Sudanese soldier in full dress uniform stepped to Christi's side and opened the door for her, ushering her into the foyer. His curved scimitar sword, sheathed at his side, slung low under a bold multicolored satin sash. Abe followed almost as an afterthought.

"Jayjan, I am so happy to see you again," Christi addressed the soldier in his native tongue of Bari. He grinned because she would be the only person here who would remember his name. And it was a delightful and charming fact that she also had bothered to master a number of phrases in his native tongue. She had spoken to him on several occasions at various functions held at the Iraqi Embassy in Washington.

"I am pleased that you remember me, Mrs. Zubayer," Jayjan replied.

As he slipped the stole off of her shoulders, he inhaled the scent of sandalwood soap with a touch of cinnamon. Despite his rigid discipline he held onto the stole just a moment too long.

"Here, I can take that. Please attend to our other guests." It was the Iraqi Ambassador, Mr. Fhad Abu Faisal. He turned and handed the stole to a male servant stationed near the stairs. "Take this up to the guest room and place it on the bed."

"Yes Sir, immediately." The young man ran up the stairs in his apparent zeal to impress the Ambassador.

"Good evening, Dr. and Mrs. Zubayer. We are pleased that you could join us. I am anxious for you to meet our guest of honor, Ms. Morelli, the new Cultural Attaché assigned to the United States embassy in Baghdad. Follow me and we will find her."

They followed along, Christi holding on to Abe's arm as they traversed the large room, weaving in and out among the milling guests. They came around the corner into what appeared to be a conservatory with a large grand piano in the corner, they both fell speechless when the Ambassador stepped to one side, and there before them was the spitting image of the young girl they had met in Iraq on the day they took their adopted daughter home to Philadelphia. They didn't even hear the Ambassador's introduction of Dulcinea Morelli.

"Safina, is it you? Christi whispered the question.

The young woman looked directly into her eyes without a hint of recognition, "What did you call me? I'm sorry but I thought I heard you call me Safina? Is that the name you used? I am Dulcinea Morelli."

"Yes", Abe stepped forward as though protecting Christi from the woman's fierce gaze. You look so much like a person that we met a long time ago in Iraq. In Basra, to be specific. We thought you might be that person. We have fond memories of her."

"Well, I can assure you that I am not the person you are referring to." Dulcinea's right hand grasped her left wrist, holding it firmly encircled by her thumb and palm. "I have never heard that name before and I have never been to Basra. I'm sorry if that is a disappointment for you." Dulcinea lied. She quickly slipped her left hand deep into her skirt pocket. She held her right hand out graciously and smiled at them in a fixed half grin. It was transparently unfriendly.

Abe took her hand and shook it, quickly releasing her. Abe was a fine doctor, and he made a quick professional evaluation. Her coloration was slightly pale, even for a darker skinned person; she had taken on a slightly gray tinge; and tiny beads of perspiration had gathered on her temples and upper lip. The room was adequately air conditioned so he made the assumption that the reaction was emotional. Her eyes were ever so slightly dilated, and when he shook her hand it felt clammy. He detected a tiny tremble on her lips. "I am anxious to hear about your expectations of this post in Iraq. Have you been there before?"

"No, unfortunately I have not visited the Persian Gulf countries. The closest I came was a brief trip to Egypt and a fact-finding State

Department visit to Gaza. However, I am well versed in multiple Arabic dialects. I have studied the Iraqi culture and the Islamic religion extensively. I'm confident that I can serve the United States adequately in this position." Her voice was even, and there was no attempt on her part to infuse it with false animation or excitement. She also failed to list her impressive credentials as a well-known scholar of Islamic history and culture. She just wanted to get away from these people. She remembered them from Yasmine's home – they had come to visit Badrae, a relative. She touched the bracelet that Christi had given her. Too bad she was not able to acknowledge this woman who had been kind and friendly to her at a time when she had no friends.

Dr. Zubayer was already partially aware of Dulcinea's background because Yasmine had kept him informed of her progress. The wise woman had recruited him for the Islamic reformation which he embraced wholeheartedly as a reflection of everything he firmly believed in. A year ago she had informed him that he should "get his affairs in order" because major global economic and security issues would be coming to the forefront. She had advised him to divest himself of stock market investments and diversify his holdings among commodities such as oil, gas, aluminum, and a sizable percentage of his portfolio and Assal's money should be in gold, silver and foreign currencies of financially stable governments. Abe held Yasmine in high regard and considered her to be an accurate forecaster of political events and financial developments. He had followed her advice and between him and Yasmine, they had quadrupled Assal's net worth during the last year, and secured it against global financial collapse.

"It was wonderful to meet you." Christi said.

"I am always intrigued by the intricacies of diplomacy in the Middle East and the Persian Gulf. I hope we will have a chance to discuss this later." Abe added.

Abe supported Christi's arm and led her away toward the buffet table.

"I like her. I'm sure she's Safina, the girl we met in Basra. I just need to figure out why she has a new identity, and what the hell she's doing here in D.C.?" Christi stated.

Christi stopped walking and turned toward her husband, "Abe, I'm afraid for Assal. I look at what's happening in the world today; at the animosity towards Islam, at the actions of extremists, and I see it blowing up in our faces. I'm afraid she'll become a victim of retribution. Abe, what if Muslims become the most hated people in the world? I think this could happen. I worry about an Islamic holocaust. What can we do to avoid such an unthinkable outcome?"

Abe looked surprised when Christi said, "…what the hell is she doing……." He almost never heard her swear. Christi was highly intelligent, but her low key demeanor and her grand southern bell manners might mislead some people into thinking she was slow to comprehend the issues. The fact was that in many ways Christi was far better equipped mentally than most of the high-society people, and many of the medical professionals he met in Philadelphia and Washington D.C.

Abe and Christi knew what Dulcinea didn't know, and were sworn to secrecy forever. That was an unavoidable requirement of Yasmine, a "deal breaker". Without a sworn promise to never reveal the circumstances of Assal's birth, he and Christi would not have been selected as her adoptive parents. The fact that Assal was Dulcinea's biological daughter, and Dulcinea had been told the baby was a stillborn was a secret. Yasmine had been right about this, it was the only way to save the mother and the baby from Khaliq and almost certain death.

Dulcinea avoided the Zubayers for the rest of the evening.

CHAPTER 21

◢ℬitterswéet Temptation

Dulcinea made sure to sit on the other side of the room from Dr. Zubayer and his wife. She was surrounded by men in the diplomatic core, along with several Secretaries of State, and Ministers of Foreign Affairs.

There was no doubt that the important people in the room had been briefed on Dulcinea Morelli and her involvement with a number of "think tanks", and top echelon CIA operatives. The men enjoyed sparring with her, and they did not dismiss her as merely the "Cultural Attaché" to Iraq. On the other hand the small number of women operatives were loathe to engage her. They were bright and articulate, but in the world of espionage and intrigue they relied heavily on their feminine charms. Most of them had no idea how to interact with a brilliant female strategist and analyst who was on a first name basis with the Director of the CIA and best friends with President Andrea Laurent of France. They could only assume that she slept with him.

The head of security for the Italian Contingency in Iraq was talking to his Polish counterpart as they sipped some alcohol-free punch, "There is a reason that such an over-qualified person has secured this diplomatic position. I spoke to a colleague of mine at the United States mission in Rome and he says the current US President never heard of her until last month. Apparently her position was part of a political deal for the deciding-vote on a piece of legislation which the President wanted to pass in the US Senate. You know how they barter legislation for political favors over there. It's kind of like the Vatican – they call it "Good Old Boys" and in the Vatican they call it "traditional offerings for pontifical endorsement".

"She's someone who the US State Department and the Senate Arms Committee is grooming for an important role. Everyone in the men's room at the mansion was speculating on her next assignment. I think this is her "coming out" party."

The Polish equivalent to the US CIA Director answered, "She is working for the UFN Council on something significant. I just can't get any information about it. The fact that it is "sealed" and everything is battened down so tightly that you can't find one memo or one communiqué that mentions her or her role, is definitely interesting." The two men stood on the other side of the room and watched Dulcinea mesmerize the dignitaries.

She hadn't even set foot on Iraqi soil and already the "shakers and movers" were plotting strategies and making encrypted telephone calls to their own embassies. So far, she seemed innocuous, but this ignited their curiosity even more. If her cover was that well constructed this had to be "big". Some of the younger men had attended IEP (*Institute d'Etudes Politiques de Paris*) with Dulcinea, and they greeted her warmly; even individuals who hadn't been that enamored of her at college. They recalled how she had decimated anyone who had the balls to debate her on any political or historical subject. Only Claude Molyneau had dared to do battle with her, being successful about half of the time.

She stood surrounded by powerful men who were genuinely engrossed in her evaluation of the current world economy, and her predictions of world shortages and how they would impact the United Free Nations. She heard a familiar, somewhat arrogant voice, "Mademoiselle Morelli, I am pleased to see you once again. May I offer my arm and steal you away from these poor bastards who are not fit to speak of monetary exchanges and world alliances, in such beautiful and articulate company?"

"*Oui* Claude Molyneau, it had to be you who would have the audacity to pluck me from this distinguished group of gentlemen, and whisk me away for yet another debate." Her Parisian French was flawless. Dulcinea was pleased to see Claude again, and as she took his arm she felt relieved. She hadn't realized how the encounter with Dr. Zubayer and his wife, coupled with the absence of Brecken, had escalated her stress level.

When they walked out onto the veranda he led her toward a secluded corner away from the lighting. Claude placed his right arm around her slender waist and boldly moved her to a position facing him, "May I kiss you Dulci? I always wanted to kiss you but you were so fierce at college." He didn't wait for her answer and he put his arms around her and stepped close to her. Dulcinea tilted her head back and he took her lips and her mouth with his. It was her first lustful kiss, and her heartbeat quickened. Her arms found their way around his neck and her fingers caressed the back of his head. It was a glorious deep kiss that lasted for a long time.

He looked surprised when he released her from his arms and opened his eyes. She had obviously sparked an unexpected response in him. Dulcinea stood there feeling decidedly light in the head, "*Wow, Tu m'etones!* (You are amazing). If I had known you could kiss like that I would've had a kissing debate with you at school!" she joked. It was a device to give her some time to compose herself. "How serious is this crush you have on me?" she laughed. Her defenses regrouped. Pretending to be coy or just playing a flirtatious game, was a device to camouflage her weakness.

Claude grasped her hand and led her down the veranda steps onto a garden patio, leaving the sounds of the recorded music of *Um Kul Tome*, the famous Egyptian singer, wafting in the background. She was reluctant to be led away. He walked along a path that led to a small unlit gazebo where he pulled her into the dark shadows and drew her close, "Pretty serious I think. There were so many reasons not to do this in college, but now it seems that you are in need of a friend. Come on Dulci, you know you were attracted to me too. Your kiss has betrayed you." Claude smiled and in the cross-hatched pattern of the gazebo hitting her moon-lit face, he raised his hand to brush a strand of hair from her eyes. "I'm not toying with you." He bent his head down and kissed her neck with moistened lips, and pressed his strong well muscled body tightly against her. His tongue explored her mouth, flicking the corners of her lips and then pulling out and tracing them slowly. His mouth was warm and soft, and smelled of spice.

She couldn't help herself as she pushed back against him. Dulci had been kissed a few times before but never like this. The men who had kissed her wanted something for themselves. Claude kissed her in a way that was all about her, her pleasure, and her satisfaction. He was an *ártiste* painting a masterpiece to surpass all art that had come before. He was confident that he would exceed even his own expectations. His mouth found her neck again and his tongue feathered her ear. He blew his hot breath into it, which caused her to arch her back and moan softly. His arms held her tightly and she felt protected in this embrace. His hands dropped down and encircled her waist. He looked into her eyes, "Dulci, why did we wait so long? How could we have missed all the signs?

Dulci felt a strange mixture of the desire to submit and the impulse to bolt and run. *What am I doing here in the arms of Claude Molyneau? He couldn't actually be attracted to me. Maybe I'm just another woman to conquer; another trophy on his bedroom wall. I don't even know how to do this.* Dulci's mind was running wild. Pictures of Khaliq's sweaty face flashed in her mind. She remembered the horrible pain of repeated raping, and the smell of dirty sweat and musky semen mixed together upon her body, so putrid she couldn't breathe without gagging. She pulled her hand down to her leg and felt through her dress for the shabria strapped to her thigh. Her emotions were scrambled and her logical mind was drowning in fear. There was an absence of the clarity that she always drew from in crisis. *If he hurts me I will kill him*, she thought.

Claude stopped kissing her and put a hand under her chin lifting it up to see her face. *He must have sensed something is wrong*, she thought. Dulci felt her body freezing up, rejecting......fighting her desires.

"Look at me Dulci! Really look at me! I won't hurt you. I promise. I won't hurt you – not ever." Claude's voice was compelling and she recognized the sincerity embodied in those strong declarations. She knew him well enough to know that he never lied. Claude Molyneau was void of deceit and trickery even when he was losing a debate. She knew he was telling the truth now too. She wanted to trust him. She wanted to surrender herself to him and to feel the touch of his hands on the most intimate parts of her body.

He slid his hand up under her skirt, upward along her hot silky thigh, and slowly found his way to the top of the lace material. Pulling her panties down slowly, he gently began to massage her as sweet juices flowed into his hand and slid down his long fingers. Dulci could not pull back. She had passed the point of refusal. She was possessed by desire. She had been denied too long. If Claude had not been supporting her with his other arm she would have slipped onto the floor. "Are you OK Dulci? Can I? She began to experience sensations coming in waves of ecstasy as he continued to massage her softly and his fingers played lightly. He slid her panties off of her hips. They dropped onto the floor. He lifted her up, laying her on a lounge in the gazebo. He unfastened his pants as he looked down upon her, and then lowered his body onto hers. Her legs wrapped around him.

"It's going to be alright Dulci. I promise it won't hurt. I will make you feel wonderful in a way that you have never felt. Whatever has happened to you before is not the same as this. Trust me to take care of you.

Dulci withdrew slightly. She was instinctively afraid. Her body remembered the pain. Her eyes opened and looked at Claude's strong, handsome face in the moonlight. His eyes reflected excitement and energy tempered with concern. He leaned down and kissed her face, her eyes, her cheeks, her forehead, her shoulders and her neck. Their lips met and his tongue found her mouth to be sweet and soft and accepting. He unzipped the side zipper of her strapless gown and lowered it down around her waist and buried his face in the rosy brown nipples, nibbling on one and using his fingers to stroke the other. Shivers traveled through her body. He remained hard and firm inside of her. Her nipples became ultra sensitive from her arousal. Dulcinea was teetering at the precipice of climax.

Claude expertly built upon this crescendo like trills up and down the keyboard of a piano. It would begin again and again but never quite reach the climax – the last note of the symphony. This was exquisite torture of Dulci's senses. *I thought there was something wrong with me. I thought I was damaged beyond ever having any kind of a normal life or experiencing love*, she thought to herself. She remembered only the horror of rape as a child bride, and later, on the Hercules when she was victimized repeatedly by the ship Captain. That is what stuck in her memory and caused her to deny her sexuality.

Claude spoke in a quiet voice, "You are as delicious as I knew you would be Dulci. You are lovely. I can play an opus of ecstasy on your body, and pleasure you beyond anything you can imagine. Dulci, all this time I have fantasized about making love to you - about giving you more pleasure than anyone else ever could, about making you come and come until you would beg me to stop. Dulci, are you happy *Mon Cheri*?" He brought his lips to her ear and whispered, "I am your lover."

"Don't stop Claude, don't stop. I can't stand to be left on this cliff. Please!" Dulci begged him. She felt her breath becoming more even, and the excitement dropping to a bearable level. He had stopped moving and stopped nibbling on her nipples while he talked to her in a soothing voice.

"Dulci, I'm slowing things down just a bit so that I can bring you with me. We are going to climax together. Just do what I ask of you." He put his hands on her breasts and massaged them, teasing her nipples. This sent more waves of sexual energy through her body. She thought she might faint from the pleasure. He took her hand and brought it down while he straddled her. "Touch me Dulci. Guide me and move with me so we reach this pinnacle together."

She eagerly responded to Claude's request. She loved the sensual feel of his smooth, taut skin. She could hear his rapid breathing. Claude was close to his climax.

His hands came down and pulled her up as he turned them over together, he lifted her up onto him and as he entered her completely, he took both of her breasts in his hands. She could no longer stand the waiting and she burst through the boundaries of control and reason and was freed from mental barriers. She was suspended in an orgasmic flood of sexual crescendo at the same moments that Claude gasped and lifted his hips, thrusting again and again. Dulci cried out as tears of release streamed down her face.

Unlike her childhood experiences, this time it was a cry of exhilaration. Dulcinea was crying from joy, and the tears splashed upon Claude's chest. She continued to produce wave after wave of tingling bliss. Simultaneously Claude's pleasure was gloriously magnified because Dulci's muscles were contracting over and over as she held him captive. "Oh *Mon Dieu*, Ohhhhhhhh dear God," Claude whispered hoarsely. When it finally ended he carefully and slowly rolled to one side and sat up on the side of the lounge holding his head in his hands. "That was different than anything I have ever felt. That was, Wow....." He searched for the appropriate expression unsuccessfully. "Special, *magnifique.......grande......*"

They were partners who both had the genetic capacity for multiple orgasms – like star bursts on a string, one after the other. This phenomenon guaranteed a successive and escalating explosion of passion each and every time they would come together. It was a new experience for Claude as well. He had never been with a woman who had achieved this level of arousal and climax – he reacted like a teenager who was doing it for the first time. She had awakened something within him that he had never known existed.

Like most upper class French gentlemen, Claude Molyneau was experienced in the pleasuring of women. He had learned from a professional in the art of sexual prowess. His father considered this to be an important part of his general education and preparation for a successful and satisfying life. But, the encounter with Dulcinea was different.

He looked around him and an expression of realization came over his face, "I can't believe that I made love to you in the dark unremarkable setting of a garden structure with lawn furniture, in a lattice enclosure without privacy. What was I thinking? You deserve better than that. *Mon Cheri*, we should have been in the penthouse suite of a swank hotel in an exotic location that would have been equal to the occasion. I'm so sorry, Dulci. I didn't plan this."

"Claude, I don't care about the setting. I was with a man that I trust. Do you know how impossible that is for me? I trusted you, and I was safe. You made my life better, and fulfilled a part of me that was empty. I had never trusted any man intimately until today. For that I'll always remember you. I'll forever feel passion with this image of you, sitting on a lounge in a Gazebo in Paris with your face aglow, and your hair damp with the perspiration of lovemaking. Don't apologize for that Claude."

"I love you Dulcinea. I never thought I'd be able to say that to anyone. But it's true. It's not just the perfect physical connection, which is incredible. I feel like I could share anything with you. The two of us make an incredible pair. I knew it from the first time we were teamed up together in college. I know that you're destined for great achievements, and that your life is not your own. I'll settle for whatever time and whatever place we can manage. I'll be true to you Dulci, I will keep my heart for you and you alone, *Mon cheri*."

Dulci looked at him, studying his expression and judging his sincerity. She was organizing herself mentally; putting back the pieces of her mind after her explosion of physical lust had been contained. "Please don't make any promises now," she said. "Just live in the moment. I don't know where this will take us – it was unexpected. I'm not sure I know what love means or how to capture love in words. Let's just give ourselves some time."

After they reassembled their clothing and rested for a few moments, it was time to return to the reception, to the world, to their own reality. Claude kissed her and turned back towards the mansion, walking briskly. Halfway up the path, he turned to look back at her, but she was gone. Instead of entering the main residence, he ducked into a side door, retrieved his coat and went out to find his driver. He had no wish to socialize with diplomats and politicians this evening. He had that satisfied look on his face, the one that reflected cat-like relaxation.

His driver grinned at him in the rear view mirror, "You got laid Monsieur. You got laid!"

"Shut up Harry. What I got was a whole lot more than just getting laid," he ran his hand through his thick hair and rested his head on the seat back. *Mon Dieu, qu'est-ce qui se passe? (My God, What happened?)* he asked himself.

Dulcinea had gone into the bathhouse off of the gazebo. She used the pool towels and running water to clean up. She put her hair back together and reapplied her simple make-up. Thankful that she had some L'Aire de Temp perfume in her evening bag, she sprayed it into the air in front of her and walked through the mist. It should diffuse the musky scent of raw sex that enveloped her. She didn't want to think about this tonight. She just wanted to savor the outrageous experience, and the revelation that she could achieve arousal and orgasm.

She pushed Claude Molyneau out of her mind and refocused her thoughts on the terrorist threats against Iraq and the United States, and the anti-terrorist commitment from member nations of the UFN. The Egyptian, Tunisian and Libyan revolutions had been received with lukewarm support by the rest of the world. They were ill-prepared to govern themselves. This created a vacuum for the Muslim Brethren to fill. If Iran had not jumped the gun with the premature attack on Israel, the Brethren might have easily gained control of those countries, but by Iran alienating the rest of the world it became impossible for the Brethren to establish dominance among rival revolutionaries. With the exception of Libya, the others were mildly westernized, at least outwardly. Dulcinea used the analytical part of her brain to drown out her personal failures and disappointments in her life. Now she was trying to use that device to quell her guilty conscience.

Dulcinea mentally pulled herself together until she remembered Brecken, and a feeling of desolation and betrayal wracked her conscience. She felt emotional fatigue coursing through her body. She knew he was in love with her, and had been for years. Brecken had sacrificed his personal feelings for the sake of the revolution. Did she really love him despite the mission and despite her intimate encounter with Claude tonight? Why were world conflicts and global politics so much easier to divine than the deepest recesses of her heart?

A few minutes later when she exited the bathhouse, Jayjan, the Sudanese soldier from the entrance door, was waiting outside the bathhouse. She looked at him and was silent.

"Don't fear, Ms. Morelli, I will keep your secrets. I am not your enemy. I am here to protect you. Please believe that." Jayjan looked down in deference. He whispered the password for Council operatives.

She suspected before this that he was somehow connected to the UFN Council, "I do believe you Jayjan. I was just startled. I didn't know anyone had followed me. I know this wasn't discrete, but it wasn't something I had planned to do either." Dulcinea wondered why she was trying to explain it to the soldier. "Do you have to report this to the Council?"

"Come with me Ms. Morelli. I have a car waiting for you on the other side of the property. I already have expressed your regrets for leaving early. I told them you were still suffering from jet lag because of your trip from Paris last night, and that you begged their forgiveness and understanding that you had to leave early." He offered his arm and motioned toward the path leading out of the back of the gazebo. "And, no – I won't report your private business to the Council. That has nothing to do with my mission, which is to facilitate your practical needs such as transportation, weapons, communications, and safe passage to your new assignment in Iraq. I have no obligations or orders to report on your personal activities."

As they stepped off the path and were making their way down a hillside to a waiting car, Jayjan stepped around a body lying close to the path and led her safely past it. "Never mind this. He was a spy sent by the Muslim Brethren to carry out surveillance on you and report back to them about who you spoke with, and to record those conversations. I knew someone was being sent, I just didn't know who it would be," he said in an unruffled voice.

"Is he dead?" She looked a little askance but she kept her comment terse and to the point, "Did you have to kill him?"

"He is dead, Ms. Morelli! My job is to make sure you are safe and any information collected about you is destroyed. It would be impossible to destroy information in his head without destroying him. You aren't going to get upset about this, are you? I was told you are quite capable of defending yourself in any manner necessary."

"No, I'm not upset. I'm curious, and concerned about who this was, and why he was following me? Won't his disappearance raise even more questions?"

Jayjan was hurrying her along the path down the hillside toward the lower road. The lights of the city sparkled as the view opened up when they came out of the trees to a narrow gate in the stone wall behind the residence. While he worked the key into the gate lock he continued speaking low, "The man didn't have any identification on him. But I recognized him from photographs and video supplied to me. He was a member of the international assassination core of the Muslim Brethren, the Chimera. He had their mark on his arm. These men work for the highest bidder. They have no real cause; anarchists, assassins, murderers, for hire basically. They funnel millions of dollars in fees into the Muslim Brethren. It's a well-organized gang. They're no different than the street gangs of America, just better funded, better organized, and better trained. They claim some fundamental blessing of Allah. This makes recruitment easier among the young uneducated Muslims around the world. I seriously doubt that the Brethren will advertise the existence of this person, let alone take responsibility for hiring him. However, his death might send a warning message – to back off."

Dulcinea was relieved. She was safe, thanks to Jayjan, and she also had her privacy intact. Dulci seldom became emotional over the death of her enemies. She wasn't the same scared little girl that she had been on the Hercules, when she killed a man. She didn't agonize over the death of an evil person. In fact she took some solace in their deaths. In some significant way it was retaliation and retribution against Islamic jihad. Revenge was almost a DNA component of Islamic hereditary makeup. Dulcinea was, after all, an Arab.

She had not been looking forward to rejoining the reception, and having all eyes upon her trying to figure out where she had been for the last hour. She was confident that as soon as she was safely delivered to the waiting car, Jayjan would dispose of the body and she would not be linked to that incident. "Thank you for your resourcefulness. I will not forget you, Jayjan. Does this mean I will see you on the airplane or will you meet me in Baghdad?

"I will see you at the US Embassy in Baghdad in three days. It is my job to guard your residence, and to accompany you on excursions from the Embassy."

"I have a bodyguard, Brecken Petersen. I won't need two."

"I'm sorry to be the one to inform you but yesterday I was told that Colonel Petersen was missing in action. Until further notice we must assume that he is dead."

Dulci felt the blood drain out of her face and she had to hold on tight to Jayjan's arm to stay upright. "That can't be, it can't be. Not Brecken, he isn't dead. If he were dead I'd know it – in my heart, I'd know it."

"You may not share this information with anyone. It is dangerous for you to have this knowledge. Just sit tight at the Embassy in Baghdad until this works its way through the organization. If I receive confirmation of Colonel Petersen's death I will communicate with you personally."

Jayjan helped her into the car, gave her a clean white handkerchief from his breast pocket, and spoke briefly with the driver. He closed the door and watched as the car drove away.

As he gazed toward the voluptuous full moon hanging low in the sky, he turned quickly and headed back down the path to the mansion. When he came upon the body lying on the path, he reached down and tapped it on the shoulder. "*Yella habib,* come on, you can get up now. She's gone. Our little charade worked. She doesn't suspect a thing. She thinks I saved her."

As the man arose he brushed off his pants and jacket front, reached into his inside coat pocket and produced an envelope. "Here, this is for you. We are working on getting you inside the UFN as her bodyguard. Just wait to hear from us." He turned and disappeared down the path. Jayjan's lips rose at the corners and his eyes wrinkled into smiling slivers. It was nice to be on the receiving end of both sides of a conflict.

For weeks Dulcinea drove herself relentlessly. She made all the necessary contacts throughout the Persian Gulf dominions. She sent coded communiques to all of the cadres across Europe and Indonesia (the country with the largest Muslim population in the world).

The UFN network was strong and constantly reinforced. There was an incredible undercurrent of dissatisfaction with traditional Islamic dogma.

Educated Muslims were ready to support reformation that would pull Islam into the twenty first century. They were anxious to excel in science and medicine. Muslims of higher learning institutions and those educated in western universities wished to pursue mathematics and quantum physics, paleontology and forensic anthropology. Women were hungry for knowledge. Just teaching Muslim women to read had already generated an important step into the present century.

Dulcinea's heart soared with optimism when she realized that the majority of Muslims would embrace freedom and liberty if they were not physically afraid to do so. This was important because it meant that if the UFN could provide the military support to sustain the revolution, it would go forward without much push from external forces. Once the tide was turned the revolution and reformation would be largely self propelled by the vast majority of the Muslim people.

"Jayjan, have you heard anything about Colonel Petersen?"

"Sorry Ma'am, I have not." He looked uncomfortable. Safina wondered why he was uncharacteristically fidgety and nervous.

She couldn't rest or stop to mourn the loss of Brecken. In her heart she knew he was alive. But Jayjan hadn't received any official notification.

Finally she called Vivian on a secure line, "Vivian, I can't sleep, I'm losing weight, and my dreams are visions of Brecken in pain. I feel that he's in trouble but I can't find out anything here. Can you investigate this for me, after all, he's your friend too. I asked Arnaud but he won't pursue it at this time......it's too dangerous under the circumstances. He can't afford to attract any unwanted attention at this juncture. Please Vivian, I can't stand the thought of Brecken suffering and me not coming to his rescue!"

"Of course, I'll do what I can," Vivian replied. "I have to hang up now, someone's watching and I think my house is bugged."

When Brecken awoke he was in pain. It was so severe that nausea overtook him as he dry-heaved over the side of the cot. Finally he was able to open his swollen eyelids enough to see a blurry scene in front of him. The room was small and there was a chair in the middle of it. The cot he was on was shoved up against a concrete wall. It was hot and stuffy. His body ached all over; every joint was swollen and sore. He stared at his hand. There was dried blood on his knuckles. "Gee, I must have given as good as I got," he blurted out to the empty room.

The door opened and a man entered the room. He was dressed like a typical *fedaheen* peasant with a red and white *kafia* scarf on his head. Brecken spoke to the man in English, "Who are you?" His voice was devoid of panic or fear. He was in trained-Marine mode. This was the automatic ingrained response to interrogation tactics. He would not let the man know that he spoke Arabic or understood it. This would give him the advantage if his captors conversed among themselves in his presence.

"Mr. Petersen, do you remember how you got here?"

"No, not really."

"It is strange story. We hope you can explain. We sit by fire in dark night with no stars. We hear horse come to camp. Think it is attack, we get guns. A big black horse walk into camp. You are on his back, on stomach with face down. When we try to come close to him, he move his head and would not let us by him. Then he go down on his back legs and slide you off of back onto ground. Horse stand by you – no will leave. We put our guns down. Then he turn and go out of camp, into desert. He go up hill looking down on camp. We see big dog running with him. We got our horses and followed them over ridge, but they were gone too fast, like *jenee* ghost. We bring you here to base. You have many injuries.... much pain, maybe broke bone or two, and head hurt bad. We see "Petersen" on shirt but no papers."

Brecken was perplexed. The man's green eyes sparkled under the single light bulb. "Try to sit." He put a glass of water on the stool next to the bed. "I be back to lead you out from here. We take you to Americans." He handed Brecken a knapsack. "We find this on your back. It has computer parts and disc. We need to leave. Whoever want you dead may try again." He left and closed the door behind him.

Brecken rose shakily and found his way to the door. His vision was still blurry and he had to feel around the door to find the doorknob. He was getting his bearings and regaining his balance. His memory was foggy but in his mind he saw the black horse standing over him in the desert. He struggled to clear his mind, to remember: *There were other bodies lying in the sand around me. Yes, there was a fire fight. I crossed the border from Kurdistan into Iraq with a unit of US Special Forces, and I brought the evidence that would prove the software forensics – the codes had come directly from the US D.O.D. I can identify the computer that transmitted the codes to the satellite that picked them up and transmitted them to al Qaeda operatives in Kurdistan. But what happened to our unit? Why were we attacked?*

Brecken knew about the horse because Dulcinea had shared her dreams with him and he saw the horse in his dreams at the hospital in Paris when Dulci was near death.

As his mind cleared he remembered that the horse came to him during the fight. There were two men beating him and asking him questions. They were Americans dressed in fatigues. They were yelling at him, "Give us the computer disc. Where is the hard drive from the computer?" They had him pinned to the ground when the black stallion suddenly appeared. He was kicking and biting. He knocked them both to the ground and trampled and stomped them to death until his hooves were covered in their blood.

The horse nudged him as he lay on the ground. He spoke to Brecken mind-to-mind like the NVC (non-verbal communication) units. Brecken wasn't equipped with NVC on this trip – and then there was the unexplainable fact that a horse communicated with him.........? It was too much to explain logically. He had tried to learn from Dulcinea to accept this second dimension as being woven almost seamlessly into reality. It was no longer impossible to suspend his disbelief.

He found the door was locked and he sat back down on the cot and drank the glass of water. A few minutes later the man came back and led him out to a waiting caravan. Within the hour Brecken was sitting atop a nasty smelling camel racing through the desert behind a Kurdish squad with automatic weapons and night goggles. He kept giggling despite his efforts not to, because the dichotomy of the highly sophisticated night vision equipment and communication equipment was so incongruent with this Kurdish military group, which appeared to be frozen in time at the turn of the last century. He also giggled because the drugs that he had been given under interrogation had not completely worn off.

He was confident that any information they had extracted from him was useless. He had been preprogrammed to address interrogation methods and psychotropic pharmaceuticals. A neuron isolation device had been surgically implanted in the cerebral cortex of his brain. This is the part of the brain that specializes in selecting, comparing, organizing and elaborating incoming information. It categorizes them as images, thoughts, and emotions and stores them as memories. Made up of about 8 million neutrons located inside a thin layer, only a few millimeters thick, and immersed inside the glia (a gelatinous substance made of a number of cells 8 times higher than the number of the cortical neurons). He activated it just before he was taken prisoner. Its purpose was to protect classified information. It was a virtual "lock-box" which encapsulated classified memory behind an impenetrable firewall, effectively shutting down his recall synapses when anyone attempted to access "coded" segments that were protected by key words. Not only did it shut down access, it produced erroneous information memories which had been embedded to camouflage the "lock box".

American intelligence had only recently incorporated this new technology in a select number of operatives. In order for it to function properly the classified information had to be appropriately tagged and downloaded to the operative after the "lock box" was implanted. This type of technological cutting edge sophistication is why Brecken never feared that America would fall to Islamic jihadist control or to recycled Marxist progressives. Only a handful of people were aware of the great chasm between American military technological capability, and the rest of the known world, who had no hope of ever catching up or exceeding America's might and American resolve to remain strong.

The improbable caravan of assorted US Army surplus jeeps, a half-track and half dozen raggedy camels took weeks to traverse the treacherous mountains of Kurdistan. The only good thing about this trip was the food. Early in the morning before the sun came up they would set up camp in some ravine or canyon. The men would unload the camels and hobble them so they could graze on the sparse vegetation. Several men would build a campfire while others took their falcons and went to hunt with them. In a few hours, as the sun rose in the sky, they would return with various doves, quail, and once they brought back a newborn goat and roasted it. There were no women in this band. The men were accomplished in making up the Kurdish dishes they were accustomed to eating in their villages. Their food reminded Brecken of his days in Amsterdam, just before they left for Paris, when Dulcinea cooked up a feast of Middle Eastern cuisine. He was definitely a fan of Kurdish dishes.

Somehow, knowing that someone ordered him to be killed and that the attempt had failed, made each breath and each moment of life sweeter. Food tasted better, colors were more vibrant, and there was a unique freedom in knowing that he was living on bonus time; time that was not allocated to him; time he had somehow been gifted. He felt like he'd won a million dollars. He dreamed of Dulcinea, Nomad and Remé as he slept under the eastern skies. Brecken was anxious to get home, and "home" was wherever Dulcinea was living.

The men were all between fifteen to thirty-five years old. It was hard to tell their ages because many of them were missing teeth, and their skin was leathered and wrinkled under their beards and mustaches. A few had green eyes, something bequeathed to them by the Crusaders more than two centuries ago. The eyes reminded Brecken of Dulcinea. She had those gray/green eyes that pierced his soul. God, he missed her so much. He was worried about her safety, but he had to admit that if anyone could take care of themselves, it was Dulci. He never quite became used to her ruthlessness; her ability to respond to threats with unflinching physical violence. She was a cold warrior.

They rendezvoused with a US Military unit out of Northern Iraq. The Kurdish warriors came over to wish Brecken a safe journey, and each man gave him something: a polished stone, a piece of dried jerky, a bag of Sunflower seeds. One man gave him a photograph of a beautiful unveiled woman with long black hair. "*Hadda Umi* he said, (that is my mother). Another man explained the gift, "His mother was caught by the Taliban, and raped and stoned by them. He wants you to punish the Taliban and kill all of them to free his country from these human lice."

Brecken understood the Kurdish code of behavior. This is how they had survived centuries of occupation and deceit. They trusted only their own clansmen. Everyone else was suspect. They were not so wrong, he thought. Even this American army was most probably going to abandon them now that they had a President who was building his own bridges with Hamas and Al Qaeda under the guise of forming a coalition with the Muslim Brethren. Brecken thought about these potential allies of the revolution and their role in the Islamic reformation. *We can save these people,* he told himself. *Yes, I know that we can. These men long for something real and worthwhile in their lives – and it is obviously not the Islam of the extremist Taliban or Al Qaeda, nor the deceit and duplicity of the Muslim Brethren.*

General Irwin, in charge of the ground forces in the area, was reluctant to debrief this CIA operative who presented himself as a United States Marine. The general was astute and had his own sources of information. Nothing significant ever got by him, even stationed on the other side of the world in a remote war zone – he had his global contacts, and unique access to communication avenues.

"Who is this Petersen fellow? For Christ's sake.....they put a hit on him?! Who the hell is this son-of-a-bitch? What did he do to piss off the New Commander in Chief? I sent for his encrypted file last night. Everything I could find on him says he's a poster boy for the perfect Marine. What can you tell me? Really! Oh God! Listen Johnson, I don't want to get within ten feet of Petersen. I know about it – you know - the IT thing. I am not going to discuss this even on a supposedly secure line. The whole world is getting ready to explode and this marine lands on my doorstep two minutes before "D" day! Geez, I think I'm going to puke here. This guy was reported neutralized as per CIC direct orders. You better get him out of here now! If you don't get him on a transport tonight, I will personally dump him in al Qaeda territory! I am just three years away from retirement. I do not want to make choices that will get me shot. OK! Just get this done NOW."

He hung up, opened his desk drawer and withdrew a small silver flask. His fingers rubbed the engraved inscription: For Sgt. Charles Irwin. In appreciation, John F. Kennedy, October 29, 1962. He took a swig of the smooth southern whiskey, and leaned back in his leather chair. *God, I miss him.*

In Kurdistan Brecken had met with high level operatives working covertly with supporters of the fight against Taliban insurgents. The Taliban were equipped with new sophisticated software programs and access to "commercial" satellite systems supposedly developed through cooperation between US software companies and a number of European and Chinese affiliates. Brecken was a master software signature expert. He could extrapolate programming anomalies and develop algorithms that would enable US Intelligence to identify the source of the sophisticated software. He had identified a source from within the D.O.D. These "players" were key members of the President's appointed support staff.

"Colonel Petersen, you must be really important to have a multi-million dollar transport sent in to evacuate you from Kurdistan in the middle of the night!" a corporal said who sat next to him in the belly of the C-130J Super Hercules behemoth. With a height of 38 ft. and a wingspan of 132 ft. it was like flying in a three story building horizontally! Until Brecken actually sat inside one of these "birds" he had never realized how massive they really are. They sat between the Jeeps and the mail bags. "Even the Speaker of the House can't get that done! I can promise you that we would never have found a ground crew for them if they landed here. This is not DC or Gitmo."

"Well Corporal, some issues of national security can't wait for political dithering. Sometimes those of us who actually live in the "real world" have to make tough decisions behind the backs of those who posture and spout rhetoric about saving the Republic. Leave that BS to the politicians. Soon you may be faced with some difficult decisions. Just remember, don't follow orders blindly. If you know that something is morally wrong, as a Marine you're obligated to decline the orders." Brecken reached out to the soldier and grasped the young man's hand solidly. He looked at him squarely in the eye as he shook it, "Always be ready for worst case scenario – things are going to heat up. Make sure you're on the right side."

Brecken looked down at the backup cell phone that was issued to him at the military base camp, and opened a disturbing reply to his coded message. His contact man in the Pentagon confirmed his suspicions that a deep mole was operating within the UFN revolutionary team, and promised a name and description to follow later. Brecken believed that whoever it was - they were the source of his detection in Afghanistan - that is how they knew he was coming and where to find him.

Dulci flew to Iraq and was installed in the Embassy as the Cultural Attaché. Marine P.F.C. John Ingrim was posted outside of her door. She was immediately bombarded with requests to attend various official functions, parties, and a never-ending string of ceremonies. The US Government was building new hospitals and schools in Iraq. She was expected to join the Ambassador to cut ribbons, make speeches, and generally represent the goodwill of the Americans to the Iraqi people. What she saw in Iraq was a horrible waste of US dollars. The hospitals were not adequately staffed; there were no trained technicians to operate the diagnostic equipment, and no trained maintenance workers for the hospitals and clinics. Everything was quickly deteriorating. It was a program management fiasco.

This was an opportunity for Dulcinea to actively pursue public recognition. For the moment they thought of her as merely someone who was extremely gifted in languages. She spoke flawless Arabic, had a wealth of Arabic literature committed to memory, and she had a personal and focused interest in the women of Iraq. She made a few calls and assigned a civilian contractor to set up a training program for hospital staff. "Report back to me in 90 days with a progress report,"

Wherever she went she addressed the women first. She defiantly refused to don an *abāya* or to be quiet when the midday prayers broadcast on loudspeakers in the streets. When the women handed her bouquets of flowers or came down a line to shake her hand, they laughed and whispered obscenities against the men into her ear. She was fast becoming their role model, their vision of what the future might hold for them and for their daughters.

She contacted Vivian by phone, "It's time for a vacation. I'm tired, and I need to be physically ready for the future. It's not just my regular duties for the embassy, but all the other special projects that require my attention. Could you put up with me for a few days? I'll route my trip through Amsterdam, and then on to DC for a week. I'll FAX my itinerary. I think I'm looking at the 20th or 21st - does that work for you?"

"Yes, I really miss you Dulci. Can't wait to see you and catch up. Have you heard anything about Brecken? I haven't been able to pry one word out of anyone. It's like he just fell off the edge of the world."

Dulci caught her breath. She had been driving thoughts of Brecken out of her mind, not wanting to consider the possibility that she would never see him again in this world. "No, I don't have any information about him or what happened to him. He's disappeared. I have to go on. I owe it to him too. He may have given the ultimate sacrifice to save the very people who murdered his parents. How ironic is that?" But, Dulci didn't believe that Brecken was dead. She felt an unbroken threat connecting them.

Dulcinea labored to establish fool-proof communications that would circumvent the conventional systems. She was being forced to delegate more and more of the groundwork in preparation for the revolution, and then for the building of a new society. She formed task teams into cohesive units that could function autonomously through the transitional phase of bureaucratic and military opposition. The cadre leaders had to be ready and able to think on their feet, and establish a strong internal chain-of-command.

She told Arnaud, "I'm finally feeling confidant that these teams can work competently and still keep our objectives in front of them. These young men and women are remarkable. Pairing them with the right mentors and providing fast AI downloads to those who elect to take advantage of that option, has made the difference."

It was crucial that no one disrupt the connections between all the revolutionary commanders in the field. Their "window-of-opportunity" after the first shots were fired was small, and precision was crucial. Some powerful dictators would immediately shut down the Internet and interrupt satellite messages between their citizens and the rest of the world. Dulci made sure there were strong anti-jamming devices in place so that the Internet would be brazenly available for everyone to participate, and for everything to be broadcast. Plans had been laid to circumvent the conventional Internet satellite connections when the time came.

All of the planned assassinations must take place as scheduled. As much as the revolutionary leaders would have preferred to simply neutralize or contain the fundamentalist extremist sector of Islam, it was simply unrealistic to adopt a negotiating or pacification path to reformation.

Dulcinea had seen Claude several times since the reception. Each time they ended up reveling in their infinite capacity for sexual satisfaction. She felt guilty and confused, and vowed to stop the encounters and to concentrate on the plans for the revolution, but try as she might she could not resist Claude. Just the thought of his hands on her body raised her body temperature. It was a powerful pull that she couldn't resist. The flame of their passion would not be extinguished, and Dulci knew it. She also acknowledged that precious time spent with Claude demanded a price.

"Claude, I can't keep doing this. I feel like a cheat. I don't love you, not in the way I love Brecken. He might be dead, but I don't believe that. How can I lose myself in your arms while my heart aches to see Brecken's face? There's something very wrong with me."

He reached out and took hold of Dulci's arm, pulling her close to him. "There's nothing wrong with you. You're sleeping with me because you are forbidden by your position in the UFN to have a physical relationship with Brecken. I know you love him. You made that clear. Yes, this is probably wrong, but tomorrow both of us could be dead. Let's be honest with each other. The probability that both of will survive the revolution is slim at best. You live under a constant threat of assassination and I spend most of my time flying around the world trying to pound financial sense into pig-headed, greedy world bankers. I've lost count of my enemies and statistically I should crash in an airplane. Brecken may already be dead. Who decides who they can hold onto in life? Don't analyze us, just go with it. You'll know when this is over. There won't be any question in your mind." He held her tight for as long as he could through the long night. They made love as though it were their last time.

She had asked Arnaud to send Brecken on more missions in the field, and to assign a new personal body guard to watch her. Her explanation was that Brecken was getting too attached to her and it was becoming increasingly awkward for both of them. Now she blamed herself for Brecken's disappearance. She had caused his deployment. With Brecken away from her she realized that a part of her was missing, a part of her that Claude could never restore. She could imagine her life without Claude Molyneau but she could not fathom her life without Brecken.

Arnaud assigned Jayjan as Brecken's replacement. The French President, Andrea Laurent, was a close friend of Dulcinea, and he was committed to the UFN agenda, "Beware, Dulcinea, this new bodyguard of yours.....Jayjan? There is something about him that I feel is bone cold....how you say... oui, 'bone chilling'. Oui, he is not to be trusted. I had him researched by my Chief Security and we found his file to be too clean, too free of any incident. He is *trei* transparent. This is an impossible achievement. All men have those sharp corners somewhere in their lives. This man's past is manufactured - a façade - it is not... *concrétiser... non vérité!* - not true."

Safina had questioned Arnaud about Jayjan, and shared the concerns of the French President, Andrei Laurent, with him. Arnaud dismissed the "too clean" record as just a case of someone who was incorruptible and careful. He managed to draft him for the position through a discreet request to the Iraqi Ambassador to the United

States. The Ambassador was privy to the UFN plans for Iraq, although he had no idea about the identity or role of Dulcinea in the Islamic Reformation. He extended all courtesy to the French diplomat.

The Iraqi Ambassador didn't know that Jayjan was a high level operative working for the UFN and assigned to protect the future President of the UFAS. Likewise, no one in the UFN knew of Jayjan's other priorities.

Dulcinea was puzzled. She had trusted Jayjan and he had been vetted by the highest level of intelligence for the UFN. Maybe Andrea was just being overly paranoid. But she tucked the comment away in the back of her mind, and promised herself to keep a closer eye on Jayjan.

On the plane ride home Brecken decided it was time to break the rules. He wasn't going to let Dulcinea get away from him. He would grab whatever moments of intimacy they could find together in the midst of an upside-down world that they were trying to fix! *I love her and I know she loves me. To hell with our orders – life is too short.* He had talked himself into it. His brush with death had made him rethink his commitments. Getting off the airplane his feet flew along the pavement as he moved toward the terminal. In a few minutes he would have her in his arms and he would tell her how he felt. Just making the decision was such a relief. He felt invigorated with new energy. He was ecstatic when he learned that Dulcinea was on a brief vacation in DC. The timing was perfect. They could spend the week together.

The moment Brecken saw Dulcinea waiting for him at the airport in DC he knew that something was wrong. At first he thought the circumstances might remind her of their meeting at the Paris airport when the terminal blew up. Dulcinea was smiling artificially and there was a barrier between them that had never been there before. It was as though she were functioning in some robotic mode. She had lost the enthusiasm that she always displayed for his arrivals. Instead of throwing her arms around him or grasping his hand in hers, she talked incessantly about nothing, and the chatter was so out of character. Dulcinea kept a physical distance from Brecken as they walked toward the exit from the passenger arrival area.

"What is it Dulci? What happened while I was gone? Something isn't right here – this isn't you, not your style at all. Tell me what's going on!" Brecken blurted out. He raised his hand to his head and ran his fingers through his hair, quizzically tilting his head at an angle.

"No, nothing is going on. I'm just distracted today. It's been hectic. I haven't been sleeping well with all the details buzzing around in my head. I just need to focus and get a break in the intensity. Don't worry about it......it's nothing. Really, it's nothing," Dulcinea repeated nervously. She was licking her lips and avoiding eye contact with him.

Brecken stopped, and reached out and grabbed her upper arm, pulling her around in front of him. He dropped his carry-on bag on the floor and grabbed her other arm, "Let's get away for a few days. As soon as I am debriefed we could go up to Camp David. This high level analyst in the Pentagon owes me a favor, and I know that the President is out of the country until next week. We could have the place to ourselves. Can you get away for a day or two?" Brecken asked.

Dulcinea looked away from him, and she stared at the ground. He could feel the change in her, and then it hit him - he figured out the rest. *She's seeing someone. She's been with someone else.* His mind was racing, and he felt like his heart was going to launch from his throat.

"Who is he? Is it someone I know? Are you in love with him?" His eyes were hard and piercing.

Dulci stared back at him. She set her jaw and swallowed, "He's someone you know of, but I don't think you have ever actually met him. His name is Claude Molyneau. I know him from college. He was on the debate team." She pulled free of him, turned and walked toward the exit. She blinked the tears back and motioned to her driver. "Put his bags in the car and take Mr. Petersen wherever he wants to go."

Before Brecken could catch up with her she hailed a Taxi, climbed in and took off. He was stunned, hurt, and confused. *She knows that I love her. How could she do this?* He climbed into the back of the limo and looked in the rear view mirror on the windshield. He saw the face of Jayjan, as he stared back at him from the driver's seat.

He hadn't planned to fall in love with her, but he never had a choice. She was everything he longed for. When he closed his eyes he imagined her warm body pressed against his, and smelled the "fresh brisk" scent that Dulci exuded. She was brave and direct, free of pretensions, and yet when it came to her mission and commitment, she was crafty and "smart like a fox". When he looked into her gray-green eyes it took every ounce of his Marine discipline to keep from taking her into his arms and kissing her passionately. Today he had thought that would all change and that he would tear down the barrier between them.

Dulcinea was independent, intelligent and analytical, yet he saw her burst into tears over the death of the dog, Remi. He watched her care for Vivian after she was shot, with the tenderness and love that a sister or mother would have exhibited. She wielded a knife with the precision of a surgeon, killing two men with the flick of her wrist before his eyes. But he was blindsided by this. He had never imagined that she would love anyone else. He hadn't considered this possibility.

"Where should I take you Colonel? Would you like to stop on the way and pick up some therapy in a bottle?"

"Sounds like a plan to me." Brecken leaned back in the seat and tried to compose himself. He was stunned. His initial anger had dissipated and was quickly replaced with self-pity and despair. His mission was to protect Dulcinea, and he was given specific orders not to allow personal attachments to develop between them that would distract her from the goals of the operation. "I followed my orders. I should have seen this coming. Now I know why I was deployed and replaced here. I foolishly thought it was because of my expertise. I never dreamed that the 'higher ups' would accommodate Dulcinea's liaison with her college chum!"

"They didn't accommodate it. They don't know anything about it. Colonel ......"

"Call me Brecken, Jayjan. We're off the record here. Tell me what is going on – at least as much as you CAN tell me."

"She doesn't love him. You should believe me about that. It's just for sex. She has her orders too, and one of them was a prohibition about sleeping with her bodyguard! Involvement with you was impossible because you were strictly 'off limits' to her." He hunched his shoulders and put up one hand in the air above the front seat, with the palm up while he kept the other one on the steering wheel and looked ahead. Brecken peered at the face in the mirror. Jayjan's mouth twisted to one side as his lips pursed. It was fairly obvious that he considered this an unsolvable dilemma. "Did you expect her to live like a Nun? Women have needs too. Can you honestly say that for the last ten years you have never found solace with another woman? If you didn't, then you are a saint. You know this is true."

Brecken stared at Jayjan. The truth was that Brecken didn't even remember their names or their faces. They meant nothing to him. When he was with another woman it was a pleasant distraction and nothing more. He loved Dulcinea, but he had not thought about this from her perspective. The limo came to a stop and Jayjan jumped out and went into the liquor store. He came out a few minutes later with a paper bag which he handed to Brecken over the back seat.

"When you went missing, she tried every way to find out what happened to you but she hit a brick wall in all directions." Jayjan turned around in his seat and looked at Brecken. "She was told that you were probably dead and your body would not be found if you had been dumped in the desert." Jayjan fell quiet as he turned around and put the limo in gear.

Brecken looked in the bag and saw it was a bottle of Jack Daniels. *Do I really need this?* He pondered in silence.

A few minutes later they pulled up in front of a local hotel. "Take it easy Brecken, life is full of surprises. Nothing turns out exactly as you plan it."

After Brecken got out and headed toward the entrance. Jayjan sighed and got back into the limo. He punched his code into Control, "We're down for the night. The second string is center front now." He looked over toward the car parked across the street. The lights flashed once. He was officially off duty until tomorrow morning. He drove off toward home and a cup of hot tea. His wife would be glad to see him. One of the perks in guarding Dulcinea was the fact that she was quite capable of taking care of herself. She had a sixth sense when it came to the anticipation of danger. It had been a long time since he had a night off. His thoughts turned to Brecken, "Poor bastard. What a lousy deal," he said under his breath.

Jayjan's wife was a beautiful woman with silky hips and long black hair, a woman who would help a man forget himself and the intrigues of the world. Jayjan had made a deal with the devil, or so it could be interpreted. He would surely die for this decision. Later, as he lay in the arms of his beloved, he wondered how they had been able to recruit him as an assassin. As he drifted into sleep, he saw the haunting eyes of a great horse boring into his soul as it pawed at his chest relentlessly as though it were attempting to awaken his heart.

"What's troubling you my love, did you have a really horrible time at the party? I wish you would be at home more. We could make our own party." Jayjan's wife ran her fingers behind his ears and kissed his eyelids. The horse's face faded from his thoughts.

CHAPTER 22

The Furrow

The winter crept stealthily across the land and vegetation took refuge beneath the earth with only spindly brown carcasses left to litter the surface. It seemed the world was sinking into its own hibernation cycle. Blankets of snow and icy frost were pulled up around the stubble on the chin of man-made interruptions in the landscape, and a season of reflection and silence began. The stubborn thorny holly with its cheerful poisonous berries and the misleading lushness of deadly hemlocks were beckoning and promising that everything would be good for everyone, like politicians campaigning to justify their existence in the darkness of the long winter yet to be traversed.

Dulcinea wrote it all down in her journal:

The soldiers hunker down in their fox holes and in their tents - and wait, grimacing, and bearing the burdens of a war they only slightly understand. Too bad no one is brave enough to tell them it is an absolutely just and necessary war; a war that is holding off the vultures until the revolution; holding the line until reinforcements will take their place and finally be allowed to fight to win! I think those who survive will be proud,

and those who do not make it will see their sacrifice through the eyes of Nomad and they too will be glad they held the line.
D Morelli, 2020

The UFN Council had spun off a successful organization: FMEW (Federation of Middle Eastern Women) that had received enthusiastic moral and financial support from free nations around the world. It was headed by Latifa Shmaiya, a dedicated and tireless soldier in the battle for women's liberation. Even Muslim women who were held captive within their own luxurious estates in Bel Air California or Riyadh, Saudi Arabia, found ways to contribute to the organization and to communicate among themselves. The network was strong and paramount to the success of the revolution. Women who had organized cadres in their own communities had been issued unique cell phones for emergency use. These were not controlled by their husbands and they didn't have to have their own credit accounts to own one. These were prepaid signal phones, and their codes had been locked in. If someone were to find one of these phones they would believe it to be broken.

Dulcinea had engineered an ocular implant similar to the ones used in the airline industry for emergency signals. When women came to the free clinics set up by the FMEW throughout the sphere of Islamic controlled regions – they were given the option of making this connection if they chose it. Once a month during the hours that their husbands would be at prayers in the local mosques the signals were tested. Brief messages were broadcast on coded frequencies.

In the city of Jericho, Jordan, Halimah walked down the path that led through the main gardens of the city. The huge Sycamore

Fig trees were laden with red flowers resting in clusters on every branch. It was a beautiful sight to behold. Jericho is known for their extensive collection of Sycamore Fig trees dispersed between the Jericho Palms. The path zigzagged between the trees. Benches were located throughout the parkway so that one may sit and contemplate the beauty of Allah. It was a warm morning, but later in the day it would be much hotter and almost impossible to venture out in the traditional thick *abāya* that women were required to wear. Halimah longed to feel the warmth of the morning sun upon her arms and face. She looked around and saw that no one was out and about yet. It was still a few hours until the midmorning prayers. She reached up and unfastened her thick veil and lowered it. Then she pulled back the black scarf that covered her head and left it resting around her neck and shoulders. She felt invigorated as the sunlight brushed her hair and the warm sun reflected on her face. Her lips curled in pleasure. Halimah reached down and rolled up her sleeves, one at a time, revealing her lower arms. The sensation was unbelievable. All of her senses were aroused and sharpened. She could hear the birds singing in the trees as they celebrated her experience with her. Suddenly she heard a voice speaking to her from inside her head. It was the signal from her ocular implant. She had gotten it a few months before when she was at the clinic with her youngest son. He was suffering from teething. Her husband beat her for not keeping the child silent at night. He had threatened to smother the baby if she did not keep him quiet.

At the clinic the woman in charge listened to her story – and examined her baby boy. His gums were red and swollen and his first teeth would surely erupt soon. But the mother was a different story. She had multiple bruises and welts on her face and arms, and one of her eyes appeared to have hemorrhaged. "Can you see out of that eye?" the nurse asked her.

"*La,* (No), I cannot see out of it. The eye is painful and swollen but my husband will not allow me to put ice on it. He says I am being spoiled and making a fuss over nothing. He says I need only one eye to do my work and fulfill my obligations as a wife. He allowed me to come to the clinic because I told him that the nurse would give me something to quiet the baby."

The nurse was not surprised. This was a common occurrence among Muslim women. They were beaten unmercifully by their husbands and then deprived of medical care for their injuries. "Let me call the doctor in to take a look at this. I will stay with you during the examination. Don't worry." She went out and came back with Dr. Bejhari.

The doctor looked inside of her eye with a PSL portable slit lamp that he held up to her eye. "You will not see with this eye again. The damage is extensive. I am worried about infection that could spread to your other eye. The eye should be surgically removed. I can do it in a few weeks. I am going to give you some antibiotics. It is important that you take them twice a day until they are all gone. Swallow this pill after your first meal of the day, and another one after you eat the last meal of the day." Halimah nodded. The doctor looked at Halimah's oldest son who stood in the doorway. He was about ten or eleven years old. Obviously he was sent to accompany Halimah so that she would not be walking outside without a male chaperon. "*Wal-led!* (boy) make sure your mother takes her pills in the morning and at night!" The boy nodded and looked down at the ground. He was not used to being addressed by a stranger.

"How does the rest of your body feel? Do you have pain anywhere else?"

Halimah was afraid. She needed to get back home before her husband returned from the Mosque. He would beat her again if his meal was not waiting for him on the table. "I have to go home now." She said.

"OK, but come back tomorrow whenever you can get away. Now I am going to give you something that will take away your baby's teething pain and he will sleep tonight. I want to talk to you about something much more important. Don't forget – come back tomorrow." The doctor said.

When she came back the next day, the doctor asked her son to wait outside the building, "Go outside and wait by the front door. Your mother will be out soon. Here is a basketball – and there is a hoop attached to the building, in the courtyard. You are welcome to shoot baskets while your mother is being attended to." It was important to talk to Halimah without her son listening. Halimah reached into her pocket and pulled out a lump of sugar. She handed it to her son. "Here have this treat because you are waiting for me."

The doctor and the nurse escorted her to an examination room in the back of the clinic. They sat down with her. "What I am going to tell you is a secret. Do you understand this?" the doctor spoke solemnly.

"Iyawah, I can keep a secret."

"Halimah, if anyone should find out about this we would be killed. I need you to understand how important this is. We are getting ready to change Islam. The New Islam will be different. In the New Islam it will be against the law to beat anyone. In the New Islam *Muta'a* will be forbidden. In the New Islam women will not be sold as child brides for men to rape and beat. In the New Islam no one will be able to say that they are beating their wives because the Prophet gave the command to do it. No one will be made to feel less important because their ancestors were not directly related to Mohammad. There will no longer be "Shia" or "Sunni" Muslims. All Muslims will be respected in the same way.

The nurse offered Halimah a glass of water. She took it gratefully. She was overheated and fatigued. She was worried about the time, and getting back home as soon as possible. She looked up at the nurse with pleading eyes, "Help me. Please help me. I am so tired of being beaten. My life is not worth living. So many days I am sad when I wake up in the morning because I dream about death and I beg Allah for death."

"Halimah, by changing Islam to a religion of peace and love, we will save ourselves," the nurse said. "We must all help with the change."

Doctor Bejhari continued, "There are clinics like this one around the world. In the clinics we are putting small receivers deep inside the ears of brave women. From those devices they will be able to hear information about their Islamic sisters everywhere. We want you to be one of those women. Halimah, this will give you purpose in your life and it will provide you with hope for a future where women will be equal to men."

They offered her an ocular implant which would keep her connected to her sisters of Islam who longed to be free. The nurse grasped Halimah's hand and said, "When the change is completed, no husband will ever beat his wife again and go free – not for any reason. Your husband will be warned in the next few weeks. If he beats you again you must squeeze this small device that we will sew into the hem of your robe. Then go about your business as usual. Do not try to fight him or threaten him. We will take care of him. You need to take care of your children and teach your sons that beating women is not allowed."

A few weeks later Halimah's husband beat her because his food was not hot enough. She lay on the floor while he kicked her in the stomach and head repeatedly. Her children stood in the doorway and watched their father beat Halimah. She was ashamed and turned her face away from them. She reached down and found the tiny lump in the hem of her skirt and squeezed it hard.

When her husband finished beating her he left to go play *Shesh Besh* (Backgammon) with the other men of the neighborhood. After dinner they sat outside the local coffee house and smoked Turkish cigarettes, drank thick muddy boiled coffee with lots of sugar, and gambled as they played tournaments against each other until it was too dark to play.

Halimah's husband rose from the table at the end of his game, collected his bet, grinned and said, "*Allah hu Akbar.* I will go home and have my pleasure with my wife now. Too bad she is so old and ugly. I need a girl to replace that hag. I have my eye on one in Bethlehem – she is still fresh, a virgin - ten years old." His friends grinned because they now had something to look forward to. After he was finished deflowering the girl, she would be available for them to enjoy in the practice of *muta'a* (the use of any woman to satisfy their needs).

Muslim men love the Prophet for his sacred teachings, and his clear understanding of the basest nature of men. All of Islam was enslaved based on the testosterone driven lust that ruled the Islamic religion.

On his way home Halimah's husband had to walk through a narrow passageway between the main street and his own courtyard gate. As he walked through it, he was attacked by two strong men. Both of his legs were broken, and one of his eyes was gouged. Although he cried out in the darkness, no one came to his rescue. One of his testicles was cut off, and placed on his chest with a note stapled to his forehead:

No man shall beat or rape his wife without severe punishment to his person.

From this day forward there will be an eye-for-an-eye and a-tooth-for-a-tooth.

Allah has heard the lamentations of the women.

Halimah's husband spent several months in the hospital. He walked unsteadily after his legs mended, and the doctors were unable to save his damaged eye. He wore a black patch over the socket. Halimah cared for his children and kept his house clean and tidy. But, she never spoke to him or acknowledged his presence. She put meals on the table when he left money for food in the kitchen jar. He went off to work each day in silence. He worked as a baker. He did not go to the coffee house to play Shesh Besh, gloat about beating and raping his wife, or obtaining another wife. He was a broken man. His older sons ignored him. They treated their mother with respect and they brought home money and presents for Halimah. She became the matriarch of the family.

All the men of the neighborhood were terrified. Many of them were habitual wife beaters in the past. They raped women without thinking twice. It was their right. Women never fought them – because it was a death sentence to fight back. Their husbands would be the first to stone them if they reported being raped.

Because of the Islamic practice of *Muta'a*, it was hard to say who the fathers of the resulting children of the village were. It was quite possible that Muslim men were marrying their daughters; they had no way of knowing which children they fathered and which children were products of married couplings. Dr. Bejhari who worked in the local clinic had foolishly brought this question up to the Muktar of Jericho. The doctor was accused of blasphemy, his clinic was trashed, and he was beaten. Muslim men were unwilling to give up their raping and abusing of women – it was the core of their religion.

After the beating of Halimah's husband the way of life in the village changed. Men did not congregate at the coffee house. *Shesh Besh* was only played on holidays or at family gatherings. Men were afraid to beat their wives, and they no longer forced themselves on women.

Gradually the fear gave way to respect, and the family was becoming more central in their lives. They were learning, through fear, that women were not going to be victimized without painful consequences to their abusers. No one wanted to be subjected to revenge. Muslims understood the power of revenge. They discovered that women who were treated with respect and protected, created tranquility and peace within their homes. These basic lessons in humility and responsibility were effective. This project was central to the FMEW (Federation of Middle Eastern Women) plan. It was laying the foundation for a new Islamic society – this was the core of the Islamic reformation.

On the day that Halimah sat on a bench under a Sycamore Fig tree and was enjoying the feeling of the sun and the air on her arms and face, she closed her eyes and imagined herself a free woman, riding a big black horse along the beach. She fell asleep as she sat there.

Suddenly she awoke to yelling and screaming. As she opened her eyes she saw a circle of men and boys from her village yelling and screeching obscenities at her, "Whore! Infidel! Bitch! ...." They came at her as a horde, pulling her off of the bench and placing her body roughly on a sheet spread on the ground. The men wrapped this shroud tightly around her head and knotted the ends around her neck and around her ankles like a bound mummy. Then they stood her upright and shoved her feet and legs into a hole that was dug in the ground. She felt shovels of dirt being piled upon her feet. She could not move. The hands that had held her body let go of her and she was planted like a tree in the dirt. A sharp rock hit her painfully on the forehead knocking her head back, another rock hit her on her chest, another and another. Soon hundreds of jagged rocks were crashing into her body. The pain washed over her in wave after wave, and she screamed a blood curdling primitive survival siren as the rocks broke her nose, slashed her ears, and crushed her skull. Her body was battered and pulverized. The shroud turned bright red with her blood and her body collapsed spilling out of the shroud as it was shredded into pieces by the hail of rocks cutting it into thousands of ripped threads. The pelting continued for almost fifteen minutes. The bloody mass that was her lifeless body was a lump on the sandy soil, surrounded by a mound of red-pink rocks. The dry, cracked earth eagerly sucked up her warm blood as it flowed endlessly down through the earth and reached the thirsty roots of the flowering Sycamore Fig tree. Halimah's bloody fingers still held the hem of her blood soaked black skirt as they pinched the hem tightly, frozen in time. A far away voice within her ear canal was repeating, *"Allah hu Akbar, the revolution is at hand. Be not fearful, be not timid, we are your sisters of Islam. United we are millions strong and our voices will be heard............"* Halimah's voice was never to be heard again in the town of Jericho where the paths are shaded by blood-red Sycamore blooms and the shame of Islam stains the earth forever in this garden of hell.

On the day that Halimah was stoned to death, her young son had grabbed the family video camera and hid behind a low wall at the edge of the park, across from the murderers. He filmed the stoning and the faces of those who participated in the killing frenzy. There were twenty two individuals in that mob: sixteen adult men, and six young boys over the age of ten participated. Her son was frozen in fear, and as he watched his mother's brutal murder by this mob of fanatical men, he retched and gagged. The boy loved his mother but there was nothing he could do. He saw his father grinning grotesquely among the crowd, and throwing rocks as quickly as he could pick up the stones and hurl them at her. He and other men around him were holding onto their penises as they hurled the stones. It was an exciting orgasmic arousal for a Muslim male to participate in the brutal stoning of a defenseless woman. This was the reason that they were not anxious and willing to reform Islam – the deepest core of this religion was founded on the edicts that glorified pedophilia, rape, incest, and sadistic violent torturous murder. Chief among Muslim degradation was their firm belief in the righteousness of the ownership and abuse of females. The Qur'an commanded them to beat their wives, commanded them to kill infidels, and commanded them to murder wives and daughters who are accused of bringing dishonor to their families by disobeying the men.

Halimah pulled her veil off and flung it into the wind. She kicked off her long pantaloons and strode across the sand bare-legged and bare-footed. The sun warmed her naked arms as she pulled off the great black *abāya* and flung it into the sea wind where it was carried far past the surf by the angry winds. Without being imprisoned inside that evil black cloak, she revealed the simple white sleeveless shimmy which she wore under her Islamic garb. The great black horse stood near a boulder, "Climb up onto this boulder and onto my back." Nomad said.

Halimah climbed onto the horse's broad back and took hold of his silky long mane, "Run Nomad, run. The revolution has begun! My daughters and my granddaughters will be free, and my son's wives will be free."

As they galloped along the sandy beach a small stocky red mare ran to meet them. Her name was Quallil and she carried the seed of Nomad in her womb. Halimah laughed into the wind with her mouth open and her arms spread wide against the gusts of sea air. She was happy. At last she was truly happy. She understood. *Freedom is the source of all happiness in the Universe. Freedom and liberty are words unspoken by Muslim women for over 1,400 years of Islamic bondage and slavery. She was at last free in death, free of fear, free of pain, free of ignorance, and free of MEN!* Nomad carried her to safety, and into the light of Allah's love.

Halimah's son hid the video tape until a few weeks had passed. Then he took it to the doctor who had treated his mother, "I think my mother would have wanted you to have this video tape. I was teaching her to read, and one day she told me that in the future women would be free to attend schools, work in offices, and even become doctors. Each day she made my favorite foods, and each day she worked hard to learn the letters of the alphabet. She was a good student, better than the boys in my class with the Muktar. My mother was a good person and she did not deserve to be murdered. Do what you can with this video; let the world know what was done here in Jericho. Let them see the true face of Islam, not the face they show to visitors who come to sit under the red flowers of the Sycamore Fig trees.

CHAPTER 23

The Steps to Revolution

Seven signals were intercepted, and local *shurtah* (police) and elders of the villages and towns were unable to decipher the messages or to understand how the women were listening to these jammed devices, or even why they had them. Although these women were beaten and tortured by the *shurtah*, they did not divulge the secret of their ocular implants. It became a badge of courage to have the device, and more and more women were asking for them at local clinics, markets, and hospitals. The password to obtain an implant was only given to those who already had one, so they were cautious about referring any woman that they did not trust completely.

A subtle, yet significant, change occurred in the Islamic culture. Women in every Islamic community were viewed differently than before. It was no longer customary to beat one's wife. Proclamations of Qur'anic commands to beat women, or kill wives and daughters, for perceived violations of family honor were regarded as highly dangerous to men. Muslim males who made such proclamations or espoused such rhetoric from the pulpits of the mosques, or sitting in the courtyards playing s*hesh besh* (backgammon), were beaten and warned to refrain from such blatant disregard for the rights of women. Those who engaged in wife beating were castrated.

Public stoning guaranteed a death sentence to any man, boy or woman who engaged in such activity. The message was clear and unequivocal – stoning was not permissible for any reason. The punishment for it was death and it was swift. All of the participants of the stoning of Halimah were shot through the head. Twenty-two men and adolescents were murdered in Jericho, and their bodies were piled in a heap in front of the local mosque, it sent a chill through the Muslim community throughout the Middle East. The UFN Council had dispatched a squad of revolutionary soldiers to ensure that justice and vengeance were swiftly carried out. They swept into the town overnight and were gone like a cold wind within 30 minutes. Every single man or boy who had participated was killed and castrated. The women and girls were silent as their husbands and evil sons were dragged out into the streets. Later, they all claimed that they saw nothing, and heard nothing.

"I make hard decisions; decisions that have global ramifications. Women's rights in the reformation will be held in the highest regard. After the revolution is completed and the reformation is law, the vigilante excesses will be a thing of the past. But, until that day when legal and just courts of law are established, our army of avengers will be out in force to facilitate a change in the culture and philosophy of Islam." Dulcinea sat back down at the head of the Council table. There was no disagreement because everyone sitting there knew it was the only option in the face of uncontrolled fanaticism and absolute power. The world had turned a blind eye to the enslavement of half of the Islamic population – the women! If half of all Americans or half of all Europeans were enslaved, there would be an outcry of unfettered support. This was much worse than apartheid in South Africa, much worse than slavery in America before the Civil War, far worse than anything anyone was willing to admit. They ignored this injustice under the guise of religious freedom. But the religious freedom was only for men! This was unforgivable, and the world was paying its debt in the form of violent terrorist attacks upon them. It wasn't enough for extremist Muslims to enslave their own people; they were determined to enslave the entire world.

The President of the United States was sitting at his desk in the Oval Office, tying up end-of-term commitments. He picked up his private unrecorded telephone and entered a special code. He folded his hands together on the desk in the Oval Office.

He looked around the room, taking his time as though committing the surroundings to memory. Soon it would be time to give up this historic room where he had wielded the reins of power. The President unlocked the bottom drawer of the desk and pulled out a cell phone. It was a device given to him by Arnaud Fournier a few months ago at a meeting in London. The phone transmitter had the capability to send an encrypted verification code – piggybacked onto a commercial signal to a satellite relay system. It was untraceable. He walked out onto the breezeway, toward the East Wing as though heading to his private quarters. He motioned his secret service man to move away from him. He punched the number into the keypad that would put his call through to Arnaud. He waited several minutes while the decryption system decoded Arnaud's voice, "Yes, Mr. President, we are ready here."

"We were friends once, Arny. Can you forgive me? You were right. I don't know if I can live with what I've done. They used me - and you know what? ......I knew it, I knew it all long. I let myself be manipulated. I pretended......even to myself......for the power, the prestige, the accolades. Arny, can you really do this from your end? Can you pull this one off?"

He could hear Arnaud breathing. "Yes, Henry, I believe we can do it. We can save the world and we can save the Islamic nations. With your help here and now - we can begin taking down this intricate pyramid of destruction, and replace it with sanity. Yes, we can save the world." The line was silent for a moment.

"Henry, activate the presidential executive deployment orders for Lieutenant Colonel Brecken Petersen, by inputting 07142856112 on this phone. Follow my instructions. Listen carefully. Keep this phone turned on. Open the bottom drawer of your presidential desk in the Oval Office. You will find an electronic notebook in the back. When you open it, a screen will appear asking for a password. It is the name of the cat we had in college - the one who liked to sleep on top of the television at the fraternity house. Authorize top security clearance for the four men listed in the UFN folder. All you have to do is click on each name as it appears and punch in your Exec One security code. As soon as you hit the 'send' key at the bottom of the screen, delete all the files, and enter the computer code that I am transmitting to you now, which will verify the orders and remove the code and the file from the memory." An alpha-numeric code appeared on the small screen of his cell phone.

"When you have completed these steps, put the notebook back in your desk. When you disconnect this phone all connection between us will end permanently. The phone will have no traceable records, turn off the cell phone and put it with the notebook and close the compartment.

When you walk out those doors next week don't look back. Leave the notebook there. No matter what happens now, you know nothing. If they don't suspect you they won't question you. And, Henry, good luck to you. We will meet again after the revolution. Don't blame yourself too much. Better men than you have succumbed to power and greed. Find a place to disappear until this is over. Your name will be on the hit list of the revolutionary forces - so you need to find deep sanctuary. Keep your head down - Monroe will come after you too. I'll find you after this is all over."

"How did you know Arny? Monroe doesn't have a vision for peace and prosperity for the world. He's a man so consumed with achieving power that he plotted with the Muslim Brethren to rule the world. I was a pawn in his global game. Good-bye, my friend, we'll meet again in this world or the next. You know me Arny, I always hedge my bets. Thank God I'm an atheist!"

"Henry, do you know how crazy that sounds? I see you still have your sense of humor even in the face of this pending nightmare. Just do what I told you and you'll be OK. Protect your kid Henry - just believe me when I tell you that the First Lady is not your partner or your friend or even a staunch supporter. When you go deep, take the kid with you and let your wife fend for herself. She's a Monroe operative."

He followed Arnaud's instructions and then went into the washroom off the oval office. He was profoundly saddened as he viewed his own reflection in the bathroom mirror. He peered at his face, the face of a scared man. He had fulfilled his part of the bargain. Monroe's voice penetrated the President's mind: "Undermine, collapse, disavow, and destroy - the fabric of the United States of America." He had laid out his detailed and brilliant plan on how to take over the most powerful country in the world without firing a bullet. He was using the Muslim Brethren to do his dirty work, with assurances from them that there would be no overlapping into his realm of authority. He had promised his friends riches beyond dreams, and power so great that Kings would bow to them. He convinced them it would be best for the common people: "Government by the people is absurd. I know what they need."

The President and his fellow conspirators had cleverly orchestrated the intricate plan given to them by Monroe, and now they controlled almost every aspect of American life. From the cars people drove to the food they fed their children - everything was uniform and regulated. It was like a horrible science fiction 'B' movie. Any business who opposed him was shut down by the EPA and the Labor Relations Board. He had implemented a huge mileage tax - to control the population movement - the most efficient way to put down any grassroots opposition, and to prohibit free assembly without actually passing laws against it. He had usurped control of the Internet and the search engines - taking away the ability of the opposition to communicate. He had instituted open borders and amnesty by Executive Orders without congressional or constitutional authority to do so. He took over the USA!

The USA was perched on the cusp of financial ruin. The conservative TV shows and radio talk shows were gone. The Federal government had taken over the networks and media outlets - some were openly federalized under the guise of equality and fairness laws, and some under veiled control by presidential appointees who used federal grants and federal protections to shut down opposition through heavy fines, taxation and outrageous licensing fees. Printed literature of any kind was prohibited by law under EPA regulations (save the trees, eliminate book distribution, stop global warming and minimize the carbon footprint). Electronic readers were licensed and monitored by the Federal Communications Board. It was genius – how easy to track the entire population, regulate their access to information and screen editorial comment. An Executive Order was all that was needed.

He could feel the dogs of Islam breathing down his neck, using threats of terrorism, and he knew that the dogs of Peking were salivating over the spoils of their labor as they edged up the interest rates on their loans. They were ready to squeeze America. These strange bedfellows had plotted successfully to bring the US to her knees. The President had bartered the country away in exchange for notoriety, lavish life style, and the adulation of the nonworking poor. The elitists 'progressives' who longed to rule in this new monarchy of greed and excess, waited impatiently for their spoils.

The President walked into his private living quarters and found his wife standing near the window, looking out. He didn't believe what Arny had said about her. He loved her and trusted her. He walked up behind her and folded her into his arms. "We're through here, Sweet Thing. I…..can't believe it ended like this. Eight years passed like……..," He snapped his fingers in the air.

She pulled away from him and turned around facing him. She was a big woman with strong upper arms and a pronounced jaw line that almost suggested an under bite. She wore bold fire-engine red lipstick and big bulky jewelry - expensive but definitely gaudy *neuveau riche*.

The President's personal aid had once described her to Arnaud Fournier as: "Flashy, with a street-gang sluttish flavor." All the President could see was her big glossy mouth with over-sized chemically whitened teeth, shouting at him, "I told Bill Monroe you'd never stay the course. I knew you wouldn't have the guts to suspend the elections and declare a state of emergency so you could stay in office permanently. I knew you were weak, indecisive, and incompetent. He made me marry you, Henry. I even had a kid to make it look good. I never cared anything for you - you should know what I am. I'm not into guys, but you're too in love with yourself to notice that."

She walked away from him into the bedroom. She was packing her bags - her ten thousand dollar set of red Moroccan leather, hand-sewn luggage was bulging with the loot from her reign in the Capitol. Just as quickly as her outburst had ignited - her voice fell silent. She got a quirky little smirk on her face as she eyed her husband, who had followed her and stopped in the doorway.

She picked up her cell phone up off the bed and punched in a number. "Hi baby, I'll be there by 10:00 pm. Send your limo to O'Hare. I can't use the President's fleet anymore - too many paparazzi. Wear that little red negligee of yours - you know how it turns me on darl'n. And, sweetheart, how is my little Cocker Spaniel puppy? I can't wait to meet him - you have the best puppies." She paused while she listened to the response. "Yes you do - even Caesar says so." Another pause lasted just a few seconds. "No, I'm done with that. I'm leaving the brat with his father, let him play daddy for a change." She paused briefly and then said, "Love ya too baby." She pursed her lips and kissed air with a loud "puck" sound, and threw the cell phone on the bed.

The wood of the conference table was still dark and shiny, and it sparkled in its austerity and polished elegance just as it had five years before when Dulcinea was assigned to the American Embassy in Baghdad. Back in Paris, sitting at the head of this table once again, marked an awesome journey.

"Arnaud, please show the council the video that was made in Jericho." Dulci looked at Arnaud. They had argued about showing the footage of Halimah. But, in the end Dulcinea won the argument. "They will only be committed completely and irrevocably if they come to hate this barbarism as much as we do." She argued. People all over the world have heard of stoning and they say they are against it, but they do nothing to stop it. They need to see these videos, not just the snips and blurred 30-second tapes on U-Tube, but the real thing in full HD color. Once they actually see this atrocity they will not be able to ignore it.

The members were surprised, "I thought our commitment to the revolution was obvious. What could a video tape do to indoctrinate us any more? We heard all the logical arguments for the revolution and we made our support known. Why should we waste our time on a video?" The Indonesian Secretary of Foreign Affairs sounded annoyed. He did not want to think that atrocities of such magnitude were actually real; actually happening in this century. Dulcinea had documentation of this practice in the countries of each participant. She handed each member the file for their country, with the documentation, dates, names, etc. In America they could not stone the girls, so they ran over them with their cars or slit their throats and threw their bodies in the alleys. The courts were merciful to these men giving them imprisonment instead of death sentences. The defense was one of cultural preconditioning. In other words, they could do it because they were Muslims.

About half way into the stoning footage, several of the council members were retching and had to leave the room. One or two others had their hands over their mouths and looked uncomfortable. One female member from Egypt was so shaken by what she saw on the screen that she burst into tears. Stoning was outlawed in Egypt. If they happened at all, it was in outlying villages secluded from the general population. She had heard rumors, but had never believed they actually still happened in any Islamic countries.

Dulcinea departed Paris on a direct flight to Baghdad She wasn't flying first class under her regular passport. There was only one person on the flight who knew who she was – an Israeli Mousad agent, Yoram Levy. He was an Air Marshal for international flights, a fully armed and trained counter terrorist operative. Israel had become a preferred source of personal body guard protection operations for the United States, Canada, UK, and Germany. The IAF trained air marshals were deployed to provide security details for high-level personnel traveling on International flights. The demand for these unique protection units had escalated since the world financial constraints had curtailed the use of private jets and military transporters. Another factor in having VIPs, or those with high level security clearances, travel incognito on commercial airlines was the reality that private jets and military aircraft were potential terrorist missile targets.

When Yoram Levy seated himself across the isle from Dulcinea she paid careful attention to him, and was aware that he was not a typical civilian passenger. She prepared for a possible attack, and she consciously shut down her panic mode, and activated her self-preservation plan. When the seatbelt sign went off, she rose to visit the forward restroom facility. She almost fell over the seat she was trying to step around. When she looked down at the passenger seated on the isle she found herself looking into the smiling eyes of Abraheem, son of the Silversmith from Basra. He was completely westernized, dark blue suit, starched white collar, navy blue tie, and jet black short hair with a clean- shaved face. He quickly looked away from her, but not before he gave her a wicked wink.

So I am now part of his game …...but what is the game? She just had to trust him; he saved her life more than once. She moved down the aisle paying close attention to passengers sitting on both sides. Were there others here to protect her? Or maybe the opposite, assassins sent to destroy the revolution before it was launched. Dulci entered the small "water closet" (Americans called them restrooms or toilets) just to the right and before the cockpit door. The cockpit doors were reinforced, bullet proof, and impenetrable from the passenger side. She knew they were armed with handguns, and she also knew there was a hidden device in the passenger cabin that could be activated by the pilot or co-pilot which would render all the passengers unconscious. It was a sonic transmission that would affect their brains, putting them all to sleep immediately. It posed some serious dangers to passengers with internal electronic devices such as pace makers and electro/mechanical heart valves. It was only to be used in extreme emergencies.

Once inside she removed her shabria from the necklace around her neck. She unscrewed one of the beads on the decorative sheath and placed it inside of a hollow enamel dental crown in her mouth. It contained a powerful pressurized sedative that she could squeeze into the face of an assailant and paralyze them on the spot. She placed the shabria in an insert sewn into the interior of her sleeve, where she could draw it out quickly if necessary. She punched a code into her cell phone which activated her ocular implant device. She then text messaged the following encoded inquiry to UFN Control: airborne to IDA #3429, possible engagement on board, please advise.

Someone knocked on the door: "Are you OK Madam? Is anything wrong?" the stewardess asked.

"*J'ai tre bien.* I will be out soon."

Dulcinea exited the restroom and headed back down the isle toward her seat. About halfway down the aisle her ocular implant messaging feature activated. She listened as she walked, "Proceed to rear, jostle arm of passenger in seat 23D and say *Pardon Monsieur* as you pass him. Wait in back of plane for instructions."

When Dulci reached the rear of the plane the back seat was empty. She sat down and found a large envelope in the pocket of the seat in front of her that was marked, *Dulcinea Morelli.*

She looked around to see if the man had followed her, but he didn't appear to have budged from his seat. There was only one person sitting in the rear of the airplane. They were tucked up in the opposite corner sound asleep with a blanket tossed over them. She carefully lifted the seal from the back flap and opened it. There was a folder inside. Dulci pulled the seat back tray down, and laid the envelope on the seat next to her. She placed the folder on the tray and started flipping the pages one by one. Satisfied that it was written in UFN code, she took out a pair of black rimmed reading glasses from the pocket of her jacket, and looked around to see if anyone was watching her. The glasses were "smart glasses" with a hi-tech double factor authentication system built into the frames. They were just one of the bi-products of the UFN's biometric technology program. Pretending to clean the lens with a tissue, she squeezed the mid section of the right ear piece on the glasses, held them up to check the lens before she put them on. Her fingerprint on the ear piece was the primary authenticating scan and the lens recognition of her iris provided the second required factor to activate the special lens. The pages were now readable through these glasses. The benefit of having the eye glasses only read the encryption with Dulci's living eyes made them doubly secure. Dulci read them in English. She was holding the master plan of the revolution. It was a detailed time line that laid out each step sequentially. There were subheading priority tabs that showed the prerequisite operations essential to each stage of the main objective. Highlighted entries were those that had already been achieved.

Dulcinea had memorized the contact code names of the cadre leaders across Europe and America. She possessed eidetic memory which made the task a matter of reading all of the data. She also remembered the names of the villages throughout Iraq where loyal operatives were in preparation and anticipation of the revolution. There were over five thousand active cells across Europe, into the

Persian Gulf area, and throughout the African countries of Islamic influence. It was organized like a typical calling tree, but with layers of redundancy back-ups in case any link was broken.

Dulcinea deactivated the glasses and returned them to her pocket. She put the papers back in the folder and placed them in her carry-on briefcase and engaged the locking device.

Yoram Levy rose and moved to the back of the plane. He sat down next to Dulcinea. "I'm here to keep you safe and escort you to the rendezvous point in Baghdad. We are two operatives; you know the other one, Abraheem. He will be right behind you as you exit the airplane, and he will ride with you. Jayjan will be waiting in the Limo. I will meet you at the Palace just before you present your US credentials. If for any reason I fail to show up, consider the mission postponed. Read the directions on page 34 in the folder."

"All right, I know the drill. What I don't have is the exact timing. It sounds overly theatrical but, could we synchronize our watches. I don't want to announce too soon. I want to make sure that our international program is underway and progressing according to our plans," Dulci said. She looked at her wrist watch and Yoram Levy looked at his. "It's 8:20 right now. Set your watch as I count down to 8:25: five, four, three, two, one, 8:25. Yoram looked up, "We're now in chromatic sync. We'll follow the planned sequence exactly. Remember not to make your final announcement until precisely 10:00, and to complete it in under 5 minutes. We'll exit the main room at 10:06, and your helicopter will land on the roof at 10:10.

If gunshots start up, keep moving. Your job is to get from the first floor to the roof, and into the helicopter. Jayjan will take you up but you must be focused. Do not deviate from the plan. If Jayjan or your other body guard falls, you will not stop to assist them. Your mission is to lead the revolution and not to be martyred for it. We will handle casualties."

Dulcinea had one opportunity, and all of the earth's inhabitants would be affected by the success of the UFN and their commitment to the world-wide Islamic coup that she would lead. It was 7:00 am, and she was scheduled to speak at 10:00 am in front of the Iraqi 375 member COR (Council of Representatives), the President of Iraq and his full cabinet, the US Secretary of State and the Ambassadors of almost every foreign consulate in Baghdad. She was being installed as the American Ambassador to Iraq. The appointment had been announced in Washington DC just hours after the withdrawal of the last US combat troops began their pull out from Iraq. Phased withdrawals were also taking place in Afghanistan and bases in Saudi Arabia and Kuwait were being downsized. A full press compliment would be attending as well.

The US Secretary of State had arrived late the night before, and was briefed on the ceremony. Dulcinea's UFN security team had secretly prepared the Secretary's security contingency and given them specific exit directions that would ensure the protection of the US Secretary. They were also instructed to withhold that information from the Secretary. In doubt as to the Secretary's cooperation, the UFN Council made a decision to review the facts after the revolution's launch. They had no interest in assassinating anyone who was "outside" the power grid. An attempt to avoid collateral damage had been pursued as conscientiously as possible, however there was no intention of bending over backwards to avoid it when this position could endanger the success of the revolution. Dulcinea was clear about the rules of engagement, "Nothing should be tolerated that could compromise our operatives in the field, or could later surface as a counter revolutionary force. We are not going to take prisoners, hold trials, or interrogate those who stand in the way of freedom. We don't have the resources, the time, or the ability to verify or discredit alibis, motivations, or religious convictions. The proponents of jihad need to understand that no quarter will be given to them."

Dulcinea's appointment as the new American Ambassador to Iraq brought her back full circle to the country of her origin. She had spent twenty years preparing herself for this day. She was terrified when she allowed herself to think about this. *How can I lead the revolution? What can they be thinking? I don't want this role; I don't want to save Islam. I hate Islam and everything it stands for. Why should I save a religion that enslaved me and took away my childhood? I want to marry Brecken and live in the countryside of Holland with a garden filled with flowers and birds. I want to have mad passionate sex with my lover in a gazebo in Paris.* These were the honest yearnings of a woman taking an irreversible step into a future more demanding and more historic than any undertaking in recorded history.

The ceremony was scheduled to take place in downtown Baghdad. The building was three stories of chipped hand hewed stone blocks. Ornate stone work with Arabic script cut in relief adorned the borders of its tall narrow windows. The building had survived numerous battles and even some nearby bomb shelling had pitted one side of it. No one had bothered to repair the damage, as though they expected more attacks. The windows had all been upgraded with out-of-place darkened glass which made it impossible for anyone to target people working or visiting inside the Palace. The entrance was wide with broad steps leading up to it from the sidewalk. There was a wide bridge that rose over a type of moat, leading to the entrance. Thick decorated columns of sandstone rocks anchored the porch and held up the covering of wooden timbers and terracotta shingles.

There were no images or statues, but a colorful blue border of hand-made ceramic tiles decorated the border around the twin heavy oak entrance doors. Two half-tracks with manned machine guns on their roofs were parked at angles in the front of the building on each side of the bridge.

Dulci exited the black Escalade on the right side when Abraheem opened the vehicle's door, helped her out and motioned her toward the front doors. Two bodyguards armed with TDI Vector K10's, capable of firing 1200 rounds per minute and loaded with 30 round cartridges, flanked her all the way up the steps. They were taller and wider than Dulci, effectively shielding her. Half way up the steps to the entrance, she turned and looked up to the buildings on the other side of the bridge. She could see soldiers with their guns pacing back and forth on the roof, and several army installations set up on the corners of adjacent buildings. Dulci was not afraid. "Ma'am, please enter the building now, we can't protect you out here in the open," her bodyguard reminded her.

"It's OK John, I am coming now," she replied. Abraheem followed her up the steps. His left hand was locked onto his shabria and his Glock rested securely against his body just below his left armpit. Beads of perspiration dotted his upper lip as his fingers twitched slightly at his side. His tongue licked his lips nervously as his eyes darted from one side to the other, looking; looking for anything unusual or unexpected.

They went up the granite steps and entered a small ante room off the main entrance hall where Brecken and Jayjan were waiting for them. As soon as they entered, Brecken stepped behind Dulci and reached to remove her jacket. She grabbed the front lapels, "What are you doing?" she asked. Her voice sounded shrill and nervous.

"I'm removing your jacket so that you can put on a light weight, but highly effective bullet proof vest! And then we can arm you to the teeth! Is that OK with you?!" his voice was sarcastic, unusual for him.

"Yes, of course. I just didn't get to that for a minute. What would I do without you?" She grinned at Brecken. She knew he could never resist her grin. She saw his face soften and his jaw relax. He helped her get the vest properly fastened, and then held her jacket behind her so she could slip into it. As he straightened the back of her collar, he slid both hands down her shoulders and cupped his hands around them. He stepped close to her, leaned down and whispered into her ear, "You'll be OK. I had a dream last night. I saw your horse standing near you, keeping you safe." Dulci reached up and grasped his fingers that curled around her shoulder. She squeezed them gently, and stepped forward as his hands slid off.

She paced the small room, silently invoking Allah to give her strength. Dulci nodded to Jayjan who was standing stiffly in the corner of the room. She noticed that he seemed distracted and uncharacteristically agitated. Yoram and Abraheem stared at her, waiting for instructions. Brecken was checking his own weapons and making sure everything was loaded and safeties were off. He loaded up on extra ammunition and a few extra Ninja-type surprises, "Just in case! Pay attention." he held up a small cannister, just a few inches in diameter. "This is a mini grenade. It is impact-activated, and disperses a burst of powerful nerve gas when it collides with any obstacle in its path. You will each have four of these babies in your pocket. All you have to do is squeeze it between your thumb and forefinger, then throw it at your assailant. Don't forget to shoot them as soon as you can. The paralyzing gas wears off in about 5 minutes. That's a safety feature in case the enemy throws it back at you, or it ends up hitting an innocent bystander."

Brecken was always a Marine first. He handed out some more Ninja stars that fit inside their sleeves, and a sonic device that would momentarily disable any individual it was aimed at.

An impressive cache of small arms was spread out on the table in the center of the room. Dulcinea eyed them as she circled the table. She chose wisely: a light weight automatic Beretta with a clever spandex thigh holster to secure it under her skirt. A tiny, one-shot Dillinger fit neatly between her breasts, in a quick release pouch. A pair of attractive low-heeled shoes was displayed on the table as well.

"Tell me about these shoes," she said. "I know they must be a weapon of some kind."

Brecken picked up one of the shoes and reached his fingers down into the toe of the shoe. With his hand inside he twisted the body of the shoe with his other hand. The shoe split into two halves. He pulled it apart and extended both halves towards Dulci. She leaned toward him and peered into the shoe halves. She could see several wires and a tiny black cube with a flashing LED light barely visible embedded in the body of the heel. "What is that?" she asked.

"That is a sophisticated missile control device." Brecken reconnected the two halves of the shoe, pushed the interior button and placed the reassembled shoe back onto the table next to the other shoe. "If you remove your shoes, push the interior activation button and disassemble the two halves – the signal will trigger a missile response within twenty minutes depending on the distance from the launch site. Both shoes contain the same signaling capability and trigger responses from two different missile origination points. If the shoe is reassembled within thirty seconds of activation the launch code will not be generated. That is your window of deactivation." Dulcinea took the weapons and carefully secured each one. She kicked off her shoes and put on the pair from the table. She checked her watch and nodded toward Jayjan and Yoram Levy.

Abraheem interrupted their discourse, he walked over to Dulci and Brecken and whispered in a very quiet voice, "There are four assassins in the main room. They are here to kill you and the other Americans and Europeans in the audience, those considered to be infidels. These assassins are sent by the Islamic Brethren and were trained and financed by the Islamic/American Relations Syndicate. I have infiltrated this organization and am appointed by them as one of the four killers. However, as you know, I vowed to Yasmine to protect you. There is another unidentified shooter present, but I don't know who it is. We must be ready for anything."

Abraheem stepped back and surveyed the group. "Dulci, when you enter the main conference room you will be taken to a seat behind the podium. I will be positioned behind those seats. Their plan is to have me stab you in the back and slice your neck when you return to your seat after presenting your credentials. This is a planned terrorist attack upon the Ambassador of the United States. They have no intelligence regarding the revolution. It is remarkable but they are so confident that Allah guides them, to the point where they simply cannot fathom an Islamic reformation or any type of revolution."

"Let's roll!" Dulci set her jaw, put a hand on her shabria, strapped to her thigh, and headed toward the door.

"Not quite yet." Abraheem said. He took a small plastic container from his pocket, removed two flesh colored patches, the size of a dime, and he said, "Hold still Safina, I need to put one of these on your throat and one just behind your ear."

"What are they for? I am not a smoker and I don't need a nicotine fix."

"This is a communication patch known as an SVC – Subverbal Communication device. You will be able to communicate silently to me as long as you think in words in your head – as though you were talking to me. Your neurons will fire, sending the correct signals to your voice box and mouth, but instead of reaching and activating your verbal audible speech, the messages will be intercepted by this device and transmitted to the matching patch just behind my ear. My patch will receive those neurological messages and transmit them to my brain as though I perceived them through my ocular nerve. I can send you messages in the same way. The only drawback to this device is that the optimum SVC range is within 50 yards of the receiver. Transmitting further may be garbled and the message may not be understood." Abraheem was confidant that Safina would quickly grasp the concept and adapt. She was remarkably tech oriented. "Brecken, Jayjan, you and I, are all equipped. If you say the name of the person you want to communicate with before you speak, the communication will remain between you and the designated person. If you do not designate an individual, the device will transmit to everyone in the unit." Abraheem took 4 wrist watches out of his pocket and handed them out. Dulcinea's had a narrow band on it, but the others were very bulky. "This is your on/off switch for the SVC system. Push the button on the face once to activate, and twice to turn it off." Do you have any questions?"

"No, I have already read the original prototype description about a year ago. It's extremely user friendly," Safina answered.

Yoram Levy remained in the ante room where he cleared it of any personal belongings, placing them in a plastic bag and handing them to the driver who waited outside the exit door, "Put these in the car and get your vehicle and yourself ready for combat." The car was well equipped for battle. It was a cleverly disguised mini tank. "When you hear the first shots you are engaged." Yoram used this time to plant some weapons and ammunition on the stairs behind some of the plants and instructed one of the Marines to be ready for action and to station himself on the roof next to the exit. "You'll be expected to provide cover for the Ambassador and whoever takes her up the stairwell to the roof. When they exit to the roof you'll continue to fire. Don't surrender your position no matter what. Make sure you have extra ammunition at the top of the stairs and keep your weapon ready to fire. Aim small and don't miss. They will be wearing body armor so hit them in the face or neck or bring them down by hitting their ankles first. Good luck soldier!"

CHAPTER 24

Shots Are Fired

Applause was coming from the main meeting room. She could hear Arabic voices, and some loud shouting. But she couldn't make out the words. Abraheem started to go over the planned exit again.

"I read the brief, I know what to do. I'll go back through the ante room and exit to the stairs. From there you'll cover me in front as we work our way up to the roof. Brecken will make sure that no one from the meeting hall gets through the anteroom to the stairwell. We'll fight our way to the third floor. Brecken will cover our rear until we reach the third floor. He'll withdraw back down the stairwell to reinforce Jayjan and the Marines."

Abraheem opened the door leading to the large hall. He quickly made his way up the steps to the stage and slipped unnoticed behind the draperies at the back of the stage. Dulcinea followed him up the short flight of steps and was greeted on the stage by a smiling young man. He was dressed in western attire and his beard was trimmed quite short. *"Ahallan ou Sahalan* (Greetings and peace). Ambassador Morelli, we are so pleased to welcome you. Be seated here behind the podium until our President introduces you to the Council and our guests." He spoke to her in Arabic. He motioned to the straight-backed chair. Dulcinea walked to the chair and carefully seated herself in such a way as to have ready access to her Beretta if necessary. "May I get you something Ma'am?"

"No, *shukran,* I am fine. I will wait for the President," Dulcinea replied. She looked away from the young man, and it was clear that she was dismissing him. He smiled and walked away from her to the other end of the stage and down a flight of steps to the floor of the hall. She watched him locate a seat in the front row and settle into it, crossing his legs and folding his arms possibly in anticipation of a long and boring session. *He's in for a surprise,* she thought to herself. She took in a deep breath, and rehearsed her timetable again in her head. Jayjan stepped out of the anteroom and found his way to the ground level near the steps to the stage.

The Iraqi President, Hasan Mohammad Abu Yousef, climbed the steps to the stage and walked straight-backed to the podium. He drank from a glass of water that was placed on the table next to the podium. The President cleared his throat. He gazed out at the large audience. "*Sabach al chir,* (Good Morning) to all of you who have gathered here to celebrate the arrival of the new American Ambassador, Ms. Dulcinea Morelli. I am pleased to accept the Ambassador's credentials. Ambassador Morelli is well respected in the international community. She is a graduate of *Institute d'Etudes Politiques de Paris* and an acclaimed author of several excellent works regarding International Law and the Political Power Bases in Europe and the Persian Gulf. Along with her impeccable academic and publishing credits, we are impressed with the Ambassador's vast knowledge of Islamic Culture, Arts, Literature and History. To crown all of these accomplishments and qualifications, Madam Morelli is also fluent in Arabic. I am particularly delighted with her mastery of languages because the nuances of language are also the mirror of a nation's soul."

Dulcinea looked at her watch and activated her SVC, *"Abraheem, how long will he drone on?"* Time was passing quickly. If she didn't get to the podium soon, their sequence of events would be off, and risked jeopardizing the mission.

"You have to stop him in one minute. Do not allow him to waste time, we are on a tight sequence."

She hit the button on her watch to deactivate the SVC. Suddenly she rose from her seat and approached the podium. She smiled broadly at the shocked President. He had never before been interrupted by a woman!

Provisions had been made to disable the Iraqi President immediately after Safina completed her statement. The consensus within UFN was that this Iraqi President had been primarily a puppet for the American President, and was not particularly political or fanatical about Islamic Jihad. He appeared to be a pompous, yet amicable fellow with limited understanding of world politics or any formal diplomatic education. He was born to a wealthy Baghdad merchant family. He was more of a ceremonial leader – the White House pulled his strings. The Revolutionary Planning Committee had decided to spare him, if at all possible. Honestly, Dulcinea could never feel ambivalent about any Iraqi man who ruled over women in such an evil society, and did nothing to improve upon their lot. She would have killed him in a heartbeat if she thought it was in the best interests of the mission.

"Thank you President Abu Yousef. You are too kind," she gave him a big white toothy smile as she physically nudged him away from the podium. "Fellow Ambassadors, diplomats, Iraqi government officials, and US Embassy personnel, and the outgoing American Ambassador, Mr. Kipling, I have presented my credentials to the Iraqi President under false pretenses." There was a rumble and whispering around the room. "Yes, you heard me right – FALSE PRETENSES!"

"Pay attention you media/press people! This is probably going to be the most important announcement in the last one hundred years!" This statement sparked rapid movement of the few Press Corps reporters present in the front row, and several network set-ups in the rear of the hall. Suddenly flashes of light were going off as they snapped photographs of her. TV cameramen yelled out orders to their gophers, and a hundred cell phones flipped open at the same time.

Dulcinea held up her arms signaling everyone to be quiet. A hush fell over the crowd. She began speaking in Arabic as translators donned their earphones and began to translate in English and French, "My real name is Safina, daughter of Latifa. I was born in a small village in Northern Iraq near the border with Kurdistan. My mother died when I was a baby and I was raised by my father's other wives. At the age of eleven, my father sold me as a child bride to a pedophile from Basra. This evil man forced me to walk all the way from an encampment in an Oasis in the middle of the desert to his villa in Basra. After we arrived at his villa I was repeatedly raped and beaten by him. Abdul Khaliq Abu El Haj forced me to perform acts of perversion on him, and he impregnated me, as a child. Five times a day, after his prayers, he raped me. I ran away from his villa trying to survive, he caught me and broke all of my toes so that I could barely walk. As soon as I could hobble I ran away again. I found refuge with a kind woman until I gave birth to a full-term stillborn baby.

In Iraq, as a child bride, I had no rights, no recourse, and no protection from this evil man. The people who saved me took pity on me, and arranged passage for me to Europe to escape death if my Iraqi husband found me. I survived, was educated, and I vowed to avenge all the child brides and the oppressed women of Islam!" Safina raised her fist into the air and shook it at the crowd as she looked into the cameras. Her face was angry, and she spoke in a passionate and loud voice. "Today the wrath of the Islamic women who are abused, beaten, and stoned, deprived of basic human rights, and treated worse than cattle, in the name of the Prophet, is unleashed! The revenge of the world community that has endured a generation of suicide jihad, unprovoked attacks, kidnappings, mass murder of the innocent, endless destruction of peace and prosperity in the name of fanatical ignorance and stupidity will purge the world of ALL Islamic jihad-ists. ALL Islamic dictators, all radical religious leaders and all of their allies will be eradicated. This is happening as I am speaking, NOW."

People started to rise from their chairs and move toward the exits. There was a look on their faces that registered as panic. Some women were screaming, and some of the guards around the room were mov-ing towards the podium as they drew their weapons.

"Silence!" She pointed to the windows around the perimeter of the room, "Listen to the gun shots, listen to the falling rockets, listen to the armies of the world who are coming after the despots, the rapists, the pedophiles, the wife beaters, the mad dictators, the evil, enslaving mullahs! This is the Islamic Revolution that will bring about the Ref-ormation of Islam!! We are the REVOLUTION. THE REVOLU-TION HAS BEGUN! Get out of our way or be killed. No prisoners, no tolerance for radical Muslims anywhere in the world. No need to blow yourselves up because we are going to send all of you to Paradise as quickly as possible!"

The assassins had all the time they needed; one double-clicked a throat microphone for the assassination to begin. Jayjan's face showed anger. He lost his focus for a split second. His training, his knowledge, his reflexes were honed to the point of a superior killer; hired as an assassin, he froze and could not carry out his orders. He looked into the eyes of his charge - Safina. She had just finished her announce-ment of the revolution, and his focus was on her, instead of his job - the environment in this room. Safina pulled out her Beretta from under her skirt, swiveled around and ducked. The assassin came at her from the side of the stage. She shot him between the eyes and he fell at her feet. Pandemonium erupted. She felt like someone had socked her in the ribs as a bullet hit her vest, but she got back up. Automatic weapon's fire was coming from outside the hall. Abraheem was communicating with her through the SVC (Sub Vocal Communications) system. *"Get to the door. Go up the steps to the left. Are you ready?"*

"Yes, I hear you. Watch out! Someone is coming up from behind you. Hit the floor so I can shoot him!" Abraheem dropped to the floor and Safina fired two rounds, and dropped the attacker cold.

The first shot went to Jayjan's left and drew his attention until the second struck Safina's bulletproof vest, and the third was deflected at an angle by the podium's microphone. Safina was having a hard time catching her breath. She'd been hit twice. The throbbing pain was excruciating. Jayjan shouted towards Brecken while shoving Safina into the ground, "Cover her. Abraheem, get her to the stairs!" Jayjan rose and took off down the main isle of the hall, shooting to the left and right as he advanced. He made a split second decision to turn from traitor to defender. He saw it now - for the first time he understood the revolution - the sacrifice of Safina, Abraheem, Brecken, and thousands of others who had put their lives on hold, put their lives on the line, for a cause bigger than any that had ever been undertaken in the history of the world. He wasn't fighting a war to go to Paradise to deflower virgins - he was fighting for a life on earth for his children and grandchildren. He took out half a dozen palace guards on both sides of the isle, and several terrorists who had infiltrated the guests and were brandishing guns.

Abraheem activated his SVC, *"Stay down until I can take this guy out. Then find a way to get to the door, I'll be right behind you. Safina, we are now strictly on SVC."*

Brecken pushed ambassadors and other political figures aside, keeping eye contact with one of the shooters who had leaped onto the stage. Before Brecken knew it, the man had a bloody knife in his left hand and Brecken had taken a cut but he couldn't afford to check it. The man reversed his grip on the knife while slashing to the left side of Brecken's neck, then brought the knife down to the outside of his right knee which made contact. Brecken nearly stumbled when the assassin kicked his knee again then stabbed downward with the knife. Thinking quickly, Brecken crossed his arms above his head at the wrists and caught the man's forearms, and then he grabbed the man's left arm and brought both of his arms down with the knife and shoved the blade into the man's abdomen. Brecken reached into his shoulder holster and brought the butt of his firearm into the assassin's jaw then ended the fight by pointing the barrel at the assassin's head and with a quick double-tap of the trigger he fired into the man's skull. Blood splattered on everything behind him as the back of the attacker's head was blown away.

Outside, the primary suicide bomber acknowledged a signal to start the attack and activated the 30 second timer on his bomb, then he ran at the compound's gate.

The US Marines outside the building deployed at the sound of the blast taking out the gate into the compound, when an RPG hit the same location. One Marine turned back towards the compound's entrance in time for a palace guard's bullet to pierce his forehead. A second Marine leaned to his right as the same palace guard aimed the rifle at him. The guard didn't realize his shot had missed until he felt a blunt sword pushing through his gut. He looked down and saw a shinny ceremonial Marine sword stuck into his stomach; the Marine twisted the sword's handle and shoved the guard's lifeless body with his boot. It slide off the sword, freeing the blade and falling back onto the ground.

Abraheem moved up behind the third assassin and brought the chair he carried into the back of the man's legs then swatted the man's gun aside again when the assassin brought his firearm around in his direction. That gave the assassin time to bring his legs around into Abraheem, and bring him down. The assassin placed his legs on top of Abraheem's chest while grabbing the bodyguard's left arm into his grip and pulling. Abraheem yelled as the assassin executed the jujitsu move and Abraheem could only watch as the man released his gun arm, and brought the barrel in line with his head; Abraheem refused to close his eyes, if he was going to die then he would not die without his courage. A bystander scrambling backwards tripped over the assassin's body. The shot came but went wide, missing Abraheem. The fallen bystander's leg knocked the gun out of the man's grip. In the assassin's struggle to shove the bystander off, he had let go of Abraheem. The bodyguard took advantage of the situation and rolled on top of the heap, keeping his gun aimed beneath his left armpit and double tapped the trigger, the assassin went down with two shots in his skull. Abraheem bounded to his feet and continued the struggle for Safina's life.

Jayjan yelled in Brecken's direction, "Clear the stairs, we need to get her to the bird on the roof!"

Safina was already almost at the door to the anteroom and Abraheem was close behind. The Special Forces Marine leaped off the stage and headed toward Safina as they converged on the exit. Brecken reached inside Safina's shirt, "Sorry, gonna need that Dillinger!" Safina gasped while Brecken grabbed hold of the firearm. He came around into a palace guard and his left foot swung out in a short arc that knocked the guard's gun cleanly out of his grip, then Brecken stepped in to knee the guard in the stomach, and brought the barrel of the holdout gun into the man's body and fired.

Jayjan dragged Safina up the stairs with Abraheem bringing up the rear and Brecken leading the way. Abraheem was grabbing the hidden ammo on the way up, and dropping the spent clip from his Glock.

From the bottom of the stairwell came gunfire. *"Do we have anyone we don't know about, helping us?"* Abraheem SV'd.

Safina SV'd back, *"I do believe those would be the US Marines that were guarding this place."*

Jayjan chimed in, *"Won't be much of this place left by the time this is all over."*

Abraheem agreed: *"Those guys will probably be seeing a lot of kitchen duty if they survive."*

Gunfire erupted ahead as two palace guards burst from a door way at the top of the stairs, and then pulled back when they saw Brecken, *"Someone give me covering fire."* Brecken said.

Jayjan pushed Safina behind him and fired two shots toward the doorway. Brecken leaped onto the landing and ran across the door opening to the other side. He reached around the door frame and sprayed the room with bullets. He heard one hit the ground with a thud. The other one staggered out the doorway but collapsed on the floor, motionless. Brecken looked into the room and motioned the others to follow him on down the corridor. The quartet had reached the floor of the heliport. *"Should be two more doors then we take a left."* Brecken was still leading the way as Safina came behind him trailing by a few feet. A man jumped out from a doorway behind Brecken and slammed him into the wall.

Safina reached for the blade hidden inside her left wrist band, but Jayjan grabbed her hand, *"No."*. Brecken jammed his left leg against the wall and pushed backward as the attacker slid one arm beneath his chin in a choke hold. The move jolted the attacker against the other side of the hall; Brecken seized the man's arm with his left hand while sliding out from the hold. He held the man's wrist and twisted it around his back then turned his head aside while aiming his gun into the back of the man's head and pulled the trigger. Two more men jumped out as a pair, aiming high and low, Brecken grunted as his left shoulder and right foot took the hits. He slammed into the other side of the hall again as one of the men took aim, Brecken's head slumped down and he closed his eyes.

Safina watched as Brecken was hit twice and crashed against the opposite wall. She slid out her blade that was hidden inside her left sleeve and grabbed hold of the Beretta stuck inside her waistband. With one smooth motion she threw the blade into the left side of the man aiming at Brecken, while shooting the man just behind him. Brecken by then had pulled the gun inside the holster strapped against his left leg and shot the man that had been stabbed by Safina. She dropped on the floor by Brecken but was shoved back, *"Keep going!"*

"You're hit, we can go together." She slipped by his side but was again shoved back.

Brecken was adamant, *"You're more important – without you this whole thing falls apart and our people die for nothing."* Anger came to her face, but Brecken took the gun holstered behind his back and aimed it at her, *"Go or I'll shoot you myself. Jayjan, take her and get her to the landing pad."* The other man nodded, grabbed Safina and dragged her away. "Disconnect SVC". Brecken said. The link went dead.

Safina's mouth was open but whatever she had to say was drowned out by two gunshots that went wide of both her and Jayjan. Brecken lowered his head, "Semper Fi." He jumped up, turning around to face the oncoming palace guards. Abraheem popped up behind them and killed them. "Jayjan's taking her to the landing pad. Go, I can hold this position." Brecken screamed.

Abraheem stood ready with his Glock in one hand and his saber in the other, "I think not. The palace guards have taken out the last Marines at the bottom of the building. The remaining guards are close behind me." With those last words, a bullet came bouncing off the wall at the stairwell and went through Abraheem's left shoulder. He looked up, "I'm afraid there is no retreat for either of us." Another shot came up the stairwell and hit Brecken's shoulder holster. The bullet only partially penetrated the holster but the impact carried him into the wall again, his vision went dark but not before darker visions passed by him.

Jayjan dragged Safina to her helicopter and shoved her in, even as she continued firing. "Get in you idiot! Pilot, get her out of here!" He grabbed a hold of her shoes, triggered the homing beacon inside them, and swung them in the direction of the stairwell entrance.

Safina had to yell to be heard over the helicopter's engines, "Jayjan come on, you'll kill yourself!"

"...along with everyone who's pointing a pistol at your head. Now get going!"

"*Spang*" a bullet bounced off the helicopter's reinforced hull. Time slowed down as Jayjan swiveled around, sinking to his right knee; the gun aimed itself until a shot hit him in the right shoulder, he aimed again with a bullet hitting his left thigh, again his gun came up as a bullet tore into his chest then one final shot came in his direction. Safina shouted just as the pilot took the helicopter around the street corner, he didn't turn in time for her not to watch Jayjan take a final shot to the head.

Brecken finally came to, and found Abraheem over him, firing. Abraheem held both his gun and Brecken's, firing in two directions, but time was not in his favor. He could feel something wrong inside him; the round he took had hit something important. He felt one gun being taken from him as Brecken sat up and started pumping out covering fire towards the direction of the vacant helipad. "I feared you were dead my friend." Abraheem panted to him.

"You wouldn't happen to have a spare gun would you; I seem to have lost one of mine." Brecken yelled.

Abraheem smiled, "I may have thrown one at a passing assassin."

Brecken spun around and shouted at the back of Abraheem's head, "WHAT!"

"I thought I had run out of ammunition. And there was your gun, I did not think to check it for ammo and I just threw it at one of the bad guys."

"Did you hit him?"

"I believe I did trip him momentarily. At least we can say we fought tooth and nail." Abraheem grinned and blood seeped from the corner of his mouth. He coughed.

"I think there's a saying that's appropriate here: someth'n about throwing everything you have at the enemy, including the kitchen sink."

"Couldn't you have at least looked for a kitchen sink before throwing a loaded gun at these guys?"

"I...... didn't ....know ....it was loaded......." Abraheem was gasping for air."

That sobered Brecken, "I'm just saying those were nice guns, that's all." Gunfire started at the bottom of the stairs, "Ya hear that? Those would be our fellow revolutionaries. It's not time to die just yet *habibi*." Brecken saw a gun in the hand of a dead palace guard, he threw himself as hard as he could across the hall, taking the gun and squishing himself against the body for whatever cover it could provide. "Can you still shoot?"

"I can still hold a gun.....I think....." Abraheem answered.

"Let's push for the stairwell and meet up with our friends. I think our fight has just begun."

Abraheem perked up for a second, "Say...., do you hear a beeping sound?"

Brecken stopped for a second, "I think I do," he looked around at the direction of the heli-pad and could see the outline of two shoes, "Hey, aren't those Dulci's shoes?"

Abraheem stopped for a moment and squinted, "*Iyawah*, I think those are hers."

"Didn't she say something about a homing beacon inside her shoes that could be activated?" Brecken said.

"Yes, a missile strike would hit the spot where the homing beacon is."

"What's that whistling sound?" Abraheem grabbed Brecken, "Those would be the missiles you mentioned."

Brecken hopped along, "SHIT, I THOUGHT THOSE THINGS HAD A 20 MINUTE DELAY!"

"It could have been shorter.," Abraheem answered. They jumped down the stairwell as the floor where they just were, disappeared. A few seconds later they opened their eyes from about the second floor, and open sky greeted them. Gunfire could be heard everywhere, "It would seem that the battle for the city has begun." Abraheem commented as he lie crumpled on a pile of rubble. His face was blackened and singed. He was dragging one arm as he crawled toward Brecken, and blood was gushing out of a deep slash on his forehead. His shirt was soaked in it.

Brecken looked gray, "It was never about the city, it was about our cause." Chanting started around them for blocks, the cries of victory. "Lalalalalalal......" The revolution inside the city had been won. "Can't those idiots see that this building still has enemies in it?"

A blood soaked Marine crawled toward them through the dust and debris, "Not anymore guys, we killed the last of them just before the missiles hit."

Brecken grabbed Abraheem with his good hand, "WE'VE WON!" Abraheem didn't answer, "Abraheem?" Brecken shook him,

"We won!" Brecken tilted Abraheem's head back, his open eyes stared up and a smile was on his face, but there was no life. Brecken closed Abraheem's eyes, holding his hand gently over Abraheem's face. Brecken coughed, trying to clear his throat. "You had the heart of a Marine, my brother," he rasped. "Semper Fi."

Safina's flight was covered by two F16-E jets packing maximum fire power. Miles from the scene she heard the blast of the explosion, and immediately after that, a missile from one of the escort jets took out the terrorist gunship that was pursuing them.

The copter headed to an oil tanker anchored in the Persian Gulf where it refueled and proceeded to Eilat, the Southern port of Israel in the Gulf of Akaba in the Red Sea. From there they flew to Cairo. She didn't know what happened to Brecken or Abraheem, but she knew that Jayjan was dead.

Safina's heart seemed to rise into her throat and the tears tore through her soul. She could barely stay conscious, as though she were drowning in the magnitude of her despair. It was the fatigue of extreme emotion that was sapping her strength. The loss of men who had protected her, saved her, championed the cause, was pulverizing her spirit. To make it far worse, she did not have time to mourn them. There was no segment on the bar graphs or the meticulously calculated time lines that made appropriate allocations of resources for the mourning of the patriots who would give their lives for the freedom of Islam. She curled up on top of a pile of parachutes in the space behind the pilot, and fell asleep.

Safina was now the President of the United Federation of Arab States. The UFAS encompassed over 360 million people in 25 countries and territories (which was similar to the makeup of the defunct Arab League but included about 80 million more people). The reformation of Islam would change the lives of 1.4 billion Muslims in every country of the world.

The UFAS had established Cairo as the Capitol. The geographical region stretched from the Atlantic Ocean in the West, to the Arabian Sea in the East, and from the Mediterranean Sea in the North to the Horn of African and the Indian Ocean in the Southeast.

Safina's helicopter landed at the International Airport in Cairo. She awoke and smoothed her hair as best she could. She was shivering from a combination of cold and stress induced fatigue. Safina almost fell out of the helicopter, and landed in the arms of Claude Molyneau, "Claude! I was not expecting YOU to be here....." Claude scooped her up into his arms and planted a big sloppy kiss right on her lips in front of her guards and her generals. "Claude, stop it! This isn't the place or the time!" She struggled to get free of him. Her body guards stepped forward threateningly. He placed her back on the tarmac and stepped back. A sudden gust of wind came up and blew sand and debris into their eyes and hair. He grabbed her arm and led her toward the airplane hangar nearby.

The body guards ran along on each side of them with their K10's clutched tightly to their bodies, and their HD eye shields pulled down from their very sophisticated electronically equipped helmets. These eye shields enhanced human sight by a magnification and sharpness of X10. The helmets were fed live audio that defined their environment from all sides because it was linked to the satellite surveillance system that protected the new President. Sharpshooters were stationed on top of the hangar and a few were tucked into the corners of the terminal about 200 yards away from them. Satellite surveillance monitored the surroundings within a 5 kilometer radius. It would be almost impossible for any assassin to target the new President under the protection program that was in place once she arrived in Cairo.

As she turned and looked at the helicopter she saw laser slashes and the deep dents from shells that did not penetrate the reinforced hull along the whole length of the aircraft, and the scorched rear props that had survived the blast of the enemy aircraft as it blew up in midair just before it was about to shoot them down. They entered the hangar's main door and Safina watched as a tow vehicle hooked onto the helicopter and pulled it into the adjacent opening in the maintenance facility.

"Oh my God!" Claude yelled out. "Somebody get us a medic, the President is injured."

Safina looked down at her blouse and saw that it was splotched with blood, and her hands were also bleeding. She didn't feel any pain at all. Jayjan's last words were still ringing in her ears. He was gone. One of her aides came over and began to examine her wounds, "They look worse than they are Madam President. You will just need a few stitches and some prophylactic antibiotics." He peered at Claude. "She will be OK. Don't panic Monsieur. You are as pale as a sheet." The aide turned toward Safina, "President, Ma'am. What should we call you Ma'am? We weren't told during the briefing."

"I hadn't thought about it before. I think.......yes! You shall address me as President Abussani. I am Safina Morelli Abusanni."

"Very good, President Abusanni. That sounds so much better than: The Eagle has landed!" He grinned at her.

Dulcinea couldn't help herself, she burst out laughing: "Thank you Lieutenant, I needed that." She continued to chuckle, and put her fist to her mouth to stifle any bout of uncontrolled laughter. Everything in her life was so serious that she was almost at the breaking point. It provided a pressure release valve to laugh at a corny joke.

She decided to ignore the knot in her stomach. Jayjan had been a loyal guard and a respected friend. She called his home. When his wife came on the line Safina asked her to sit down. She expressed her sincere condolences and told her that under different circumstances she would have delivered this message in person. "After the war we will sit down together and remember Jayjan as he deserves to be remembered. At this time I must do everything I can to make sure his life was given in service to a great cause and a triumph of good over evil that will stand for centuries as a tribute to him."

There was no time for mourning casualties of the revolution. If she allowed herself to become enmeshed in grief it would paralyze her. She had to look forward each day from now on. The question of Brecken and Abraheem's survival remained unanswered. She could only pray that they made it. When the revolution was over and the reformation was in place, she would take the time to grieve those who gave the supreme sacrifice.

"Your staff is waiting for you in the conference room here. Information is coming into the UFN Command Center from all of your commanders in the field that the mission is on track in all locations around the globe. We are at 45% completion of phase I. Unfortunately the collateral damage in Afghanistan is extensive. Al Qaeda is no more, all of their strongholds were wiped out. Most of the women and children made it out before the deep laser satellite strikes hit. But, there were still hundreds of families that did not heed the warning, or were not allowed to leave. I will bring you a full written report in ten minutes." He turned and walked briskly out of the hangar, jumped into a waiting jeep and drove toward the terminal.

An ambulance pulled up to the hangar door and a medic took Safina to the vehicle. Claude followed along, not saying anything. He appeared to be struck silent by all the deference being proffered to Safina. Two gigantic bodyguards armed to the teeth and looking ferocious were not having a calming influence on him either.

The airport was secured, and friendly forces manned the perimeter. Opposition to the revolution was non-existent. This lack of seri-

ous resistance in Egyptian jurisdiction was unexpected. They anticipated a bigger fight until they realized that the people of Egypt were
hungry for Islamic reformation. The work they had been doing with
the Muslim women of the Middle East over the last five years had
paved the way. The women and the younger generation were well
aware of the plans for reformation. They hungered for the freedom
it would bring to their lives. The majority of young men between
the ages of 16 and 25 were requesting combat training. The young
revolutionaries joined cadres in their respective geographic areas during the preparation of the revolution, and were active in removing
Sharia clerics from their communities. These young men were not
afraid to confront their fathers, uncles and grandfathers in changing
the social structure of their villages and towns. They also revealed
the facts regarding the Prophet of Islam, distributing fact sheets and
posting on the Internet social networks about who he really was and
how he gained his power. The facts could not be buried any longer.
The true story of Muhammad was exposed for the whole world to
see. A few of them had been caught and killed, but it served only to
inspire others to join the cause and free their nation from the bonds
of the fanatical extremists.

Safina had developed good working relations with the Egyptian
scientific community and the Minister of Science and Technology
through her work on the Morelli Foundation for the Treatment and
Cure of Cancer. She presented them with a cooperative plan, working
with Israel, to develop and distribute Dr. Morelli's cancer cure. The
Egyptian people were well aware of the fact that together with Israeli
scientists they were responsible for curing cancer on a global scale.
Egypt was also fully funded for all medical research through the pro-
ceeds from their cancer protocols and formulas. The Egyptian people took great pride in this achievement, and it brought cancer cures
to the people of Egypt – something they truly appreciated. Egypt

and Israel were the first countries in the world to be completely free of cancer related fatalities. Travel between Tel Aviv and Cairo was opened up and although the security screening was arduous, an effort was made to simplify and shorten the process.

The UFAS had structured the government to oversee and secure the autonomy of each country who would now be named States. They would have State Constitutions, Presidents, Cabinets, and Courts. They would be funded through their own State Revenue Services.

The President of Egypt had been given a simple choice: join and support the reformation, or die. He chose freedom and a more broad definition of democracy than the Egyptian mini-revolution had accomplished less than a decade earlier. A plan to set up an expanded democratic government in Egypt was handed to him. He was told to select his cabinet for an interim government until fair and honest elections could be convened. He signed a letter of intent to ratify a new peace treaty with Israel, and instructed his head of security to supply a list of radical jihadist activists within his government and in the opposition party. That information was more for personal preservation than for the sake of the revolution. The Egyptian leader was pragmatic. He was not a zealot.

Before dawn on a Friday, six Israeli F-15E aircraft flying at Mach 1.6 under the radar executed an accurate strike on twenty three nuclear facilities in Iran. They took off from two different locations and converged on the targets sequentially, the most threatening facilities being hit first. The F-15E's were enhanced with TEWs (Tactical Electronic Warfare Systems), and RWR (Radar Warning Device APG-70 Radar systems, and AESA – Active Electronic Scanned Array, Radar – AN/APG-82(v)1. They were on direct link to the UFN Command HQ.

The dictator and the Ayatollah were executed by operatives on the ground. Revolutionary internal forces in Iran were given full power to establish a new democratic government without the dictates of the Islamic extremists. There was to be a full separation between secular rule and clerical laws. The revolutionary forces had moved rapidly through Tehran with surgical precision. The jihadist strongholds were raided simultaneously. It was a day of bloodletting; a day of purging Islam of the malignancies that had almost destroyed its people. Exposed in the light of day, documented with accurate historical documents, only the hysterical fanatical warmongers persisted. They were released from this earth-bound existence and ushered off to Paradise as per their religious convictions. The Iranians were free at last, free to excel in all spheres of science and art. This was their true heritage and they could now cultivate the rich and bountiful talents that they possessed. The Persian people could once again flourish and enrich the lives of humanity.

The missile targets were hidden in almost every corner of Iran; one in the heart of Tehran. Some of them were low level research and development operations, while others were Uranium enrichment centers and weapons development facilities. Israel was the obvious choice to execute this operation. Israel also had the most exposure if Iran were to attack again. She had the right to defend herself. The United States government was publicly indignant, condemned the violence and the collateral damage – but behind closed doors the entire free world was celebrating the success of this mission officially titled "Operation Wipeout".

The Iranian scientists deemed themselves "experts" in nuclear weapon development, they were light years behind the capability of the United States intelligence community in detection and targeting of nuclear operations anywhere in the world. The US satellite defense array was technologically far beyond anything else in the global arsenal. To save the planet, they had the capability to obliterate entire countries.

To sustain the illusion of world cooperation and the facade of multi-national sovereignty, the United States had postured, speechified, and gone through hoops of diplomatic negotiations to obtain concessions that they could easily usurp without any real threat to US interests. Unbeknown to the American people or the duly elected procession of temporary American presidents who passed through the White House, a small group of dedicated guardians had long been protecting the security of America and the free world.

President Kennedy and President Ronald Reagan were the only US Presidents who were aware of the role that NASA played in the defense of the American Republic, and even they were not briefed on the Guardians. The Founding Fathers had worked hard to ensure the continuity of the country they had created. Although they had built in a huge margin for change and adaptation into the fabric of the Guardians, they had also marked clear, defensible lines in the sand. When those lines were threatened, the Guardians were activated.

The Guardians prepared and certified a list of targets in Iran and presented it to the Israeli generals with coordinates and satellite laser depth readings. The source was simply "classified" counter intelligence data:

1. Bonab: Nuclear Research and Development Center

2. Mo-Allem Kalayeh: Nuclear Research Center

3. Karaj: Cyclon Accelerator Research

4. Kalaye Electric enrichment Nuclear Research Center/ Sharif University Research Atomic energy of Iran.

5. Chalus: Weapons Develoment Facility

6. Jabr iban hagan: Research and Conversion.

7. Gorgan: Research Facility

8. Damarand: Plasma Physics Research.

9. Tabriz: Engineering Defense Research.

10. Ramandeh Uranium Enrichment.

11. Lashkar-Abad Uranium Enrichment.

12. Khondab: Heavy Water Plant

13. Arak: Heavy Water Reactor.

14. Darkhouin: Uranium enrichment Site.

15. Ardakan: Uranium Ore Purification.

16. Bushehr: Light Water Nuclear Reactor 1000MW.

17. Fasa: Uranium Conversion.

18. Natanz: Enrichment Facility.

19. Esfahan: Nuclear Researdch UCF Facilities.

20. Saghand: Uranium Mine.

21. Nrigan: Uranium Mine.

22. Zarigan: Uranium Mine.

23. Yazd: Milling Plant.

"That crazy Iranian mad man thinks he can take over the world. He's out-of-control. Let the Israelis do the dirty work." The President's chief advisor was speaking to the Joint Chiefs of Staff at a meeting being held in the War Room of the White House.

The generals and admiral sat stone-faced. There was no reply and no change in their expressions. The last time the Chief Advisor to the President had met with them, they were given orders to shoot down any Israeli planes flying over Iraqi air space. The UFAS Revolution was already in progress. It was just a matter of minutes until the President got the news. Their plan was to remain neutral and delay acknowledgment of the executive order to shoot down Israeli planes. With all the chaos and confusion going on in the American White House it would be easy to blame it on the Attorney General. They could say that he countermanded the President or they could simply say that they could not authenticate the message and therefore they were unable access the strike codes to execute his orders.

Brecken was still missing and it had been a month since anyone heard from him. Safina assumed that he had been evacuated with the other Marines who had been injured or killed in Baghdad on the day the revolution began. She had tried all of her connections in the State Department but they had not found any trace of him. He was officially listed as MIA but only with the top level of the CIA. He did not exist in any other data base.

Jayjan's and Abraheem's bodies were recovered and transported to their families for burial. Safina sent her condolences.

Safina didn't allow herself to mourn for Brecken, because she didn't believe he was dead. When she dreamed of Nomad she always saw those who moved through that Universe to the next dimension. Nomad never appeared with Brecken, and his familiar face was not there when Abraheem and Jayjan walked along the beach in that other world. They had effortlessly moved through that dimension on their way to another level of "being". She selfishly regretted their absence from her daily physical existence.

She replayed the battles of her life in her dreams at night, and searched for Brecken on the bloody fields of war, and in the dark shadows of her childhood village. She looked for him moving away from her through crowds at airports, and running on the beaches of Lebanon with Rémi where he had once come to rescue her when she was faced with moving on or returning to him in life. Safina eyed the cliffs and rocks above the beach looking for Nomad as a confirmation of Brecken's passing. But the symbol of strength and purpose in her life, the magnificent black horse that had altered her time line, never appeared in her dreams with her soul mate, Brecken. She could not bring herself to ask Nomad, for fear of the answer she might receive.

CHAPTER 25

The Healing of the West

Safina addressed her newly formed cabinet and the representatives sent from each of the 25 States in the UFAS, "They will make it. The American people will get their government back on the path to prosperity. I know them well enough to trust that their foundations are rooted in freedom just as they were when their founders launched the unique and bold experiment of a new form of representative government by the people. Don't be overly pessimistic – the US Military will stand fast. A call for early elections will be honored. The American people are basically sound. It takes time to awaken them but once they are aware of the realities – they will meet the challenges ahead of them. There are competent and ethical men and women standing ready to serve. The second American Revolution was a purging of the Islamic/Monroe takeover in North America and Mexico. The corruption and the shredding of their constitution necessitated a strong, concerted and organized "take back" of their American Republic. The UFN stood by them in support of democracy.

It is time for us to build our own bastion of freedom and democracy. With the reformation of Islam into a religion of compassion and justice, we made a huge historical leap into the 21st Century. This could never be an easy transformation. There will be continuous pockets of fierce and violent resistance. We can expect suicide bomber attempts to terrorize the population. Schools will be targeted because education is the key to representative government.

When we deal with these issues and address these problems we must understand that to be successful in the removal of these 'cancer cells' from the body of our society, we will be forced to take radical and decisive steps. There is no place for mercy and patience. If we allow one remnant of organized terrorism to exist we endanger the entire reformation and hence the entire world. This terrible task has been allocated to us – we are chosen to cleanse the world of this hate-mongering fanaticism. These people justify their actions with promises of martyrdom and being transported to Paradise – so what we will do is facilitate their desire to die.

While the Islamic Revolution and Reformation were underway, China mistakenly decided it was an opportunity to proclaim their superiority among nations, and as the leader, usurp their rightful place as the chief architect and policy maker of the world.

The American Joint Chiefs of Staff vowed to unleash Armageddon, a preemptive nuclear strike that would wipe China off the face of the globe if they did not back down immediately. They gave the Chinese and the rest of the international bullies such as Russia and Turkey, the following ultimatum, "If you activate even one launch system or transport even one missile toward a launch point; if you load one missile onto a truck, open one silo door, activate any long-range scanning device, move a nuclear submarine through an underwater channel, or turn an aircraft carrier into the wind, or if you capture one satellite photo of our defenses or our cities, we will blow you to "smithereens"! With 80,000+ armed nuclear warheads aimed at your cities, ports, factories, water supplies, food storage facilities, electrical power grids, etc., you should be holding your breath and praying that we do not twitch!"

The Joint Chiefs sent a coded message to President Morelli Abusanni of the newly established UFAS, and to all members of the UFN, which outlined the steps they were taking to safeguard the sovereignty of the United States and her allies, and requesting membership in the UFN.

Safina had reciprocated with a full report of the Islamic Revolution and the progress of the Reformation Council. "We are on track with a 75% completion of the revolutionary stages. All extreme jihadist dictatorships have been neutralized. Enemies of the UFN have been killed. Interim state governments within the United Federation of Arab States have been established and communications and utilities have been re-established in 90% of confrontational/combat areas. We are now on stage 4 of our domestic agenda. This is to establish reliable distribution of food, clothing, clean water, and set up clinics and hospitals in all of our member states. It would appear that we have a 90% rate of active cooperation from the inhabitants of almost every UFAS member state.

She answered the US request with a promise, "Establish a new democratic government under the US Constitution, re-institute free elections, and appoint a new judiciary body of honest men and women who will be dedicated to preserving your constitutional law. When all of those steps have been taken, and your new elected Senate and House representatives are in place, and a new US President is elected by the people and sworn into office - you can count on immediate membership in the UFN. We will be honored to accept you into our family of United Free Nations."

The US State Department delivered its ultimatum to the Chinese via live satellite hook-up from NORAD directly into the Chinese command post in Beijing, and the Japanese secret stronghold in Osaka. Turkey was already under US/NATO control, and martial law had been established under a territorial governor. The Chinese were so taken aback by the US capability of cutting directly into their internal communications network and blasting this message across everything in the Chinese system that they immediately called for their forces to stand down.

"We are watching you with an eagle eye," was the follow-up statement by Admiral Taylor on the USS Nimitz standing by in the Indian Ocean on full alert. It was broadcast to the Chinese, Japanese and North Koreans. The Chinese attempted negotiations with their liaison in the remnants of the American administration only to realize that the administration was no longer at the helm.

The Joint Chiefs of Staff had called on retired military generals to set up a temporary interim government in Dallas Texas. National general elections were being organized. The Marine Corps was restoring public and private communications and the broadcasting capability that had been dismantled over the last 3 years. Law enforcement personnel were asked to return to their stations and re-establish civil order as quickly as possible after the failed attempt by the Brethren and Monroe partnership to take over and control the United States of America.

The Chinese Ambassador issued a terse statement, "We will stand down at this time. We do not wish to pursue a confrontation. Please advise us of your terms. We wish to open a dialog with the appropriate representatives of the USA."

Safina evaluated the situation in depth. She was acquainted with many of the "players" and knew the Islamic plan inside-out. She had the support of the Guardians in the CIA and in the State Department. Together they had formulated a simple three prong plan. Safina met with former classmates from her Paris days, who were struggling to work within what was left of the US Federal Government. State governments had systematically been broken down and, in some states, the coffers were empty and law and order were nonexistent.

The UFN had requested a charter for the New US Government to be filed as an applicant for membership.

A coordinated operation was underway in all branches of the US Military. In accordance with the provisions of the Constitution of the United States, the Joint Chief's of Staff had determined that their oath to defend the United States against all enemies, foreign and domestic must be honored.

The Islamic terrorist cell that was a growing cancer inside the US Military was dealt with quickly and decisively through military tribunals. Sentences were carried out immediately. A list of subversive operatives of the Islamic Brethren, and the Organization for American Islamic Relations was handed to the CIA special ops unit.

The French intelligence community was anxious to participate. They opened all their files to the American CIA operation's HQ. Arnaud made sure that all the players were properly vetted.

CHAPTER 26

The Balance of Power

Eighteen months had passed and Brecken was still MIA. Safina tried not to think about him but it was impossible. Alone in her bed at night she clutched the pillow and shed her tears deep within its soft cushion. *I should have told you how much I love you Brecken. I should have demanded the moments of passion that we could have had,* she agonized. It was the first time in her life that she truly considered an existence beyond this earthly tether. If Nomad and Rémi existed in that "other" place she had to believe her heart. If Brecken were with Nomad and Rémi she would have met him in her dreams. *He's alive. I'd know if he were dead. When he went missing in Kurdistan I knew he was alive,* Safina reasoned in her mind.

The price I am forced to pay is too much. When she tried to remember Brecken's eyes she suddenly forgot what color they were. Safina no longer hugged her pillow at night, imagining she was pressed against his chest. Even her cat took his place next to her each night and she did not imagine that his soft purr was Brecken's breath. *I'm forgetting how to love him,* she cried. There was nothing to remember, nothing to replace the ache in her heart. They had never consummated their physical union. The completeness she felt, only with

Brecken, was a merging of mind and soul in a profound coupling that she believed few people would ever imagine or experience. It made physical sex pale in comparison. Without Brecken in her life, she was reduced to being a shallow, flawed, unexceptional, struggling being.

One night she had a vivid dream of making love with Claude. She felt ashamed and guilty when she awoke flushed and sweaty. Safina had to accept the fact that her body had its own demands that could be disassociated from her spiritual and emotional need for human connection and love. She had discovered a powerful carnal appetite within her that continued to amaze and attract her. It was obvious to her that the sensual electricity between her and Claude Molyneau had very little to do with love.

There was so much to do that she couldn't take time to mourn the loss of her friends. So many heroic men and women had died in the struggle to save Islam from itself that, at the end of the day, their faces blurred in her mind.

Safina was barraged by requests for mediation, advice and support throughout the newly formed UFAS. Leaders attempting to cope with the intricacies and hurdles of governance were anxious to access her council and advice. The UFN Charter was a foundational document for many of the States. They also had the military backing of the UFN forces when pockets of resistance or insurgencies surfaced. She was skilled at delegation and although she directed her resources in a superior fashion, she always worried about how well her assignments were addressed.

Safina held the first post-revolutionary press conference in front of her offices in Baghdad. It was broadcast around the world. She spoke in Arabic. Simultaneous translations were broadcast in every language.

She started with the basics, "I am Safina Morelli Abussani, the Provisional President of the United Federation of Arab States, holding this office until national elections can be held. Hopefully in just a few months from now a new President will be elected to a single term of six years.

The birth of democracy is not an easy accomplishment. The revolution and mandated by the excesses of extremest religious power and corruption. Although we strive to achieve a democratic-representative government, we are forced to establish foundation rules and laws to protect the Federation in its infancy.

State and local elections are to be protected and certified by the Federation.

Women of Islam, you are valiant. Your thirst for freedom has been acknowledged. I ask you to hold tight to your hope and enthusiasm for the future. You have been deprived of education for 1,400 years. Within 5 years we intend to wipe out the educational gap caused by your enslavement. Women are lining up each day to accept the implantation of a tiny receiver chip that will impart vast amounts of knowledge in incremental feeds. Men under the age of 25 are also invited to participate in this voluntary free program. The UFN has funded the program and will supply hand-held devices with LCD screens that will demonstrate the data feeds being streamed to those who wish to be educated in this manner. The program is voluntary. However, if any husband or father is caught depriving the females in their family from participation – the full force of the law will fall upon them.

I ask that you consider this path as a choice you can make freely. These chips may be removed anytime you decide you don't want it. If you would rather attend the UFAS schools being set up throughout the Federation States, that is also your choice. Education is a gift – you can accept it or refuse it. I beg you to accept this gift that will free women from the bondage of 1,400 years.

Arnaud and Safina were having an argument, "You always think about everything in terms of the global impact. What about the people of this Federation? How are they going to survive without the money from oil production? It's not like they can drink the sand. They can't even raise enough food to meet their basic needs. These states were countries where everything except the oil was imported – even gasoline, for God's sake! They eat Big Macs in Riyadh and have Cocoa Puffs for breakfast in The United Arab Emirates," Safina pointed out. "They're not all desert nomadic tribes, these are nations that have become completely dependent on oil production and exportation."

"Safina, there are other natural resources within the Federation! We have uranium and copper mines, cotton, dates, olives, and wheat! And don't forget the Morelli Foundation and the pharmaceutical Research & Development. We have the manpower for manufacturing; we just need the money to build the production lines.

We have to destroy the poppy fields. That business will only tear the Federation apart. The Federation will have to supply the Afghans with other sources of livelihood. I think we need to look at the Israeli experience. They would be willing to assist us in setting up light manufacturing as they did in Israel. They are also experts in agriculture and the development of pest and drought resistant crops. We should take advantage of their years of expertise, their strong desire to make peace with their neighbors, and their support of the UFAS! Isn't that the main justification for massive global changes in the balance of power – to create the opportunity for world peace to develop and create prosperity?"

Arnaud was convincing. She knew he had logic behind his words. But Safina also liked to stir things up, just to get the mental juices flowing.

Arnaud addressed the members of the UFN, "I formed a unit consisting of forensic financial wizards. Their task was to find the "golden needles" in the financial haystacks all over the world. Oil revenues are gone from many of the states in the UFAS. We need to seek out and seize the vast monetary reserves that the OPEC nations accumulated in so few hands."

The advantage that Arnaud had was a handful of good guys who refused to work for the "sleaze bags" of New York Wall Street and London's Canary Wharf. Those were the men he recruited. They were modern day "technical knights" equipped with artificial intelligence that was fast and accurate. They unleashed their tiny robots in the trillions. They spread out along the communication networks of the globe, traveling to remote satellite systems in the virtual universe and back to earth, in the blink of a nanosecond. They gathered minuscule bits of relevant data which were processed and combined, putting the puzzles together to locate vast sums of money that had been allocated and hidden, to build the "New World Order". The consensus of the UFN members was that the Building of the New World Order was a euphemism for 'lining the pockets' of a coalition of elitist progressives while enslaving the citizens of the world.

Once the UFN financial team pierced the subterfuge and eliminated millions of false markers, the way was clear to drain off the accumulated assets and collapse the virtual banks. Just like a house of cards – it all came down, a century of deceit and conspiracy. The missing gold and other valuable assets of the world economy have been located and seized!" There was a loud spontaneous applause. All the delegates stood up. The world had never smiled so broadly and been so universally positive about the future. Arnaud was gleaming with obvious satisfaction. He raised his hands and signaled the audience to be seated.

"President Morelli of the UFAS and President Kalian of the USA have jointly sponsored a recommendation that a UFN monetary board be established temporarily that would be comprised of representatives from all the member nations of the UFN. This board would establish the fair allocation of the funds to member nations who complete their electoral process in certified legitimate elections. When all of the funds are disbursed to the membership States, the UFN Monetary Board would be disbanded. We do not want to establish a version of a "World Bank". We have an interim transitional period of three years to implement disbursements. A copy of this proposed UFN ruling has been provided to the members. We will meet here again in one month to discuss this proposal and vote on the finalized version."

Arnaud took a sip from a water glass and coughed into his handkerchief politely. He grinned almost boyishly – obviously pleased with the tidings he was about to share, "China was crippled by a major pandemic. We disarmed their nuclear capability after their military coalition with the Muslim Brethren collapsed. With the cooperation of the Americans we have been assisting the counter revolutionary Chinese government to restructure their distribution network and get their people on a track to self sufficiency. The trade agreements between UFN nations have been suspended permanently, and new agreements will be negotiated as required. Member countries of the UFN will adhere to the UFN ban on agreements that would seek to undermine or damage the sovereignty or solvency of any member nation. You all know that the penalty for circumvention of this foundational rule will be met with UFN intervention – both financially and militarily.

You will be glad to hear that the nuclear capability of Korea and Iran has been removed. The dictators who threatened humanity have been executed. Their countries are under UFN restructuring for a transition to democracy as soon as possible." Loud applause broke out again and flashing camera lights lit up the podium.

Arnaud stepped back a few feet from the microphone. He motioned to Safina as she stood up and came to the microphone. "I give you President Safina Morelli Abussani of the UFAS!" Everyone in the great hall stood and the applause was deafening. It continued for at least a full ten minutes. Tears streamed down Safina's face. She had fulfilled her mission. Islam was saved, the world was saved. Her life and her sacrifice had not been wasted.

Meticulous planning each step of the way and sound analytical ability had made the difference. They were not "out of the woods" yet, but the wave of progress they were riding was going to take them far in a short time. Daily Safina was faced with the harsh statistics of those brave revolutionaries who had made the final sacrifice. They had given their lives to free their people, end the slavery of women, and ensure the survival of the Islamic Reformation.

Safina had brokered a tight political, economic and military coalition with Poland, Czechoslovakia, Hungary, Yugoslavia, Germany, and the USA. Those countries were strong allies of the UFAS. Together they had changed the balance of power in the world, making it a safer and potentially more prosperous planet. France and Britain were still under martial law as all remnants of the Muslim Brethren occupation were removed. There were still cells of jihadist opposition and the fighting was not over in many locations across the Islamic sphere of influence – but they were incapable of regrouping and reorganizing. Each pocket of insurgency was being handled the same way – obliteration of all combatants and their supporting networks.

Japan, Turkey, Russia and Norway were put on a watch list by the UFN. Most uninformed leaders were unaware of the duplicitous actions of Norway as they attempted to cash in on their fabricated scientific documentation of a long laundry list of supposed and imagined hazardous materials around the globe. They were major contributors to the global financial collapse, and it was done by design – not just through the promotion of erroneous science. The Japanese application to join the UFN was on probationary status for 5 years. Turkey was required to disarm and join the UFAS accepting the UFAS Constitution. Their government was disbanded and a military governor was assigned to oversee elections and the establishment of a new state constitution. Safina was well aware of the duplicity of the Turks and their pretense of allegiance to the United States. Their aspirations to establish the Third Caliphate in Istanbul were a matter of record in the CIA documentation of classified communications between Al Qaeda and the Turkish Government. She had read them herself over ten years ago. They were deceitful back stabbers.

If Arnaud had not intervened on behalf of the Turkish people, Safina would have included Turkey on the nuclear hit list that took out the oil fields and most of Iran. Instead of addressing the Turkish issue with military force, the decision had been made by the UFN Council to integrate the same program that had initially been put in place for the UFAS educational revolution. The Islamic Reformation was a reality in the Islamic world; embraced wholeheartedly by the vast majority of Muslims. The reformation was centuries overdue, and modern day Muslims were fully aware of this. Even in Turkey, once the fanatical fundamentalists were pulled down from their powerful positions, the Turkish Muslims were free to join the reformation.

Russia was considered by the UFN to be a threat to world stability. Although Russia had agreed to disarm, there was evidence to the contrary. It appeared that the "Russian Bear" adhered to the old adage that 'one cannot teach an old bear new tricks'. Organized crime in Russia was a major obstacle to Russia's development and their peaceful co-existence within the world community. Russia was a stumbling block to maintaining the peace. Safina had appointed a commission of military and strategic experts to come up with a plan to get Russian on the right track. Economic opportunity would go a long way to convert the Russian people into the concept of taking care of themselves instead of their generational dependence on the government to babysit them.

CHAPTER 27

Fantasy of Love

S afina looked at the telephone, willing it to ring; willing it to be Brecken on the line. She refused to accept his death. She yawned and decided to lie down for a few minutes on the sofa in her office. She locked the door and told her aid to hold all calls for at least two hours. "Only wake me if there is any word about Colonel Petersen."

She was just nodding off when the telephone rang. "*Bonjour je-sais-tout.*" It was Claude Molyneau on the line. He was talking to the most powerful woman in the world, yet referring to her as a "smart-arse". "*Je t'aime mon amour.* I miss you – no, that's not really true – I miss your body. You can't debate that! I can feel my hands on it right now. Are you dressed? Tell me what you are wearing."

"Claude, stop it. My panties are getting wet. How I have missed you!"

"*Je ressens la même chose pour toi mon amour* (I feel the same for you my love)." Claude laughed over the telephone. "What are you wearing? Come on now, tell me, *mon petite cheri.*"

"Alright, I'm wearing a dark colored suit of some kind of shinny soft gabardine. There's a short skirt that reaches just below my knee. It fits fairly tight. If you look closely you can see my thong line and maybe the outline of my leather gun holster. The jacket is tailored with wide lapels and it hugs my bust line. Under that I have a thin white blouse that plunges slightly in the front so that you can just barely discern the hint of cleavage.

Under the blouse I'm wearing a chantilly lace bra with delicate wires under the breast to push them up as though they were an offering, with not much coverage on the top – just deep enough to hold my breasts in place, with the edge of my nipples peaking out from under the lace.

Between my breasts a lace pocket is hidden that conceals a bejeweled silver shabria. The cold metal sheath that protects the razor sharp blade is tucked against my breast. The studded handle is snuggly positioned by my right nipple so that it is easily accessible. Sometimes when I am nervous I lick my index finger and rub my nipples with the wet tip lightly until they get so hard that I become dripping wet. This relaxes me and relieves tension.

Claude.......... I'm licking my fingers and rubbing my nipples. I'm lying on the sofa in my office with my legs apart. What should I do now?" She could hear him breathing hard on the phone. He inhaled deeply.

"Reach down inside your waist band and down to your sweet place. Rub in a slow circular motion. Oh.....oh......oh. I can't stand this. Tell me more Safina. Keep going. What else are you wearing?"

Safina purred softly. "Under the skirt I am wearing my black leather Barretta holster around the left thigh – it is strapped tightly with one strap from my waist going down the crack in my buttocks and it is strapped between my legs, pressing against my crotch whenever I move. Under the holster I have on thin black satin panties.

"Oh My God, Safina you make me crazy. Now do me a big favor, get up and walk to the door and open it. Imagine that I am standing in the doorway."

When she opened the door Claude was standing there just as she had imagined him. He came into her office and locked the door behind him.

Safina was speechless. She knew she should throw him out of her office, but she was so hot by now that she couldn't restrain herself. He closed all the shutters in the room. Took off his jacket and draped it on the back of a chair. Then he took her into his arms and kissed her long and deep, pushing his tongue gently down her throat and then pulling it out while he pressed his hips against her.

She could feel him growing large. He slipped off her jacket and unzipped the back of her skirt. It fell to the floor. She stepped away from it. Then Claude slowly unbuttoned her blouse and pulled it off of her shoulders and let it fall. He carefully removed the Barretta from her thigh holster and laid it on the desk. Then he unbuckled the gun holster and slipped his hand between her legs to guide the holster strap out. As he carefully and slowly pulled the holster between her legs to free it, his thumb gently brushed her. She gasped.

Safina stepped out of her shoes and kicked them away. Claude removed her shabria from the pocket in her bra and placed the dagger carefully on the desk. He reached behind her and unfastened the bra. He held it up to his lips and kissed the lace, and tossed it aside. He loosened his tie and pulled it off from under his collar, and slowly unbuttoned the shirt down the front as he stared lustfully at her bare breasts and the perfect rose nipples. He removed his silver cuff links and carefully put them in his jacket pocket that was draped on the back of the chair. He took his shirt off, hanging it over the jacket on the back of the chair and put his tie over it. His movements were slow and deliberate. Claude's muscular tanned body, with brown hair on his chest, was magnificent.

Safina ran her fingers over his chest. Then Safina reached down and unfastened his belt, pulling it out of his pant loops. She tossed it on the floor and unfastened the clip at his pants waist, and unzipped the zipper that constrained him. She could see him bulging behind the white cotton boxer shorts as she slipped his pants off onto the carpet and then she pulled the boxers off too, freeing him.

Claude stepped out of the shorts, turned her around with her back facing him and pulled her against his body. He spaced his stance wide and put his arms around her and ran his hands up and down her breasts and stomach, down into the soft curls of her mound, and then up to her breasts as he pinched her nipples gently and slid his hands back down to her waist. He nibbled on her neck and blew soft hot breaths into her ears. He was pressed tightly between her buttocks from the rear. He ran his fingers up and down her breasts and back down as far as he could reach. He stepped back slowly, pulling himself from between her smooth cheeks, and gently turned her around to face him.

Claude pulled her up on her toes, pushed her head back and kissed her lovingly on the mouth and then with extreme tenderness he began kissing her neck and ears, moved down to her shoulders. His muscles were hard and built up from years of fencing and lifting weights. He cupped both of her breasts in his hands and kissed each nipple, licking and nipping at them until they became hard and extended. He lifted her up easily and sat her on the desk; pushing her papers aside. Claude laid her all the way back onto the desk top with her legs over the side. He placed his warm hands on the inside of her thighs and pushed her legs apart forcibly. Safina moaned and stretched her arms above her head. He began to stroke her breasts and her stomach with his hands pushing her breasts upward with force and then smoothing them back downward with a feather touch several times. He began massaging her with his hand. She watched his face as he manipulated and stroked her. She was holding back the tidal wave that he had set in motion. She wanted to climax with Claude. Safina was breathing hard as her excitement mounted.

He worked her nipples with his lips, sucking on them and giving her gentle love bites. Then he lifted her off of the table, supporting her weight easily with his strong hands under her bare silky buttocks and her slender firm arms wound around his neck, his thrusts were hard and long, over and over, until it took all of her will power not to scream out in total rapture as he reached that deep contact place at the end of her tunnel. It was the place where ecstasy is jealously harbored. The place ignored by amateur lovers; a treasure that nature reserves for superior males. Safina could stand it no longer and she climaxed repeatedly, one spasm after another until she could not catch her breath.

He raised her body off of his and laid her on the sofa naked. He stood there just taking in her beauty and her musky scent. She wanted him to look at her naked. She was excited by the lust on his face, with his mouth slightly open, and his tongue licking his lips. His damp softly wavy locks of hair spilled over his forehead across his eyebrows and eyes.

They were both silent as they dressed. The thoughts swirling in their minds were almost palpable as uncertainties about their feelings hung in the air. Would this obsession for physical union push them apart or pull them together? Was this purely sexual magnetism or was it far more for both of them? Claude smiled at her, but his eyes did not have their usual nonchalant sparkle, and his chin was not locked in his familiar determined "I know what I'm doing" tilt. These two powerful individuals could delay answering these questions, but eventually resolution would not be avoided.

"Claude, this has to be the last time we do this. I know it sounds deceitful under the circumstances, but I love Brecken and I can't do this to him. It would devastate him. I need you to stay away from me. I just can't resist this uncontrollable attraction that we have for each other."

They both dressed and Claude kissed her again before he left.

"I'll call you tomorrow!" Claude winked at her uncharacteristically as he unlocked the door and left. Safina had never seen him behave in that manner before. She thought it odd.

The telephone was ringing and ringing and someone was knocking on her door as she rose from the sofa and unlocked it from inside. "What is going on?"

President Abussani, Are you OK?

"Was anyone here while I was sleeping?"

"No, Ma'am – no one. I knew you were tired and I kept everyone out. I have been guarding your door for the last 4 hours!"

Safina looked down at her clothing. She was fully dressed. *Thank God, it was just an erotic dream. I don't have to feel guilty about a dream. Do I?* Safina was flushed and she felt slightly disoriented. *It seemed so real – so vivid.* Her body felt limp and relaxed.

CHAPTER 28

Dream of Peace

Safina met with three generals in charge of military deployment throughout the UFAS and four exceptional multi-national commanders of the UFN. They were 'exceptional' because they had worked together in harmony to achieve phenomenal results.

She knew each one of these commanders well. She had spent the last five years communicating, planning and implementing strategies in productive cooperation with these seven military strategic experts. At first they expressed skepticism about taking advice from an inexperienced civilian regarding military strategy, but they quickly came around to relying heavily on Safina for raw data evaluations. She could put the pieces of a puzzle together and come up with a logical and workable scenario.

They were summoned by her to discuss the recommendations of the UFN commission on Russia. This was a technically sophisticated virtual meeting via secure satellite connections. Safina was convinced that educational and economic methods were not going to be sufficient to neutralize the Russian underworld. better known as the *Russian Mafia*. They were organized on two fronts: Drug and contraband distribution, and enforcement tactics. It was crucial to break up this organization that undermined the basic tenets of democracy. Safina had a comprehensive plan to assassinate their leaders and their lieutenants, destroy their networks and replace their economic role in their communities with viable alternatives for legitimate business and commerce.

The UFN commanders were men and women of integrity, people of action and resolve, and they were largely non-political. She sat at the head of the conference table facing the web cam. Each participant was represented by their own video square on the display monitor in a simple grid pattern. She mentally sized up each one of them. *Which one of these men or women will carry this torch after me?* she pondered.

"I believe that the UFN must mount a joint military operation to dismantle the Russian nuclear arsenal and establish a functional democratic government in the entire geographic area. Prague appears to be a logical choice for the capital, and I want to hear your thoughts on that today." Safina believed it would benefit the USAF and the UFN if all of the Eastern block countries, and their satellites, were declared independent states in a federation, with a legitimate central-ized federal government, and subsequently encouraged to join the UFN. She wanted to hear all sides of this debate and weigh the alter-natives. The economic structure of that proposed federation would determine it's feasibility.

She held her hand up to forestall questions, "It will not be a sim-ple task to find cohesiveness and common ground to rebuild this region. There are vast cultural, religious and philosophical divides. I believe that the reformation of Islam will continue to be a healing factor throughout this diverse community. Economic stability and opportunities for growth, will contribute positively as the base needs of the population are more easily obtained through commerce and educational programs. These things take time and investment. In the interim we must provide security and civil order. Your role will be to maintain the peace throughout the region while this process unfolds. You must secure the borders and prevent the infiltration of the Russian mobsters and gangs along our UFAS boundaries with Russian controlled areas. I want to discuss the development of a detailed military plan to eradicate the Russian Mafia from Eastern Europe."

The conference continued for several days, and a plan was agreed upon and a time line set up to commence the operational phase. Not one to sit on an operational plan, Safina gave the order to assassinate the Mafia leaders immediately. She already had men in place to do the job. Capture and tribunals were not going to expedite the democratization of Easter Europe. The people of the region were tired of waiting for prosperity and liberty – someone had to clean up the mess that was allowed to flourish for decades after the collapse of the Soviet Union.

After taking questions, Safina closed down the virtual conference, "Those of you who are involved in the military leadership of the UFAS must focus on our objective to destroy any remnants of al Qaeda, Hamas, and the Taliban. No insurgency can be tolerated. Deal with this immediately using extreme prejudice."

The timing was right, the leadership was battle-tested, and the teams who operated so cohesively during the revolutionary war were now well-prepared to deal with the "hot spots" left over from the death of Islamic jihad aspirations.

North Korean communism was surgically excised and the new United Korean Republic was officially recognized on a probationary status by the UFN. The military was dismantled and the nuclear threat neutralized. The North Korean dictator and his heirs and supporters were executed.

China was a surprise. When the American and Islamic revolutions were in process, the people of China were coming out of a devastating pandemic which killed at least 25% of their population. The survivors rose up and took back their country. The communist leadership, that had enslaved them since the Mao Tse Tung communist revolution, were dragged into the streets and hung. The red flags and banners of communism were burned. Mao Tse Tung's face no longer glared at the Chinese from every building and on every corner. His little red books with their "Mao-isms" were burned voluntarily. There was an organized new leadership and a communication network already in place. Safina was encouraged by the smooth transition to democratic rule. The young people of China had been preparing for liberty; they were educated, informed, and technologically hungry for change. The people of China were entrepreneurs, farmers, engineers, doctors, artists, writers, musicians and freedom lovers. They were hungry for liberty and self determination. The Chinese had unlimited talent and resourcefulness. They also had huge natural resources and some skilled workers in their urban centers. At last they could be partners in world commerce. Safina challenged the Chinese to engage themselves in solving the world energy issues. She encouraged them to join the UFN on a provisional basis with a plan to become full members within 5 years. They had the money and the human resources to emerge as a strong world power and to be a force for freedom and enterprise. The heavy yoke of communism had finally been lifted.

Safina sat at her desk in the comfortable office of the UFAS in Cairo. She was in the habit of spending half the week in Cairo and the other half in Baghdad or Tehran. Since the revolution there was a contagious atmosphere of hope and a new vitality as Islam emerged from the oppression of fanatical fundamentalism, and from the enslavement of women across the Muslim world. There were smaller offices set aside for her in both cities. She also visited the other states of the United Federation of Arab States as often as she could. Safina had a proven talent for matching resources with problem solving. She promoted a kind of mentoring relationship between experienced governors and those who were less experienced in functioning in a democratic state government environment.

She was having a long telephone conversation with one of her closest advisors who was staying in Libya to help with the reformation process there, "I am optimistic about Libya rebuilding at last, since Qaddafi came close to destroying that country. He murdered thousands of rebels while I could do nothing to stop it until my own revolutionary troops from around the region were available to put an end to the carnage and stop the Muslim Brethren in their quest to usurp power as dictators toppled. It was one of the most frustrating moments since this revolution began," Safina shared.

The advisor responded, "Libyans are beginning to educate their young people with a goal to bring that country up to speed with other more advanced Muslim states in the UFN. The process is proving slower than the Iranian transition because the Libyan population is culturally and technologically delayed due to their long period under the dictatorial oppression of a raving maniac."

He continued, "It's rumored in the intelligence community that Omar Qaddafi suffered permanent brain damage from the ravages of syphilis that went dormant, and then resurfaced as a virulent brain virus. Listening to his speeches, it's obvious that he was quite definitely insane. Did you know that this was the case with the notorious tyrant Idi Amin in Uganda years ago? But in that instance it was documented by the foreign physicians who were brought in to treat him at one point."

She knew it was important to be vigilant and connected, with those who were vested with the powers of leadership in each state. She provided guidance and financial support as warranted. Safina expediently dispatched military support when necessary. Her tactic was to come in quickly, displace or destroy the tyrants/insurgents and hand the governance and enforcement over to the citizens as quickly as an interim government could be seated. Elections were scheduled within six to eight months – so that the citizens would understand that the success of their democracy lay with them and their ability to exercise their freedoms responsibly. Educated women were recruited to participate in all of the interim governments. It was important that Muslim women and men learn to work side by side as equals – and to see how women could contribute and stand shoulder to shoulder with male leaders. Safina had actively recruited Islamic women from the United States and Europe. "We need you, the women of Islam need you to come and help them become full-fledged citizens, it is your turn to give something back in exchange for the educational opportunities that you had in the West." Every night before she went home she made a phone call to some educated, intelligent Muslim woman on the other side of the world and personally begged them to help their Muslim sisters back in their countries of origin.

There were stacks of projects and correspondence to handle. Even with two full-time aides and a large competent staff, it was difficult to stay current on all the developments in the large geographic area of the Federation, and still maintain her connections in the rest of the world. She relied heavily on the quality and dedication of the core revolutionaries. She found young men and women with vision and dedication who were anxious to step up and reform their countries through education, hard work, and innovative uses of technology. She encouraged audacity and taking ownership of a problem and finding a way to solve it. The greatest resource the UFAS had were its people who were hungry for freedom from oppressive, and nonproductive, uninspiring lives.

CHAPTER 29

Whispers from the Past

"President Abussani! There is someone here to see you."
"Make an appointment for them. Maybe I can get them in by
tomorrow afternoon. Find out what they wish to speak to me about.
Please!"

"This cannot wait Safina," Arnaud said from the doorway.

She went over to him and put her arms around him, "When did
you get in? You should have called – I would have sent someone to
pick you up from the airport. This is a wonderful surprise!" *It isn't bad
news about Brecken that he is bringing to me personally! He wouldn't be
looking so cheerful if he were about to tell me that Brecken is dead.*

He gently disengaged from her embrace, "I have someone I want
you to meet. This is important Safina. I think you should sit down."
He led her over to the ornate blue sofa against the wall next to her
desk. He put his hat on her desk and sat down beside her and held
her hand between his hands. As he looked at the doorway he called
out, "It's OK, you can come in now."

She hadn't seen Arnaud for months, since a series of meetings
after the revolution began the year before. They had talked via telephone and even conducted teleconferences with other governments

on the other side of the world. Lately he had called her several times to talk about having Latifa and Yehiye Shmaiya visit her. She had put him off because she simply had too much on her plate right now. "Perhaps during the Holidays or if I make a trip to London, I can have lunch or dinner with them," she told him.

It was clear to her that he didn't understand how busy she was, trying to keep the reformation alive and progressing while dealing with the old corrupt habits of officials throughout the Federation. She had recruited Iranians and Egyptians to assist her because many of them were already well educated. Her newest program was to have each one of her vetted recruits mentor at least two potential leaders from other Federation countries: Kuwait, Saudi Arabia, Libya, Jordan, Yemen, Afghanistan, etc. Her greatest challenge was to embrace Turkey and its more secular history while guarding against the Turkish ambitions of absorbing the UFAS into a Turkish Empire. They had much to offer but they also had their own grandiose agenda to rule. Their demonstrated duplicity tainted the possibility of trust.

Then there was the task of setting up timely elections in each state, and ensuring there were elected representatives in the Federation Congress. Her position as President of the UFAS was also provisional and elections should be held within a year to legitimize her position or elect a replacement. "Arnaud, we are chairing a new School of Political Science at the University of Baghdad. It is so exciting, and I wanted to ask you to become a guest lecturer."

Arnaud was looking like the cat that got the cream. He had a mischievous smile on his face. Safina began to stand up but he pulled her back down. "Sit down Safina, I know you are happy to see me and I feel the same. I didn't come all this way just for a hug. I have a surprise for you.

Latifa and Yehiye Shmaiya came into the room. Latifa looked pale and she wiped her eyes, but her mouth was smiling. It was difficult for Safina to understand why Arnaud had brought them here, and what was going on that she had to sit down! *"Ahalan ou sahalan"* she greeted them. "Welcome, it is good to see you again." Safina said. "Can you believe that we actually did it?! We had a revolution and now we are building a democratic society for the next generation. We have freed Islam and saved the children of Islam. Oh, Latifa and Yehiye, I am so grateful for all of your help. I know how hard you worked to get international support and to coordinate so many intricate meetings, and welding your influence and reputations to help the cause of freedom. I haven't had time to thank you before now."

Arnaud stepped forward and looked into Safina's eyes, "Safina, this is Latifa, your mother!"

Safina put her hand over her mouth. The silence held the room in virtual suspended animation. Frozen in time, somewhere inside of her she knew it was true. Safina broke out in a cold sweat and a physical ache spread across her back and shoulders. She remembered the unsettling feeling she experienced when she met Latifa for the first time at the diplomatic party in Paris. She had dismissed it as just something she ate that didn't agree with her or perhaps the stress and excitement of having prepared that event from beginning to end and the let down when it finally happened. Now she knew it was because her heart recognized her true mother. She sank down farther into the soft cushions of the sofa.

Latifa sat down next to Safina on the sofa and put her arms around her. There was no way to express her feelings. They just sat that way for a long time. Everyone was teary eyed. Arnaud gave Latifa his handkerchief. He walked over to the desk to retrieve some tissues which he discreetly applied to the corners of his own eyes. Yehiye was not embarrassed to be sobbing as he saw the joy of his beloved wife. It had been almost a decade since Latifa had discovered that Safina was her lost daughter. She had bravely kept the secret so that the cause of freedom would not be jeopardized. It was a huge sacrifice and one that he knew was almost unbearable at times. Now there was no reason to keep the secret anymore.

"Prove it!" Safina said. She had regained her equilibrium, and her natural skepticism surfaced.

Latifa spent the next hours telling Safina the story of her life; the rescue by Yehiye and why she had not been able to take her daughter with her. She told of their attempts to find Safina and how El Sighi had lied about what had happened to her. She told her about the anklet and how she had recognized it at the house in Paris.

Yasmine sat on the veranda in her villa on the outskirts of Basra. She had just received the text message from Safina regarding the confirmed death of Abraheem, son of the Silversmith Farouq. She could see his face in her mind's eye: a fine young Arab man with thick curly black hair and a shinny trimmed beard. His silver shabria, studded with precious gems was tucked into his white sash. Everything about Abraheem bespoke his honesty and honor. He had died to save Islam from annihilation from a threatened global backlash against Islamic terror and fundamentalism. She knew his family well – his father was a good man but like many Muslim men, he had several wives. He had ignored the plight of Abraheem when his mother died in childbirth, and he had blindly followed Islamic tradition and ostracized her when she failed to produce another male child.

When Yasmine needed Farouq's help to get Safina out of Iraq, she had used his guilty feelings about Abraheem's mother to get his cooperation. Now she had to go to him and tell him that his son, Abraheem, had died in Baghdad, fighting in the revolution. They would have seven days of mourning and then Abraheem would again be forgotten by his family. But Safina, Brecken, Vivian and Yasmine would never forget him. He had sacrificed everything to save Islam.

There was something else important that Yasmine needed to address for Safina. She dispatched two men to a small village just south of the border with Kurdistan, "Find a woman named Farka who is married to the local sheik, El Sighi, and bring her to me. If she has children bring them as well. If the husband refuses to let her go, terminate him."

Farka was Safina's only childhood friend. She was the child bride of Safina's father, El Sighi. Safina had promised Farka that she would not forget her and that one day they would see each other again. Yasmine would keep that promise to Farka.

A week later the men returned with Farka and her son. El Sighi had not only opposed them, he had attacked them. They had killed him and his older adult sons. All of the wives and children living at the villa were told they were free to stay or leave. The local police had investigated and decided that no arrests would be made. The men had fired in self defense.

When the men brought Farka to Yasmine's villa she was almost comatose in her reactions. The leader of Yasmine's men had collected information in the village, and interviewed the local police. He gave Yasmine the report. As she read it she began to understand Farka's mental and physical condition. According to the information collected, Farka had produced ten live babies during her life. Her son was 17 years old. All of her four daughters had been sold to older men as child brides. Two had died giving birth at 13 and 14 years-of-age. One had been beaten to death by her husband. Three of Farka's children had died as infants or young children. Farka had no front teeth. Her husband had knocked them out of her mouth during a beating. Her face was scared and lacked expression or animation.

Yasmine had been kind and gentle with the woman. She thought she would give Farka a chance to live without fear for the first time in her life and see if that would bring healing.

"She's an amazing woman," Yasmine wrote to Vivian. "She can't read or write, and she has no sense of individualism, but she expresses a persistent desire for her son to be educated and allowed to pursue his own path in life. Farka loves to be read to. She remembers everything she hears. She was deprived of almost everything, yet she found joy in her children and in the most simple pleasures in life. I found out that she can imitate all the desert birds, and can differentiate between the males and females. She understands their calls and songs. She was born to be an ornithologist. If she had been afforded the opportunities of education, she would have made a remarkable biologist. Her powers of observation are far superior to the average person."

A month later Yasmine traveled to Baghdad to meet with Safina.

"I have something important to share with you Safina. I will be at your house in Baghdad this evening. Badrai has also sent you a treat!" Yasmine told Safina over the telephone.

"OK, I won't be home until around 8:00 pm. But someone will be there to open up for you, and I will send a dinner ahead. Don't wait for me to eat – just help yourself. I am having a working dinner here," Safina said.

A few hours later Safina was finally on her way home. Sitting in the back seat of the bullet proof Escalade and watching her motorcycle escorts on both sides of the vehicle, she was going over the past days in her mind. Having her mother in her life was an incredible experience. For years she had worn Latifa's anklet and believed her mother was dead despite Nomad's insistence that she was alive. They planned to spend the New Year together in London. It would give her some time to get to know her mother.

It had been an exhausting week and she was looking forward to a hot bath and a good night's sleep. Yasmine would be waiting for her at the apartment. She decided she would call her office later and inform them that she was taking the day off.

Spending a day with Yasmine would be a pleasurable break from the mental grind that she had been living since the beginning of the revolution.

CHAPTER 30

A Security Breach

Abodyguard detail of six heavily armed men provided round-the-clock security for Safina. Since the loss of Brecken and Jayjan, she was at greater risk for attacks. As they neared the apartment complex two of the motorcycles peeled off. The complex was only about a mile away. As Safina glanced toward the front of the vehicle she noticed that the driver had pushed up his sleeves as he held onto the steering wheel quite high on the wheel which was an unusual grasp for a professional driver. She saw a tattoo on the inside of his left arm – only a small portion of it was exposed but she was sure it was the outline of a snake head that was attached to a larger tattoo still hidden by the man's sleeve. Was it the ancient Chimera tattoo that she knew was the mark of a trained assassin working for the Muslim Brethren? She decided it was best to assume that this was an attempt on her life.

Safina pushed a button on the handle of the Shabria strapped to her right thigh as she pulled it from its sheath. This activated a silent alarm in the lead vehicle and an automated signal for back-up from Security HQ.

"You're a new driver aren't you?" she asked him.

"*Iyawah*, I started today. My cousin, Achmad, who usually drives you, is with his wife at the hospital – she is having a baby," the man replied. He looked into the rear view mirror and smiled at her.

She smiled back, unfastened her seat belt, and moved forward to the edge of her seat as though wanting to engage him in more conversation. He looked back at the road. She leaned over the seat and ran her hand down his shoulder and across his chest. "My! You are a big strong fellow. Do you have any plans for tonight?" she asked in a throaty voice.

The vehicle slowed down. He hesitated for a moment. "Keep driving, cousin of Achmad. I am feeling friendly tonight. Just look ahead at the road and enjoy the ride." He was grinning now and slowing the vehicle as she reached down and opened his belt and slowly pulled his pants zipper down inch-by-inch. She put her hand on the back of his seat and tickled his ear with her finger, moving her lips close to his neck. His penis was enlarged and ready to burst from his pants. She leaned over the seat as though she were going to use both hands to massage him. "Can you see the road?" Safina whispered into his ear. She saw the barrel of a handgun sticking out from under his left thigh on the outside of the driver's seat. His hand was reaching slowly for the gun.

"I can see it," he moaned.

In one fell swoop she reached forward and pulled the gear out of drive, slipping it into neutral and pulled the keys out of the ignition. The engine died immediately. She slipped her shabria out of her palm and jammed it between his legs. He doubled over in pain, screaming as she managed to pull the knife out and stab him in the side of his neck. His left hand came up with the gun firing. He was attempting to twist the barrel around to point it at her head.

The vehicle veered to the right of the road, jumped the curb, and rolled down a steep hillside toward a low wall. Safina pulled the blade out of his neck, fell back into the back seat, found the door handle and pulled. It would not open. It was locked from the driver's master lock. The SUV hit the wall going about 80 kph. The rear portion of the SUV rose high in the air, causing the vehicle to flip over onto the other side of the low wall, and fall to its side and continue over-turning down the hillside doing several death rolls, and finally landing with its wheels in the air. The driver was strapped inside upside down, still screaming obscenities while blood spurt all over the windows on the driver's side and the windshield. The gun in his left hand kept firing until it ran out of shells. The bullet proof windows did not allow any of the rounds to escape. Some were ricocheting off of metal and glass surfaces inside the car.

Safina was bruised and bleeding from the somersaulting and rolling of the car, but she was still conscious and trying to get out of the vehicle. She kicked the windows but it was futile. She looked through the windshield and saw flames coming out of the mangled front section of the vehicle. Yanking her Berretta from the holster, she fired into the door lock. It still wouldn't open. She fired into the windows but they were bullet proof. Smoke was starting to fill the vehicle. She could see people running around the car, and heard them trying to open the doors to no avail. Coughing she was running out of options, yet still trying hard to maintain a clear head. The driver had lost consciousness. She crawled along the upside down roof of the vehicle, under the front seat trying to get to the master lock next to the dead inverted driver. She pounded her palm upwards on the buttons on the driver's side. The windows were electric and without the key in the ignition they would not work. Panic began to set in: *Find the keys stupid! What did I do with them after I pulled them out of the ignition?!* She felt around the front passenger side interior roof which was now the floor. Her fingers brushed something, she felt around some more and found them. *Is there an automatic opener on the key ring – please Allah, there has to be one.*

Someone was hitting the back side window with something loud, she could hear the window cracking but it wasn't breaking. Bullet proof windows are layers of sandwiched plastic and thick glass, they crack but don't break into pieces.

The smoke was toxic and it was getting dense. Being trapped inside an upside down vehicle was disorienting and she found it difficult to keep her bearings. She could barely breathe now, and the flames were starting to come through the firewall under the dashboard. Safina crawled back to the rear of the vehicle and got down on the ceiling to keep her head low. She finally found the smooth round plastic door opener on the key ring and pressed it twice just before she passed out.

A backup security car drove straight down the hillside and stopped next to the low stone wall. A large man dressed in a military uniform got out and leaped over the wall. He ran toward the car. Flames were shooting out of the engine compartment and flickers of red flames inside the front seat area were visible. The driver was hanging upside down strapped into his seat in the overturned vehicle. Suddenly a big bang rocked the car as the driver's air bag deployed. The man ran to the back door and yanked it open. He reached inside and grabbed Safina's arms and pulled her out of the burning car onto the grass. Then he scooped her up in his arms and ran to the wall and jumped over it, still tightly holding on to her. At the moment he hit the ground and ducked down behind the wall the SUV exploded in a ball of fire. There were several smaller explosions that followed.

As fresh clean air entered her lungs, Safina began to wake up. She coughed trying to clear her lungs of the toxic smoke. As her eyes opened she looked up at the man who had pulled her from the burning car. "Brecken, is it really you? Am I dreaming or am I dead?"

As he cradled her in his arms, he took his handkerchief out of the inside of his uniform pocket and wiped her tears. "You're OK honey, you're gonna be fine." He held her tightly in his arms. Fire trucks had pulled up to the scene and the firemen asked him to move away from the area. He rose with her in his arms and carried her to the waiting ambulance, sitting her on a gurney inside the vehicle. The paramedic gave her a drink of water, and strapped an oxygen mask to her face. "Breath deep, Ma'am. We want to make sure all that soot clears from your lungs." The paramedic got out his stethoscope and was getting ready to get her vital signs and treat her cuts.

"They said you were dead Brecken............. I knew it wasn't true.......... I never gave up believing you would come......... back to me..........." she was unable to talk because of the coughing. It was getting worse and she was turning blue around her lips as she gasped for air. Brecken noticed that the arm of his jacket was soaked in blood where he had carried her away from the vehicle.

"Safina! Breathe and listen to me. I was in a coma for weeks and weeks and no one had any record of me in the Marines because of my high level CIA assignment. I'm not in anyone's computer system. I couldn't remember much of anything at first but as the months went by I began to piece things together. Then I was watching television in the convalescent hospital and I saw your speech to the UFN. The minute I saw your face my memory returned. Everything came flooding back within the next 24 hours. I made my contact call – and the CIA picked me up from the hospital almost immediately. They flew me back here this morning. I couldn't wait to get back to you, to hold you in my arms, and tell you how much I love you."

She pressed her face into his shoulder and inhaled deeply. He was in full dress Marine uniform. Safina realized that she had missed this most wonderful scent in the world – the masculine clean aroma of a United States Marine. It was a unique subtle combination of soap, leather, aftershave, peppermint toothpaste, gun oil, and the black polish that Marines use to make their shoes shine as brightly as any mirror. He held her tight and at last she felt safe. It was the embrace of a man who never wanted to let go again. He held his life's desire in his arms.

Safina pulled her head out of his shoulder and held her head back with an open mouth. Brecken leaned down and caressed her sweet lips with his own. Love so freely offered washed over him as he closed his eyes.

This purest love had patiently stood by, unconsummated. This was the breaking of all the barriers that had prevented them from following their hearts. They were soul mates. Brecken and Safina were destined to be together from the first time they had met in that wonderful country kitchen in Hilversum, Holland. Two decades had passed since then; her seventeenth birthday. Tomorrow she was turning thirty seven.

She closed her eyes and her body went limp as she lost consciousness in his arms. She stopped breathing. He put his fingers on her neck and couldn't feel her pulse. Brecken yelled, "MEDIC! MEDIC! She's in trouble here!"

Brecken was waging war with the pull of that other dimension. *NO, you can't have her. I've waited all these years for her. Give us time dear God. Give us time.* Despite decades of secular training and the exposure to all the pressures of the modern, hedonistic American culture, Brecken still believed. He invoked his Marine oath, "God, Country, Corp." *I kept my promise God, now it's your turn.*

Safina had been "surviving" for all of her life. She had reached her limits of endurance. The fight was over. She couldn't find the strength to hang on any more. Her mission was accomplished; revenge was taken, and Brecken was safe. Nomad stood on a hill and waited for her. Rémi beckoned her with loud barks, bouncing up and down on his front paws. She began to walk down the beach toward them. She saw Abraheem and Jayjan standing high above, on the rocks overlooking the sea. The tide changed and the waves hit the beach closer and closer to the rocks. The wind pummeled her, and Safina shivered in the damp cold December mist of the Mediterranean winter.

Security posted two fully armed Commandos outside the door of Safina's modest house in Baghdad. Yasmine was waiting for Safina with hot tea. She had run a bubbly herbal bath. She turned to Farka, "The responsibility of her position must be exhausting for her."

The telephone rang and Yasmine hesitated to pick it up. It wasn't her house so perhaps she should leave it for the machine to answer. She heard the answering message, "You have reached the message service of the President. She is unavailable at this time. Please leave a message or contact her office."

"Yasmine, pick up the phone. This is Brecken! If you can hear me – pick up the phone!"

He gave her instructions to come to the hospital as quickly as possible, and he asked Yasmine to hand the phone to one of the guards outside the door. He spoke with the guard briefly giving him a password known only to Safina's personal guards. Then he hung up. The guards escorted Yasmine and Farka to a waiting car and they sped off to the hospital, hoping to arrive before it was too late. When they got there Safina was in surgery.

A ricocheted bullet inside the vehicle had pierced her back, broke a rib and lodged directly against her heart. The internal bleeding had accumulated behind her lungs until the pressure prevented her from breathing. She hadn't felt the pain and she was bleeding from the entry wound at the back so Brecken and the paramedic hadn't realized immediately that she was mortally wounded.

The paramedic had resuscitated her twice on the way to the hospital. Brecken wasn't confident about the Al-Jirahat Surgical Specialty Hospital or the ER doctors. Despite almost $53 billion spent on reconstruction in Iraq, the hospitals were abandoned and looted almost immediately after being handed over to Iraqi control. The medical care was substandard in all aspects. There was a severe shortage of doctors and trained hospital workers. Like so many well-intentioned programs the rebuilding of Iraq did not take into account the poor educational level of the entire population. The shortage of trained medical personnel, engineers, electrical and electronic experts was appalling.

He had contacted the Marine base hospital and used his rank to demand an American surgeon and surgical team be dispatched to the hospital. "The life of the President of the UFAS is crucial to the security of the United States. We must offer our assistance," he told the hospital C.O. When that request fell on deaf ears, Brecken played his last card. He called the President of the United States directly on the classified executive line that was to be used only for grave national security threats. The President spoke with him briefly. She was in total agreement with Brecken – the United States would offer assistance.

Within minutes an ambulance arrived at the hospital with a mobile unit, and surgical staff. As Safina was wheeled into the O.R. the American surgeon turned to Brecken, "Who the hell is this? I got a call directly from the President of the United States telling me to get my ass and my surgical staff down here immediately!"

Brecken was coping by finding something he could do to stack the odds in Safina's favor. He rounded up a dozen soldiers from the base that had the same blood type as Safina, and put them on call because the blood banks of Iraq were non-existent.

Yasmine told him about Latifa being Safina's birth mother – so he contacted Latifa in London and gave her the information he had so far.

"I'll be on the next plane – I can find my own way to the hospital. I'm going to ask Madeleine to come with me. After all she is Safina's mentor.

When Latifa got off the phone with Brecken she made a discreet call to Claude Molyneau. She was aware of the relationship between Claude and Safina. She had incorrectly assumed that they were more than lovers. At various diplomatic events she had observed them brushing hands in the midst of cocktail crowds, standing close to each other in the refreshment line, and looking at each other over cocktail glasses. At the Ambassador's ball in London she saw them each head out, one after the other, to the gardens and disappear down the same path that led to the arboretum. They returned over an hour later within ten minutes of each other. She noticed that Safina's body guard, Jayjan always positioned himself outside the exit door whenever the two left a party or official function.

Later the pair danced one slow dance at the ball – and she saw the way Claude pulled Safina close to him and ran his hand down her back. She observed Safina's head falling back with her mouth open while her knee found its way to the inside of his leg. Their encounters were brief but there was a sexual-electricity in those connections.

"Hello Claude, this is Latifa Shmaiya. I hope you remember me…….. Of course, thank you Claude for the compliment. I don't have much time so I need to be blunt. Please forgive me for this personal intrusion. I wanted you to know that President Safina Morelli Abussani of the UFAS has been shot. She is in critical condition at the Al-Jirahat Hospital in Bab Al-Moatham, Baghdad. They don't expect her to survive. ………. Claude, are you still there?" The phone went dead. She tried to call him again but the line just went directly to voice mail.

Brecken called Vivian in Holland. She was unable to travel as she had just had back surgery. She tried to reassure him on the telephone, "You know how strong she is – remember how she took on all those assassins in Amsterdam, and how she was fearless in the battle of Baghdad. Keep talking to her Brecken, when she comes out of the surgery, keep calling her back to you. Don't give her up! Don't let go of her! You know about Nomad? Yes? Do you understand that Nomad will come for her – and she will be drawn to him? You are strong enough to overcome that pull, Brecken. I know that you are. I know that she loves you with all of her heart, and she has always loved you."

"How many times do you think Safina can cheat death? Brecken asked.

In the cocoon of her coma, Safina's mind replayed recent incidents in slow motion as she floated in that fragile delicate ebb and flow between life and death. A month had passed since she had returned home, stressed, and found Yasmine waiting for her. She relived the incident when she was too tired to listen to Yasmine and begged off, saying she would speak to her in the morning. That night Safina slept like a baby. She couldn't remember her dreams. As she opened her eyes and stretched her arms out she forgot about Yasmine and her mention of someone else she wanted Safina to meet.

Safina washed her face and wrapped herself in a soft chenille robe and padded barefoot toward the kitchen for a cup of coffee.

Her large "mushy" Blue Mink Ragamuffin cat was waiting for her. He wound his body around her ankles and purred loudly. "Raoul, you are such a big baby." She lifted all twenty pounds of him into her arms as he rubbed his fat whisker pads against her neck and placed his big soft paw against her cheek. He was the *purrrrrrfect* "de-stressor." She had named him "Raoul" for an exiled Liberal left-wing Cuban writer she had met at a debate in college. She liked him, and appreciated his measured and thoughtful debating style. Of course, he never won a debate with her. Raoul, the cat, always won the debate with Safina regarding treats, or cuddling. He had her wrapped around his paw.

The morning coffee ritual was a vice that Brecken had taught her. He was a connoisseur of gourmet coffees. He taught her to use a French coffee press which he claimed was the only way to truly preserve the perfect flavor and aroma of the coffee beans. He made sure she had a whole cupboard full of various exotic flavors and brews. He ground and blended his own unique combinations of whole roasted beans.

She was delighted to see that Yasmine had used Safina's finjan to brew an aromatic thick, cinnamon flavored sweet Turkish coffee. It was steaming hot and she poured some into a delicate porcelain cup and went toward the breakfast room to curl up with a Cairo newspaper.

As she entered the room, she saw the back of someone's head as they sat on the sofa in the living room. She entered and cleared her throat so as not to startle them. The person rose and turned around. Safina almost dropped her coffee as the newspaper fell on the floor. Her hand was shaky and she put the cup on a sideboard. "Is it you? Is it really you?" she exclaimed in Arabic. "*Allah hu akbar!*"

The woman began to smile shyly, and she looked down at the floor. Safina ran over to her and threw her arms around the woman. They both began to cry and laugh at the same time.

"Safina, I saw you on the TV box in our village store. You are an important person. You saved the women in Iraq. No one believed me that I know you. When I said that you are my friend, everyone laughed at me."

"Farka, I thought about you so many times. I sent someone to the village but El Sighi said you were dead and he refused to talk to the person I sent."

It was a world of surprises. She found her mother and she found Farka. Only Brecken was missing. Farka and Safina talked almost all day, and Yasmine joined in. They had so much to catch up on. Living twenty five years in a few hours is not possible but they made a good dent in the renewal of their friendship.

Safina felt like an aunt to Farka's son, Kareem. He was a tall, shy young man. But she noticed that when she addressed him he looked her squarely in the eye. She also saw how solicitous he was of his mother. He was protective of Farka, and Safina imagined that he had been upset when his father beat her. *It must have been hard for the boy to watch that, and not be able to do anything to protect his mother*, she thought. This had been the basic strategy of the pre-revolutionary conditioning – preparing the young sons to rebel as they saw a different type of society.

"I want you and your son to stay with me. I want you to live here and be my family." And, we need to get your teeth repaired. You are a beautiful woman, Farka – you can't go around with your front teeth missing."

Farka covered her mouth self-consciously. She had almost forgotten about her missing teeth. It would be nice to have teeth again.

Safina remained in a coma. Brecken sat by her bed just as he had in Paris when she was injured in the explosion there. This was like a recurring nightmare. Again he was helpless to affect the outcome. All he could do was to plead with God to bring her back to him.

He talked to her constantly, "Come back Safina. Don't leave now, it's our time...... it's our chance ..... I need you so much." He held her hand and felt her growing colder and farther away from him. He didn't want to ever let go of her. He felt powerless. Brecken wanted to scream and shake his fists at God, and then he realized how insignificant his supplications were compared to the task that had been given to Safina. All that really mattered was the question of whether her leadership was still crucial to the delicate balance of power in a world hungry for lasting peace.

Brecken had, at long last, grasped the purpose for which Safina was born, and he understood the circumstances of his own birth, and his adoptive parent's death. All of those complicated and intricate threads had been woven together to create the fabric of the revolution and the reformation of Islam. His destiny, Safina's fate, and the destruction and obliteration of jihad had been crafted into a promise of a new path for mankind. The revelation took his breath away, and gave him the courage to accept any outcome.

Yasmine entered the room, "Go get something to eat and drink. You won't do Safina any good if you collapse."

After he left the room, Yasmine pulled the chair closer to the bed and she took Safina's hand into hers. "You have a daughter – the baby you gave birth to when I found you – she is alive. You need to see her, to hold her in your arms and tell her how much you love her. You need to come back to her! Listen Safina! YOU HAVE A DAUGHTER!"

Deep in her coma Safina was transported to the shoreline with her arms around Nomad. He was pushing her toward the water. The incoming tide was at her ankles but the more he pushed her the higher it rose. Soon it was almost at her waist. She tried to shove him back toward the shore but he refused to budge. Safina had never felt so weak and she knew that her effort to push the horse was killing her. It was so difficult to inhale, as the water rose to her neck she understood that she only had minutes left before it would be higher than her head. She tried to swim but her feet were too heavy to kick and her arms weighed her down. Anger swelled in her heart and she wailed at Allah for all the pain and disappointments of her life: "Why do we praise Allah? Why do we say that Allah is great, merciful, and wondrous? Where is your mercy now? How are you glorified through the suffering of humanity? Why did you choose me to be the instrument of this bloody revolution?" She was tired of fighting killing, struggling, and questioning everything.

"Oh my God, it never ends. I want to see Brecken!" She was becoming agitated, and the shock of what had just happened to her was setting in. "Someone tried to kill me and I killed him instead. Can't you just leave me alone?!"

Just before the water was about to cover her head, she heard a woman calling to her from the shoreline. She strained to see the woman's face. Safina realized it was Christi, the woman she had met in Basra, the woman who had given her a silver bracelet to remember their friendship. "Go back Safina, our daughter needs you. Our daughter needs you!" Safina whispered in Nomad's ear, "Take me back my friend, take me back. My destination is not yet reached."

The big horse swam ashore with her holding onto his mane. She let go at the shoreline and dropped onto the sand, gasping for air. Nomad galloped down the beach. Rémi, the big dog was standing over her, licking her face. She pushed him away and sat up. He looked at her with his tongue hanging out and his tail wagging happily, then he took off after Nomad. Christi waved to her from the cliffs farther down the shoreline.

Claude Molyneau arrived at the airport in Baghdad in the afternoon. He took a waiting limo to the hospital. He had arrived in a private jet owned by his father. He rarely took advantage of his father's extravagant lifestyle, but it was the only way to get to Safina quickly. He sat back in the cab and thought about his relationship with Safina and what it would be like if she were gone from his life.

They were perfect lovers. Their bodies were in complete synchronization. When they came together they were like ballroom dancers who had been together forever, each intricate move seamlessly choreographed, or a school of tropical fish turning and diving, swirling as one in a silvery explosion. Each intricate orchestrated degree of sensuous arousal was played out in a symphony of highly charged sexual energy unlike anything that Claude had ever experienced, heard of, or thought was even remotely possible.

Safina was exquisitely in tune with Claude's body. She touched him in ways that were unexpected and delightful. Her fingers were delicate instruments of pleasures untold. He couldn't think about her without being aroused. It didn't matter how long it had been between encounters. When he walked into a room where she was present, even when five hundred people were there, the electricity between them was charged with anticipation. They had to be cautious and discreet because someone who was sensitive to those vibrations would have felt their connection. Just touching her fingertips in a crowded room was enough to raise his heartbeat and increase his respiration.

As the limo neared the hospital Claude was beginning to wonder how he would deal with Brecken. He knew that if Brecken were alive he would not tolerate Safina's lover. Brecken was still MIA as far as Claude knew. Safina had told him all about the unconsummated love between her and her bodyguard. She had been clear about her devotion to Brecken Petersen. Claude was not jealous. He was glad that Safina knew who she loved with all of her heart. He envied her unquestioning commitment to Brecken. Because of her intense sexuality she had made the decision to accept Claude as her lover. She was able to separate her love for Brecken from her physical need for Claude. Claude thought he was comfortable with this.

Claude Molyneau had been careful to keep his relationship with Safina in a mental box that precluded falling in love with her. He loved her as a friend and as a sexual partner. He told himself that he was not "in love" with her. There were other females in his life, but no one was the 'love of his life'. He was still seeking that woman. He realized that after his relationship with Safina it would be difficult to give her up whether in death or because of her commitment to a marriage with Brecken.

Yasmine had intended to tell Safina about Assal, Safina's daughter, but didn't do it. Maybe she thought it was just too much information at once since Safina had found her mother, and then she had been reunited with Farka. The secret of Assal wouldn't die with Yasmine. Dr. Zubayer, who had adopted Safina's daughter, had been instructed to give Assal the key to Yasmine's safety deposit box in New York City on Assal's 25st birthday. She would open the safety deposit box in just a few months, and she would know the truth about her identity.

She was Safina's daughter: analytical, highly intelligent, quick witted, and logical. But her grace and style were definitely gifts from her adopted mother, Christi. Yasmine believed that she would continue the struggle that her birth mother had fought so hard for.

While the main battles of the revolution were over and the world was headed in a positive direction, there were still major obstacles and problems to address. European and American Progressives continued to plot the overthrow of the European Alliance and the new government of the United States of America. They also had their sights set on dismantling the UFAS and undermining all attempts to fold Russia into an Eastern block federation under the UFN umbrella. There had to be a strong leader in place who would carry on the advocacy for the women of Islam and sustain the reformation. The day was coming when Safina would no longer be able to carry the heavy load. The reformation needed continued nurturing and direction so that it never lost its momentum or its relevance.

Whether Assal would reveal herself to Safina was a decision that only Assal could make. Yasmine, Badrai (the sister of Assal's adoptive father), and the servant Riya, were the only people who knew the true identity of Assal.

When Dr. Zubayer was called and told that Safina was hospitalized and not expected to survive an assassination attempt – he had to decide if he would take Assal to see her birth mother or let that opportunity pass.

On his way to the hospital Claude was forced to admit to himself that his relationship with Safina was much more than a sexual liaison. He loved her. Considering the possibility that she might be lost to him forever caused him to realize how deeply he cared for her. He rationalized his failure to understand this earlier because neither of them were utterly consumed by it. They were both committed to two of the most important tasks in the world. Safina WAS "The Revolution" and she was the only person who could have brought the UFAS into being and the only woman who had the technical and cultural understanding to bring about the FMEW's rapid growth and success.

Claude was a financial genius and had the resources and the guts to go up against George Monroe's financial machine and beat it. He had put the free world back on track financially and had found a way to fast track a world-wide recovery plan. His father's international banking connections and Claude's audacity and financial wizardry had pulled the world back from the brink of global collapse after the third pitiful attempt by the Americans to pull themselves out of a bottomless pit of financial demise. The free markets were functioning and the future of capitalism was beginning to look positive. China had been subdued and harnessed; its new leadership was convinced that it was in their best interests to cultivate a new free-market relationship with the West. The Chinese people were reaping the rewards of new opportunities. Their future looked bright indeed. But the most gratifying outcome of the revolution and the financial restructuring back to the original free market principles was the fall of George Monroe's financial empire and the subsequent wipe-out of his vast network of radical Progressives who had blindly invested every cent of their ill-gotten gains in his "World Government" scheme. George Monroe was still "at large" but Claude was confident that he would be hunted down and brought to justice. The most recent piece of intelligence indicated that Monroe was hiding at sea. Claude smiled when he thought of that – a dumb place to hide since the US Navy "owned" the oceans and seas of the entire world.

Safina turned away from the blue Mediterranean Sea and opened her eyes to a stark white room with bottles, tubes and wires hanging all around her behind white canvas curtains like the complicated rigging of a clipper ship in full sail. The odor of antiseptic and disinfectant was too strong to ignore. "Where is this place?" she asked weakly.

"You're in the hospital Safina. You've been here for days, sleeping," Brecken answered. He took hold of her hand.

Her mouth was dry and sticky as though she had a ball of damp cotton in her mouth. Her throat was sore, and there was a thick yucky coating on her teeth. Brecken slipped a small piece of ice between her lips. "Here, suck on this. I know your mouth is dry, but this'll help." He took a damp wash cloth and wiped off her face and gently wiped the inside of each of her wrists, trying to cool her off. "You almost decided not to come back to me, Safina. I was so worried about you. I love you so much. I need you. I couldn't bear to let you go." His voice cracked as he tried to "keep it together" for her sake. He fought back his tears of relief.

"Brecken, I love you too much to leave you. Don't you know you're the love of my life, my best friend, and the person I trust most in the world? In my dream I was fighting with Nomad to let me get back to you. Jayjan and Abraheem were there, and Remi too. But, I refused to go with them. You're my life. Without you I'm a boat without an oar, a bird without wings, a nation without God."

He leaned down and softly brushed his lips on her cheek. "I must go tell the others that you're awake. They'll be so happy!"

"What others? Who's here?" Safina questioned him.

"Yasmine, Farka, Madeleine, Arnaud, Latifa and Yehiye have been camped out in the visitors lounge for three days. Even Claude Molyneau is scheduled to arrive this morning. I understand he's coming in on his father's private jet."

As weak as she was she couldn't help but blush slightly when she heard Claude's name. Something deep inside of her quivered ever so slightly. He was the first man to make love to her in a way that awakened her body and her emotions. She would always remember his words whispered with hot breath into her ear as he made love to her in a gazebo in Paris, "Safina, I am your lover." But Brecken was the man she was destined to love and destined to be with in sickness and in health.

It had taken over forty minutes for Claude to get through the heavy security at the hospital to enter the wing where Safina was a patient. As he walked briskly down the long corridor to her room and approached the door he saw Brecken bending over Safina and kissing her. He stood just outside the door and listened to Safina's declaration of her love for Brecken.

Claude knew that Safina was Brecken's soul mate. She had made that clear to him the last time they were together. He might be able to win over her body but he was positive that he would never win her heart. Not in the way that Brecken held it in the palm of his hand. There was only one option. Claude turned around and walked back out of the hospital, got in the limo and headed back to the airport. He would let her go. It was the right thing to do. As much as he felt a gapping rip in the center of his heart and felt it spreading through his being, he was also smiling through the pain. Safina was alive! She was in love with a good man, a man of honor and integrity. Claude would step aside. He wouldn't interfere. If things should ever change, he would be there to pick up the pieces. He wished them happiness together.

In the process of consoling himself his thoughts turned to self magnification: *I am better in bed ......but one cannot blame Brecken for that........after all, he is an American. They have no patience to create sexual artistry. Safina will need to teach him, but alas....students rarely reach the level of the Master craftsman.* This internal monologue was Claude's way of encapsulating his feelings in a tightly buried place deep in his heart. He knew he was doing that, and he smiled at his own devices to hold onto his male ego with his honor intact. He had used the same tactics in his old college debates. If you couldn't win the debate logically your next best ploy was to diminish the importance of the subject at hand, and feign disinterest in the actual outcome.

The sleek dark haired stewardess working this flight on his father's jet, stopped next to Claude's seat and offered him a drink. "Oui, Mademoiselle, I would love a lemony Cuba Libra with tons of ice, but only if you will join me." He looked at her appreciatively and with a feigned hopeful adolescent grin. He had not lost his self confidence or his masculine wiles.

Claude could have any woman he had ever desired, yet he walked away from the person who he knew to be the love of his life. He thought: *I'm not that noble. If I have the chance to hold Safina once more in my arms and feel the beat of her heart pressed against mine, I will take it.* Claude grinned at his own seductive nature despite a lingering feeling of shame that tarnished his unselfish gesture.

Abe and Assal slowly exited the Boeing 747 in Cairo. Their connecting flight to Baghdad was scheduled to leave in an hour. She was a bit shaky coming down the ramp into the terminal. So much had happened to her this past year. They had lost Christi, the cornerstone of their small family. It was just Assal and Abe now. He was a wonderful father and an exceptional orthopedic surgeon, but since the loss of his beloved wife he was floundering. Assal had been away at school when she learned of her mother's death in an automobile accident. Death had been swift and Christi had not suffered. No one was prepared for this devastating loss, least of all Assal. She didn't have the chance to say good-bye to her mother. Christi and Assal were not simply mother and daughter. They had been best friends.

She had known she was adopted from the time she was old enough to understand it. Abe and Christi had been open about it. They celebrated her adoption as a fabulous gift that they treasured. Every year on her birthday they retold the story of their journey to Iraq and the journey home with their daughter. Assal had always felt cherished and loved. People who were not close to the family had no idea she was not their natural child. They assumed she simply took after her father in her bronzed coloration and features. Her parents had made sure that she was bi-lingual in English and Arabic. Later she mastered several other languages. Like her biological mother, Safina, she had an ear for languages. She was a tall girl with green eyes. She wore her black hair in thick braided loops high on her head, or she let it down where it draped her shoulders and back, and framed her face as though it were a classical painting from the turn of the century. She was memorable, with a widow's peak hairline. There was something commanding about the way Assal moved and how she stood out in a crowd. She had an understated eloquence derived from her heritage, and the influence of her cultured and educated adoptive mother. Assal possessed the gift of critical thinking. It was a rare and valuable trait.

When Abe first received the news about Safina, he sat down with Assal, "Your biological mother was critically injured and she is in a Baghdad hospital fighting for her life."

Assal was astounded that her father even knew who her birth mother was, let alone having some ongoing connection to her. "Who is she? Do I know her?" Assal asked.

"She is President Safina Morelli Abussani of the UFAS."

Assal had sat frozen and stunned for several minutes, trying to restructure her self-image. She had thought she knew who she was. She hadn't thought much about her adoption except to wonder what her birth parents looked like. To find out that her birth mother was a famous revolutionary, and the President of the Federation of United Arab States was astounding. It had occurred to her that President Abussani was too young to have a 25 year old daughter! Her father had to be mistaken. Assal had read about President Abussani and greatly admired the woman.

"Why'd she give me up Dad? Why didn't she want me?"

Abe looked at his daughter intently. *Should I tell her the whole thing? Will she be able to deal with the enormity of the event of her birth..... and how it changed the entire world? Will that be too much for a young woman to take in?* His thoughts were filled with apprehension. But, in the end he quietly revealed the details of her birth and adoption.

"So Safina doesn't know that you exist. She was never told that her baby survived. She never married and never had any more children. She was too busy saving the world! I am telling you all of this because you would have been given this information on your birthday anyway; your birth mother may not survive her injuries, I thought you deserved the opportunity to see her now. Only you can make that decision. I will respect whatever you decide. But the decision has to be made soon, it will take almost a whole day to reach her location, and we cannot be sure she will still be alive or awake once we get there. It's up to you if you want to try."

He handed her the photograph of Safina holding Assal as a baby. Safina was laughing at the baby who was tightly gripping her finger. "We took these photos on the night we took you home from Iraq. Safina didn't know you were her daughter. She was only told that we came to visit with our baby. It was the only time she ever got to hold you in her arms. Even though she didn't know, you can see in the photo how she connected with you. It was one of the most difficult things your mother and I ever had to do, not to reveal to her that she was holding her own child that night."

"Oh Dad, how could you do that? Was it truly that dangerous for her to know? Do you think she would've stayed in Iraq and risked death if she'd known about me? I can't imagine having to deal with all of that when she was only twelve years old. How horrible it must have been for her to go through those things." she began to sob. "Yes, I want to leave now and go see her while there's still time." Abe handed Assal his handkerchief. " Dad, I need to let her know that I'm OK and that she has a daughter. I know that Mom would have wanted me to do that."

When they arrived the next day in Baghdad, Abe placed a call to the office of the President. He wanted an update on her condition and details about getting to the hospital. They didn't want to give him any information because he was not a relative. That is when he told them that Assal was the daughter of President Abussani. There was a momentary silence and a clicking sound on the line. The voice on the other end of the line told them she had been transferred to a different hospital and gave them directions from the airport. They said the President was still unconscious.

The taxi let them out at the front entrance to the hospital. Abe was surprised that it wasn't crawling with reporters and security. Inside the hospital it was strangely quiet. Abe had expected to be confronted with layers of security and all kinds of check points to get in to see the President, but except for one regular guard at the front gate, no added security was visible. As they entered the foyer of the hospital they saw a guard sitting at the information desk in the center. Abe and Assal approached him.

"Yes Sir. What can I do for you?" the man asked.

"I am here to see President Abussani. We are family members," Abe answered.

"The President is gone. All of her security and staff have vacated the hospital hours ago. I'm sorry that no one bothered to contact you with this information. It was all over the news: the shooting and then the death of the President. You will have to contact the UFAS headquarters for more information. I am truly sorry for your loss."

Abe walked over to an empty bench and sat down. He held his head in his hands trying to get a handle on his feelings. He had temporarily forgotten Assal until he felt her hand on his back.

"Oh Dad, I so wanted to see her and speak to her. I wanted to tell her how proud I am to be her daughter." She sank onto the bench next to him. He reached over and put his arm around her.

"It's OK Assal, she knows.....now she knows the truth. She knows that you love her and that her sacrifice was not wasted."

The guard from the front desk approached them, "Excuse me, but are you sure you are relatives of President Abussani?"

"Yes, I am her daughter. I mean, I was her daughter........" Assal began to tear up.

"Please, don't cry. Here, take a tissue." He towered over her. His breath reeked of garlic and tobacco.

"Do you folks need a ride to the Presidential headquarters? I can take you there, it's on my way home and my shift is ending in just a few minutes. Your taxi has left and you won't get another one out here for hours." His lips remained slightly open as he breathed through his mouth, and his eyes narrowed under thick black brows.

As he handed Assal the box and she pulled a single tissue from it. She noticed a strange tattoo on the inside of his left arm, just below his elbow. It looked like some kind of a goat with the head of a lion and the tail of a snake. It was pretty weird looking – and as she stared at it, a creepy chill ran up her spine.

The End

BIBLIOGRAPHY

Ahmed, Ahmed S, *Islam Today, A Short Introduction to the Muslim World* (London, Tauris & Co., New York, St. Martin Press, 2001).

Baer, Martha; Heron, Katrina; Morton, Oliver; Ratliff, Evan, *Safe, The Race to Protect Ourselves in a Newly Dangerous World* (Harper Collins, 2005).

Ferguson, Niall, *Colossus, The Price of America's Empire* (The Penguin Press, 2004).

Fregosi, Paul, *Jihad in the West, Muslim Conquests from the 78th to the 21st Centuries* (Prometheus Books, New York 1998).

Friedman, George, *The Next 100 Years, A Forecast for the 21st Century* (Doubleday, 2009).

Gabriel, Brigitte, *They Must Be Stopped, Why We Must Defeat Radical Islam and How We Can Do It* (St. Martin's Press, 2008).

Hirsi Ali, Ayaan, *Infidel* (Free Press, Simon & Schuester, Inc., 2008).

Hourani, Albert, *A History of the Arab Peoples* (Warner Books, 1992).

Kennedy, Hugh, *When Baghdad Ruled the Muslim World* (De Capo Press, 2005).

Kurzweil, Ray, *The Singularity is Near, When Humans Transcend Biology* (Viking, 2005).

Lacey, Robert, *The Kingdom, Arabia & the House of Sa'ud* (Avon Books, 1981).

Lings, Martin, *Muhammad, His Life Based on the Earliest Sources* (Inner Traditions, 2006).

Mernissi, Fatima, *The Veil and the Male Elite, A Feminist Interpretation of Women's Rights in Islam* (Perseus Books, 1991).

Spencer, Robert, *Islam Unveiled, Disturbing Questions About the World's Fastest-Growing Faith* (Encounter Books, 2002).

Spencer, Robert, *The Myth of Islamic Tolerance, How Islamic Law Treats Non-Muslims* (Prometheus Books, 2005.

Wahdud, Amina, *Inside the Gender Jihad, Women's Reform in Islam* (Oneworld Publications, 2006).

Walther, Wiebke, *Women in Islam, From Medieval to Modern Times* (Markus Wiener Publishers, 1999).

ALPHABETICAL LIST OF CHARACTERS
SAFINA, DAUGHTER OF ISLAM, BOOK I

Main characters are underlined.

Abdul Khaliq Abu El Haj: (antagonist) Safina's husband

Abdul Zabayer: doctor and adoptive father of Assal

Abraheem: son of silversmith in Basra and revolutionary soldier

Arnaud Fournier: French diplomat, UFN Council member

Assal: biological daughter of Safina

Badrai: cook in the house of Yasmine

Brecken Petersen: U.S. Marine Lieutenant Colonel, body guard, soul mate of Safina

Casper Van Vleit: Dutch First Mate on the Hercules

Charlemagne: French bull dog of Arnaud Fournier

Claude Molyneau: French banker and Safina's lover

Christi Zabayer: American wife of Dr. Zabayer and adoptive mother of Assal

Demetrius: (antagonist) Captain of the Hercules

Dulcinea: alias of Safina, main protagonist

El Sighi: antagonist and father of Safina

Farka: youngest wife of El Sighi

Gerard: Bull Mastiff dog of Arnaud

Jamillah: mare belonging to El Sighi, also an abused woman

JayJan: body guard, spy, revolutionary soldier

Latifa: biological mother of Safina, President of the FMEW

Luigi Morelli: Italian researcher, doctor aboard the Hercules, adoptive father of Dulcinea

Madeliene Fournier: wife of Arnaud Fournier

Nomad: black stallion horse – (Bedoui)

Prodromos: cook on the Hercules

Quallil: mare of El Sighi, purchased by Abdul Khaliq Abu El Haj

Rembrandt: Vivian Von Stetton's dog

Remi: Bull Mastiff dog of Arnaud

Riya: servant girl in house of Yasmine

Safina: main protagonist – Iraqi girl who becomes the leader of the Islamic Revolution, Pres. UFAS

Vivian Von Stetton: Dutch women who mentors Safina (Dulcinea), member of the UFN council

William Monroe: antagonist, multi billionaire.

Yasmine: woman in Basra who saved Safina, member of the UFN Council, mentor of Safina

Yehiya Shmaiya: Jewish Yemenite jeweler and husband of Latifa

Youssef: Safina's oldest brother, and horse whisperer

Made in the USA
San Bernardino, CA
13 December 2014